MINE TO SHARE

PROTECTION SERIES
BOOK 7

KENNEDY L. MITCHELL

To my amazing readers,
Thank you for waiting for Jameson's story. I might be a little
biased but its totally worth the wait.
I hope you enjoy Jameson's unconventional happily ever after.

PROLOGUE

UNKNOWN

A lone car whizzed past, tires splashing along the wet street, making me dip farther into the shadows to stay hidden from any curious eyes. A block over, a car alarm blared, amping up my nerves as I hurried along the sidewalk, heart hammering in my chest with each quick breath. Shadows shifted across the street as transients and homeless searched covered alcoves for a place to rest for what remained of the soggy night. At well past two in the morning, it was only me and them out in this area of town, those with a home or not hiding in the shadows tucked in their warm beds.

Water soaked through the worn soles of the thrift store tennis shoes from the shallow puddles along the sidewalk. The oversized, thick coat I'd scored at Goodwill not only helped me blend in with the others wandering the street but warded off the chilled breeze that carried the hint of salt and sand. The Santa Coasta nights turned cool, all the blissful warmth from the day gone the moment the sun dipped beneath the horizon, and tonight was no different.

My lungs were tight, each quick breath like inhaling

shards of glass instead of air. Every sound had me jerking like the addict I'd passed two blocks back. Even the buzz of the lamps was too loud, the soft glow too bright for someone hyped on anxiety and nerves. Gripping the ball cap bill, I wiggled it lower on my brow and kept my face downturned toward the crumbling sidewalk, only chancing a look over my shoulder when the urge became too insistent to resist.

Like now. The distinct sound of heavy wheezing breaths, the splash of a step in a shallow puddle—all too close for my nerves to not demand I check who followed me on the otherwise empty street.

Unable to fight the urge, I shot a quick glance over my shoulder, scanning the shadows only to find a slim frame several feet behind me but gaining ground. The person weaved in and out of the circles of light cast by the few working lampposts.

Movement tight, I jerked back around, a lump forming in my throat making it difficult to swallow as I picked up my already-quick pace.

An angry bark down the alley I'd just passed had me swallowing a startled curse, my steps stumbling. Choking down the rising fear threatening to suffocate me right here on the sidewalk, I shifted to a slow jog, hurrying toward the next alley and slipping around the corner, the rough edge of the brick catching on my coat sleeve, ripping the worn material. Not until the darkness concealed my hiding spot did I pause, leaning back against the building for support. Fingers trembling, sweaty palm wrapped around the knife's cheap plastic hilt, I slid the weapon free of its sheath.

Blood thundered in my ears as I waited. A deep inhale whistled through my clenched teeth over and over as I attempted to calm my racing heart. The faint sound of approaching steps had me widening my stance, prepared to fight the person following me. Muscles tensed and ready, I watched a hunched figure, mumbling incoherent words to no one I could see, pass by the alley, not pausing or looking my way once.

The held breath burning my lungs blew past my dry lips as I slumped against the hot brick.

Thirty seconds.

That was all I could afford to calm the hell down and get my shit together enough to keep going. I couldn't freeze, not now. I had to keep moving.

At the thirty-second mark, I placed both hands on the brick and shoved off, forcing myself out of my hiding spot and back onto the sidewalk.

Four more blocks. Four blocks and I would be safe. The night would be over.

I needed to keep moving.

The motel's half-lit neon sign blinked in dismal welcoming when I rounded the corner, causing me to pick up the pace. Cautious that others might be watching from the various windows despite the hour, I rounded both shoulders, ensuring anyone looking couldn't positively identify my height, and fluffed out the jacket to give my frame a bulkier appearance. Halfway across the crumbling parking lot, I slid my hand into the deep pocket of my loose pants. My heart rate slowed as my fingers wrapped around the cheap plastic key ring, assuring myself it was still there as I weaved around the motel's cameras, having reviewed the layout first thing earlier in the day.

I planned tonight down to the second, and so far, everything had gone according to plan.

But I wasn't out of the woods yet.

It took two tries to get the metal key into the lock. The

loud thud of the door closing behind me rattled through the room. With the lock engaged and a cheap plastic chair shoved beneath the door handle, I allowed myself to take the first full breath since setting out on tonight's mission. Hands by my side, I stood in the middle of the room, listening to the faint sounds of a couple fighting nearby mixed with the normal grunts and moans of what went on in these pay-by-the-hour places.

What I didn't hear or see through the break in the curtains covering the front window had a knowing smirk tugging at my thin lips.

No police sirens cut through the night.

No red and flashing blue lights flickered in the parking lot.

A relieved sigh brushed across my dry lips as I forced my tense muscles to relax, the adrenaline from the night's events slowly draining away, leaving me exhausted yet sated, knowing I did what had to be done. From the moment I'd left home earlier, knowing exactly what tonight would bring, my frayed nerves kept me from taking a full breath. The weeks of watching, waiting, and diligently planning the perfect moment were the easiest part of all this. It was nights like tonight, when my targets found true justice for their past crimes, that were equally exhilarating and terrifying.

Though not nearly as horrifying as that first time. Unprepared, startled by the anger and fear coursing through my veins, the knife had trembled in my hand, making the wounds sloppy.

Nothing like they were now.

Deep. Calculated. Deadly.

Each strike of my blade ensuring maximum pain for the

sick bastard unlucky enough to be on my radar and a very slow death as they bled out with me watching.

The pain was exactly what they deserved.

Becoming a serial killer wasn't a top career choice, but things happened, fate changed the course of my future, and here I was. Alone, covered in blood that wasn't my own, and smiling into the dark. Though unlike other multi-victim killers, I wasn't a psychopath, narcissist, or insane.

Or so I thought. Though it was all based on perspective.

Mine, I was doing the community a service. To others, they might only see the bodies left in my wake, uncaring about the destructive lives the victims lived before I took matters into my own hands.

Someone had to.

Shrugging off the thick coat, I shoved it into the black plastic garbage bag I'd brought with me, followed by the cheap tennis shoes and soggy socks. Fingers wrapped around the thin plastic, I dragged it off the single queen bed I had no plans to sleep in, then padded to the tiny bathroom and flipped the light switch.

The yellowed fluorescent bulb flickered, buzzing to life above the cracked mirror.

Hips digging into the sink as I leaned toward the mirror, I tilted my face one way and then the other, studying my pale reflection. The tiny crimson flecks along my cheek held my focus as flickers of the night's events ran on repeat.

The beautiful, muffled screams, desperate pleas for me to stop, and insistent begging to spare their pathetic life were quickly becoming my favorite facet of this justice mission.

The sticky, thick blood that sprayed with each plunge of the knife, not so much. It made cleanup a fucking bitch. Remembering my first time had me scoffing at my idiot self as I tugged the sink's stopper closed. Reaching beneath the sink, I looped a finger through the handle of the jug of bleach I'd brought from home. The chemical vapors burned my nostrils and lungs with every inhale as I filled the bowl halfway, saving the rest for the shower, as my routine required destroying any lingering evidence.

Not caring about splashing bleach on the clothes that would soon be scattered around the city, I tossed the still-bloody knife and sheath into the sink, watching as the liquid shifted from its original yellowish color to pink as it stripped the dried blood and all DNA from everything it touched. Hat first, followed by my shirt, pants, and underwear, I removed each article of clothing before shoving it all into the black trash bag. The cheap clear plastic shower curtain crinkled, the hooks screeching across the metal bar as I reached inside the shower and twisted the knob all the way to the right.

As the water heated, I forced my gaze to stay on my face instead of slipping lower to the still-puffy scars littering my stomach. Bile rose along my throat. My fingers wrapped around the sink, catching me before I could fall to the floor as memories from the worst night of my life tried to bombard me.

I wasn't born a monster. I was made into one.

This wasn't what I wanted from life, but what I wanted and what I'd become all changed in a single night.

The night my old life ended and this one began.

Of hunting, watching, and taking.

Just like they had.

The first time was an accident. I'd only brought the pitiful kitchen knife to scare him, but the fear rushing through my veins had made me jumpy. Feeling cornered, he lunged, and so did I, but I had something he didn't. The sensation of fresh blood pouring over my hand, seeping between my shaking fingers, made my stomach roll. But his pleas for mercy, begging me to spare his life, resurrected my strength, a sense of power I hadn't felt since someone just like him stripped it from me.

That was what made me do it again and again, the pull that kept me hunting and killing those I deemed worthy of my blood justice. I craved the power I gained by taking these bastards' lives, even if it was for only a little while. It was wrong, but that wouldn't stop me. I was in too deep now, too many bodies in my wake to turn back and pretend like nothing happened. To act like my new hobby wouldn't put me behind bars for the rest of my life.

Not that I planned to go to jail. That was a death sentence for someone like me. No, if it came down to it, if that asshole detective and too-smart-for-her-own-good ME ever figured me out, then... well, I hadn't gotten that far.

Because outside the thrill of the hunt and removing another sick bastard from this world, I wasn't living.

Jerking my gaze away, cutting off my depressing thoughts, I yanked the curtain aside and stepped beneath the dismal spray, allowing the barely warm water to slide over my skin, erasing the minuscule drops of blood I knew would be damning evidence if I were caught. After washing my hair three times, I grabbed the bottle of bleach and tipped it until the toxic contents splashed over the opposite hand. The liquid burned my already-raw skin, but I fought through the pain, knowing it was necessary.

Getting caught because of a sloppy mistake wasn't an option.

Not when there was more work to do.

1

JAMESON

My eyes pinched, and a sharp hiss that whistled through my clenched teeth covered the sound of the manila file folder crumpling beneath my tightening grip as a fiery pain raced down my arm, making the tips of my fingers tingle.

Being shot sucked hairy balls.

Not that I'd ever actually sucked balls, shaved or hairy. I just assumed it was as terrible as taking a bullet.

The spot where the slug pierced through my bicep pulsed in a reminder that I didn't take pain medication before boarding the jet. The wound was healed enough for me to be cleared for duty last week, and the last few days only a barely noticeable ache reminded me of what happened. But not today. Which I should have expected, considering I was always tense as hell while soaring tens of thousands of miles above the ground in a luxurious sardine can with engines.

"Are you sure you're up for a solo case?" Smoothing out the now-bent folder along the table, I shot my boss, SSA Rhyan Riggs, a wounded look at her question. "Stop. I know you can do it. I'm not doubting that. It's just that the last case you went on with Cooper ended with both of you shot. I'm being a good boss and double-checking that I'm not pushing you too hard, too fast."

"It was just a through and through," I grumbled under my breath. "We're down a profiler until Cooper is cleared for duty, and based on how that asshole won't follow a single one of the doctor's orders, we'll be short for a while."

Rhyan smirked on the iPad's screen I had propped up on the table. At that moment, the entire jet shook, hitting turbulence or the precursor for crashing to our fiery death, causing the device to tip forward. I jerked my hand out, but the iPad smacked the table before I could catch it. After propping it back up, I leaned back in the chair, both hands gripping the armrests until my knuckles ached.

"Since you're doing this one solo, I also want to make sure you have all the support you need. This case is interesting, to say the least."

"With you and Charlie at my back, plus the others on the team waiting in the wings to offer help, I have all the support I could need." Releasing my death grip on the chair, I pulled the file folder to the edge of the table to scan the pictures inside for what felt like the hundredth time since Rhyan dropped them on my desk that afternoon. "Interesting case indeed. We have little to go on except that all the murders were committed by the same unsub." I held up the picture of the most recent victim. "Little to no evidence and a decent amount of time between kills. This unsub is a planner."

Which made my job that much harder.

Four male victims all stabbed to death, all with different knives and blades, with no sign of sexual assault. The two found outdoors, one in an alley and the other in a parking lot, still had their watches, wallets, and keys. The two found in their respective homes had nothing taken or displaced, outside the bloody scenes in their bedrooms.

Wrapping my sweaty palm around the drinking glass on the table, I downed several gulps of the cold water to ease the building nausea.

I fucking hated flying.

Too bad it was part of my job now.

If I had known how much I would fly around the US as an FBI profiler, I might not have accepted Rhyan's offer. But when we're called, we go, and the BSU's private jet was the quickest way to get to those who needed our expertise.

Well, the others' expertise. I wasn't there yet. Eight months out of training at Quantico did not make me an expert by any means. My years working as a cop, then a detective in Nashville, helped, though. It was how Rhyan even knew I existed in the first place to offer me a job on her new team, based out of the Dallas office.

"I agree. Looks like a single unsub," Rhyan mused while looking off-screen, no doubt scanning the same pictures as me. "Once you land in Santa Coasta, you'll head to the main police station, where you'll meet with the lead on these cases, Detective Slade Taylor. He's the one who reached out for help after their ME noticed similarities in the cases."

I nodded along, letting her know I understood as I continued to scan the four case files. There wasn't any evidence or connection between victims to go on. No matching DNA—hell, no DNA at all besides the victims'— and no consistent fibers. A few foreign hairs, but the initial analysis pointed to those being cat hairs, the particular breed not yet identified. It was a surprise the ME even noticed that the cases were connected. Most were too over-worked and overwhelmed to have connected these dots.

Their ME was a damn good one.

And I would know, considering I'd worked with her before. It shocked me to see her name listed on all the autopsy reports, which morphed into excitement at seeing her again when Rhyan assigned me this case.

Just thinking about Dr. Rain Evans had memories from those two years working together flickering to life. Slightly awkward in an adorable, quirky way, Rain drew me to the morgue more often than needed. She was married, so nothing happened between us, but that didn't stop the spark our friendship struck within me. Her easygoing nature, the strange things she'd blurt, the genuineness of her laughter, and her personality made me wish I'd met her before her asshole of a husband did.

If I were to settle down with anyone, it would have to be someone as amazing as Rain. Which I'd yet to find.

My shaggy, light-brown hair swept across my forehead as I shook my head, hoping to dislodge the ever-present loneliness her memory stirred to the surface. Between Tallon and Remy busy working on their new relationship and the new job that sent me hundreds of miles from my family in Nashville to Dallas, the glaring solitude in my life was almost too much to shove to the background.

I was too focused on completing training at the top of my class, then learning the ins and outs of the profiler role to even think about anything other than work. The past several months, my personal life took a back seat to advancing my career. Besides, it was tough to find a partner—or partners, really—who enjoyed the type of relationship I did.

"Check in once you've met with everyone and had a chance to get set up. I requested a room set aside for you at the station, but apparently, they're busting at the seams.

Detective Slade offered to kick someone out of their office, but...."

Yeah, starting off a challenging case with some officer or detective already hating me for taking their space wasn't ideal. Not everyone agreed with the FBI coming in and poking around their cases, claiming to know more than the local police force, so adding to the tension wasn't what I wanted at all.

"The last case, Cooper and I worked mostly from our hotel rooms," I said absentmindedly. "But that wasn't great since we couldn't let housekeeping in with pictures of the missing women plastered all over the walls." Considering I didn't know how long it would take for me to come up with a solid profile, not having housekeeping wasn't an option. "I'll figure something out once I'm there and let you know where I end up."

"So, what else is going on in life?" Rhyan asked, her odd tone triggering all the red flags.

"Nothing much, but what's all this about? Not that I don't enjoy talking to you, boss, but I really need to review these case files before landing in an hour."

On the screen, her eyes cut to the side. "Um...."

"She's trying to keep you distracted since you're afraid of flying" came the familiar voice of Special Agent Charlie Bekham, our tech genius and Rhyan's romantic partner, from somewhere off-screen.

Rhyan cringed, validating his announcement.

"I'm not afraid," I said through gritted teeth. "I just hate not being in control."

"There is so much to profile from that statement," Rhyan said with a sly grin.

There was.

Too much, which was why this conversation needed to end before she tried to profile me.

"Thank you, but I'm good. I'll reach out once I've landed and settled."

Her lips parted, brows pulled in tight as she started to respond, but I ended the video call before she could get a word out. I'd no doubt get a text shortly with her apologizing for overstepping, but I knew she only meant well.

Rolling my shoulders, I shifted in the plush leather seat, but it didn't help me refocus on the case. Instead, my admission to Rhyan kept nagging at me to look deeper into my self-identified issue. I wanted control in most aspects of my life, but I wasn't controlling toward others. Unless they didn't have a plan in place—then I'd shift into an annoying, controlling asshole to get shit done. I was a sucker for a solid, easily executable plan. Which all made me a damn good detective because I hated loose ends.

Though none of that translated into what I wanted behind closed doors.

There, I didn't want to think, have to decide or overanalyze everything like I did in every other aspect of my life. Which made Tallon and me perfect partners those years we'd shared lovers. He liked to control every aspect of the scene, and I enjoyed rolling with his orders, knowing he'd keep everything mutually beneficial for everyone involved.

It was a unique relationship; one I'd only had with him. Until it all ended the first time when his sister went missing, then again most recently when he started a solo relationship with Remy, a past hookup of ours. When I wasn't sharing with Tallon, I settled for one-night stands, which was fine, just not as exciting or fulfilling on my own. Though I wouldn't say my unique interests in the bedroom were the only reason my relationships never worked out long term.

The demanding job of a homicide detective in a large city like Nashville and now as a profiler, flying around the US with little to no notice, didn't make relationships easy. No woman wanted to be constantly left behind or ignored for a new murder case, or plans always changing because of a fresh lead. The job as a detective was all-consuming, and so far from what I'd seen, so was being an FBI profiler.

Which meant I was shit out of luck in the love life department.

Pinching the bridge of my nose, I closed my eyes and forced myself to relax into the seat. The random hookups were fine, scratching an itch for myself and my partner for the night. Though, if I was honest with myself, even those were becoming draining instead of leaving me recharged for a few weeks.

I longed for a connection with a partner beyond the initial physical attraction. Missed the deeper aspects of a relationship, a friend and lover wrapped in one. I wanted that in someone—or really two someones—long term. But that wasn't possible.

Not for someone with fucked-up needs like mine.

What I craved in a relationship wasn't what people wanted in the long run. Group activities in the bedroom were just a fling, a way to check something wild off their sexual bucket list.

No one wanted to share in a committed relationship. To have one woman you both gave everything to because your everything was only half of what they truly deserved.

No one but me.

2

RAIN

"I know it's a risk, okay?" I admitted with an exaggerated sigh. "It's just... I'm not meeting anyone the traditional way, so online dating it is." My chair rolled along the floor with each of my jerky movements, unable to keep myself still. Eyeing the clock, I cringed. I needed to leave soon if I wanted to go home and freshen up before the date I was half dreading, half excited for. "No one here looks at me in that way, not when they know what I do."

Inhaling a slow, calming breath, I allowed my lids to flutter closed and counted to ten before releasing it through tight lips.

"I chose a busy bar just down the road, just in case he turns out to be a serial killer and wants to turn me into a skin suit. I'll be fine." Not sure who I was convincing here. "I just need to remember to not say anything weird," I grumbled as I stood. Shooting Caroline Pickard a sad smile, I strode toward the steel table she lay on. "So that means no talking about work. At all." Which sucked since work was basically my whole life. "Don't blurt any random, awkward-as-hell-even-in-*my*-mind comments or thoughts. And most of all, do not compare this guy to you-know-who."

Because no one could. I knew that. Hell, even Caroline knew that, and she was dead.

As if the simple act of thinking about him conjured his overwhelming presence, the door behind me swung open, nearly banging against the opposite wall. It had taken me the last eighteen months to get Detective Slade Taylor to consciously use less force when entering the morgue. As a result, the wall hadn't needed repairs in weeks.

"You got anything for me, Rain?"

My name on his lips sent a shiver racing down my spine like it always did. Something about his deep rumbling tone did strange things to my body, making it tingle and pulse with just a few words.

This was clue number one out of a hundred that I needed to jump back into the dating game, to find a man who I was not only crazy-attracted to but also available. The always-grouchy, built-like-a-Roman-gladiator Detective Slade was only one of those two things. Not because he was married or engaged or even dating anyone, but he wasn't available to me.

And only me, considering the line of women he'd left in his wake for the two years we'd worked together.

It was painful, having this intense crush on a man I worked with day in and day out only to remain invisible in his eyes. Sure, he valued me as the only ME in Santa Coasta, but that was all Slade saw. He'd never come right out and said he wasn't as attracted to me as I was to him, but I knew without him having to tell me. There were no long looks, no striking up casual conversations to get to know me better. Though, being fair, he didn't do that with anyone at the station. Plus, the man who could easily be an underwear model instead of a detective was way out of my league. He went out with gorgeous actresses or runway models, not women like me.

Normal.

Well, normal was subjective.

I did just have a one-sided conversation about my dating life with a dead woman, so....

With my back to him, an attempt to keep my focus on work instead of noting every perfect inch of the massive man, I scanned the body in front of me, mentally cataloging everything I'd just written in my report. Though the report was a formality, considering Slade preferred to hear my findings straight from me.

Holding a shallow breath, I dared a quick glance over my shoulder. Standing at six foot five, he seemed to loom over me with his height and wide frame, even with the distance between us. With a lovesick sigh, I stared a little too long to be professional. His trimmed beard did nothing to hide the strong jaw beneath. Somehow his slightly crooked nose from one too many injuries added to his good looks instead of the opposite, and the penetrating green eyes highlighted by his thick dark lashes made him breathtaking.

He was and always would be completely out of my league.

As usual, a deep scowl lined his ruggedly handsome face, intense gaze locked on the woman's feet. Not on my ass like I desperately wanted.

Air rushed past my pursed lips with a deflating breath.

Yes, this somewhat-blind date was terrifying but absolutely necessary. I needed to get over this insane and unrequited crush. This was no way to live day in and day out, working side by side with someone while desperate for their attention, knowing it would never happen.

Slade wasn't an asshole about his lack of attraction toward his socially awkward medical examiner. If he treated me like my worthless ex-husband had, it would be easy to move on from this infatuation. Instead, he was a grumpy gentleman. Not cold, but clear on the professional boundaries he kept firmly in place between us.

"Hey, Slade," I said, trying to keep the swoon in my tone to a minimum. This was ridiculous. I was an educated, thirtysomething woman. I did not swoon. Yet every time I allowed my imagination to wander on how his large hands would feel skimming up and down my lean frame, caressing what little curves I did have, the idiotic swooning happened. "You're stopping by later than usual. Didn't expect to see you to go over my findings until the morning."

He grunted something as he moved closer to where I stood over the body, careful to keep a very wide professional bubble between us.

Instead of wrapping his thick arms around me and squeezing me to his hard chest.

Talk about a scalpel to the heart.

Clearing my throat, I forced my focus back on the reason he stopped by.

"I was just about to hit Send on my report and put her away for the night."

On the other side of the table, he nodded, dark brows pulled in tight as he scanned the dead woman's face. "Leaving at a decent hour tonight, Rain. That's as odd for you as it is for me. Hot date to get ready for?"

I stood a little straighter. "Well, actually, yeah. Though I wouldn't say 'hot' since I haven't met the guy in person yet. Though, based on his profile picture, he's—"

His green eyes flicked up from the body between us, drilling into my hazel ones. "Are you fucking with me? You're meeting up with a guy you met online?"

Embarrassment heated my cheeks at his words and incredulous tone. I swallowed hard to calm my racing pulse, giving me a second to form a response. How the hell did a few pointed words from him make me squirm like I'd done something wrong? I longed for his attention, yet when I had Slade's full focus, I ended up tongue-tied and unable to think straight.

Thankfully, I could always talk about work. Autopsies, pathology reports, and case-breaking evidence I'd found on the body were my comfort zone. Want to discuss the size and shape of a stab wound or the bodily fluids I found on a body? I was ready all day, every day.

A normal conversation about anything else... not so much.

Hence the pep talk I'd had earlier.

With a dead woman.

"You were right." Slade's narrowed eyes scanned my face. My shifting the conversation from my date back to work to avoid answering his question clearly didn't go unnoticed. Like he wanted to know about the date and how I met the guy anyway. He was probably more confused about why someone would use the internet to find a date, considering Slade could walk into any bar—hell, out in public anywhere—and every available, and sometimes not, woman would flock to his side, desperate for his attention.

I would, too, if he didn't only see me as a coworker.

Most nights I dreamed of him realizing he wanted me as much as I wanted him, that I'd wake up to him banging down my door, ready to test out all my dirty fantasies of us together. But that was all it was, a dream.

Men in my past claimed I was too tall and thin, not curvy enough to be considered conventionally pretty for a woman. Which, with almost zero hips, baby hills for boobs, and feet the size of water skis, I had to agree with them.

"Rain?" I jerked my head up, his gruff tone startling me out of my rambling thoughts. "You said I was right, so what was I right about?"

"Sorry about that. Lots on my mind," I sighed.

"Because of the date?"

"Yes and no. You know me." I tapped the side of my temple with a single finger. "This right here never stops. Speaking of stopping, do you think we could talk the chief into going more ecofriendly and stop printing out reports?"

Long, dark lashes fanned up and down with his slow blinks, clearly confused on where the hell that thought came from.

"Sorry, I read an article about the Amazon being destroyed last week, and it just popped into my head." My awkward, nervous laugh echoed around the morgue.

Right. Moving on.

Clearing my throat, I waved a hand over the body draped with a white sheet like a morbid Vanna White. "As I was saying before I spaced out and brought up the destruction of a vital part of our ecosystem, you were right about Mrs. Pickard here. She did not hit her head and drown in her home bathtub like her husband claimed happened."

Slade's intense green eyes stayed locked on me for several seconds before he gave a subtle shake of his head, breaking eye contact to stare down at the murder victim.

"So, no water in her lungs?" I dipped my chin in confirmation. "So, what was the cause of death, then?" he asked, features hardening as he took in the dead woman's face. "Are those bruises pre or postmortem?"

"The slight bruising on her face and shoulder was healing, so it wasn't part of the trauma inflicted at time of death." Pulling a pen free from my lab coat, I pointed the cap end at her neck. "Here is where I found the cause of death. The hyoid bone is fractured—"

His string of muttered curses cut me off. "That motherfucker strangled his wife and staged the whole fucking thing."

The vibrating anger in his harsh tone had me sucking in a sharp breath.

Sure, Slade was sinfully good-looking, but his unapologetic protective side was his most alluring feature from my perspective. Mess with women or kids and growly Slade came out in full force, and I had to lock my knees to keep from melting to the floor. I was as attracted to this emotional side of him as I was physically.

Hands curled into tight fists, he pressed them to the side of the steel table, the black ink designs along each finger standing out as the color bled from his normally tan skin.

"What else did you find?" he rasped, clearly restraining his growing rage at the man who killed his young wife in cold blood.

"Based on the bruising on her back, I'd say he held her down with a knee or hand between the shoulder blades while he strangled her from behind with either a towel or sheet, maybe. Not his hands or rope—I would've found distinctive bruising. I pulled a few white cotton fibers out of her hair and off the skin around her neck and sent them to the forensics lab in San Diego for analysis. Did you guys collect anything from their apartment that I could pull a sample from to test for a match on the fibers I found on her?"

"We bagged and tagged so much shit from their apartment that I lost count of what all we have. But I'll go through the evidence and see if anything matches what you're describing."

I nodded, knowing he'd be up here all night sifting through evidence, looking for anything that could help the case. "If you find something, let me know. I'll also swab it for DNA. It might not do much in court since they both lived in the apartment, so both sets of DNA would be on the item, but I might be able to prove where it was placed around her neck and where he gripped it based on the heavy presence of skin cells. Better than nothing."

The muscle along his jaw ticked, something that happened when he ground his teeth in frustration. Reaching up, he rubbed a wide palm over his short jet-black hair.

"This evidence, along with the hospital reports from previous domestic abuse, should be enough to convince a jury that her bastard of a husband did this on purpose."

The soles of my shoes squeaked along the floor when I twisted to check the time. When I turned back, Slade's attention was no longer on the woman between us but locked on me.

"Where are you going to meet this guy?"

I shoved both hands into the pockets of my lab coat to keep from fidgeting under the intensity in his gaze. "The Lager."

The corners of his lips twitched. "You chose a known cop bar for a date?"

I nodded, not understanding the humor lining his tone. "Well, yeah. I'm new to this online dating thing, and I wanted to go somewhere safe. I've heard some others talk about it...." I licked my lips. "Is that a terrible choice? Should I change—"

"It's fine."

Disappointment rushed through me, sinking into my stomach. Not sure what I was hoping for, but him saying it was fine that I was about to go out on a date with a complete stranger wasn't it.

"Right, well, I need to get things wrapped up here so I can get home and change."

That intense gaze slid down my body, taking in my simple baby blue blouse and black pants. "You look fine."

Fine. Again with that damn word.

Not *good.* Not *beautiful.* Not *hot.*

Just *fine.*

Wasn't that always the case with me? Not ugly, but not really attractive. Not too tall, but tall enough to scare most men off. I was stuck in this middle zone where men saw me as the quirky friend, not the one they wanted a relationship with. Maybe that was why I married Josh despite the red flags he'd waved early in our relationship. He gave me attention, said all the right words, and I fell hook, line, and sinker.

"Doesn't the fish only fall for the bait? Not really the hook or line, or even the sinker, for that matter."

"Do I even want to know?" Slade chuckled.

"Probably not. Even if I explained it wouldn't make sense." Wasn't that the truth? Explaining the random thoughts that popped in my head, refusing to leave me alone, was impossible since even I didn't understand most of them.

Intrusive thoughts. That was the term they used nowadays. And aptly named for me. These random thoughts usually came from some memory that randomly popped up, sometimes relevant, other times not.

When I was in the zone, alone with a body—which

sounded way worse than it actually was—I could focus. It was when I was alone that my mind wandered, which was most of my time outside work since I had zero friends or family in town. Most nights were spent at home with yet another delivered meal while I watched whatever latest Netflix show caught my attention.

And maybe that was all I was destined for in this life. Though I would take the lonely nights over walking on eggshells every day like I had with Josh.

"I also came down here to fill you in on those four cases you linked," Slade stated.

"Oh?" I checked the clock and sighed. If I stayed to hear what he had to say, there wouldn't be enough time to go home and change, but I really wanted to know what Slade thought of my findings. "Do you want some coffee?"

"If it's your good stuff, not the shit upstairs."

"Of course, it's my good stuff," I said, a smirk pulling at my lips. I'd already cleaned and put away all my tools, so the only thing left was to send my report and log off. And with Slade's help, I stored the body in her assigned drawer in record time.

Slade followed closely as I pushed through the swinging doors of the morgue and stepped across the hall to my small office. It wasn't a large space, but I didn't need much since most of my time was spent next door with the bodies. Grabbing two mugs, I placed one under the Nespresso machine, popped a caramel-flavored pod I knew Slade liked into it, and pushed the lever down.

Turning, I found Slade already sitting on the small teal love seat, leaning back with both arms stretched out along the back. My stomach flipped at the delicious vision. The top button of his white dress shirt was undone, giving a glimpse of the golden tan skin beneath. Both large, tattooed hands dangled on either side of the couch, drawing my attention to each thick digit.

"You okay there, Rain?"

"Yep," I wheezed, my breathing too shallow as I imagined those fingers dancing along my fair skin.

Not in my league. Not in my league.

"So, tell me more about this dead fucker you're meeting with tonight." My gaze jerked from his thrumming fingers to his jade-green eyes. I narrowed my own, not understanding his words. "You're taking this guy to a bar where everyone knows you and is over-the-top protective of their own."

This time, the wave of disappointment had a thick ball of emotions clogging my throat.

Of course, he didn't say that because he was possessive of me but because of all the cops who would be there tonight. And me working as their only ME in Santa Coasta meant I was one of them. Even if most gave me a wide berth when we passed in the hall or at crime scenes.

I liked to think it was because of my job, though I knew most thought I was on the wrong side of quirky, leaning more toward fucking weird.

"Right. Should've thought about that before choosing a location. Um, he lives close to San Diego, so he's driving up to meet me here and does something in accounting." Slade's incredulous huff cut off my next words. "Is his job funny?"

"For someone like you, yeah."

Hands on my hips, I shot him an annoyed glare across the room, ignoring the freshly brewed coffee at my back. "And what's that supposed to mean?"

Leaning forward, he pressed both elbows onto his thick thighs, his clasped hands dangling between his spread knees. "He won't understand you."

With an eye roll, I whirled around. Finger hooked into

the handle, I held the steaming mug and turned back, a response on the tip of my tongue.

But all words fled my brain upon finding him just a step away instead of on the couch where I last saw him. Eyes locked on me, he carefully took the mug, a single hand completely engulfing the hot ceramic.

"I didn't mean that the way you're taking it. I'm saying he won't understand what goes into our jobs. No one does unless they're in this life."

"So, you're saying all those women you date, they *understand* you?" I arched a brow and crossed both arms over my chest.

His gaze dipped lower before locking back on my face.

"I don't date," he whispered, closing the short distance between us.

Heat flushed beneath my skin at his proximity. "Yes, you do," I whispered.

"Dating and fucking are different things, Rain." I swallowed down the whimper that wanted to escape at hearing that word in his deep, gruff voice. "So no, I don't date. Not when I know it would be pointless."

"Why is that?" Needing to break the strange intensity building between us, I turned, my shaking fingers gripping the other mug and placing it beneath the machine.

"I know how it would turn out." The disappointment in his tone had my movements pausing. "And it's never the way I intended."

My throat worked as I swallowed hard. What in the hell was going on here? We never had these types of conversations. It was always about work, the cases and evidence. I didn't know how to process this Slade with the grumpy detective I'd known since arriving in Santa Coasta.

"What did you want to talk to me about?" I asked to get

us back into safe territory. Discussing the various homicide cases he and I worked on together was way easier than whatever this oddity was. Pressing the power button on the machine, I skirted around him to sit in the small armchair that sat catty-corner to the love seat.

He tracked my every move until I was settled. Lips pressed in a tight line, he returned to his seat, spreading his knees wide, taking up most of the space.

"After reviewing your notes and going back through mine of the crime scenes, I agree with you. One perp committed those four unsolved homicides."

The machine beeped, signaling my coffee was ready, but I ignored it. Instead, I leaned forward, eager for Slade to continue.

"I think we have a serial killer in Santa Coasta."

All the air rushed from my lungs in a forced breath.

"Wow," I said, flopping backward. Rubbing at the back of my neck, I stared at the wall behind Slade, mind racing with what this meant. "Damnit, I didn't want to be right."

"I know. But whether or not you wanted it, you were."

"What do we do now?" I leveled a pleading stare his way. "I've never worked on something of that scale. What if I miss something and—"

"Neither have I, Rain. Which is why I called the Behavioral Science Unit."

I wrinkled my nose. "The who?"

"The FBI." My dark brows flew up my forehead at that. "The unit leader in Dallas reviewed the case files and agreed with us. They're sending someone from the team to help." Switching the mug to his other hand, Slade glanced at his watch. "With the storms rolling in, he won't land until late tonight, so we can meet him here tomorrow morning."

Serial killer.

The FBI coming in to help.

Slade acting strange.

Why did I get a feeling my boring, predictable life was about to get a lot more interesting?

3

RAIN

"You must be Rain."

I glanced up from the sticky laminated menu to the man standing beside the high-top table I'd scored five minutes ago. When I arrived ten minutes late. Which meant he was fifteen. Not a great first impression, but I was late, too, so I couldn't hold it against him.

Too much.

I sure as hell wasn't about to lower my standards on punctuality—or anything else, for that matter. This was my chance to start over.

Instead of standing from the tall barstool for an awkward hug I absolutely didn't want, I held out my hand. "And you must be Tyler. Pleasure to meet you."

His fingertips slid along my palm as he released his limp handshake in an icky way that made me wipe my hand along my black slacks.

"I apologize for being late," he said with a half smile. "Traffic getting out of San Diego was a nightmare."

A server approached and asked for our order. Instead of

motioning for me to go first, Tyler spoke up. "We'll have two dirty martinis, please." He sat up straighter and pulled the menu from my loose hold.

"I don't like vodka," I offered with a brittle smile. "I'll have—"

"It's okay," he said, cutting me off and waving the server away. "I'm sure you'll love this. It's my favorite drink."

My left eyelid twitched, something that happened when I was annoyed or angry.

"Actually," I said, calling out to the server before she could walk away, "I'll have a Blue Moon draft, no fruit."

When I refocused my attention on Tyler, I found his lips pressed in a thin line, clearly unimpressed that I changed the order.

"I just assumed you'd want something low calorie. Most women I've been on these types of dates with have all wanted something similar." A tight smile pulled at his lips. "It's okay, though."

"Yeah, it is," I responded with my own razor-sharp grin, "because I don't like vodka."

"Whoa," Tyler scoffed, holding both hands up. "You don't have to get all emotional about it."

"I'm not emotional." The opposite, in fact. I was calm. After years of being gaslighted by Josh, I was well equipped to stop it immediately. "I'm just standing up for myself and what I want. So, you mentioned you're in accounting. Tell me what you love about your job."

Worst. Question. Ever.

Thirty long minutes later, I'd almost finished my second tall draft and had yet to say a word. He really, really liked Excel. While nodding along, feigning interest in his one-sided conversation about the software program, I scanned the crowded bar, hoping to see a familiar face.

Anyone who would save me from this agonizing death by talking of cells and pivot tables.

Hope sparked, making me sit up straight, when I met the gaze of a veteran officer I'd seen around the precinct. Only for that hope to be dashed, my shoulders rounding in defeat when he simply dipped his chin in acknowledgment before turning his attention back to the group he'd been talking to.

With a sigh, I tapped my phone screen to check the time, hoping we had shifted into warp speed at some point and this date was almost over.

Nope. Forty-two minutes and counting since I sat down.

"You worried about patients?" I jerked my gaze to Tyler, who gave a pointed look at my phone. "Isn't that why you're checking your phone mid-conversation?"

First, "conversation" indicated two parties speaking. That was not the case here. Second, was it lying if you omitted the truth just a smidge? Sure, I could toss out that my job was touching dead people all day, every day, and I liked it....

Shit, I really needed to rephrase that stuff. Even in my own head, it sounded creepy.

"I'm positive they're fine," I stated honestly. They *were* fine, tucked into their individual coolers for the night.

Knowing I needed to divert his attention from asking more questions about my work, I went with a standard first-date question. "So, did you grow up in California?"

"No, I actually grew up in Texas," he responded with an eye roll. "Glad I got out of there when I did. Backwoods hill-billies."

"Oh, I grew up in Dallas...." I trailed off when it was clear he wasn't stopping his own backstory.

Maybe I should tell him I touch dead people just to get this over with.

Blowing a semi-quiet raspberry in annoyance, I pressed an elbow to the top of the table and plopped my chin in my palm. My eyes glazed over as he continued to tell me his life story. It didn't take long for my focus to narrow in on the large mole on his neck.

Has he seen a dermatologist about it?

Damn, when was the last time I had a full scan to check for skin cancer?

I should call and schedule an appointment. Or book online right now.

My fingers twitched to swipe the screen and get this one now-nagging item off my to-do list.

"Don't you think?"

"Hmm?" I distractedly responded. *Damnit, what was he talking about?*

"I said we should limit who moves here. Set up a screening process."

The last swallow of my now-warm beer caught in my throat. Covering my mouth with a loose fist, I coughed, trying to clear my airway.

"Didn't you say you moved here?" I said once I could talk.

"Well, yeah, but—"

"Hey there, Dr. Evans." I twisted in my seat, smiling up at the young officer who'd stepped up to our table. "Good to see you out with the living tonight instead of being stuck in the morgue."

If this date had been going well, that statement would've made me cringe. But as it stood, I was grateful and didn't give two shits that the officer had just outed me.

"Yeah, well." I shrugged. "Can't let you guys have all the fun, and I'm not the dead one unable to go out and live life."

"Just those you spend your days with?" He chuckled with a genuine smile that made his icy blue eyes sparkle.

"What the hell is he talking about?" Tyler asked. *Oh shit, forgot he was here.* "What does he mean 'out with the living' and 'the morgue'?"

The officer's smile fell as he turned to my so-called date. "Meaning she's the queen of the dead, man. If there was foul play involved, this amazing woman will figure it out. She's the best medical examiner ever to come through Santa Coasta—hell, maybe the entire state of California."

I almost preened at the officer's words until I noticed all the blood had suddenly drained from Tyler's face. I scooted to the edge of the stool, prepared to catch him if he passed out.

I am totally "not it" for administering CPR if he falls off the barstool and hits his head.

"You said you were a doctor," he accused, eyes narrowed in my direction as he slowly inched back, putting more distance between us, as if that would change the reality of my job.

A job that he, and most people, were repulsed by but I liked, thank you very much. Even if others saw it as disturbing. I didn't. I gave a voice to the dead, helped grieving family members find closure, put bad guys away because of things I found.

So, screw this Excel-obsessed jackass for making me feel anything but proud of my career choice.

"I *am* a doctor. I have the medical degree to prove it."

His trembling fingers rose to hover in front of his face. "Oh fuck. I touched you." His eyes were now the size of saucers. It would be funny if it weren't insulting.

My abrasive snort snagged his attention back to me

instead of the hand he was certain would melt off because it pressed against my skin. This man was the most ridiculous person I'd ever met. "You can't catch death, you idiot. Plus, I washed my hands before leaving work." Teeth sunk into my lower lip, I searched the ceiling as if trying to remember. "At least I think I did."

"Oh fuck no. I'm out of here." With a scathing glare, he hopped off the stool and shoved his way toward the front door, not caring who he pushed out of his way in his desperate attempt to leave my orbit.

Just like that, my first date in almost two years walked out of the bar.

And I wasn't sad about it.

Slowly, the rolling laughter and loud voices filtered in, reminding me that I was in the middle of a packed bar. Embarrassment heated my cheeks. Hopefully, no one but the officer still hovering close by noticed me getting left in the middle of a date.

"Sorry I just ruined your night," he offered, kind enough to glance away as my embarrassment mounted.

Reaching up, I patted his shoulder, loving that he didn't instinctually flinch away from my touch. "You actually made it better. Want to stick around and have a drink with me?"

His eyes widened ever so slightly. "Um, no. Can't."

"Right." I waved him off with a lopsided smile. "I'm sure you're here meeting friends or something. Don't worry about me. Go have fun. Live life to the fullest and all that. Enjoy your youth."

His laugh carried over the other sounds of the loud bar. "Enjoy my youth? Who says that?"

"Me, apparently," I grumbled. "Please go before I say anything else embarrassing that will confirm I belong with the dead more than I do the living."

"Jenson, what the hell are you doing bothering the good doctor here?" A familiar female detective bumped her slim shoulder against the officer's. "Did you really run off her date?"

"He saved me from my date," I corrected while flagging down our server and ordering another beer.

The detective's dark brown eyes narrowed. "Why did you need saving? What did he do, Dr. Evans? I can arrest—"

"Nothing besides being an arrogant, self-centered asshole."

A smile pulled at the corners of her lips. "Seems to be the norm with the gender, honestly. Based on the ones I've dated, at least."

"Hey," Officer Jenson protested. "Not all of us."

"You want to come hang out with me and my friends? I'm Jennifer—Jennifer Gray—by the way. I've seen you around, but I don't work homicides, so we haven't really met."

I started to lift my hand but noticed she didn't extend hers, so I quickly tucked it under the table. "Nice to meet you officially, Jennifer. What friends?"

I followed where the detective hooked her thumb over her shoulder. A group of four women sat around a small high-top table, three of them talking while one stared our direction with an unreadable expression on her face. A chill ran down my spine as I held the woman's gaze.

"Thank you for the invite, but I'm just going to drink this beer, pay the tab, and go home. It's been a long day, and tomorrow will be worse, no doubt."

I smiled at the server as she set my beer down.

"Why do you say that?" Jennifer nodded to Officer Jenson as he covertly removed himself from the conversation, slipping into the growing crowd of people.

"Just lots going on," I said evasively and took a sip of the cold liquid. Sure, she was a detective, but I wasn't about to tell her about the FBI coming in since she wasn't directly involved.

"I heard about the uptick in homicides." I studied her features, waiting to hear where she was going with that statement. She laughed at whatever she saw on my face. "The gossip mill is alive and well at the precinct. That's how I know, but thankfully we have you to help get all those solved." She glanced over her shoulder. "I better get back before the girls order me a shot for ditching them so long on our night off. Bye, Dr. Evans."

"It's Rain, please."

"Cool. See ya, Rain."

Turning back to the table, I studied the full pint glass. *That wasn't so bad. Wait, did I just make a new friend?* Jennifer didn't shy away from me, even though she was well aware of what I did for a living. I said nothing random or embarrassing, which was because she made me comfortable—or the two beers had taken the edge off, making me somewhat normal.

Female friends in the past were not only hard to come by but even harder to keep. At this point in my life, I'd stopped trying, knowing it would end with me heartbroken that another person I considered a close friend went radio silent, or I found out they just wanted to use me for something. Usually, it was to get close to one of the officers or detectives I worked alongside.

After finishing the beer and paying the full tab—that Excel-loving asshole's shitty drink included—I weaved through the happy throng of people, easily slipping out the front door without being noticed. Once outside, I relaxed, embracing the chilled breeze that had goose bumps popping along my bare arms. Hands wrapped around the opposite biceps, I started down the sidewalk, eager to get home and soak in a steaming-hot bath like any other night.

By the end of my normal ten-hour day, my lower back hurt from standing all day, my brain was mush, and, since I normally worked through lunch, I was starving.

Like now.

My stomach growled at that moment, so loud that anyone close would think I had a tiny bear tucked in my purse. The thin leather strap of my handbag shifted off my shoulder from the jostling of my quick pace. Normally at nine o'clock I was tucked in bed, reading or watching TV.

And that was completely fine by me.

Thankfully, being an ME meant I made enough to not need a roommate, even with the crazy-high prices in Southern California. I enjoyed the quiet solitude living by myself offered. Even if sometimes the quiet was too much and the solitude was more ominous than relaxing. A roommate wouldn't fix that, though, only someone I was excited to see and hang out with at the end of a long day, not just a warm body.

Turning the corner of a two-story brick building without looking, I clipped the edge with my shoulder.

"Oh shit, I'm sorry." I looked up at the building, then smacked my forehead. "Sorry, I apologized like you're a person." My feet slowed to a stop. "But you're not, so I'm going to keep walking."

Why the hell am I so strange? No wonder I didn't have friends. I was talking to buildings, for fuck's sake.

The short walk home was fine until I turned the corner, my townhome within sight. My steps slowed as the hairs on the back of my neck stood on end, an unsettling feeling sitting heavy in my gut. The straps of my bag dug into my palm as I held it close to my side. A frantic look over my shoulder for the cause of my spike in anxiety came up empty. Turning back around, I picked up the pace, the soles of my Golden Goose tennis shoes slapping the damp sidewalk with every step.

At the stoop to my place, I leaped up the steps, the keys to unlock the front door already in hand. The keys to the morgue and office clinked together, my hands shaking as I shoved the thin metal into the lock and twisted hard.

The solid dark wood front door swung open, me stumbling in after it to get inside as quickly as possible. It slammed shut behind me, the click of the deadbolt echoing in the pristine entryway and up the stairs. Ass pressed against the wall, hands on my knees, I sucked down gulps of air, my eyes trained on the door handle, fully expecting to see it wiggle as someone outside tried to follow me inside.

Gaze glued to the lever, I blindly felt around the umbrella holder in the corner, fingers searching for the only weapon on this level. The smooth wood of the bat dragged against the rough edge of the stainless-steel container as I pulled it free.

I wrapped one palm followed by the other around the base of the bat, fingers flexing and tightening to adjust my hold. Needing to be ready to attack, I raised it high over my right shoulder, prepared to smash the skull of anyone who dared enter my sanctuary.

A slight scrape, a barely-there sound, had my heart sinking into my stomach. I swallowed hard, hoping that would calm my ragged breaths, which were so loud it was impossible to hear anything else.

Sixty seconds passed with me at the ready, standing as still as a statue, listening and waiting.

But nothing happened.

No one knocked, not a single thump of a fist or shoulder against the wood to break down the barrier between me and the threat.

My muscles were locked from holding the rigid position too long, and I had to force myself to lower the bat. Keeping a hold on my weapon, I backed away from the door, gaze still locked on the handle, watching for the smallest movement. When the rubber heel of my shoe hit the first step that would take me to the main living area, I slowly backed up the steep stairs, never looking away from the door. At the top landing, I peeled my fingers free, setting the Louisville Slugger against the wall that led to the living room and kitchen.

As I glanced around the large open space, the tight tension slowly eased, allowing my shoulders to drop from around my ears and the first full breath since I felt eyes on me outside to fill my lungs. I dug through my bag for my phone as I made my way to the kitchen. With it clenched tight in my fist, I dropped the large carry-all bag onto a tall clear plastic counter stool and immediately opened the fridge.

Various take-out food boxes lined the shelves from the past week, but nothing grabbed my attention except for the few beer bottles on the door shelf. After snagging one dark bottle, I popped the lid off and slid a thumb across my phone screen, desperate to figure out dinner and move on from the terrible night. Smooth glass pressed to my lips, I tipped the bottle back. Cool liquid slipped down my throat, erasing any lingering fear as I scrolled through my favorite delivery options for dinner.

Before I could confirm the delicious sushi order, the screen flashed with an incoming call.

"Hey, Mom," I said, my voice echoing around me as I pressed the phone to my ear.

"How did the date go?"

"My day was great, thank you for asking," I responded sarcastically, rolling my eyes, though a crooked smile pulled at my lips.

"Rain Day Evans." Yep, that was my full name. My parents were hippies. When I got old enough, I thanked them for abstaining from naming me Rainy Day. Which, per my "uncle," was his call. "I've waited months for you to get back out there and live your life. Don't make us waste our valuable time with common pleasantries."

"So, you don't want to hear that I was right about those cases being linked?" I arched a brow as I took a slow sip of my beer.

Silence filtered from her end of the line, making my smile grow. It wasn't every day that I could stun my mother into silence. I relished the moment, knowing all hell was about to break loose once she came to her senses. We had a great relationship. My dad and uncle too. Maybe because I was an only child, and with that, I was their world.

"Really? Rain, that's... amazing sounds like a terrible word, but it is. You pieced together the clues. I'm so proud of you. James," Mom yelled into the receiver. I grimaced and pulled the phone away from my ear to save my eardrums. "Rain has a serial killer case!"

"Oh hell," I grumbled. Walking around the large marble-top island, I pulled out a stool and plopped down, knowing this call would take a while.

"Honey," my dad's voice joined Mom's. "I know you can't discuss specifics of the case." As the police chief of a small town outside Dallas, he understood the rules I had to follow. "But are you safe?"

The beer bottle hovered halfway between my lips and the counter. I slid my gaze to the baseball bat. "Why do you ask?"

"You're a single woman and the ME who just connected several homicides. If this suspect wanted to take out the person who identified his killing spree, you're an easy target."

"Wow," I mouthed, then spoke into the phone. "Thanks for the confidence boost, Dad. I'm not an easy target."

"One karate class when you were six does not mean you're capable of—"

"Get your facts straight. I was eight, and it was two classes." He didn't need to know about the self-defense classes I'd taken since leaving Josh. He'd question why I needed to feel strong and safe again. Dad didn't need anything else on his plate.

"The date, Rain. How did it go?" Mom pleaded.

Not sure what it said about me that I would rather talk about homicide than how the date went. It was just hard. They wanted me to be happy like they were. All three were successful in their careers and living life to the fullest. And I meant full. Despite being crazy busy, they maintained a healthy marriage, still disgustingly happy.

All three of them.

"Not great, Mom." After taking a swig, I twirled the bottle along the smooth marble. Neither said a word, and I knew they were doing that silent conversation thing on the other end of the line. "It's fine. I'm only thirty-two. I have plenty of time to keep looking."

"I just want you to be happy," Mom sighed.

"Who says I'm not?"

"Your tone, for one. The fact that all you have is work, no friends, and no family out there is another—"

"You guys, I'm fine. I'm building my career, enjoying my freedom from that soul-devouring marriage. I'll figure out the happily ever after thing some other time."

Right now, I had a serial killer to help catch.

And no clue how to do it.

4

———————

SLADE

Annoying-as-hell alternating chimes filtered through my dead-to-the-world sleep, their sound rising the longer I ignored the damn alarm as I lay sprawled on the bed, struggling to get my stiff body to move. I slapped the mattress, searching for the phone lost somewhere on my king bed. A frustrated grunt escaped me, deflecting off the silk pillowcase and sending my own hot morning breath wafting over my face. Every single one of my muscles protested as I rolled to my back, the ever-constant reminder of the beating I'd put my body through playing football for half my life.

Peeling one eye open, I held the phone an inch from my face, then tapped Snooze before letting it tumble onto the pillow beside my head, narrowly missing my cheek. But like every morning, there was no point hitting Snooze. I was up whether or not I liked it.

Eyes closed, I stretched my neck one way, then the other, slowly warming the muscles for the long day ahead. A few years ago, I'd learned if I gave myself time to wake up slowly, ease my banged-up body into motion instead of popping out of bed, I could prevent hours of painful, stiff muscles and joints.

Playing tackle football from the age of eleven to when I was forced to retire fifteen years ago left me dealing with a body that felt older than my actual age of forty-five. Hell, the career I chose after football had aged my mind and soul too. All the violence I saw on the field and now in Santa Coasta wore me down to this.

An irritable, old-ass motherfucker who needed the max dose of over-the-counter pain relievers and the hope of seeing the most interesting woman I'd ever encountered to edge me out of my too-comfortable bed every damn day.

I peeled my lids back and blinked up at the ceiling as I started my morning muscle warm-up routine, rolling both shoulders forward and back.

Dr. Rain Evans was the only reason I'd stuck around Santa Coasta as a homicide detective. I was so close to resigning when she arrived fresh from completing her forensic pathology fellowship, ready to start her career as our medical examiner.

She was young, innocent, and way too good a woman for someone like me, but I was drawn to her the moment she'd walked through the station introducing herself to the officers and other detectives. The wide smile on her face, her bright shining light that was so at odds with her career choice, I immediately felt the urge to protect her any way I could. Shield her infectious joy from the violent shit we dealt with on a daily basis. Which was dumb as fuck considering she chose her career, not the other way around, but it didn't stop me from wanting to keep this job from corrupting her.

At first, I told myself the protective urge came from a fatherly type instinct since she was almost thirteen years younger than me. But the way my heart pounded and cock twitched every time we were in the same room was constant proof that there was nothing fatherly about my feelings for Rain.

Though I didn't want the job to corrupt her, I wanted to debase her slowly, make her crave me like I did her. Not that she knew. That professional line was firmly in place, something I had to remind myself of daily. I wouldn't bring her down by giving in to everything I wanted, not when she had her whole young life ahead of her.

The muscle that never failed to come alive first thing in the morning slowly hardened as her beautiful petite face floated through my mind. Though it was her wide, guileless smile that got me every time I was on the receiving end of one, which was often since she thought my grumpy attitude was hilarious. No fucking clue why.

Then, of course, there was her brilliant mind that usually rendered me speechless. She said the strangest shit, which oddly enough was a breath of fresh air compared to the dull, shallow women who flocked my way expecting the man I was years ago instead of this washed-up version.

Rain didn't care what she said or what she wore. Rain was Rain. And she was fucking perfect that way. Too good for an old bastard like me.

She deserved someone as amazing as her, not an old asshole who couldn't walk first thing in the morning, had been married and divorced three times, and was dumb as hell compared to her clever brain. Not only did I not deserve a chance with someone like her, but neither did the assholes who I worked with every day.

Which was why I told them all to stay the fuck away from her the day after she arrived in Santa Coasta. It was either my large intimidating size or the look of promised death when I clearly explained that she was off-limits, or possibly both, because no one had risked asking her out or making a pass at her since that day.

Did it make me an asshole for shutting down all her dating options? Probably. Didn't change the fact that I still shook down every new officer or detective twenty-four months later, letting them know the "stay the hell away from Rain" rule and the consequences if it was broken.

"Fuck." My groan vibrated around the empty room. The insistent throb had me moving a hand beneath the sheets to wrap a calloused palm around my rock-hard cock, tightening my fingers until a sharp pinch of pain sent a hiss whistling through my clenched teeth.

Imagining her tall frame, those long, lean legs encircling my waist while I sucked on her perfect tits, thick fingers stuffed in her soaked cunt, had my hand jerking along my shaft. There was nothing fake about Rain Evans. No hard implants, no too-full lips with filler that were fucking disgusting to kiss. No, her naturally thick lips were perfect, too easy to picture wrapped around my cock as those hazel eyes gazed up at me with an eagerness to learn exactly what I wanted from her. That wild mane of dark brown hair clenched in my fist as I held her at the perfect angle. Or my hand collaring her neck as I slammed into her tight pussy, squeezing ever so slightly as she detonated around me.

The sharp, ear-piercing ringtone I'd programmed for when dispatch called shrieked near my ear, shattering the fantasy. Cursing a string of grumbled words, I swiped the phone off the bed and answered the call.

"Taylor," I bit out while shoving against the mattress until my spine hit the headboard. Eyes closed, I dropped my head back, resting it against the smooth leather.

"Good morning to you, too, Detective." The corner of my

lip curled in an annoyed snarl. I was not in the mood at seven in the damn morning for petty chitchat. Not that I ever really was. "A wellness check was called in by a neighbor. Responding officers found a bloody mess inside. Time to get to work. Sending you the address now, and Dr. Evans is on her way as well."

Tapping the red circle on the screen, I flicked over to the messaging app to update the FBI agent of the change in plans for the morning.

A pitiful cry from somewhere down the hall reminded me my only friend was hungry. Damn spoiled cat.

With everything squared away, I tossed the phone to the other side of the bed and slowly untangled my legs from the black sheet. Pops and cracks reverberated around the room as I stood, stretching my arms high above my head.

I frowned down at my bobbing cock, still standing at full attention. There wasn't time to finish what the fantasies of a naked and begging Rain started.

Nothing like beginning the day with murder and a case of blue balls.

CLOSE TO FORTY MINUTES LATER, I waited outside a cheap-ass motel, thumb impatiently tapping against the shitty sedan's steering wheel. I shouldn't complain since the car wasn't mine and got me from point A to point B, but I really hated the ugly-as-hell city-issued shit they forced me to drive while working. Tan four-door basic sedan with brown cloth seats that reeked of stale coffee. It was as embarrassing as a fucking minivan with a little stick figure family on the back windshield.

I'd much rather drive my blacked-out G-Wagon, everything about it perfect for someone with my build, but Chief said it was too flashy to use on the job. Though I figured the asshole was just jealous since he did, in fact, drive a mini-van. I was proud of the fucker, though, for taking one in the balls for his family and driving that dad-mobile.

I didn't have a family, so no hellion wagon for me.

Ever.

My attention swept from the man wandering around the other side of the parking lot to the one approaching who looked completely out of place at the rent-by-the-hour motel. Dressed in navy slacks and a pristine white dress shirt with a tie tucked into a vest, I immediately knew he was the agent I was here for. Our gazes clashed through the windshield, and I hitched my chin, indicating I was his ride for the morning.

I cringed at the ear-piercing screech the door hinge ground out as Agent Bend opened the passenger-side door. With more grace than my extra-large frame ever allowed me, the agent folded himself into the seat and slammed the door shut.

"Detective Taylor?" he questioned, shifting to face me.

"That's me." I slapped my hand in his and squeezed, which he matched, upping my opinion of the man. You could tell a lot about someone by their handshake. "I have a feeling we'll be together long enough to skip the fucking titles, so just Slade from here on out."

"Jameson Bend." He eyed the half-empty disposable coffee cup in his hand. "Please tell me there's a decent coffee place around here. I can't drink any more of this shit."

"It's on our way. You got everything you need?" At his nod, I shifted the car into Drive and slammed on the gas, shooting us out of the parking lot and onto the nearly empty street. I smirked at his barked curse as he held the cup in the air to keep the liquid from sloshing over the edge. "I didn't want to linger any longer than needed. I saw a few guys eyeing my tires, which would've been a pain in the ass to explain if they got stolen. You picked the shadiest motel in Santa Coasta, you know that? The FBI have you on an airtight budget or something?"

Keeping his death grip around the oh-shit handle, Jameson huffed. "I didn't choose the motel, one of our admins did. Clearly not realizing he'd booked me somewhere that the bedbugs were the size of miniature fucking dogs."

Pulling into the coffee shop I knew Rain favored, I directed the car toward the drive-through line.

"So, you're in from Dallas?" I asked, relaxing back against the seat while waiting for the car in front of us to finish ordering.

"That's right, but I recently moved from Nashville. I've only been with the Bureau about a year. Before that, I was a homicide detective."

My opinion of the man increased with that bit of information, which he probably knew would happen. He was establishing camaraderie, letting me know he understood firsthand the difficulties of my job. Damn, the guy was in my car five minutes and I already liked him better than half the men I worked with daily.

"Did dispatch say if this homicide was connected to the others or random?" he asked.

I held up a finger as I slowed the car in front of the speaker and ordered for me and Rain. "What do you want?"

"Largest coffee they have. No room for cream."

I nodded and added it to the order. As I pulled forward toward the window to collect the drinks, his stare burned into the side of my head. I shot him a look out of the corner of my eye. "What?"

"Large unicorn Frappuccino with extra whipped cream, caramel drizzle, and only blue sprinkles?"

My jaw clenched at the laughter in his tone.

"It's for our ME. She likes the sweet shit." I could still feel his eyes on me as I took the drinks from the woman at the window. "Don't start profiling me, jackass. That's a good way to get tossed out of my car."

"Fine," he said, still fucking smirking. "Speaking of your ME"—I shot him a questioning look at his odd tone when he mentioned Rain, having no damn clue what that was about—"her findings impressed me. I'm looking forward to digging into the cases with her."

My tattooed fingers tightened around the hard steering wheel. "To answer your earlier question, no, they didn't say if this was linked to the cases that brought you here. But I didn't want to leave you sitting around the station with your thumb up your ass while we worked this fresh case."

"Thanks," he laughed. He pried the lid off his coffee and inhaled the steam, lids closing like the aroma was pure fucking heaven. "Fuck, I need this. The flight in was long as hell last night. The only positive was it gave me more time to dive deeper into each case while we circled for an hour waiting to land."

"What's your take on the suspect?" The driver's seat protested as I shifted, trying to get comfortable.

"I have a few theories, though I want to hear yours first."

I glanced over with a raised brow. "Isn't giving us insight into this guy the reason you're here?"

Jameson took a sip of his coffee and shrugged. "I'm here to help identify the unsub's traits that will help you catch the fucker. But I'm not arrogant to think I can read a few files and know everything about the four cases. I need your firsthand knowledge to help piece it all together before the unsub turns this from four murders to a dozen or more."

I nodded. Everything he said made sense. Him not being an arrogant asshole, assuming he knew better because he had a fancy profiler title and federal badge, definitely won him even more points in my book. I could never trust someone who didn't keep an open mind with each homicide case. If this job had taught me anything, it was to expect the unexpected, because we humans were good at finding inventive ways to hurt one another.

"Okay, here's the CliffsNotes version of what I've picked up. One suspect—or unsub, as you called him—no partner based on only one type of knife used in each murder, even though the style of knife changes with each new victim." I slowed the car to a stop at a red light and took a quick sip of my steaming coffee, groaning as the bitter taste cleared the remaining fog from my still-groggy brain.

"It feels personal, don't you think?" Jameson mused from the passenger seat, staring out the window, watching the businesses and restaurants pass by.

"Huh?" I questioned, hitting the blinker before taking a sharp right down a residential street.

"Stabbing someone is personal, very hands-on. A gun would have the same result—death. The unsub could shoot them several times to ease the rage. So why a knife?"

"Too loud? We're not like Texas. Nothing is spread out. If you fire a shot, at least ten people will report the noise."

"True." He nodded. "Or the unsub enjoys being up close while they bleed out. The initial stab wounds on the recent victims were to incapacitate and inflict maximum pain, not kill quickly. Which again makes me think there are some personal reasons the unsub chose these specific victims, even though we can't find a connection."

I slowed the sedan, pulling alongside the curb and parking behind a police cruiser. Hand on the door handle, I paused before pushing it open to glance over to the passenger seat. "Don't think I haven't noticed that you're carefully choosing to not call the suspect him or her."

Jameson just smirked.

I raised a brow. "You don't think it's a male suspect?"

He fixed a contemplative stare out the windshield. "I don't have enough information yet, and I don't want to sway any future theories by pigeonholing us into one way of thinking. There are contradicting pieces of evidence I haven't figured out." He narrowed his eyes like that statement pissed the hell out of him. "*Yet.* Haven't figured it out *yet.*"

At that, he swung his door open and stepped out onto the sidewalk.

A low groan rumbled in my throat as I did the same, lumbering out of the low car with my coffee and Rain's in hand. With the side of my thick thigh, I slammed the door shut, not bothering to lock it with five squad cars around.

The June gloom was in full force, casting a gray haze over the normally bright sun, which helped keep the heat to a nice seventy degrees. I took the lead, Jameson falling a step behind me on the sidewalk as we approached the taped-off area. I nodded at the officer keeping the perimeter secure from nosy neighbors and gestured to Jameson. "He's with me."

The young officer nodded, though something shifty about his behavior had me pausing before ducking under the yellow tape.

"He's FBI," I continued. "No need to think you'll get in trouble for letting him into the crime scene."

"I don't think the fear in his eyes has anything to do with me," Jameson mumbled at my side, smirking behind the disposable coffee cup.

I glared down at the officer. "Out with it."

"I didn't hit on her," the kid blurted, hands raised in surrender. "I just stopped by her table to say hi. She looked uncomfortable."

My stomach dropped, realizing this idiot was about to out my "keep your distance from Rain" rule to the FBI agent listening to every damn word. "Please don't kill me. Sir."

Jameson barked a startled laugh but covered it quickly with a fake-as-hell cough. I shot him an annoyed look that only had his smile widening.

What the hell does this jackass find so fucking funny?

With a huff, I turned my attention back to the officer. "I'm not going to kill you, kid. Thanks for making sure she was okay. We're all good."

His narrow shoulders dropped, and a relieved smile pulled his lips upward. "Fuck, I was nervous. I grew up watching you plow down men twice my size on Sundays with my dad and—"

"Fucking hell," I grumbled and stormed toward the front walk that led to the house where the victim waited. "Don't say a fucking word," I shot at Jameson.

"Fancy unicorn drink and warning people to stay away," he mused as we stomped up the three concrete steps to the front porch. I nodded at the officer manning the door. Motioning for Jameson to go first, I followed him down the narrow hall toward the click of cameras and the stench of death. "She must be someone special."

He had no fucking idea. Though he would as soon as I had the "keep your fucking hands off Rain" talk with him.

"No way." Rain's voice came from the bedroom I'd yet to enter since Jameson had paused in the doorway. "Detective Jameson Bend. What in the hell are you doing at my crime scene?"

I shifted to look over his shoulder just as Rain slowly straightened from where she leaned over the body sprawled on the bed.

"Dr. Evans," Jameson drawled, finally moving so I could enter the room alongside him. Based on the smirk and knowing look in his eyes, the bastard wasn't surprised to see her like she was him. "It's been a while, Raindrop."

It was the wonder and hope in his fucking tone that had my gut churning and my hands squeezing around our drinks.

What the hell is going on here?

5

RAIN

Hand still hovering over the temperature gauge that helped me determine the time of death, I blinked at Jameson Bend, fully expecting the mirage to fade. But it never did. Jameson was there in the flesh, staring at me with that sexy-as-hell smirk that I remembered all too well. It had been almost two years since I last saw him, and damn, did that time do him well. Still as handsome as I remembered with his chiseled jaw, strong nose, lush lips, and ever-present humor behind those almond-shaped honey-brown eyes. The shaggy brown hair that looked in need of a haircut was different, though. So was the hardness to his features that stripped away the previous cuteness, leaving handsome as fuck behind.

I shook my head, sections of long dark hair slipping over my shoulders with the movement.

"You grew your hair out," he said, that smile of his growing. "I like it."

"Thank you. And you took on the *GQ* look." I gestured toward his trendy ensemble. Gone were the ill-fitted, off-the-rack suits and bargain-bin ties. The vest that perfectly matched his tailored navy slacks stressed his lean waist and firm chest. He wasn't wearing a jacket, and both sleeves of his crisp white dress shirt were rolled up, sitting snug around muscular forearms. "What are you doing here?"

Slade shifted, moving to block my view of Jameson. I sent him a confused look before my gaze landed on the yummy frozen concoction in his hand.

"Here," he grumbled.

I swallowed down the squeal of delight that wanted to escape at the sight of my favorite drink. It was exactly what I needed after sleeping terribly the night before. I ripped one glove off and gratefully took the drink from his extended hand.

"And to answer your question, why he's here. Bend here is the profiler the FBI sent to help us." His green eyes slid to the body on the bed. "Our guy do this?"

My lids fluttered closed in pure bliss as I sucked down the delicious liquid before answering. When I peeled both eyes open, their attention was locked on me, clearly waiting for a response.

Right, work first, then finish the yummy drink.

"FBI. Fancy." I winked at Jameson. "Seems we have a lot to get caught up on." Jameson flicked his honey-brown eyes between me and Slade, lips tugging down in a slight frown. "Yes, Detective Slade, this looks to be another one of our suspect's victims. I can't say for sure until I complete the autopsy, but all the similarities to the last cases are here."

The snap of latex sounded behind me as I turned my focus back to the thermometer jabbed in the victim's liver.

"Our unsub doesn't care about the mess left behind," Jameson muttered as he eased around the bedroom, studying the blood splatter.

"It's been like that at the other scenes, too, which I'm sure you saw in the crime scene photos."

Jameson only hummed a response, which made my lips quirk upward. When we worked together, me in my final forensic pathology fellowship needed to be a fully licensed ME and him a rising-star detective, he was the same way. Took his time examining every detail and committing them to memory to piece together later.

"Time of death is tricky." I scribbled the reading down on my notes. "Based on the liver temperature, I estimate it around forty-eight hours ago."

"But," Slade drawled as he inclined his head toward the AC vent, "the air is kicked down, keeping it cold enough to throw off his body temperature." I grinned, pride swelling at him noticing before I could point it out. Gesturing a crime scene tech over, Slade pointed down the hall. "Find the thermostat, document the temperature for Dr. Evans. She'll need it to identify an accurate time of death."

"What are other similarities from the previous murders?" Jameson leaned in close to study the body sprawled out on the full-size bed. Even with gloves on, he knew not to touch my body. Well, the dead body, which was mine. Though he could touch my actual body.

Wait, this is getting confusing.

"I suspect I'll find some kind of blunt force trauma to somewhere on the head beneath all that blood once I wash him down, if this is the same as the others," I stated.

"To disorient or incapacitate?" Jameson asked, though it sounded like he was asking himself instead of me and Slade.

"Did you read the reports on the other victims?" I sent a pointed look across the blood-soaked bed to Jameson. "Or barely skim them like another certain detective I know?"

"I read them," Slade grumbled as he stalked around the

room. He plucked a heavy-looking watch off the dresser between two latex-covered fingers. "Nothing looks disturbed, similar to the other crime scenes. Except for the gore-fest you're standing over."

"I read them, Rain." My heart did this strange flutter thing in my chest at hearing my name in Jameson's smooth voice. "But I'm sure like Slade over there, I prefer to hear the details straight from the ME so I can ask questions as they come up."

"And here I thought you came to the morgue just to see me," I chided Slade with a half grin. I knew that wasn't the case, but it was fun to hope. "I can't tell how many stab wounds this victim has, but if he's like the others, it will be thirty or more, most postmortem."

"Damn," Jameson muttered.

"I think I got something." Jameson and I both turned to where Slade squatted near the end of the bed. Careful to avoid blood splatter, I tiptoed closer and leaned over his broad shoulders, following the direction he pointed. "It's not much, but it looks like a shoe print to me."

My hair shifted with each tilt of my head, trying to see the faint crimson impression from various angles. "Could be. I'll put a marker on it for the CSU team to photograph."

"No physical evidence left behind. Air temp turned down to throw off not only the time of death reading but also to slow decomposition to not alert neighbors with the smell, and nothing taken that could eventually be traced back to the victim." Slade slowly stood, and I cringed at the sounds coming from his knees. "Anyone else annoyed with this fucker?"

I raised a blue-gloved hand and nodded.

Jameson huffed a laugh, shaking his head. "I've seen enough here. You good?" he asked Slade, who nodded. "SSA

Riggs asked for a place for me to set up, large enough for a murder board, but she said y'all are out of space?"

"Yeah, we've hired a bunch more officers and detectives in the past year."

"You can use my office." Both men slowly turned to face me. Slade was his normal grumpy self while Jameson wore a surprised expression. "What? I do most of my work in the morgue. The office is more of a formality. It's not much, but...."

Jameson nodded. "Sounds good to me. I'll try to keep the mess contained to not take over your space. We'll be working close together since there's little evidence to go on. The bodies will have to tell us everything."

"I'll finish up here." I gestured around the room. "And make sure the shoe print is documented."

Slade edged toward the bedroom door, tugging off his gloves as he spoke to Jameson. "Do you want to talk to the neighbors with me or head to the station with a uniform?"

I couldn't hear Jameson's response as they walked down the hall, the words muffled. That didn't stop me from watching them leave, though. Two very different body types, neither less attractive than the other.

Slade had the massive build with broad shoulders, thick thighs, and muscular arms, and I could picture him tossing me around, manhandling me the way only men in my dreams could accomplish. Whereas Jameson had a cockiness about him that spoke to knowing exactly how to use his lean frame to make you crave more.

"Excuse me, Dr. Evans."

"Yes." I turned, jumping back a bit when I nearly bumped into the crime scene tech. I inched backward, slightly uncomfortable with the way he stared at the body. "Did you need something?"

A chill swept down my spine when his bloodshot eyes slid from the dead man to me. His dry lips cracked with a slow smile as he tucked a few stringy locks of greasy dark hair behind his ear. "Is there anything else you want me to focus on?" He lifted the camera between us and gave it a shake. "I photographed the scene and the shoe print."

"What happened to your hands?" I asked, ignoring his words, focused on the exposed patch of irritated skin between the standard-issue latex gloves and the cuff of his long-sleeve shirt.

"Nothing's wrong," he said in a rush, dropping the camera so it dangled from the strap around his neck to yank both sleeves down. "Just eczema."

I nodded slowly, letting him think I bought the lie. Because I knew for a fact that it wasn't eczema. It was a chemical reaction. Clearing my throat, I forced my gaze anywhere else to keep from badgering the poor guy.

"Take pictures of the hallway and the point of entry that the officers pointed out earlier. Zoom in on the locks used on the back door. Detective Taylor will want to compare them to the other crime scenes."

With a clipped "Okay," he hurried off down the hall.

Odd man.

Though that wasn't uncommon in this line of work.

After releasing the body to be transported to the morgue, I grabbed my bag and carefully made my way out of the house and onto the quaint front porch, sipping the mostly melted drink that Slade brought as I walked.

That man was an enigma. I couldn't figure Slade out no matter how much time we spent together. Which was the complete opposite of Jameson. We'd flirted a lot while working together in Nashville, though it never turned into more since I was married. But now I wasn't, Josh somewhere far away from here, no doubt still pissed that I found the courage to leave him. After years of his backhanded comments and—

Oh shit. Did I turn my hair straightener off?

My stomach dropped. I thought I did. I usually did out of habit. Yet....

"What are the odds of a major fire starting because of a flat iron being left on?" I asked the officer who stood beside my white Tesla. "And if a fire starts and takes out the entire row of townhomes, will I be held liable? There could be animals trapped inside," I said, voice rising with my panicked thoughts. "Or people. Sleeping. It's still a little early. Shit, I can't go to jail for manslaughter. I don't even know how to make a shank!"

Ignoring his slightly alarmed, more confused stare, I hurried around to the driver's side and swung the door open. After tossing the black bag into the back seat, I pulled away from the curb and zipped quietly through the residential streets. As I drove from the crime scene toward home, all kinds of devastating scenarios played out in my head. The worst being that I stood trial facing the death penalty because my careless mistake caused the loss of hundreds of innocent lives.

Sure, there were only four townhomes in my section, but I didn't know how many people lived in the other three units. I'd never done a census of my neighbors. Hell, I didn't even know what my neighbors looked like. Between the long hours at work and having an unhealthy obsession with Netflix true crime documentaries, I'd never run into anyone.

A relieved sigh rushed past my lips as I parked along the curb in front of my house, no visible flames or smoke emitting from the roof. Chuckling at my idiot self, the crazy things my vivid imagination came up with which would no doubt give me a heart attack one day, I climbed the concrete steps, keys in hand, only to pause when something caught my eye.

The toe of my sparkly shoe nudged the frayed edge of my Christmas-themed welcome mat where an unfamiliar slip of paper lay tucked beneath.

Shit. I really need to switch out the doormat, considering Christmas was six months ago. But is it too late to put out the spring one? It was technically summer, even if the daily fog and gloom didn't make it feel that way.

With a quick headshake to refocus on the pressing issue I'd rushed over here for, I bent forward, the wind whipping several strands of dark hair against my face, obscuring my vision, as I reached for the white paper that was stuck beneath the top corner of the mat. My confusion grew as I plucked it between two fingertips. It wasn't thick cardstock, like a mailer for a local business would use, like I'd expected. Instead, it was a folded piece of lined notebook paper, the edges torn as if ripped from a spiral binding.

With a shrug, I shoved the paper into the back pocket of my pants and threw the door open. Inside, I dumped my purse and bag onto the floor and raced up the first flight of stairs. Death grip on the railing, I launched myself around the corner and hurried up the next flight to the bedrooms and potential fire hazard.

Nostrils flaring with each struggling breath, I jogged past the two guest bedrooms and the full bath toward the main bedroom at the end. Dirty clothes littered the floor, the pile of clean laundry still waiting to be folded on the side of the bed I didn't sleep on. Nothing differed from how I'd left it earlier that morning. No smoke or orange flames crawling across the room.

I blew out a loud relieved breath, the ball of worry in my

gut vanishing as I stepped into the bathroom, quickly scanning the open area and finding it just like the bedroom. Various bottles and tiny glass jars filled with expensive face oils lined the counter right next to the reason I'd almost died of lethal injection for mass manslaughter. The flat iron seemed to evilly cackle at me from where it sat on the counter, turned off and cool as a cucumber.

My eyes rolled to the celling. *I knew I'd turned it off.*

Rounded cord between my fingers, I yanked it free from the socket and then tossed the whole thing into the bottom drawer, slamming it closed with my foot like it was its fault I was this overanxious crazy person.

"Damnit," I groaned, tossing my head back.

This frantic, all-consuming worry had to stop. It wouldn't be bad if this only happened now and then. But the panicky episodes, overthinking, and questioning myself happened almost daily lately.

If it wasn't me freaking out about something I'd left on, it was if I'd locked the front door, or the car door, or my office. And if I couldn't remember, all the worst-case scenarios of what could happen would work their way into my thoughts and dig in until that was all I could focus on.

Double and triple-checking myself made me damn good at my job...

But a fucking nutcase in my personal life.

Maybe Josh was right that he was the only one who would put up with my increasing level of crazy.

Elbows pressed onto the cool counter, I smacked my face into both palms and raked my fingers back until they tugged through my loose strands.

No. Josh was not right. He was a manipulating asshole who made me dependent on him by making me feel unwanted and unlovable.

Though it was difficult to not see a sliver of truth in his blunt words. Who would want to put up with someone like me long term? My mental state most days was the definition of a shit show, not a hot mess. Looking back, I knew that was why I'd settled for Josh—I thought he was the best someone like me could do.

After that first time he cheated on me, then blamed me, claiming he did it because I worked too much and was never home, I should've left. But by that point, I believed his lies, questioning myself and what I had to offer anyone else.

Until a smirking, good-looking detective strolled into the morgue one day.

The man who helped me see through Josh's lies and manipulations was now back in my life, this time as an FBI agent here to help identify a serial killer. Back then, Jameson was casual about uncovering the issues in my marriage that I wanted to keep hidden. Not sure how he put everything together, but he did. Six months after we first met, our innocent flirting turned pointed, even uplifting in a way. He would constantly build me up, telling me over and over that I was enough.

Not enough for him or anyone else, but for me.

In his own unique way, Jameson gave me the strength to be okay with loving myself just the way I am, quirks and all. I didn't have to conform to Josh's needs or wants if they didn't align with my own—which they never did.

And now that amazing man was here.

My past crush working side by side with my current one.

"Fuck," I muttered to my reflection. "I can't even keep my heart rate normal with Slade in the room. I'll turn into a puddle of mush when it's both of them." One hand slipped down my neck, fingers wrapping around the base of my throat. "Both of them," I whispered, licking my lips. "Me between them—"

The familiar vibration of an incoming text jerked me out of losing myself to the very dirty fantasy.

Pulling out my cell, I skimmed the text letting me know the body was back at the morgue and waiting for me. Time to get back to work now that I knew for certain my house wouldn't turn into ground zero for setting the entire state of California on fire.

As I turned to head for the door, my fingers shifted along a texture different from my smooth cell phone case. Pausing, I rotated my hand to see what was stuck back there.

The note.

What if all my worrying projected into the universe and this was from a neighbor wanting to get to know me? Which could be great, but my nose wrinkled at the thought of all the effort it took to build friendships. An extrovert I was not, so starting a flimsy acquaintance with this unknown neighbor sounded exhausting.

Preparing for the worst, I unfolded the notebook paper.

Three words.

That was all it took to erase all concerns of the hypothetical neighbor friendship, douse the smoldering flames the thoughts of Slade, Jameson, and me together stoked, and make me forget all about the dead body waiting for me at the morgue.

I found you

"Damnit," I whispered, the paper shaking between my fingers.

Was my dad right about being worried for my safety?

Was I in danger?

6

JAMESON

I trailed a step behind the large detective as he lumbered up the short concrete walkway to the cottage-style home's front porch. Based on his stiff posture and occasional glares he'd shot my way since we started canvassing the neighbors, the man desperately wanted to ask how in the hell I knew Rain. And like the cheeky asshole I was, I wasn't about to give up any information until he finally broke down and asked.

I shouldn't find it entertaining to withhold the information, but there was an instant camaraderie with Slade that made me want to mess with him like I would my best friend, Tallon. And fucking hell, it had been a while since I had someone I could say that about.

The soles of my leather shoes scuffed along the porch as I slowed to a stop right behind Slade, rocking onto the balls of my feet with a wide smile when he lifted a massive hand and pounded it against the wooden front door.

"What the fuck are you smiling about?" he grumbled. Reaching into the inside pocket of his jacket, he pulled out the small spiral-bound notepad he'd used to take notes at the last few houses. "Murder scenes your happy place or some shit?"

I huffed a laugh, shaking my head. "Not my kink." He twisted to look over his shoulder, a single brow lifted. "I'm just wondering how long you're going to resist asking me."

"I don't know what you're talking about."

The click of a deadbolt being disengaged snapped our attention to the front door, and all my earlier humor faded.

Time to work. I can harass his stubborn ass after.

A blue-haired elderly woman peered through the three-inch gap between the slightly open door and frame. "What do you want?"

I held up my badge at the same time Slade did, introducing himself first, then me.

"We're here because of an incident about two houses down. Did you notice anything odd the last few nights? Anyone lurking around you didn't recognize, or a car, maybe?" Slade asked, his tone warm, the earlier annoyance gone. Though that didn't stop the look of sheer horror on her face as she stared up at Slade, who towered over her.

I sighed, knowing what was about to happen.

"No, sorry." With that, she slammed the door in Slade's face and quickly secured the lock.

And another one bites the dust.

"I should ask the questions from now on," I said, turning around and heading back toward the street. "All we've gotten so far is he was loud and had female visitors often. Pretty sure they're scared you'll grind their bones to dust if they don't answer right."

Slade chuckled behind me. "You say this *after* we're done canvassing the area." Up ahead, blue lights still flashed on the cruisers parked out front of the victim's home. "We'll have all the information on the victim pulled by the time we get back to the station. By the look of the other bedroom, he had a roommate who we'll need to question."

"Odd, isn't it?" I mused, stopping to take in the entire block of houses as questions filled my mind. "Some are killed outside bars, others in their homes. Once we get everything laid out in chronological order, hopefully it will make sense why."

"I'll do whatever you need to help identify this fucker," Slade stated, and I nodded my thanks. "You hungry?"

"Starving." My stomach twisted at the mention of food. "That shit motel didn't even have a vending machine to grab a granola bar out of this morning."

Back in his ugly-ass car, I buckled in as he turned the key, starting the engine. But instead of pulling away from the curb, he stared out the windshield, knuckles white from where he held the steering wheel in a death grip.

I sighed. "Come on, ask me. I know you're dying to know."

His low, annoyed growl made me smile. "Fine. Fuck it. How do you know her?"

"Her being...?" Of course, I knew who he referred to, but if he wanted the details on Rain and me, he needed to fucking ask the right questions.

"For fuck's sake," he growled and ran a hand through his short dark hair. "Rain. Dr. Evans. How do you know her?"

"I think you want to know more than that, but we'll start there. We met during her forensic pathology fellowship. She was working with the ME there in Nashville, where I was a homicide detective. Now I have a question." Slade shifted, putting his back to the door to face me fully as he motioned for me to get on with it. *Impatient fucker.* "I couldn't really tell because of the gloves, but it didn't look like she was wearing a wedding ring."

Slade blinked, the corner of his lips curling upward, probably loving that he knew information I didn't. Asshole. "That's not a question."

Touché, fucker. Touché.

"Is she still married?"

"Nope."

"Hence you memorizing her favorite drink and warning the other male officers to stay the hell away from her or risk your wrath."

Grumbling something under his breath, Slade shifted the car into Drive and pulled away from the curb. "I know nothing about her ex. She showed up here out of nowhere, full of so much fucking sunshine despite the dark that comes with her job. So yeah, I might have warned some assholes I work with about approaching her, but I didn't want anyone mixing business and pleasure."

"Right," I drawled. "And that's the only reason."

I cursed, hand jerking to grip the oh-shit handle so I didn't fall out of the seat as he took a turn too tight. "So, no more husband. Thank fuck."

"Did he hurt her?"

Now, if my Glock weren't sitting at my hip and I didn't know the vengeful wrath in Slade's voice wasn't directed at me, I might have shit my pants. Because holy fuck, the menace in his tone was intimidating as hell.

"Depends on your definition of hurt," I hedged, watching for his reaction to that evasive answer. As expected, he shot me a pointed glare that promised intense pain if I didn't get on with it. "Emotionally abusive, sure. Manipulative as fuck. Filled her brilliant little head with all kinds of lies and shit that I spent every day that year we worked together trying to untangle. But physically? I saw no evidence of that in how she acted around me or any visible bruises."

"Name." With just one word, I knew if I told him, he'd find Rain's asshole ex-husband and make sure he disappeared for good.

"I'm not giving you that."

"Why. Not?"

"Because from what I saw earlier at the crime scene, the connection you two have, you mean something to Rain. I won't be somewhat responsible for you getting tossed in jail for murdering the fucker."

"Only if I get caught," he stated with a sharp grin.

"Believe me, I fucking get it. Do you know how many times I debated making him disappear so he couldn't keep hurting her? I had to watch it all first-fucking-hand for a year, witness the confused looks and doubt as I worked to unravel his lies. The fact that I didn't murder that bastard should've won me some kind of damn citizenship award."

"I'll get you a cookie after lunch."

My lips curled into a smile. "Thank you. I feel seen."

He thumped his thumb on the top of the steering wheel while we waited at a red light. "So, you two never...?"

I swallowed the memories of how much I wanted her, making my throat dry, and turned to look out the passenger window so he wouldn't see how guilty I still felt for pining over a married woman. "No. That amazing woman, even though she was treated like shit and knew it, she remained faithful to him. That's the person she is. If she would've given me any sign that the flirting could've turned to more, I would've been all over her, but she didn't. And you know, as much as I hated it, her keeping those boundaries made me respect her even more."

He rubbed a hand across his mouth and slowly nodded

in agreement. Tense silence filled the car as we both thought about that amazing woman.

"Not trying to take us too far off-topic, but this car is terrible." Slade's barked laugh echoed in the interior. "I thought the one I had in Nashville was bad. It had been impounded after a body was found in the back seat. You really can't get the smell of death out of cloth upholstery."

A humor-filled smirk tugged at his lips. "I'll never make fun of this rolling turd again. At least it never had a dead body in it."

"How long have you been a detective?" I asked as we pulled into a diner-style restaurant parking lot. The few empty spaces hopefully spoke to the good food served inside.

"Seven years. Been on the force for almost twelve now."

He shoved the car door open and stepped out into the crisp morning air. I followed suit, taking a deep inhale of the cool breeze, a vast difference from Texas, which was preheating for summer.

Slade noticed my pause. "Can't beat the weather out here, even with the haze. Next month it'll be all sunny skies and warm weather, but the nights are always amazing."

The glass door opened with a silent whoosh, but the bell overhead had the hostess's head popping up at our arrival. A groan rumbled in my throat at the amazing smells that wafted over me. The younger blonde woman took one look at Slade, completely ignoring me, and literally sighed, slumping over the little wooden stand as she visually devoured him.

"How many?" she asked, twirling a lock of bleached-blonde hair around a finger. I snorted when she squeezed her arms, pushing her hard, round tits together.

Not using his big boy words, Slade held up two fingers

and motioned to an open booth in the back. One I noticed offered both sides the ability to see most of the restaurant's dining area and entrance. Once seated, I shifted along the fake leather bench to lean back against the wall, keeping one eye on the busy diner and the other on Slade.

"Here are your menus." I blinked, having forgotten the hostess was still there. "Is there anything else I can get you?" She was completely ignoring me yet again. Apparently, she had a thing for tatted giants. She fluttered her long fake eyelashes at Slade, who refused to make eye contact, simply waving her off while glaring at the menu.

I gave a low whistle when she finally took the hint and walked away with a huff. "You have it that bad for Rain that you won't even acknowledge someone like her?" I inclined my head back the way we came.

"Been there, done that," he muttered without looking up.

"Her specifically or...?"

"Her type."

"Which is...?"

"You always ask this many fucking questions to someone you just met?" I just shrugged in response, and he released an exasperated sigh that, for some reason, made me happy. "That type. Looking for something shallow, a one-night type thing. I'm too old for that shit. Plus, they all think they're getting the man I was fifteen years ago."

There was so much to profile from what all he'd just revealed. But first, I needed to verify if my assumptions about him and Rain were correct.

"You asked me, and I'll turn that question on you now. You and Rain, there anything beyond what I saw today?"

A harried, older waitress appeared before he could answer, asking for our orders. Having not even glanced at the menu, I ordered the breakfast special, knowing whatever came I would scarf down. I was so fucking hungry, the pain in my stomach was distracting. The amazing smells of greasy food and fresh coffee made my mouth water to the point that I worried about drooling in front of my new friend. Slade ordered some complex egg white omelet with a side of fruit and whole grain toast, then handed off the laminated menu.

He caught me watching him. "What? Some habits are hard to break from those years of watching every damn thing I put in my body. Plus, since I can't work out like I used to, my wrecked body making me feel every hit I took those years playing football, I have to watch what I eat if I want to fit into the clothes I spent way too much fucking money on."

I snorted. "College or pro?"

"Both. I loved it, every aspect of the game. The strategy and expecting your opponent's next move, plus wiping the fucking turf with their asses, was a blast. But then the wear and tear all those years of playing started showing. One critical hit to my knee and I was done."

His gaze took a far-off look. It was clear he missed it and hated that he had to give it up. That had to be difficult, loving something you'd done your whole life only for it to not be an option anymore one day.

"Football makes sense," I said, spinning the tightly wrapped paper napkin and silverware along the table between us. "You're a big fucker."

Slade's lips curled into what I now considered his version of a smile. "You'd be smart to remember that if you get any ideas of starting something with Rain while you're here."

"So, you two are together?"

A lost, almost sad expression flashed across his face, erasing his normal scowl. "No."

"Because you're not into beautiful women who are brilliant, funny, and quirky as hell?"

"Why are we discussing this instead of the dead man we left back at that house?"

The squeak of rubber soles against the floor jerked our attention to the now-frozen, wide-eyed waitress who held a glass of water in each hand. With what I hoped was a calming smile, I grabbed both from her with a mumbled thank-you. Sometimes I forgot how our casual conversations about murder and crime scenes sounded to those around us. Hopefully, she wouldn't call the cops on us. That was always a hassle.

"We're discussing your interest in the good doctor because I've looked over these cases a dozen times now and still can't nail down enough for a specific profile. There are too many contradicting elements. Each case varies just enough. I have a feeling that with these complications, I'll be here a while, and if I am, working side by side with you and Rain, I need to know what I'm walking into."

"Plus, you're interested," he hedged with a dark glint in his green eyes.

"Plus, I'm very interested." And I hopefully wasn't imagining things back there at the house. The spark that smoldered when we'd worked together in Nashville seemed to still be there for her too. Now I just needed to know if Slade would be a hindrance if I wanted to pursue Rain. "You obviously like her. You wouldn't do all the shit I've already witnessed just because you want to keep her safe. There's more to it than that."

His massive shoulders rose and fell in a noncommittal shrug, and he took a slow sip of water. "Even if there was more than me just wanting to protect her, it doesn't matter. We're colleagues, and that's all we'll ever be."

His dejected tone made a sharp pinch radiate in my chest. With a pained wince, I rubbed at my sternum, trying to ease the ache.

Why in the hell did a man like Slade Taylor think he didn't deserve a chance with someone like Rain?

But more importantly, why in the hell did I care?

7

SLADE

Fingers searching inside the side pocket of my slacks, I dragged out six painkillers and tossed them into my open mouth, swallowing them dry. After doing this several times a day for too many years, it was easy to force the small brown pills down with nothing to drink.

"Was it worth it?" Jameson asked, focus never lifting from the crime scene photos on top of Rain's desk.

Stretching my neck one way, then the other to relieve some of the tension, I relaxed back against the stiff couch. "Was what worth it?"

Face still downturned, he peered up and lifted both brows. "I wouldn't be much of a profiler if I hadn't noticed you're in pain every time you move and the handful of pills you take throughout the day to help." His brows pulled in tight as if an unwelcomed thought just popped up. "Those are all over-the-counter pills, right?"

"Would it matter?" I adjusted along the couch, slightly uncomfortable with his perceptive-ass stare directed at me.

It was *my* job to make people squirm the longer I glared at them.

Jameson straightened from where he was bent over Rain's desk, sorting the pictures, and tugged at the bottom of his vest. "It matters to me, yeah."

"Why?" I could easily tell him they were common over-the-counter pills I'd bought in bulk, but his agitation made me curious. Now I needed to know why he cared. This side of me, the drive to uncover the answers, was what made me want to be a detective.

"Detective Taylor, are you trying to profile the profiler?"

I lifted a single shoulder before leaning forward, the couch complaining beneath my weight. The thing was barely big enough to fit my enormous frame, and most of the time, I worried the peg legs would give out under my heavier-than-normal mass.

"Several reasons it would bother me," Jameson went on. "First, you're working alongside Rain daily, and I don't want that shit around her. It would make you unpredictable, and with your size compared to hers, it's not safe."

I dipped my chin, agreeing with him. If I found out any prescription junkie was hanging around Rain, I'd make sure they found their way out of town quick.

"Second, it's illegal, and I'm pretty sure that goes against everything we stand for."

I snorted. Another correct assumption. I'd hate any hypocrite in this precinct who thought they were above the law or could sneak around it to fit their needs.

"And third." His unfocused gaze flicked to the side, staring just over my shoulder. "My best friend's baby sister."

I stilled, waiting for him to continue, but he turned back to the pictures, leaving me hanging, curious as hell for more.

"Want to talk about it?" I asked. Jameson just shot me an incredulous look and rolled his eyes. "Fine. I get that. I have baggage, too, that I don't like to talk about. But explain what you're doing over there and if there's anything you need from me."

His narrow shoulders relaxed, clearly relieved that I didn't push it, which only made me want to ask again. I wouldn't, though. I'd only known this guy for a total of seven hours, but somehow it felt like longer than that. Hell if I knew why. I didn't have friends or want them, but then in walked this fucker. We'd been stuck together since he hopped in my car earlier, and surprisingly enough, I wasn't annoyed with him.

Yet.

"I'm sorting the photos and case files to set up a visual timeline on the wall behind me. It helps me to see it in chronological order."

"That something they taught you at the academy?" I stifled the grunt that wanted to escape as I shoved off the low couch and shuffled my way to Rain's desk.

"Yes and no. I would do this, but on a much smaller scale, at my desk as a homicide detective. But now, working multiple cases instead of single, the academy taught me to organize it better, to help it make sense. Once it's all up, you'll find me in here staring at the wall of pictures and notes for hours. It's my thing."

"If it works, I don't give a fuck what you stare at." Catching a glimpse of one of the photos, I pressed a finger to the edge and spun it to face me. "The first victim." Jameson pulled it free and turned to tape it to the wall. "What does that first case tell you about this guy?"

"Unsub," he corrected. "And it tells us a lot now that there are other victims to compare it to. The erratic placement of the shallow stab wounds, hesitation marks, and where the body was found point toward victim number one being unplanned, an accident maybe."

"An accident? I've never accidentally murdered anyone, despite the urge."

Jameson huffed a laugh and nodded. "Same. And by 'accident,' I mean maybe the unsub went there only intending to scare the victim or confront him about something, but then things got out of hand." After taping the crime scene picture to the wall, he turned, crossing both arms over his chest. "My theory is it triggered something in this unsub. I don't know what yet, and that's bothering the shit out of me. It would help if we could find a connection between any or all of the victims."

The desk dug into my ass and thigh as I perched on the edge while scanning the pictures Jameson had taped along the wall.

"I'm not sure about the connection angle with the victim from this morning. We're still running his background and all that shit. As far as the others go, the only connections they seem to share are their gender and, from what we can tell, being heterosexual. They held different jobs, some were in relationships, others not, and they lived in different locations in the city. Hell, they didn't even go to the same bars or restaurants. They lived totally different lives."

"Hopefully, Rain will have something new for us after the autopsy. If anyone can find something for us to go off of, it's her." His eyes cut my way, and I rolled mine, knowing this conversation was about to take a drastic detour. "Is she dating anyone?"

"Had a date last night," I grumbled. "Not sure how that went, but she's not in a relationship that I know of."

"Maybe I'll see if she's free tonight, then." He studied me, no doubt watching for even the smallest reaction. I gritted my teeth to not say a word. "You wouldn't have a problem with that, would you?"

"Why would I?" He shrugged, but it was that damn knowing smirk that pissed me right off. "Guessing you don't have someone at home waiting for you." That cocky attitude of his vanished, turning more introspective the longer I watched him. *Well, fuck, now I feel bad.* "Don't worry. Me neither."

"Ever been?" he asked. "Married, that is."

I held up three fingers. His sharp whistle cut through the office, and I snorted. "Tell me about it. Though they got their money and stay out of my life, which is fine by me— and them." Glancing around the small office, I released a humorless chuckle. "Guess that means I'm not cut out for long-term commitment, right?"

When he didn't immediately respond, I swung my gaze back his way, which he held for a split second before going back to sorting the notes and files. "Not necessarily. Are you wanting me to profile you and tell you what I see? Initial take, of course."

Shit. Was I?

Did I want to hear someone like him verify what I already knew?

"Nah, I know what happened. No mystery there," I said, not wanting him to list all my shortfalls. We'd be here all fucking day. "The first two, well, they married a pro football player but didn't realize that playing ball, being part of a team, wasn't only my job but my life. I spent hours on the field and in the gym, working with my coaches and studying playbooks. Though wife number two left after my injury, knowing I would never play again."

"Ouch. That's harsh."

I nodded, completely agreeing, though why should I

have expected her to stick around when I needed her support when I was never there in our marriage before the injury? "And basically, the same thing happened with wife number three, but slightly different. That time I was married to this job and didn't have time for her. At least that's what she told me all the fucking time."

"Same," he grumbled. "Especially now, flying across the country, spending weeks away from home. I can't even have a fucking dog."

"That's why I have a cat."

Jameson's hands froze, the papers dropping from his loose hold.

Ah shit. I just admitted that. What was it about this fucker that had me opening up? I hadn't talked this much in a twelve-hour period since maybe high school.

"You. Have a cat." I nodded carefully while he studied me. A slow smile pulled at his lips as he shook his head. "Damn, I did not see that coming."

"Does that mean something about my mental state?" Because I loved that damn moody-ass cat. We gave each other space but knew the other was there if we ever got the urge to interact.

"Nah. Now if you had a bird or something...." He gave me a worried look, making us both laugh.

Tossing the papers aside, he pulled out the office chair and plopped down, the pictures and murder board forgotten for now. "Please tell me this pussy's name is something adorable, like Snickers or Sprinkles." I sealed my lips together and worked my jaw back and forth, which only made his howl of responding laughter echo around the office. "Oh fuck, this is officially my new favorite assignment."

"It's Sneakers because he's all black—" I narrowed my

eyes at his laughing ass. "—like my soul, except for his paws, which are white. But I normally call him Sneaks. When I see him, anyway. He's fairly antisocial."

"And you don't think you're made for relationships," he chuckled. Twisting one way, then the other, he tilted his head, studying me. "Or maybe you've been doing it wrong."

"No, the sex was fucking phenomenal. I wasn't doing that wrong."

He rolled his eyes. "Thanks for that bit of unsolicited information, but that's not what I'm talking about. I'm saying the relationship as a whole. Maybe you're like me. I realized early on that I'm first married to what I do. It's part of me, so I'll never give what a relationship needs to make it work. Alone, that is."

Alone? What the fuck did that mean? Of course, he wasn't alone if he was in a relationship.

"So, nothing long term," I clarified. "No commitment, just a bunch of one-night stands to get your rocks off, not really caring who the person is." Which was fine, no judgment. But recently I wanted more than that, even though I knew long term wasn't in the cards. Maybe when I retired, I would finally settle down with someone special.

"Yep." Jameson popped the *P*, still twisting in his seat.

"That means if you pursue Rain, you'll do that to her. Use her while you're here." I didn't like that. Not at all.

Would the FBI notice if an agent went missing?

"If she's open to the idea," he continued, "fully understanding that what happens between us is short term, then I think we'd be using each other."

Fuck, I didn't like that either.

8

———————

RAIN

Hands wrapped around the edge of the steel table, I forced my emotions down to remain analytical as I surveyed the body. A deep ache bloomed in my chest for the young man whose life was taken before he'd really lived it. Him being the fifth victim almost made it harder. One individual not only snuffed out the five victims' lives before their time but altered the lives of so many others. Each victim who died at the killer's hands was a son, brother, friend. One moment they were alive, had a future and plans, and the next, gone.

It could happen to anyone, yet most always assumed it would happen to someone else.

"We'll find out who did this to you," I whispered while covering his lower half with a white sheet. "Detective Taylor is amazing at what he does. And Agent Bend." I paused. "Well, that is odd to say. Agent. Seems so official, right?"

Shaking my head, I turned to count my tools, making sure the number was the same as when I started the autopsy. I'd never left a tool in a body, but it freaked me out thinking I might. Plus, right now, the repetitive counting helped distract me from thinking about the damn note.

After staring at it for way longer than I wanted to admit, my gut told me it was Josh. But if it was my ex-husband, why leave a note? And why now?

The verbiage didn't make sense either. It wasn't like I'd hid my location or changed names. All Josh needed to do was google my name and he'd know exactly where I was. Unless this was him toying with me, which I absolutely wouldn't put past him. He was never violent, but there were times toward the end of our marriage, when the recently opened handle of vodka was nearly empty in a single night, that I wondered if that was when he'd change tactics from verbal to physical abuse to get me to bend to his will.

Josh, when in his right state of mind, was a manipulating, victim-mentality asshole who was incapable of taking responsibility for anything in his life. The world was out to get him, and it was always someone else's fault when shit went wrong. But when he was almost blackout drunk? That was the unknown I never wanted to gamble with and find out. And what ultimately, along with Jameson's validation and confidence-boosting comments, was what made me leave.

Whoever said divorce was the easy way out of a marriage must have never been through it. Though even with the high cost, giving him so much of my damn money to get him to go away, and the endless stress, divorce was better than the alternative, which often ended with a victim for me to determine cause of death for.

Approaching muffled voices drew me out of the past before the morgue doors swung open. It was as if the air conditioning suddenly broke, the normally cold room heating as they strode inside.

Gaze locked on the body, hands stuffed in the pockets of my lab coat to keep from fidgeting, I forced myself to think about anything other than the two hot-as-hell men at my back.

"I should start running," I said, not giving in to the insistent urge to turn around and sneak a peek.

"If it were anyone else"—Jameson's voice grew closer, making a shiver race down my spine—"I'd think that comment was a trap. But knowing Rain...."

"It's just her, and we need to figure out what the hell triggered that train of thought."

My lips curled at the edges. "What exactly are you saying, Slade?"

Finally, his wide frame rounded the end of the table as he stepped into view. I studied his face, hoping to get a read on what he was thinking.

"That for the slow fucks like me and Jameson here, our brains have to work overtime to even attempt to keep up with yours."

"Ah." I bit my lip to keep from laughing. "Well, I appreciate that, but I was just thinking it could help me meet my neighbors. You know, in case of emergencies."

"What happened?" A startled gasp caught in my throat at Slade's harsh tone. "What fucking emergency do you need help with?"

"Erm." I cut my gaze to anywhere other than his bright green eyes bearing down on me. "An imaginary one."

Somewhere behind me, Jameson chuckled.

"An imaginary.... So, you're all right? Do you need a doctor?"

The concern in Slade's voice had me almost melting into a puddle on the floor. With a quick inhale, I parted my lips, ready to explain how I'd created a whole worst-case scenario in my head, when Jameson spoke up.

"Well, I'm glad you're okay. Are you done with the autopsy of our guy here?" I licked my lips and nodded. "Great, then can you walk me through your findings, please?"

When I turned to where Jameson stood at the end of the table near the victim's feet, I found his full attention on me instead of the body.

The building tension slowly eased, and my held breath rushed past my pursed lips. As much as I loved Slade's intensity and concern, the topic change was appreciated. Which, knowing Jameson, he'd probably done on purpose, enjoying seeing me get flustered.

"I ran his prints through the database but came up empty." I bounced my gaze between the two men, giving them a chance to fill me in on what they'd found while I was busy here in the morgue.

Clearing his throat, Slade slid a small spiral-bound note-book from the side pocket of his slacks and flipped it open.

"Matthew Brewster. Thirty-two years old, single from what his friends say, though his neighbors had something different to say about that." I filed that away to ask about later. "We talked to his landlord. He and another male rented the house. Been there a year, always paid on time, no complaints from his end."

"The roommate wasn't there last night. He's in Los Angeles visiting his girlfriend," Jameson added. "Solid alibi since he's been with her the last week and has several people to corroborate his whereabouts."

"Matthew," I said, staring at his pale face, "was stabbed thirty-eight times after an initial blow to the right temple." I pointed a gloved finger at the bruising. "After the blunt force trauma, which probably dazed him or even knocked him out for a few seconds, the first penetration wounds were to the kidneys. If he was unconscious from the blow to the head, that kind of pain would've woken him up. And I think that's why this guy chose that location." I worried at my lower lip, imagining how painful the last few moments of his life were. "The pain would've left him almost immobile while the killer carefully inflicted the next wounds to his lungs. He bled out, like the others, and the other stab wounds were postmortem." I shook my head, the tip of my ponytail swaying with the movement as I ripped off my gloves. "I've noticed something with each new victim."

"Any defensive wounds?" Slade asked, coming to stand beside me while slapping on a pair of gloves. Tossing the sheet back to expose a hand, he carefully picked it up and rotated it, inspecting the knuckles. "None on the hands or forearms, like he fought back." He narrowed his eyes at the light bruising around both wrists.

"I noted those in my report. With lack of fibers or indentions or even residue, I don't think he was restrained during the attack. With an object, at least." My lips twisted down in a frown as I remembered how the body from the other day didn't have obvious strangulation marks on her skin, yet she was.

"How does he keep them from fighting back?" Slade mused beside me. "Though I guess the victims *are* on the smaller side."

"Everyone is compared to you," I joked. "We can't all have the build of a lineman."

"Left tackle," he stated with a smirk. "If you want to get technical about it."

"I think you were about to say," Jameson cut in, breaking off my wayward side conversation with Slade, "that you've noticed the murders are more violent but almost clinical at the same time. The stab wounds are precise, calculated even." I nodded in agreement. "Makes sense. This is the fifth body we've found, so it's safe to assume the unsub is more confident, maybe even did research on the circulatory system or anatomy to inflict maximum pain without, what I'm thinking, the unsub's favorite part being cut short by the victim dying too soon."

I studied the body while Jameson spoke. Damnit, there were too many unanswered questions still, and we were on victim number five. How many more would there be before we caught him?

"What do you think is his favorite part?" Slade asked. "Are you saying the actual murder isn't?"

"No. Not after seeing this body."

"What, then?" I questioned. "With the number of stab wounds and the crazy scene he leaves behind, how can the murder not be what this person enjoys? He's left almost half a dozen bodies in his wake."

"Is this victim like the others, no residue or marks around the mouth area?" I dipped my chin in acknowledgment. "What if it's not the act of the murder that keeps this unsub going but their screams or something else the unsub is coaxing out of the victims?"

"Screams," I mused. Flipping the sheet down to expose the torso, I pointed to one of the many wounds. "That one right there punctured the lung, so screaming couldn't happen. He wouldn't have been able to take a full breath. That's why I say he's getting better. Each wound is precise, at least until the victims are dead."

"How many are postmortem?" Slade asked as he moved around the table. He flipped the sheet back, exposing the victim's legs.

"It's hard to say exactly since I'd wager some were made just before he fully bled out, which would've taken a while. So, in the moments immediately prior to death and then after, I'd say thirty to thirty-five."

"Why the overkill?" Jameson mused. With a groan, he interlaced his fingers behind his head and stared at the ceiling. "This case is so fucking contradicting. Just when I think I have a read on this asshole everything changes."

"What are these?"

My shoulder brushed against Slade's side as I shifted closer to the table to see what he was pointing at along the victim's legs.

"I noticed faint bruising there too. I noted it in my report."

His green eyes flicked from the shins to the bruises on the wrists, back and forth, brows pulling together even tighter with each pass.

"Do you have a theory?" I asked.

I couldn't help but stare at Slade as he inspected the body. Damn, he was sexy without even trying. The light blue dress shirt made his smooth, naturally tan skin stand out. The cuffs of both sleeves were rolled up to his forearms, showcasing the black ink designs that decorated both arms. I'd never seen him without his shirt—well, not in person. The pictures I'd found online during training camps or after games displayed his fully inked chest and back in all its glory.

"Maybe." He locked that intense gaze on me. "Come with me." After ripping off the latex gloves, he tossed them into the trash and wrapped his thick fingers around my wrist, tugging me toward the door.

My sneakers scuffed against the floor as I stumbled after Slade out of the morgue, across the hall, and into my office. I barely looked at the morbid pictures and notecards taped to the wall behind the desk before I was whirled around.

"Get on the floor."

My heart skipped as I blinked up at Slade, sure I'd heard him wrong. "What?"

"I have a theory on how this guy—" Jameson cleared his throat, making Slade respond with a dramatic eye roll. I stifled a laugh. "On how this *unsub* restrained the victim while he bled out, and I need to visualize it." Slade gestured to the rug and arched a brow. "Don't worry, Rain. I won't hurt you."

"I know that," I sighed. "It's just... unexpected."

Eyeing both men in case this was some strange joke, I slowly lowered to the floor. On my knees, I looked up at him through my dark lashes and waited.

Only for my mouth to dry out at the dark expression I found on his face.

My heart kicked into overdrive, hammering against my chest as heat licked beneath my skin. This was so not the time to be this turned on, but it was a visceral response. There was no stopping the way my core fluttered, or the desperation of wanting him to weave those thick fingers into my hair, guiding me exactly where he wanted. Too many times, this happened in my dreams. Him standing over me, ordering me to do whatever he said. Which I did, oh so willingly.

And now with the bonus of Jameson watching.

Maybe joining.

With a curse, he jerked around, breaking our heated stare and putting his back to me. All the hope and desire that had swelled within me with his hooded green eyes directed at me turned to lead and dropped in my gut, making my stomach roll. I flicked a worried look to Jameson, who leaned against the doorframe, lips pursed as if he were annoyed.

Forcing a wide smile, I cleared my throat.

"Now what?" I asked, tone as raw as I felt on the inside. I probably looked pitiful staring up at him with hearts in my eyes and a blush flaming across my cheeks.

"What the hell are you doing?" Jameson muttered, now glaring at Slade.

"Lie on your back and I'll show you what I'm thinking."

Jameson popped off the doorframe and sauntered deeper into the office, falling onto the couch. "Well, this just got interesting. You okay, Raindrop?"

I huffed a laugh, shaking my head as I lay down, wiggling until I was as comfortable as I could be on my office floor with two sexy men watching my every move.

"I thought we agreed in Nashville that was a terrible nickname."

"No, *you* said it was terrible. I like it."

My hair rasped along the thick rug when I rolled my head so I could study Slade as he moved to stand over me.

"This would be better on a bed," he mused.

"Not much of an exhibitionist?" Jameson quipped, making me smile as some of the embarrassment and dejection faded away.

"I'll admit I've never been much for doing anything on the floor," I said, adding my opinion to the mix. "Too hard on your back."

Slade just blinked while Jameson's grin grew, turning almost catlike. "Then maybe you needed someone under you."

I tilted my head, brows pulled in tight. "That doesn't make sense."

"Does to me." Jameson shot me a wink before turning

his attention to Slade, all humor gone. "Get this circus back on track there, Detective. Why is Dr. Evans on the floor?"

"Do you trust me?" Slade rasped. I nodded, unable to form words as he slowly lowered. The insides of his knees pressed against the outside of my shins, holding my legs together. "Imagine you're in the same level of pain as this morning's victim." I dipped my chin. Though the pain would be hard to recreate, I somewhat understood what most nervous systems and impulses came with that kind of pain from school. "Now try to fight back."

Keeping my focus on not moving my back or my core, because of the wounds there, I thrashed on the floor. Two large hands gripped my thighs, keeping them secured to the floor like his legs were doing lower. When I swiped at him, doing anything I could to get free, he snatched my hands and pressed both to either side, keeping his hold loose enough to not bruise.

I stilled.

"You think this is how the killer kept a hundred-and-fifty-pound man pinned to the bed?" Jameson mused.

"There has to be a reason there are no defensive wounds. Even if the pain was incredible, his adrenaline would've been pumping and given him a boost. Not much of one, but long enough to get a hit or two in."

"This won't work." My gaze flicked from where Slade hovered over me to where Jameson now crouched by my head. Reaching out, he moved a rogue hair from across my eye, the tenderness in the touch sparking a need I didn't realize was there deep in my chest. "You're a mammoth, Slade, and she's not the same size as our victims. Let's switch."

Pointing at Slade, Jameson snapped his fingers and

gestured for him to stand. Once Slade was up, Jameson reached down to help me off the floor.

"Switch places?" I said, rolling my shoulders to ease the stiffness. Not only from lying on the floor but being hunched over the victim for the last several hours, looking for trace evidence and performing the autopsy. I needed to get to the gym to work some of this stiffness out, but there hadn't been time recently. An uptick in homicides would do that to an ME's downtime.

"Yeah, you get on top."

"For fuck's sake," Slade hissed.

"What?" Jameson smiled as he folded himself down onto the floor. "Okay, now mimic how Slade pinned you, trying to keep in mind the bruising you saw on the victim's legs."

Slowly lowering, I pressed my knees against his legs, but it wasn't enough. Shifting, I eased back onto my heels so I was almost sitting on his shins but was supported by my weight.

"Are you thinking this happened after the initial stab wounds?" I asked. "Because there is no way I could roll him over like this to get to the kidneys, which I established during the autopsy were the first wounds."

"Something Jameson said made me think. If taking a life isn't what gets this bastard off, then maybe it's watching them die," Slade suggested. "You said they die slowly and in pain. We'd always thought the suspect did his thing, then left because of the other crime scenes. This is the first victim who he's taken ample time with."

Hands wrapped around my waist, catching me off guard. I sucked in a breath and gripped Jameson's forearms.

"But the victim would still be conscious and fighting. I can grab the unsub." He attempted to jerk me off him, but I shifted my weight forward, my core flexing beneath his tightening fingers. "Huh. What muscles are you hiding under there, Raindrop?"

I lifted a shoulder in a nonchalant shrug but used that distraction to dislodge his hold and pin both of his hands to the floor. I stared at where my hands were and realized that was exactly where the bruises on the victim were.

"If I don't squeeze too tight, I could restrain but not leave obvious marks." I looked down at Jameson and smiled. "Try to get loose now, remembering that you're bleeding out, disoriented, and in extreme pain."

He did as I asked, wiggling beneath me, but with the way I sat on his legs plus the hold on his wrists, all he did was shift from side to side.

"Fuck," Jameson gritted out through clenched teeth after a few seconds. "Exercise over. Slade."

A simple plea and I was plucked off Jameson like I weighed nothing. When my feet were steady beneath me, the hands wrapped around my shoulders vanished.

"Sorry," I said in a rush. "I didn't mean to hurt you—"

"First," Jameson huffed as he sat up and slid along the rug until his back hit the side of the chair. Knees bent, he draped both toned forearms on top. "You didn't hurt me. It just took me off guard because of your skill. And second, well, I'm thirty-fucking-four, have done some very questionable shit, and never knew I had that kink."

"What kink?" I squeaked. *What the fuck is going on here?* I looked to Slade for help, who, shockingly enough, was smirking.

"Being held down by a beautiful woman."

The world slowed. *Did he say beautiful? No, no, he said dutiful. Because I'm good at my job. Right. Riiiiight.*

Swallowing hard, I retreated a step, feeling the full

weight of their combined intense stares. Desperate for a distraction to give me time to dissect what the hell just happened between us, I pressed a hand to my empty stomach, fingers gripping the loose fabric of my top.

"Right, well, I'm still working on the skill part. Self-defense classes for the win." When neither said anything, I sighed. "Listen, I'm starving. How about dinner, and then we come back and discuss that," I said, gesturing to the murder timeline taped along my wall. "And what we just uncovered with this little demonstration."

With a flick of his wrist, Jameson checked the time on his smart watch. "Dinner, then home. We can go over everything tomorrow." He winced. "Fuck, I forgot to change where I'm staying. I really don't want to go back there. I already feel like I need an antibiotic shot after last night." He reached up and scratched his head. "And maybe to be checked for lice."

I huffed a laugh. "It can't be that bad."

Slade shook his head. "He's not exaggerating. You know that pay-by-the-hour motel off Carter on the outside of town?"

"No," I gasped. Jameson grimaced and nodded. Reaching up, I dislodged the tie in my hair and raked my fingers through the long ends, working out a few tangles. "That place is dangerous. You should stay with me."

Slade made a noise and turned around, mumbling something under his breath.

Jameson, though, he looked like I'd just made his entire year with my offer. "Really? Fuck, that would be amazing. I won't stay with you the whole time. Just until I can work—"

I waved him off. "I have a spare bedroom. It's not a big deal."

Plus, that would put him right down the hall. Someone I

was attracted to and, I assumed, was available. Maybe this was what I needed to get over my pitiful, unrequited infatuation with Slade.

Though I wasn't sure if that was possible.

But would that be such a bad thing? Why couldn't I have my cake and eat it too?

Or, in this case, have both sexy-as-sin men.

If you asked my parents... they would say I should.

Just like them.

9

———————

RAIN

"You sure that's a good idea?" Slade questioned after Jameson walked out of the office.

After proposing that Jameson stay with me instead of finding a new hotel, it took us a few minutes to figure out the logistics. Jameson needed to grab his stuff from the motel, so he took Slade's car, which was now apparently dubbed the "turd mobile." Then he'd meet us back here and we'd all go to dinner. I volunteered to go with Jameson since I knew my way around town better, but neither of them wanted me anywhere near that shady motel, and after I thought it over, I one hundred percent agreed.

Falling into the chair with a groan, I relaxed against the back, allowing my lids to flutter closed. After a terrible night's sleep, then the roller-coaster emotions today, a bubble bath and then heading straight to bed were definitely on the agenda after dinner.

"It's not like I invited a stranger off the streets to stay with me. I know Jameson from when we worked together, not just today, and I'm positive the FBI wouldn't allow someone with a violent background to become an agent.

Plus, to be honest, the company will be nice. My house has felt empty lately, which makes me sad."

"I know what you mean." I arched a brow his way, and he rolled his eyes. "About the empty part, not the sad shit."

My lips curled into a smirk. Of course, the big mean NFL player didn't want to talk about things like being sad or lonely.

"Thank fuck for this job keeping me here most of the time," he continued.

I nodded in agreement. For several seconds, we sat in comfortable silence, both of us lost in thought. When he spoke up, I jerked in the chair, startled out of my thought tornado about the creepy note from earlier.

"You never told me how your date went."

Heels pressed against the floor, I swiveled the chair one way, then the other. "Not much to tell since it didn't last very long, which was fine by me."

"Why?"

I considered that for a second, debating which characteristic I should list for why I was okay that the date didn't go well. "Besides his love affair with Excel?" Slade snorted a laugh. "And that he thought he could catch death from touching me after he learned about my unique career?"

A grumbled "Fucker" carried around the room, making me all warm and fuzzy.

"He was the wrong dominant," I stated matter-of-factly.

This was fun. Relaxing even. Whatever caused this shift between Slade and me, I was here for it. I didn't feel as tongue-tied, his overwhelming presence not nearly as heart-stopping as it was even this time yesterday.

"What does that mean? The wrong dominant."

I slid my gaze to the couch, finding his green eyes

watching me. "Controlling dominant instead of good dominant, like… well, like you, for example."

"Me," he scoffed. "Not so sure about the accuracy of that observation, Rain."

"I know what I see, and you're protective and intense. The type of dominant that makes people feel safe around you, not smothered or bossed around. Even though we don't know each other that well—"

"We don't?" he questioned, his tone conveying his confusion on that statement.

I rolled my eyes, not stopping to dive into that conversation. "Even though we don't hang out or know each other outside of work, I know you're the guy who would be protective, not jealous and controlling. My date last night ordered me a drink and wouldn't take no for an answer after I told him I wouldn't like it. In a situation like that, someone like you, the good dominant, would let your date order but also be ready to take over if needed, and then you'd go to any means necessary to make sure she got what *she* wanted."

"Have you been following me?" Slade narrowed his eyes, though the twitch of his lips said he wasn't serious.

"What most men don't understand is that most women want our guy to be in control but not control us. I've been there, had that, and have the emotional scars to prove it. Now I know what to look for." I smiled brightly. "The good dominant."

"Someone like me."

My pulse fluttered at his deep, husky tone.

Shit, did someone kick the heat on in here? Pulling at the collar of my blouse, I shook the thin material to cool my too-warm skin.

"Well, yeah." I dropped my hand and put both beneath my thighs to keep from fidgeting. "But don't worry. I know you don't see me that way," I said in a rush. "This isn't me trying to latch on to you like a spider monkey." That ill-timed mental picture of me literally leaping on him, wrapping my arms around his neck and my legs around his waist and holding on tight sent a fresh wave of heat flashing through my veins.

"Anyway," I drawled with an uncomfortable chuckle. Moving to sit up straight, I stretched both hands high in the air, fingers wiggling. "I might need to borrow a few of those pills you take. My shoulders are killing me today."

"Hmm, I have a better idea. Come over here and I'll see if I can help." Curling a single tattooed finger, he beckoned me closer. Which, of course, I did immediately because I had zero willpower around my forever crush. As soon as I was within reaching distance, he gripped my hips and shifted me to stand between his spread thighs. "Now sit, and I'll massage your shoulders."

Right. Sit. Between his thick, muscular thighs and not spontaneously orgasm.

My extensive education said that wasn't possible, but with the way my core throbbed at our proximity and his intense stare locked on me... well, science might be wrong, because I had a feeling I'd combust the second his skin touched mine.

Palms pressed to his knees for support, I gently lowered to mine, shooting Slade a quick glance up through my lashes before twisting to put my back to him and plopping down onto the rug.

Breathing labored, muscles tighter than they were when I initially complained about the pain, I waited, staring at my desk. I jolted along the rug, breath catching in my dry throat, when his heavy hands dropped to my shoulders. Scorching heat from his calloused palms instantly soaked through the soft material of my top, making my nipples harden beneath the lace bra.

Holy shit, this is happening.

Slade fucking Taylor is touching me.

Platonically, but still.

"You okay with this?" His voice seemed to rumble against my skin, making me suppress a full-body shiver. "Rain?"

"Yes," I whispered. Though "okay" was not how I felt.

Ecstatic. Turned on more than I ever had been before in my life. About to pass out because my lungs suddenly forgot how to do their fucking job.

All of that worked better than "okay."

The rough calluses along his palms snagged on my blouse as he shifted his loose grip, angling his thumbs between my shoulder blades. Delicious pain radiated outward as he applied pressure, carefully digging into the muscles. A pitiful, guttural moan vibrated in my throat as the pain shifted to relief, the tight knots slowly easing beneath his talented fingers.

"Holy hell," I whimpered, no longer caring what he thought of my sounds and words. "Please don't stop, ever. Follow me everywhere I go and just do this, all day, every day." His hands shook as a low chuckle sounded in my ears. "You missed your calling. You've barely touched me and it's the best massage I've ever had. Though I'm not telling a single soul about this talent of yours."

Scooping my long hair into one hand, he swept it to the side, draping it over my shoulder to give him better access to the base of my neck. Goose bumps sprouted at the direct contact as he worked his magic. My head drooped forward, and all worries of the creepy note, serial killers, and intrusive thoughts vanished.

Time ceased to exist as I soaked up the unexpected gift of blissful silence in my head.

"Why haven't you ever talked about this ex of yours?" he asked, shattering my peaceful bubble.

My brows pulled together. "What made you think of him?" Though I had a feeling I knew the answer to my question.

"Jameson."

"Why were you two talking about me and my ex?" The tension from earlier crept back in at the thought of them discussing me.

"He wanted to know if you were still with him." Slade cleared his throat. "I think he wanted to know if you were single or not."

Oh.

Well, okay, now I was totally fine with them talking about me.

"I never mentioned Josh because we don't really talk, Slade. Like ever." Or touch, even by accident, which made this current moment beyond atypical. Though I wasn't complaining, because my recurring fantasy of his hands on me finally came true. Sure, they were caressing my shoulders instead of much lower, but beggars couldn't be choosers.

And for Slade's touch, I'd be a beggar all day, every day.

Well, between autopsies.

His thumbs dug into a knot, making me hiss at the sudden burst of pain. "We talk," he grumbled. "Almost every day."

"About work, not personal stuff like ex-husbands, or ex-wives in your case."

He hummed a noncommittal response. What the hell did that even mean?

Rolling my eyes, I studied the geometric pattern on the rug. "Plus, when I moved here, leaving all that behind, I decided I wanted a fresh start. Didn't want anyone to know who I'd become with him. I'm stronger now, more the me I was meant to be, if that makes sense. I know divorce happens to a lot of people, but because of my situation, I was embarrassed."

"Why?" A puff of warm breath brushed down the back of my neck. This time there was no hiding my involuntary shiver.

"Because I married him. It was my choice," I said, digging my short nails into the rug. "Because I put up with his controlling bullshit for as long as I did. I don't know, a lot of reasons, really. Though if you ask my parents, they'd tell you it was doomed from the start."

"They saw red flags and didn't tell you before you got married?"

I sighed, relaxing back, which nestled my spine against his crotch. Feeling the heat radiating through his slacks, I lurched forward, figuring he'd want me out of his space, but both hands tightened, keeping me firmly in place. Heart slamming against my chest, I forced myself to remember what the hell we were talking about.

"Um, right, my parents? They told me, tried to warn me about Josh and his controlling tendencies even before we were married, but of course I didn't listen to them. At the time, I thought they were trying, yet again, to convince me that marriage was an outdated symbol of commitment, sealing myself in a life of unnatural monogamy."

Slade's hands stilled. "That's oddly specific. Sounds like you've been told that belief of theirs a few times."

A huff brushed past my dry lips. *A few times, my ass.* With his hands still unmoving, I gave both shoulders a shimmy to urge his magic fingers back into action. Only his loose grip tightened in warning.

"I heard that my whole life. See, my mom is an anthropologist, and after studying all different societies, she believes the ones who have committed poly relationships are the healthiest. From animals to humans, she thinks monogamy is a way to lock both women and men into relationships that are doomed to failure."

His responding silence to my family's odd beliefs kicked my worry and anxiety from the background into hyperdrive. Before my thoughts could swirl with all the terrible things he would say or do now that he knew I grew up a little different, I shifted along the rug to face him.

Those green eyes searched my face, his brows pulled in tight. One hand slipped from my shoulder to clasp the back of my neck. The tip of his thumb brushed along my throat in lazy strokes as he studied me like I was a puzzle he couldn't piece together. I licked my lips, and his hooded gaze tracked the movement.

"Slade?" There was no covering the rising desire in my breathy tone. Fuck, I wanted him. Desperately wanted him since the day I'd tripped over a rolling office chair and slammed into his hard chest. I wasn't even sure what answer I was hoping for.

"I never said I don't see you that way." My heart stuttered as he leaned closer, gaze locked on my lips. "I just know I shouldn't."

"Shouldn't?" I panted, eyes flicking from his lips to his eyes and back again.

"Because you deserve so much better than me. But...."

Oh, I liked the sound of that.

I twisted until I was fully turned toward him, on my knees between his. His hands slipped from my shoulders to rest on top of his thick thighs. Transfixed, I memorized the tattoos decorating the top of his right hand, gaze trailing up his inked forearm.

"I want to be a selfish bastard and ignore all the reasons I shouldn't."

"Shouldn't what?"

Slade's lips pulled into a knowing smirk. Pitching forward, he stilled when his face was barely an inch from mine. The tip of a single finger trailed down my jaw, dipping lower until all five fingers lightly grasped my throat.

Trembling in his hold, I swallowed, barely stifling a moan at the way my throat worked beneath his loose grip.

What would it feel like if he squeezed?

All this should have been a big, waving red flag, but instead it made my needy core throb and send another wave of desire to dampen my already-soaked panties.

Maybe I was part bull and red flags drew me in instead of warning me away.

"That I shouldn't say 'fuck it' to all the reasons for me to stay away from you and make you mine."

"Oh." A medical degree and that was the only response I could come up with.

"Ruin you for any other man."

"That sounds nice." *What the fuck is wrong with me?*

That smirk grew into a full smile. "I assure you, Rain, there is nothing nice about the things I want to do to you."

Yes. All the yeses. Is there a waiver I need to sign or—

A sharp knock on the office door had me jolting away, putting much-needed space between us as our surroundings came roaring back to my awareness.

Holy shit, we're at work, in my office.

With guarded eyes, Slade tracked my frantic movements as I stood, legs a bit wobbly from kneeling and the want still pumping through my veins. Unable to fully support my weight, I bounced between pieces of furniture, then the wall as I wobbled toward the door.

His dark chuckle at my instability filled the office. Glancing over my shoulder, I shot him a glare before twisting the doorknob and giving it a forceful tug. Fully expecting to find Jameson, I didn't cover my surprise at finding the female detective from last night standing there instead of the FBI agent.

"Hey," Jennifer said, eyeing the partially closed door.

Nervous for her to see inside my office, I tightened my hold on the edge of the door and closed it a bit more. "Hey. It's Jennifer, right?"

"Yep." She studied me for a second before shifting on her feet, attempting to see around me into the office. "You okay?"

"Yeah," I fake scoffed, which no doubt made Jennifer even more suspicious. "Yeah, of course. Why wouldn't I be? I'm not hiding anything or anyone behind me in my office...."

She pursed her lips, clearly not believing me. Not that anyone would, police officer or not. "Right, well, I wanted to invite you to dinner with me and my partner. I saw your car in the parking lot as we were leaving and thought, 'What the hell?' Interested in joining us?"

Before I could respond, a massive presence stepped behind me, and the door was gently tugged out of my tight grip. Jennifer's eyes widened before snapping to my face.

"Detective Gray," Slade rumbled in his normal grumpy tone. "Dr. Evans and I were just talking over a case." My heart sank when he moved past me, keeping a wide professional gap between us. His green eyes locked with mine over his shoulder. "Tell Agent Bend we can pick back up in the morning. I have a few other cases I need to follow up on."

Without a second glance back, he lumbered down the hall and disappeared around the corner.

"No wonder you were acting all shifty. You were stuck in this tiny room with that asshole." Jennifer stepped into my office using the wide gap Slade left between me and the door. "I've never been down here. Nice office, minus the murder scenes taped on the wall. Not my kind of decor."

Sighing, I pinched the bridge of my nose. The emotional ups and downs of the day were wearing on me, causing a low throb to pulse between my brows.

"Yeah, that's Agent Bend's work." Turning, I found her around my desk, staring at the pictures up close with a curious expression on her face. My steps slowed. "Which department do you work in?"

"Burglary," she tossed over her shoulder. "Damn, who did these guys piss off?"

"That's what we're trying to find out."

Her head bobbed, a tight smile on her face. "So dinner, yes or no? My partner is quiet, so I'd love the company."

"Actually, I already agreed to dinner with Agent Bend." And Slade, but not anymore, apparently. "But thank you for the invite."

She nodded, shifting her weight from one foot to the other with both hands hidden in the pockets of her slim gray slacks.

"Was there something else you wanted to talk about?"

The detective's gaze turned unfocused as she stared just over my shoulder.

"Jennifer?" I took a hesitant step forward, hand outstretched toward her.

With a jerk, she sidestepped my approaching touch with

a hard headshake. "Sorry. I just—" She cleared her throat and ran a hand through her short dark hair. "I've just been—"

"Hey, Rain, you ready to—oh. Sorry, didn't mean to interrupt." Jameson stood in the doorway, honey-brown eyes bouncing between Jennifer and me.

"It's fine. Maybe next time on dinner," she said.

"Sure," I mumbled, watching her hurry toward the door when just seconds ago she was frozen in place.

With a dip of her chin toward Jameson, Jennifer skirted around him and rushed out the door.

Confusion was evident on Jameson's face when he turned back to face me. "What was that about? Everything okay?"

"Yeah, I think so. She invited me to dinner, but I think there was something else on her mind. I only met her last night at the bar when she and another officer saved me from that dreadful date."

Unlike Slade, who tensed at the mention of me dating, Jameson smiled and nodded. "I can't wait to hear about this date of yours, then top it with a shit story of my own."

I snorted, shaking my head even though the movement made my building headache worse. "Deal. Though I'm not sure it'll make me feel better about venturing out into the dating world knowing it doesn't matter what gender you are, dating these days just flat-out sucks."

He stepped close, and a strong waft of cedar and spice drifted up my nose. Lids half closed, I swayed toward Jameson, eager to inhale more, only to be stopped by his hand wrapping around my bicep, his hold gentle as his thumb swiped calming strokes along my arm.

"Come on, Raindrop," he rasped, gaze searching my face. "It's been a long day for all of us. Slade texted saying he had some reports to catch up on, so how about we head to your place and order takeout instead of going out?"

The relief of not having to "people" at a restaurant had me sagging against him, resting my head on his shoulder. "Yes, please. That sounds amazing."

His fingers trailed down my arm until one hooked around my wrist. "Then that's what we're doing. I, for one, can't wait to get out of these clothes."

I stepped back to give him a slow once-over. "But they look so good on you."

Jameson's cheeks flamed red. "I promise, they look a thousand times better off." I sucked in a breath at the heat that flared in his hooded gaze as he returned my inspection. When his gaze met mine, his top teeth sank into his full lower lip. "Just like yours."

My lips popped open with a sharp gasp.

Chuckling, his smile turning salacious, Jameson winked at me. "Come on, Raindrop. Let's get you home."

Brain in full-fledged malfunction from Slade's earlier words and now Jameson's, I allowed him to lead me out of the office and toward the parking lot.

How in the hell had I gone from no prospects, every male avoiding me like I had the plague, to two dangerously attractive men openly admitting they were attracted to me?

And bonus—one of them would stay in the room next to mine for the foreseeable future.

Is there any way this doesn't end with me more of a mess than I already am?

JAMESON

"So, what do you feel like ordering?" I called out while meandering around the spacious living room, inspecting the various dying—and, in one case, completely dead—plants. A soft flick against a withering prayer plant's browning leaf sent it floating to the floor. "Huh, I always thought these types of plants were unkillable."

"Yeah, well, my ability to kill any plant I touch should not be underestimated." A smile tugged at my lips as I continued to stare at the poor plant. "And as far as food goes, what do you feel like eating? You're my guest, after all."

The soles of my shoes slid on the thick rug as I turned, eyes narrowed to where she moved around the kitchen. "Nope, that's not how this is going down tonight. It's what you want. If you don't feel like deciding, I will, but don't push aside what you want to appease me."

With a groan, Rain slumped onto one of the clear plastic stools, face to the ceiling so all her long dark hair cascaded down her back. "You can't just say shit like that, Jameson," she protested before righting herself, both elbows thumping onto the island's top. With two fingers, she massaged her temples as if warding off a headache.

For a few seconds I watched, lips pulling into a frown. Determined to help her even though I had no clue where to look, I weaved through the living room furniture, stepped into the kitchen, and began rummaging through her cabinets. "And why can't I say shit like that?"

"Because it's—what are you doing?"

"Finding you medicine for the headache you clearly have."

"I didn't...." Her hazel eyes rolled to the ceiling. "Damnit, you notice everything," she grumbled.

Sliding off the stool, she stepped beside me and pulled open the cabinet above the microwave. The large bottle of Excedrin Migraine rattled as she lowered it to the counter. While she opened the medicine, I grabbed a chilled bottle of water from the fridge, unscrewed the cap, and set it in front of her.

"Thank you. And you can't say stuff like that or do stuff like this because it's...." She circled the hand not holding the water bottle, gesturing up and down my lean frame.

"It's what you deserve?" I hedged, crossing both arms over my chest.

Edge of the bottle pressed to her lower lip, she tracked the movement before tipping it back and taking a long sip.

"Um, no, more distracting." Finger hooked around a drawer knob, she tugged it open and pulled out several to-go menus, tossing them onto the island between us. "How do you feel about Italian?"

"Sounds perfect." It took no time to narrow down what I wanted, considering I could've eaten the entire menu. Breakfast/lunch at that diner with Slade was too many hours ago. Add in the fact that the vending machine offerings in the break room at the station were dismal, and I was starving. "I know what I want. How about you write out your order and address, and I'll call it all in while you go upstairs and change."

Was it forward of me to order her around, sure, but Rain looked wiped. Something happened while I was gone, risking my life to pick up my bags, that had drained her. And since I was here, in her home, I was more than willing to help so she didn't have to do it all on her own.

The loneliness I kept shoved down deep swelled at our simple interaction and the need to take care of Rain. This was another aspect of committed long-term relationships I longed for—helping your partner, even with the smallest of actions or words, to make their day just a little easier.

At her slow nod, I swallowed down my shock, having expected her to put up a brief fight since she'd been on her own for so long and fully independent. After scribbling down her order and address on a kitchen notepad, she headed for the stairs only to pause, foot hovering over the first step.

"There are two spare bedrooms upstairs. Take whichever one you want. It'll take about forty to forty-five minutes for the food to arrive after you've ordered. I'm going to take a quick shower and change into some comfortable clothes before dinner gets here. Remote is on the coffee table, and there's beer in the fridge. Make yourself at home."

It was on the tip of my tongue to ask if I could join her, but I snapped my lips shut to keep the too-forward comment to myself. Sure, I was eager to pick up where we'd left off two years ago now that I knew she was single, but that didn't mean Rain was. The last thing I wanted to do was make her uncomfortable in her own house.

First, boundaries and expectations needed to be established. Then, if she was open to something short term between us, I could lick every inch of her skin, show her all the things I wanted to do to her back then and now could.

Like sliding my fingers through her dark hair, holding her in place while I fucking devoured her mouth, the same way I would her pussy. Or wrapping those long lean legs around my hips while I sank in balls deep, fucking her so hard the pictures rattled off the wall.

I swallowed a groan and adjusted my hardening cock.

Nothing could happen. Yet.

Food, change, then, if she wasn't too tired from this long-ass day, we could have that conversation. Asking her if she wanted a short-term fuck buddy seemed fast since I hadn't even been here twenty-four hours, but this wasn't a new connection or friendship. We were just picking up where we left off. Plus, I didn't want to waste a single moment wondering if she wanted more with me like I did her when I could have her in my arms every night.

Almost forty minutes later on the dot, the doorbell rang through the house. My stomach growled as amazing aromas of tomatoes and garlic filled the bottom landing the second I shut the door. In a rush to get the amazing-smelling food in me as soon as possible, I raced back up the steep stairs, nearly colliding with Rain at the top.

"Oh," she exclaimed, skidding to a halt to not take me and the stuffed brown paper bag I had cradled to my chest down to the floor. "I was just coming down to get that. Thank you."

My brain registered her saying words, but all I could focus on were her bare legs that disappeared into a pair of sleep shorts. The bag crumpled beneath my tightening hold to keep from running a finger along her defined thigh.

Swallowing down my rising need for more than the food

in my arms, I followed her into the kitchen like a lost puppy. A lost, horny puppy. I stifled a groan at catching a glimpse of her perky ass that barely peeked out beneath her shorts.

Tongue thick, throat dry, I forced down a swallow as a sweet vanilla scent wafted off her.

Fucking hell, she smells good enough to eat.

My nostrils flared, imagining having her as dessert.

"Sorry it took me a while," she said over her shoulder as she pulled two white plates from an upper cabinet. "One of my indulgences is soaking in a hot bath when I get home. It helps ease some of the pain in my lower back from standing all day." Taking the bag from my hand, she set it on the island, pulling out the individual plastic containers with no clue about the battle raging inside me.

With my hands free, I clasped them in front of my raging hard-on, hoping it was enough to conceal how much I enjoyed seeing her with barely any clothes on. Of course, my stupid ass pulled on sweatpants instead of jeans, wanting to be comfortable. Which I was, except for the fact that I'd pitched a very obvious tent. If I didn't get my mind out of the gutter, there would be no hope of it going down before she noticed. If she hadn't already.

Eyes locked on the ceiling, I blew out a slow breath through tight lips.

"Not a problem," I replied, trying to *not* picture her in a bath covered in bubbles with me behind her, cock deep in her wet pussy....

Fuck.

"So, tell me what you've been up to the last couple of years," she said while dishing out the steaming food onto the plates. "Obviously, lots of changes considering you're an agent now. How did that even happen?"

Clearing my throat, I ran a hand through my hair,

pulling at the longer strands until a bite of pain radiated along my scalp, hoping that would take my mind off a naked Rain. Only it did the opposite. I imagined my face between her smooth thighs, eating her delicious cunt while she yanked my hair, demanding I make her come.

"Jameson?"

"Yeah?" I croaked, unable to look at her.

"You okay?"

"Fine," I got out through clenched teeth. *Fuck, I have to get myself under control. What the fuck is wrong with me? I never lose control like this.* "The food looks and smells amazing."

When I dared a glance her way, I found her studying me.

Shit. Would she be offended that I almost came in my fucking pants like a teenager from just looking at all that bare skin?

"I don't cook, so I quickly learned which places to order from and which to avoid. It's not that I don't know how to cook, but by the time I get home and changed, I'm too exhausted."

I pulled up a plastic counter stool and slid into the comfortable seat. "And cooking for one is hard. It always ends up being too much food, and seeing all the leftovers in the fridge makes me sad."

Her bright laugh filled the kitchen, easing some of the tightness in my chest—and pants.

"Right," she agreed. "Those full containers mock you anytime you look in the fridge. So takeout is really for my mental health." Opening the fridge, she raised a brown bottle in the air. "Beer?"

"Fuck yes." I gratefully took the offered cold bottle. "So, you asked why the FBI."

She nodded, some tendrils of hair slipping from the

messy bun on top of her head as she slid onto the seat beside me.

I fisted the fork I'd just picked up, restraining myself from staring at the way her shorts rode up her thigh, tempting me to slide a finger along the cuff and follow it to where her legs pressed together.

"It's a long story," I managed to get out.

She gestured to her full plate and held up her beer with the other hand. "We've got time. Come on, tell me. I'm curious."

"To understand, I need to go back several years. Back before you were in Nashville, my best friend's sister was abducted and held by a sick son of a bitch who was obsessed with her. She was found weeks later, but we never caught the guy. My best friend, Tallon, took it hard and joined the FBI to have the access and jurisdiction all over the States to hunt the bastard who'd hurt her. Years later, the case brought him back to Nashville. We were paired up again, and somehow, I got on SSA Riggs's radar when she and another agent helped us with the case. She was impressed, asked me to join the team. I said yes, and here I am."

Stomach demanding I take a bite, I dug into the cooled lasagna. Plus, I didn't want to fill in the enormous gaps in that story. About how the woman my best friend and I shared once came back into our lives with a son and was a target of a different serial killer. That would open a whole can of worms I wasn't ready to discuss.

Was I bitter that Tallon and Remy found themselves happy together, without me? Absolutely not.

But that didn't mean I wasn't jealous that they'd found their someone.

"Wow, that's nuts. Your friend's sister, is she okay now?"

A sappy smile tugged at my lips as I chewed. "Yeah, she's

good." Very good, and happy with Tallon's friend, Bryson. It was fun managing Tallon when all that came out. "So, what about you? What have you been up to since you left Nashville?"

Her fingers twisted as she twirled the fork in the middle of her spaghetti. "As I was interviewing for a permanent ME job, I finally got up the courage to divorce my asshole husband. And I have to credit you for that. You were key in helping me see how awful he was and believing I didn't deserve any of it."

Pride swelled in my chest at her admission. Too many nights I'd lain awake wondering if I did more harm than good with all my carefully worded compliments and words of encouragement. "I'm glad I could help, but don't sell yourself short. The strength and courage to leave that bastard was all you. You did that, put in the hard work and fought through the tough times."

She huffed. "'Tough' seems like too light a word for what it's like after you've decided to file. Constantly questioning if you're doing the right thing, second-guessing yourself on the timing and if it's all worth it in the end. But I knew I had to do it and it would all work out in the long run. Once the divorce was final, he took more than half of everything I'd worked for—and even then demanded alimony." She rolled her eyes so hard I was surprised I didn't hear it. "Can you tell I'm totally not bitter?" Rain shot me a smile. "After it was over, I accepted the job out here, knowing the distance would be good, and moved across the country. Alone. To make him sign and stop his constant demands for more, I left everything we'd purchased together, only taking my oh-so-precious shoe collection and clothes. I knew I'd want to start completely fresh here, so it wasn't that big of a deal." She waved a hand around the townhome. "All this I bought once I moved in, and I love it. It's all me, what I've always wanted but couldn't have because it wasn't his style." After chewing a large bite, she jabbed the empty fork my way. "Okay, fine, I am totally bitter."

Wiping my mouth with the rough paper napkin, I tilted my head toward the living room. "And you wanted dying plants to add to this new life of yours because...?" A puff of air exploded out of my lungs when her elbow slammed into my ribs. Half faking being in pain, I rubbed at the spot. "Damn, woman. You weren't kidding about those self-defense lessons. You've got some power in those hits."

She preened, sitting up a little taller. "It helped build my confidence in living alone. I feel safe. Well, I did." I made a mental note to come back to that little admission. "But I still wanted to know that I could defend myself if needed. Plus, it's a great workout. Josh didn't like it when I went to the gym, saying the definition and hard muscles only made me look even more like a boy—"

"You do not look like a boy," I hissed.

She snorted a humorless laugh. "It's okay. You don't have to placate me. I know I don't have the curves men like or the"—she gestured toward her chest—"you know. But I've come to accept my body the way it was made. If Angie Harmon can rock this body type and still be beautiful, then why can't I?"

"I'm not placating you." My grip tightened on the fork as I stabbed at the last bite a little harder than needed. "I like the way you look, but you're more than your body, Rain. What you offer is the whole fucking package. Anyone who makes you think you're not worthy of their attention just because you don't have huge fake tits is no one who deserves your time or even a single thought. You hear me?"

I said the last three words with more bite than I

intended, but fuck, how could I not? There was no way I could sit here and listen to her think less of herself because she didn't have the curves she thought made a woman beautiful.

Because she was exactly that to me.

"Okay," she breathed, wide eyes locked on me. With a small shake of her head, she broke off my intense stare. "How do you do that, Jameson?"

"Do what?"

"Make me see the truth so clearly with just a few words. You did it back then, and you're doing it right now."

I tilted my head, debating my answer. "Back then, did I mention I have five sisters?"

And just like that, her vulnerability, the weight of our conversation, lifted. A wide grin spread across her petite face, bunching her cheeks and making those hazel eyes squint.

"No, I don't think you mentioned that. I would've remembered. That makes so much sense. You were trained." That smile of hers shone so brightly, and the joy was fucking infectious. "So, because of insider intel, you under-stand a woman's thought process."

I shook my head, a few still-damp locks of hair dropping against my forehead. "Um, fuck no. No man can claim that —or a woman, for that matter. It's always changing, and if I learned anything living with my sisters and being raised by a single mom, it was to hold on tight because the emotional roller coaster is one hell of a ride. Oh, and if you're ever asked how an outfit makes them look, do not hesitate in saying it's perfect, but maybe different shoes."

Head tipped back, mouth open, she laughed out loud, the sound making my heart thunder in my chest. What would it be like to hear that laugh every day, to know I was the one making her so damn happy that tears welled in her lower lids?

"What?" she said, still laughing. "Why shoes?"

"Simple answer. Because it shows you actually looked at the outfit, not just responding with a rehearsed answer, and shoes seem to be the only article of clothing that doesn't elicit an emotional reaction."

Rain's smile was so wide I could almost see all her straight, white teeth. "Meaning?"

"If I said to try different pants, then they thought the pants fit terrible and would never, ever wear them again. Tops? Fuck no." I faked an exaggerate grimace. "My sister once smacked me upside the head because she thought I was commenting on the way she didn't fill out the shirt. I've tried suggesting different accessories, but they saw through that because I don't know shit about pairing belts and bags together. So, shoes. Proves I'm engaged without offending any part of the outfit they pieced together."

She shook her head in disbelief. "You're unlike anyone I've ever met, Jameson."

"And that's a good thing?" *Please say yes.*

"It's a relief," she said, pushing her plate away and leaning both forearms onto the counter. "And I agree with your assessment of holding on tight during the emotional roller coaster. I took a few trips on one today, hence the headache I had earlier."

"The case?" I hedged.

"No. Well, kind of. It's all kind of mixed together." She shot me an odd look out of the corner of her eye. "It's complicated."

I hummed a noncommittal response. "Well, I'm here if you want to talk about it. I'm sure we could uncomplicate it together."

Or make it more complicated by me telling her I wanted to see where this connection between us could go while I'm in Santa Coasta.

Both finished with our meals, we cleaned up the kitchen, chatting about various things but steering clear of the heavier topics from earlier. Drying the last plate, I put it back in the cabinet she'd pulled it from and turned, leaning my ass against the edge of the counter.

"Hate to do this, but I have some work I need to get caught up on."

"The exciting life of a profiler," she joked.

"Exactly." I waited a beat to see if she wanted to use this chance to make a quick escape upstairs. When she stayed by my side, finishing her beer, I took the opportunity. "Want to keep me company?"

It sounded like an innocent question, but it wasn't. The idea of her disappearing into her room, shutting herself away until tomorrow, didn't sit well. I wanted more time with her, even if it was me working and her simply in the room with me.

It was dumb and way too soon for her to have this kind of pull over me, but I couldn't help it.

Every part of me wanted Rain.

Any way I could get her.

***

THIRTY MINUTES into the crime documentary she had started on the TV, my laptop had timed out from inactivity, my entire focus on the sleeping Rain lying on the couch beside me, softly snoring. Head draped off the cushion, arm twisted, and torso contorted, there was no way she was comfortable, but it had only taken her a few minutes to nod off, so maybe this was how she slept every night.

Careful to not disturb the sleeping beauty, I softly shut the laptop and laid it on the glass coffee table. While a witness's voice poured through the TV speakers, I took in every inch of bare skin exposed beneath the cream knit blanket she'd tugged off the back of the couch when she first lay down.

It did funny things inside me when she snuggled down on the couch, shooting me a sheepish smile before flicking on the TV. I didn't take this moment lightly. She trusted me, leaving herself vulnerable, and invited me into her comfort zone.

After everything she'd seen in her job and life with that asshole, she trusted me, a basic stranger, enough to fall asleep beside me.

Sure, it could've been from sheer exhaustion, but I told myself it was because she knew deep in her soul that she was safe with me. Despite my best effort, my hand slid forward, erasing the small gap between me and her bare feet. Without touching her soft fair skin, I traced the lines of her muscular calves, stopping at her knee, knowing that was too close to where I desperately wanted to explore.

A quiet whimper had my eyes snapping up to her face. The earlier peaceful expression was gone, replaced with furrowed brows and pursed lips. Her body jerked, feet kicking out at the same time her breathing turned labored.

Fuck, is she having a nightmare?

What in the hell had this woman gone through that those fears chased her in sleep?

The pitiful cry that escaped and following full-body twitch had me sliding down to the floor, knees pressed into the thick rug.

"Raindrop," I whispered, fingertips hovering over her shoulders, seconds away from shaking her awake.

Rain shifted along the couch, flipping so her spine molded into the cushions. Behind closed lids, her eyes jerked as if desperately searching for something. Her leg shot out, shin nailing me in the bicep.

I couldn't take it anymore. Not with me sitting right here watching would she live in fear, whether awake or in her dreams. Gently, I wrapped my fingers around a narrow shoulder, fingers tightening slightly. "Rain, wake up, sweetheart."

Her head dug into the couch, arching her neck as if begging for my lips. Another sound erupted from her lips, this time a moan.

And not one of pain but of pleasure.

I stilled, peeling my fingers off her one by one and retracting my hand.

Was this a nightmare or...?

A slow smile curled up my lips as another breathy moan filled the open living room, drowning out the sounds of the TV.

My cock twitched inside my sweats, watching her writhe along the couch, knees falling open, sending the last corner of the blanket falling to the floor by my legs.

A gentleman would grab it and cover her up. But a gentleman I was not.

I swallowed down a guttural groan, gaze scouring every inch of her long bare legs. Those tiny sleep shorts had ridden up, showcasing every dip and curve of her pussy.

My heart hammered, and I jerked my gaze to the ceiling. Fuck, I was just saying how happy I was that she trusted me, and here I was ogling at her in her sleep. If we were in a relationship, sure, I wouldn't feel bad. But we weren't. She didn't know I wanted to toss those long legs over my shoulders while I tongue-fucked her dripping core. Wasn't aware that being around her was a constant strain on my control, holding myself back from touching her, memorizing every curve of her amazing body.

Clearing my throat, I studied her face, debating whether to wake her up or let her be. Using the tips of my fingers, I brushed a few hairs from her forehead.

"Yes, Jameson...." The words were barely audible, but I stilled, knowing exactly what I'd heard.

My brows shot up over my forehead.

Well, this just got interesting.

She was dreaming of me.

I was intruding, doing something wrong, but I couldn't pull away.

Guess my voyeurism is out in full force.

"Slade," she whimpered.

A wide smile crept across my lips. What an enlightening few minutes. Seemed Rain was interested in both Slade and me together. Which worked for me. Two was great, but three was a fucking fun party.

Careful to not disturb her, not wanting to ruin her fun, I stood and stared down at the beautiful woman who was quickly filling all my waking thoughts, desperately wishing I could wake her up with my face between her legs and help her finish whatever her fantasy dream had started.

But I couldn't.

Not yet.

Tomorrow.

I would tell her I wanted more than her expertise on the case.

That I wanted it all and more.

And was open to the grumpy detective joining in on the fun.

After draping the light throw over her, I moved on silent feet through the living room and up the stairs. I was very ready to get to my room, behind a closed door so I could have my own fantasy dream, though I fully intended to be wide awake with my hand wrapped around my pulsing cock while I envisioned us together.

11

———

SLADE

The heels of my shoes slammed to the cheap tile floor as I paced up and down the hall in front of Rain's office. After glaring at the locked door, I checked my watch again, huffing at finding only three minutes had passed since I last checked. Pausing, I slumped against the wall, the drywall rattling beneath my spine.

The coarse hair along my jaw scraped across my palm as I scrubbed at my face, trying to chase away my worries and fears.

I fucked up yesterday. My slip was unprofessional and way over the line. Rain and I were colleagues. She was thirteen fucking years younger than me, had a whole bright future ahead of her, and was too damn good a woman for me to want.

She deserved someone better than me.

Someone like that fucker Agent Bend.

With a grumbled curse, I tapped the back of my head against the wall, trying to dispel the visions of what happened between them last night. With him staying at her place, how could something *not* happen?

My hands tightened into fists at my side.

It should be me with her. Giving her everything she could ever want. Memorizing every inch of her body and showing her all the ways I could make her scream until her voice cracked and tears leaked down her cheeks.

"Fuck," I groaned.

I was in such deep shit.

Was there any place worse than being caught between what you knew was best and what you wanted? If I wanted the best for her, I'd stay far away. But if I wanted the best for me... well, that was Dr. Rain Evans. Every delectable, quirky, brilliant piece of that amazing woman.

Sure, I had money and a fat cock, but also more baggage than either of those could outweigh.

Which was saying a fucking lot.

Rain's distinct boisterous laugh echoed down the hall as she and Jameson rounded the corner. I stood up straight and crossed both arms over my chest, fixing my face into my normal scowl.

Rain smiled when she saw me. Jameson... fuck, I wasn't sure what look he sent my way.

It looked like he had a secret and was damn smug about it.

"Good of you two to make it this morning," I grumbled. Like an asshole.

Rain's smile faltered.

"Don't be an ass," Jameson snapped. "She wanted to stop and get you breakfast."

My stomach dropped, making the few pills and smoothie I ate for breakfast roll like a hundred-pound lead weight.

"It's not good to take all that medicine on an empty

stomach," she said, avoiding eye contact. "Hope you like sausage and egg."

I didn't.

Not that I would say that out loud. This amazing, generous woman thought about me despite my asshole actions yesterday. She woke up, and I was on her mind. There could be raw fucking duck in that bag, and I'd swallow it whole with a wide damn smile on my face.

And to be clear, I hated duck, raw or cooked, more than sausage.

But instead of telling her how much I appreciated it, I reverted to my old grumpy-ass self that I was with everyone else. Hence why they hadn't given me a new partner after the last guy left five months ago. If that jackass didn't want to know all the ways he was doing shit wrong, then he should've done it right the first time.

"Thanks," I grumbled, snatching the brown bag with a grease stain already darkening the bottom from her hand.

"Did you get all that work done last night?" Jameson asked, a single brow raised.

Ignoring his question, knowing he saw through my reasons to bail last night, I turned and followed Rain toward her office. The keys jingled in her hand as she shoved one into the lock and twisted.

"Everything go okay last night with you two?" I asked, eyes on Rain's ass that looked amazing in her black cigarette pants. They were one of my favorite pairs on her. They molded around her firm backside and made her legs look miles long.

"Yep, we ate pizza, had a pillow fight, then braided each other's hair before writing in our diaries."

I shot Jameson the bird and plopped down on the couch.

"It was fine," Rain stated, a deep crimson blush rushing

to her cheeks. Flicking a nervous glance at me, then Jameson, she lowered her head to dig inside her purse, dark hair falling in a curtain to hide her face.

I looked to Jameson, who hid a knowing smirk behind a to-go coffee cup.

What the fuck is that all about?

Damnit. Did they fuck?

The second that thought flashed through my mind, I expected jealousy to spike, heat filling my veins and heart ramming against my chest the way it always did when I thought about another man with Rain. My Rain.

But it didn't.

Huh.

"You want a coffee, Slade?"

"Yes," I breathed. "I finished the cup I brought from home while I waited for you two."

"That was my fault," Rain admitted with a cringe. "I fell asleep on the couch, which I never do, and woke up late." Her hands stilled on the coffee machine, her gaze going glassy. With a firm shake of her head, she cleared her throat. "Won't happen again."

"I'll make sure you get into bed at a decent time tonight," Jameson offered with a wink. Rain's eyes went wide before darting back to the task at hand. "Maybe Slade could join." The round coffee pod Rain was busy putting into the machine slipped from her fingers and clattered to the ground. "You know, to brainstorm, of course."

With jerky movements, Rain picked up the dropped pod. "Sure, yeah. That sounds good. All of us together." Her laugh was strained. "At my place."

It was damn clear that I was missing something. I narrowed my eyes at Jameson, but he just offered a shrug and kept drinking his damn coffee. Looking between me and Rain, he shot me a wink and shoved off the wall. When he passed by Rain, headed for the back of the office, he brushed against her with a whispered apology. Rain stiffened, but it was the flush that crept along her cheeks and down her neck that had me swallowing a shout for him to stop making her uncomfortable.

Her fair skin darkened the same way yesterday, with my hand wrapped around her throat and my cock digging between her shoulder blades.

So, either she was uncomfortable then and now, or...

Or was a dangerous thought.

"Here," Rain said, now standing beside me with a steaming mug in her outstretched hands. She looked at the paper sack I'd tossed on the side table and completely forgotten about. "Are you not going to eat it?"

In my prime, I could outrun most men even half my size. But that speed didn't hold a candle to how fucking fast I swiped the bag off the table and ripped it open. The disgusting grease trap was in my mouth before she blinked.

"Yum," I said, slowly dying inside. But seeing her smile soften and stretch across her face made the nausea worth it. "Thank you. I feel better already."

"What hurts so bad that you have to take so many pills a day?" she questioned, crossing both arms over her chest. I darted my eyes to the side to not watch how that move pushed her tits together.

I huffed around the last bite of the sausage and egg biscuit. "What doesn't?"

"It's not good, you know. For your stomach, liver"—she waved a hand, gesturing to my chest—"everything. That medicine isn't intended for daily maximum dosage usage."

"I don't use the maximum," I grumbled. At her narrowed

eyes, I rolled mine. "I go slightly over. I'm a big guy. I can handle it."

"Slade," she admonished, pushing at my arm. And apparently, I was thirteen again because I totally flexed. "That's terrible."

"It's better than hating life every time I move. Listen, I appreciate your concern, Doc, but I'm doing what I can to get by."

Her shoulders slumped. "Just getting by doesn't sound like a way to live." What would she say if she knew the only thing that even got me out of bed anymore was the hope of seeing her? "I'm going to do some research. Surely, they have some new medical procedures that can help manage your joint pain better. Cortisone shots—"

She stopped at my wince and no-doubt pale face at the mention of a needle.

"What was that look?"

"Let's talk about the damn murders," I said, loud enough for Jameson to hear. "What are you looking at over there, Bend?"

"Oh no. I'm too invested in this," he said, pointing the end of a pen between me and Rain, "to discuss what's behind me. The case isn't going anywhere, so what was that face for, Slade?" I shot him my best death glare. One that made most men piss their pants, knowing I could snuff out their life with a single blow. But not this fucker. He just smiled. "She mentioned a shot, and then you looked physically ill."

It was on the tip of my tongue to lie and say it was the nasty fast food I just forced down, but then that would hurt Rain's feelings, so I just sealed my lips shut, refusing to answer.

"You," Rain said in surprise. "The great Slade Taylor,

capturer of all bad guys and savior to women and children everywhere, is afraid of needles."

"Am not." I winced at the pout in my tone. I cleared my throat, ensuring I sounded like the badass I was. "I just don't prefer them."

"Right." Rain drawled out the word, clearly not believing my lie.

Neither did I.

"Maybe Rain could hold your hand. Would that make it all better?" Jameson leaned a thigh against the side of Rain's desk. "Or she could even do the injection. She is a doctor, after all. You trust her, don't you, Slade?"

Fucker.

Dead motherfucker.

"Yes," I said through gritted teeth. "Of course, I trust her."

"I'd have to do some research, but it shouldn't be a problem." Her loud clap rang through the office as she leaped off the edge of the couch. "I'll start looking into it tonight. I'm assuming you've also gone through physical therapy." I nodded. "And keep up with the exercises they suggested."

That, not so much. I was a smart man. I knew it would help, but I was also a stubborn motherfucker. I wasn't sure what made me push back on all the stretches and band work they suggested to keep my ligaments and muscles loose but strong. Whatever it was, I'd tossed the step-by-step printout the moment I walked out of the door.

She sighed. "I'm taking that lack of response as a no. I'll add that to the list of things to research, but I'll need to know exactly what hurts and where."

"You should probably give him a full physical," Jameson added, shooting me a wink behind Rain's back. "Don't leave any area untouched."

A tiny squeak escaped Rain. Before I could get a read on her face, she whirled around, long dark hair floating with the quick movement.

"Then, can I be next?" His face pulled in an exaggerated grimace as he massaged his bicep. "I was shot just a few weeks ago."

"Really?" I asked, instantly concerned. I'd never been shot, but I was positive the pain was annoying as fuck if it was anything like what I lived with daily.

"For real?" Rain said, striding over to Jameson. "Where? What muscles did it penetrate?"

With Rain focused on prodding at his arm, she missed Jameson waggle his brows at her saying "penetrate." I couldn't hold back a huffed laugh. Good to know I wasn't the only one who still thought like a fucking teenager at times.

"Not sure on what muscle, but it was a through and through. Maybe you can look tonight? It would make me feel better having a second opinion on some of the tightness and occasional pain spikes."

"Yeah, we can do that."

"Great, then it's a date."

"What?" she squeaked.

Jameson waited until she tilted her face up to his. "You assess the old guy's ailments, though I have a feeling some of it can be resolved with Bengay—"

"Fuck you, motherfucker," I grumbled while trying to smother my smirk.

"And then you can look at my gunshot wound."

"Not much of a date," Rain said, shaking her head. A small grin pulled at her lips when she turned around, heading for the coffee machine. "Sounds more like work.

Though working on the living instead of what I'm used to would be a nice change of pace."

"Can we please talk about the case now?" I tossed out, ready to focus on something other than Rain's skilled hands roaming over my body. Fingers skimming along my bare skin....

Fuck.

If I could make it through the physical assessment without popping a raging boner, that would be a miracle.

But then she'd know that part of me still worked just fine.

And was very eager to break all the professional boundaries.

Boundaries that were looking more and more gray with every passing minute. If things kept progressing, it wouldn't take long for them to vanish altogether.

I wasn't sure if that terrified or thrilled me.

Maybe a bit of both. Because Rain wasn't the type for a quick fuck and leave. She was a woman to love, to cherish. To give everything for. But what would happen if my everything wasn't enough?

And I was the one fucked and left?

12

RAIN

I could do this. I was an adult—a damn doctor, for fuck's sake. A motherfucking professional.

There was no room for the tingles in my lower belly, the slamming of my heart in my chest every time I looked at Jameson and Slade. Though being inconvenient and incredibly distracting didn't seem to matter to my visceral reactions.

I just needed to think of something besides that hot-as-hell dream last night. Of the three of us together, the two men devoted to finding every place that made me tremble with need.

Ugh. Yes, a distraction was needed. Like thinking of gross things like kale or broccoli.

"What's that look for?" Jameson said, humor in his tone.

"Thinking about vegetables," I muttered before realizing I sounded like an escaped mental asylum patient.

"Cucumbers?"

"What?"

"Nothing." Jameson shook his head and ran a hand

through his light brown hair. "Should I ask why you're daydreaming about vegetables?"

"Most definitely not. I just needed a brain cleanser of sorts."

"The idea of your hands on me and the big guy made you need a distraction?"

"What?" I squeaked, the word getting caught in my throat. "No. Of course not. I'm a professional."

A professional who really wanted to see them naked—and not for a physical assessment.

Damnit. I closed my eyes, pulling all my cringe-worthy stimulants to the forefront of my brain to get my breathing under control.

Noisy, crowded restaurants.

Too-loud music while I was trying to concentrate.

Josh's nasally voice.

Yep. That last one did it.

Releasing a slow breath through pursed lips, I let my lids flutter open, finding Jameson watching me. One corner of my lips tugged upward.

"Okay, I'm ready." With a flick of my wrist, I motioned toward the wall of pictures. "Let's get started so we can stop this guy."

"Unsub," Jameson corrected. "I'm not one hundred percent sure this is a guy."

"Explain," Slade said from the couch. Leaning forward, forearms on his spread thighs, he took up the entire piece of furniture.

Turning my chair around to face Jameson straight on, I sank onto the soft cushion. After slipping off my sneakers and tucking both feet under the opposite thigh, I snagged the single decorative pillow in the couch's corner and placed it on my lap, elbows pressing onto the top as I leaned forward, giving Jameson my full attention.

"Comfortable?" Jameson laughed.

"Yes. You may continue. Actually, can you grab me a Coke from the fridge?" I pointed to the small appliance that the coffeemaker sat on. "Then I'll be ready. Need another caffeine boost."

"You know," he drawled as he yanked open the door, "with as much shit as you give Slade for those pills he pops, you're not much better with all the sugar you eat and drink."

"Yeah, but it's different because I'm a doctor and I know how bad it is for me." I accepted the chilled can. "And don't tell me that doesn't make sense because it does to me, and therefore I'm right."

"Whatever you say, Doc. Okay—"

"Oh, and my iPad. It's in my bag." Jameson shot me a look. "What? You've thrown me way off my routine this morning. Normally, I have an hour responding to emails and finishing up reports in the peaceful quiet before doing all this."

"This being...?" Slade asked.

"Talking. Interacting. Trying to act normal."

"You *are* normal, Raindrop."

I shrugged a shoulder as I took the iPad from Jameson's outstretched hand. "Then I have you all fooled." Dropping the iPad onto the pillow, I pressed my fingers together and attempted an evil laugh.

"Maybe *normal* is a strong word," Slade said with a chuckle. "No offense."

"None taken. I tell myself the same thing all the time."

"Anything else? Your laptop? A foot rub maybe?"

Though I knew Jameson was being a smartass, I kicked out one foot, raising it high until it hovered near his chest.

"That would be lovely, actually. As cute as my expensive sneakers are, they're uncomfortable until they're broken in."

My expectation of him smacking my socked foot away was dashed when he gripped it between two hands and pressed both thumbs into the arch, eliciting a whimper as the pain turned to relief.

"Oh fuck. I was kidding, but now I don't want you to stop."

"Do you two need a room?" There was a tightness in Slade's voice that had me tensing.

With one last squeeze, Jameson lowered my foot to the floor, standing with a heated look in his honey-brown eyes.

"You asked why I'm not positive this is a male unsub." Turning, Jameson strode to the far wall and pointed at a single picture. "Reasons I think it's a female unsub. The blitz attack to the head as the first injury. It makes me think the unsub isn't strong enough to subdue the young male victims without it. There's also the point of entry into the houses." He tapped the end of a pen against victim number two's house. "This window is narrow. The notes in the report said it only opened halfway, which was probably why it was left unlocked. Sure, there are lots of men out there with leaner frames that could fit through that gap, but my training makes me lean more toward a woman. But then there are the obvious contradictions."

I waited a few seconds for him to continue, but he didn't. "Okay, out with it. What are the obvious contradictions to the theory that this is a female unsub? Because it isn't obvious to me," I said without looking up from the screen as I shifted through the blunt force trauma wounds on each victim.

"The mess." I cut my eyes to Slade. Reaching over, he swiped the screen to the third crime scene. "That would bother most women. Plus, the blood splatter that would be on their clothes and coat their hands."

"That doesn't make sense." I tilted my head to the side, hoping the new angle would make me understand what they were saying. "Why would the amount of blood point to a man or a woman?"

"Typically, in female offender cases, they don't want to leave a mess for someone else to clean up. Which is why most go for poison or a tragic accident outside the home. Plus, the laundry aspect. Getting blood out of clothes is a bitch," Slade added. "What?" He looked between me and Jameson as we stared at him. "I wasn't a saint in college or after. I never started a fight, but I sure as hell finished them. And let me tell you, broken noses fucking bleed everywhere."

Oh wow, that should not be hot. Should not make me all tingly and heat spike in my veins.

Think about the case, Rain, not how hot a fist-fighting Slade was back in the day.

"I get what you're saying, and I agree to a point, but what if the unsub is like me?" Both men focused their attention on me. "I don't mind the mess or care about blood on my hands or clothes." I twirled a dark lock of hair around my index finger. "If they didn't want to bother with getting the blood spray, which they were absolutely covered in, out of their clothes, the easiest solution would be to toss everything after."

Jameson's eyes widened. "That's brilliant, Rain." Grabbing a file folder off the desk, he flipped it open and thumbed through the pages. "Maybe the unsub stripped off the bloody clothes as they left the crime scene. Did you have any officers go through trash cans in the neighborhood?"

"The neighbors', yes, but not a wide radius." Slade

pulled out his phone, thumbs flying across the screen. "I'll have a few officers head over to yesterday's victim's neighborhood and do a deeper dive. Hopefully, trash day wasn't yesterday or today."

While the two dug deeper into this new theory, I pulled up the pictures of all five victims' torsos to compare side by side. The number of stab wounds didn't change with each victim, just the wound pattern and accuracy. The unsub used a different type of knife, which was why we originally didn't connect the cases. It wasn't until victim number four that I linked them. Four young male victims with excessive postmortem trauma were like a blinking light saying "Hello, dumbass, these are connected."

"Let's talk about what we know for now. Let's start with the bodies. Rain." Jameson inclined his head my way, giving me the floor.

Shifting in my seat, I sat up straighter and cleared my throat. "All five victims were young, decently healthy single males. COD was exsanguination. The type of knife used varied with each victim. And like I said yesterday, the precision of the wounds was night and day from victim number one to the one yesterday. It took a while for victim number five to bleed out, whereas victim number one was stabbed almost directly in the heart. He bled out quickly."

"The unsub is evolving, perfecting their methods to ensure he or she gets what they want out of the kill." Jameson motioned to victim number one with the file folder. "Ten months ago, victim number one was found in an alley beside a dive bar he frequented. His alcohol level was twice the legal limit."

Slade stood and walked over to the desk, pushing aside a few files before plucking one off and snapping it open. "No one saw him leave with anyone, and he'd normally walk the couple of blocks back to his apartment after too many drinks."

"Victim number four, who was found beside his car in the parking lot of a bar, had the most traumatic head wound." Using two fingers, I zoomed in on the picture I took during the autopsy. "Which makes sense, since he was the biggest of the victims. Our unsub was probably concerned about being overpowered. Based on the positioning, the blow came from behind, and a round pipe or bat was used. I assume it was a complete surprise, which brought him to the asphalt based on the trace material I found in a few scrapes on his palms and knees. The stab wounds were inflicted while he lay prone based on the blood pattern on the victim's clothing."

Slade paced from one side of my office to the other, rubbing at his jaw. "The way the unsub kills has stayed the same. Why not a gun? If he or she can't overpower these men, why not just shoot them?"

"Sound?" Jameson mused, tapping the edge of the file in his hand against his palm as he stared at the pictures. "You mentioned that before. The homes and businesses are close together, so a gunshot would almost guarantee cops and increase the likelihood of being caught."

"And ballistics," I added. Slade paused his pacing to stare down at me. "What?" I jerked my eyes around the room, uncomfortable under his intense scrutiny.

"You sure you don't want to give up your day job and become a detective? Because you'd be damn good at it." I slouched back, relieved I hadn't said something dumb, as Slade continued. "The good doc is right. We would've tied the cases together immediately if the same gun was used instead of different knives."

"Which you can find at almost any store," Jameson

agreed, nodding. He released a frustrated groan and fell into my rolling chair. "Another piece we haven't pinpointed: Why these particular victims?"

"Victims number two and four had small misdemeanors on their records for bar fights. Other than that, they all have clean backgrounds. No drug use for any of them. Victim one had a girlfriend, though the others didn't."

"The latest victim's neighbors said he was a ladies' man. Maybe they all were and we're dealing with a pissed-off boyfriend. Or if it is a woman, they all made enemies of the same one-night stand." Slade leaned against the wall, crossing both arms over his broad chest. "Though what are the odds for either?"

"Low," Jameson sighed. "There has to be something that connects them that we're not seeing. It's not in their backgrounds or credit history. I had our tech guy go through their online history, and he didn't come up with any overlap on their spending." He huffed a laugh. "Unless you count watching hours of porn."

"I don't understand men's obsession with porn," I said, flicking through the pictures, praying something would jump out at me. "Why watch something that would never happen? And it's not like it does anything to relieve the arousal it creates. You're still having to take matters into your own hand." I smirked at my pun. "And it alters your expectations for your next sexual partner. Believe me, I've seen a lot of penises, and the equipment porn stars have—"

"Did I fall headfirst into the twilight zone?" I stopped talking, cheeks heating, finding both men's intense gazes on me. "Watched a lot of porn, have you?" Jameson questioned, exchanging a strange look with Slade.

Ugh, did I really want to talk about this with these two? Not at all, but how did I get myself out of this conversation without admitting the truth—that I watched it with popcorn and beer as a good laugh at the end of a hard day?

What? The acting was hilarious and the plots too far-fetched.

"So, ten months, five victims, and we have shit to work with to catch this fucker." I shot Slade a grateful smile. "And we can't even narrow down the gender."

Staring at the gory crime scene photos, I tilted my head, imagining myself as the unsub.

"I'd use poison," I mused. "Not that the blood and gore affect me, but it's just easier to plan, you know. Slip something into their drinks at the bar while they went to the bathroom that wouldn't take effect until hours later and isn't detected by a normal toxicology screen. Or maybe invite them over for dinner, then put it in the dessert so the poison doesn't take effect until they're home and in bed. It would look like they just died in their sleep." Twirling a lock of dark hair around my fingers, I shook my head, making those few strands tug on my scalp. "No, then I would be connected to the murder as the last person to see them alive, which means I couldn't commit multiple murders without becoming a suspect."

The responding silence was heavy. Peeking up through my lashes, I saw both men staring at me with shocked expressions.

"What?"

"Oh, nothing. Just seems like you've thought this through. In detail."

I nodded at Jameson. "Well, yeah. Hasn't everyone had that intrusive thought of how you could get away with murder?" By their horrified expressions, I took that as a no. "I would never do it," I admitted in a rush. "Just, you know... sometimes my mind wanders and.... Never mind."

"Right. Well, now I know to monitor my drinks around Rain from now on."

I rolled my eyes at Slade. "Or just don't piss me off to make me want to create a chemical compound that would be virtually undetectable with a tox screen."

"It scares me because I know you're smart enough to figure it out," Slade grumbled.

"Thank you." I beamed.

"If there are a string of sudden unexplained deaths in the area, we know who to suspect first. And, Slade, you're right—we know little about this unsub. We need to know why these victims, why knives, and what is he or she getting out of these kills? One thing we have going for us is the lengthy time period between murders."

"Why do you think that is?" Slade asked.

Jameson turned to stare at the wall of photos and notes. "Hunting the next victim? The unsub knew victim number five was home alone, that the roommate was out of town. He or she had to stake out the house for days or even be close enough to hear the roommate's plans." Jameson jumped up and rifled through the files. "For fuck's sake. Of course."

Slade and I waited, both edging closer to Jameson to hear what he'd found.

"The two killed outside their homes was because they didn't have a house but lived in apartments. With cameras and other security measures, the unsub wouldn't be able to get to the victims in their home." He straightened and ran a hand through his hair. "Which verifies the stalking aspect of the profile. Our unsub knew where they lived and planned accordingly. It also tells us these victims are special, targeted. We need to find out the why."

I leaned back in the chair, rolling my head along the stuffed cushion. "Not to throw another kink in your gender debate, but it could be a small-framed male. He could easily slip through the points of entry and would be weaker than the victims, which is why he uses the blunt force to the head."

"True. Not every male is made of pure muscle like me and Slade here." I snorted at Jameson and shook my head, sending my hair slipping over my shoulders. "And, Rain, you can toss kinks my way anytime."

Memories from last night's dreams surged forward, making the earlier quiver in my lower belly return in full force. I covertly pressed a hand to my stomach, willing the sensation to go away. Discussing gruesome murders was not the time to be turned on.

"Muscle, my ass," Slade chuckled, shooting Jameson an incredulous look. "You look like that skinny swimmer fucker."

"That narrows it down," Jameson muttered while fixing the cuffs of his dress shirt. "I want to see the crime scenes with my own eyes, walk the area and space to see if anything pops out at me. Who's down for a field trip?"

I shot my hand up in the air, fingers wiggling, though the dampness in my armpit had me slowly lowering it back down. An hour or so stuck in a small room with the two hottest males I'd ever known had me sweating more than normal. Plus, the sudden hot flashes every time pieces of last night's dreams wormed their way to the forefront of my mind. So being a little extra sweaty was okay.

Right?

Or...

Did I forget to put deodorant on earlier?

I mentally walked through my frantic morning after waking up late.

I was pretty sure I did.

I thought I did, but....

In a few minutes, I would be trapped in Slade's car with these two. What if I forgot to put deodorant on and started to smell? They would think I didn't shower and had horrible hygiene. Then any chance of the magical threesome dream would never come true. Not that I had a chance in the first place despite that, but intense body odor radiating off me in waves and making them gag would totally slash that sliver of hope I tightly clung to.

That settled it.

"Slade, can we swing by my house on our way to the first crime scene? I forgot something."

"What is it?"

In a flash, Jameson's hand came up and smacked Slade's chest, making him grunt. "Don't be so nosy, old man. What if it's personal? Do you really want to make her say she forgot tampons?"

Slade's brows pulled in tight. "Would it matter? Rain is thirtysomething and a doctor. Pretty sure she's okay with talking about menstrual cycles." I pressed three fingers to my lips to halt my growing smile while they had the oddest conversation ever. "It's not like she's thirteen and it's her first period."

"Know a lot about when girls start their periods, do you?" Jameson queried.

Slade wrapped a large hand around the back of his neck and squeezed. "I started fucking... I mean, dating earlier than most." He sighed at Jameson's pointed, raised brows. "Fine. Really young, okay? What can I say? I was always this damn good-looking." Now *that* I fully believed. Though now I really wanted to see a picture of teenage Slade. "Fuck, let's just go. And yes, Rain, we can stop by your place on the way."

Smirking, I slowly unfolded my legs and stood.

This morning had been awkward and way out of my normal routine.

And what surprised me the most?

I kind of liked it.

13

———————

RAIN

Deodorant applied—or reapplied, still hadn't remembered—I locked the front door and hopped down the concrete steps. Hand on the door handle of Slade's sedan, I tipped my face up toward the midmorning sun, soaking up the soft rays cutting through the gloomy weather. Within the next few weeks, the weather would shift to clear blue skies and all-day sun like Southern California was known for.

Today would be a good day. This was the longest I'd gone without days of solitude in what felt like years. I worked alone, hours in the morgue with only dead bodies as company. Lived alone. Zero friends. No close work colleagues.

Wait, where was I going with this?

Oh yeah, reminding myself how damn lonely my life had become. So, call me greedy or a masochist, because I would no doubt have an ulcer from nerves after spending long hours with these two, but I reveled in the constant company.

In fact, I didn't want it to end.

Though I shouldn't already be thinking about this one amazing reprieve from my lifestyle of solitude ending, I knew it would. Jameson would go back to.... Wait, where did he say he came in from?

And Slade would go back to being Mr. Grump with his one-syllable responses.

Though I still hadn't figured out what caused the one-eighty shift from the grumpy detective I'd grown used to and how he acted now. He didn't seem as concerned about it as I did. Like now, as I slid into the back seat, he didn't even glance my way, whereas I was a bundle of nerves and excitement for the togetherness day.

Who knew spending so much time with the living could be so exciting? Well, two people I was eager to hang out with, anyway. I wouldn't be nearly as thrilled at the prospect if it were anyone else.

"You all good?" Jameson asked, twisting in the front passenger seat with his normal simple grin.

"Yep. All set. Where to first, boys?"

"To where it all started. The alley where victim number one was found." Jameson held up the top file, giving it a little shake, and turned back to face the windshield. "We're good to go, driver. You may proceed to our first destination."

My giggle filled the back seat.

"Fuck off," Slade murmured, though I caught a hint of a smile in the rearview mirror, even him finding Jameson's antics somewhat amusing. Though both of our smiles faded when his intense gaze shifted to look back my way, the dark-tinted sunglasses not enough to diminish the feel of his eyes on me. "You never told us what that emergency was about yesterday. Why you needed to get to know your neighbors."

I hummed in response as I watched my neighborhood

pass by the window. "I thought I left my straightening iron on."

One dark brow rose above his wire-framed sunglasses. "And that's what you consider an emergency?"

I rolled my eyes, not bothering to turn from the window. "Well, yeah. And it was a genuine emergency to me. You weren't the one about to be some inmate's bitch while serving seventy years plus multiple consecutive life sentences for involuntary manslaughter of over a thousand innocent lives."

Silence. So much silence. Only the whir of the tires and the creak of the car's shocks filtered through the thick silence.

After a minute, Slade pulled down his glasses and shot Jameson a confused look. "Do you understand her words?"

Glancing over his shoulder, Jameson locked those honey-brown eyes on me. "Care to share with the class about how you went from a small hair tool left on to you turning into a mass murderer?"

An amused smirk tugged at my pursed lips. With a sigh, I relaxed back into the uncomfortable seat. The car was ugly as hell, but at least the inside was clean. Spotless, actually, just like Slade's appearance most days. In fact, I'd never noticed a single wrinkle or disheveled hair on the detective in the almost two years we'd worked together. He seemed to be perfectly put together, even his five o'clock shadow groomed instead of appearing lazy or unkept.

"It might not make sense to you two with normal thoughts, but sometimes I work things up in my mind. It wouldn't be so bad, but once I've escalated the what-ifs to the improbable outcome, I can't move on until I've resolved the initial trigger. In yesterday's case, I ran home and made sure I'd turned my straightener off. And I unplugged it so later in the day when I questioned myself again, which I knew I would, I could tell myself not to freak out. Over that, at least."

"You say 'sometimes,' but it must be fairly often if you've created a workaround to resolve the trigger of your anxious thoughts." Jameson's brows pulled in tight as he spoke, not in confusion, really, but more concern.

I nodded and shrugged. "It's definitely gotten worse recently because... well, as depressing as this sounds, I think it's because I don't have anyone here to talk me off that ledge. If I had someone to call, anyone to listen and dispel my crazy fears over something as simple as leaving a hair straightener turned on, then it wouldn't escalate to me googling ways to make a shank."

Slade barked a sharp laugh while Jameson continued to study me. "You don't have anyone to talk to?"

"Well, I do, but the dead aren't great conversation partners."

Jameson snorted and twisted back around, a hand coming up to rub at the back of his neck. "I mean a breathing, 'able to actually talk back to you' friend. Either here or back home?"

An ache bloomed in my chest at his harmless question. It was sad as hell, but I didn't. Not a single one here, past coworkers I grew close to who I still kept in contact with, or anyone from medical school. This job not only isolated me because of what I did but also the sheer amount of work on our plates that kept me from having the time or energy to foster solid friendships.

My friendless state wasn't intentional, by any means, but that didn't change the outcome.

Sure, I had family, but they were just as busy. I was lucky

to talk to them once a week, but sometimes we went way longer with only check-in texts exchanged.

"Not really," I muttered in answer to his question after the lengthy pause.

Mumbling something under his breath, Jameson shifted in his seat, hips rising a few inches so he could dig something out of his suit pocket. At an awkward angle, he held out his cell phone and waved it wildly in front of my face.

"Take it and put your phone number in my contacts. I never asked for your number when we worked together because you were married, and I believed that was crossing a line. But now you're not married and back in my life, so there isn't a reason that I shouldn't have your info stored in my favorites list."

A sharp breath raced down my throat at my quick inhale. I held it until the air burned in my lungs as I plucked the offered cell phone from his grasp.

"I'll be your friend, Raindrop. Be the one you can call when you need someone to talk to, or hell, just don't want to feel so damn alone. Any time, any day. You call me. Because believe me, I get it. Not the anxious thoughts but the suffocating weight of not having anyone close to lean on."

"I can't ask you to do that," I said, though my fingers flying over the screen, inputting my cell, full name, and address into his contact list, spoke to the way I desperately wanted what he sincerely offered. "What if you're busy or with someone?"

Like a woman.

Hot jealousy coursed through me thinking about his jokes, cocky smirks and sweet words directed to someone else.

Once again, Jameson turned in the seat, the belt across his

chest catching, making him curse at the damn thing. "You clearly don't understand the lengths I'll go for you, Raindrop. Enter your phone number, please. That way, when this case is solved and I'm in another city chasing another serial killer, you'll still be a part of my life. I hated you leaving and not having a way to reach out when you left Nashville. Please don't make me go through those horrible Raindrop withdrawals again."

"Fine," I sighed, like it was a chore to accept his friendship.

My gaze flicked to Slade's hands, the white-knuckled grip he had on the steering wheel. He hadn't uttered a single word or given any clue to how he felt about the conversation between Jameson and me. He shouldn't feel obligated to offer his friendship, too, yet his stony silence made me feel rejected all the same.

Guess that meant he didn't feel the same way as Jameson.

Which was fine. Totally and hurtfully fine. I now had one friend who I could call, and that was more than I woke up with this morning. I should be content with the new addition to my life, but a part of me still felt empty, and somehow, I knew Slade needed to be the one to fill that void. Within the last twenty-four hours, my unrequited crush on the growly man had shifted from a physical attraction to wanting more.

I wanted everything both of them had to offer.

The car slowing pulled me out of my thoughts. I blinked to refocus my eyes, a wide smile spreading across my face as my favorite coffee shop's sign appeared outside the window. At the speaker, Slade ordered my special unicorn drink and two regular coffees. I was practically bouncing in my seat when he passed back the delicious concoction.

"You're encouraging destructive behavior," Jameson

commented while taking one of the large black coffees from Slade.

Delicious sugary goodness slid over my tongue, the various flavors bursting to life as I sucked several long pulls up the straw. With a content sigh, I slumped against the door, pressing my forehead against the glass. "Destructive behavior. What does that even mean? You act like giving me sugar is equivalent to getting me wet." The moment the words leaped off my numb tongue, they registered. My spine went ramrod straight, gaze jerking from one suddenly too-still man to the other. "Like a gremlin." In sync, they each twisted their heads toward the other, exchanging silent words and making my pulse race. "Seriously, you two, stop whatever you're thinking. Get your minds out of the gutter." I smacked Jameson's shoulder, then Slade's. "You both know what I meant."

When Slade's shoulders trembled, I realized he was silently laughing. He looked at me through the rearview mirror and shook his head. "Sorry, Rain. We only get bigger as we grow up, not more mature. There are some things we will always find funny."

"Yeah, like a friend telling you how they shit their pants, or anyone saying the word *penetration* out loud." Jameson chuckled, focus on the phone in his hands. "There, I just sent you a text. Though I changed your contact to Raindrop. Did you really need to put all those acronyms behind your name?"

Letting the icy mixture melt in my mouth, savoring every burst of flavor, I waited until I swallowed before responding. "I wanted to make sure you knew it was me. In case you got me confused with another Rain in your life."

Jameson snorted. "Well, don't worry, that's not an issue, Raindrop. I've never met another Rain, and even if I did, I know they could never compare to the original. You're one of a kind, sweetheart. Now and always."

Rolling my forehead against the glass, I used my hair as a dark curtain to hide my giddy grin and shoved the straw between my lips.

Every single inch of me pulsed at Jameson's declaration. My heart, which seemed to need a jolt of electricity to get the rhythm beating normally again, especially loved knowing I was one of a kind to him.

THERE WAS NO REAL scientific evidence that supported my claim, but it was official.

I was fucking hangry.

We had little time between visiting the first four crime scenes. Jameson took his sweet-ass time scrutinizing and walking around, so for lunch, all we had time to grab were protein smoothies from a place Slade liked. Which wasn't enough for me then, even less so now.

That sorry excuse for sustainable nutrients was over five hours ago. Clearly these two men hadn't worked closely with a female in a while—if ever. If they did, they would know we needed to be fed and watered regularly.

Damn, I made us women sound like high-maintenance houseplants.

Oh, maybe that was what I was missing with my plants. I needed to stroke them, love them, maybe even talk to them like I did my dead bodies. Maybe then I could inch my vegetation survival rating above zero percent.

While I was eyeing the precinct as it grew larger in the windshield, my stomach growled, the sound like two boulders colliding in a violent fight to the death.

"I'm hungry," I complained with a hint of whine while pressing both hands to my empty stomach. My education told me it would take several days before the lack of actual food would lead to starvation, yet my body was telling me death was imminent if I didn't ingest proper food as soon as possible. "How about we grab dinner first, then come back here to finish work?"

"I could eat," Slade said, heel of his hand pressed to the steering wheel, turning it with a practiced ease as he paral-lel-parked across the street from the station. "What about you, Bend?"

"Huh?" he asked, barely pulling his rapt attention from the iPad in his lap, where he'd written all his notes and questions from the day. "Oh, we're here. Great." Jameson wrapped his fingers around the door handle, but Slade's massive hand gripped his shoulder, keeping him from exiting the car.

"Earth to Jameson. Rain just mentioned she's hungry, and I agreed. Let's go grab an early dinner, then come back here to finish up."

I loved how he claimed this dinner as "early." Only workaholics like us would consider six o'clock an early dinner.

"Um," Jameson murmured as he lifted his wrist to check his watch, "I'd love to go, but I really wanted to focus on piecing together the profile while the crime scenes are fresh on my mind. Plus, I plan to reach out to our technical profiler to see if he's come up with any connections between the victims."

If it weren't for my stomach lining eating itself, I would've said I could wait for dinner.

But this was now a life-and-death situation.

Which was super dramatic since that wasn't possible

after going five hours without food. Meaning the quick escalation of me dying right there in the back seat wouldn't even be a thought. No anxious thoughts when I knew for a fact that I would live.

Maybe.

Highly likely.

"I'm not sure how long I'll be," Jameson continued. "How about I meet you back at your place, Rain? I can call a rideshare once I'm done if you have a spare key to your townhome."

Without hesitation, I dug through the bottomless pit also known as my purse for my car keys. Grabbing the ring, I dangled the little fob over his shoulder. "Here, take my car. Park in the garage around back and you'll be able to get in through that door since I don't keep it locked."

"Thanks, Rain. See you two later. I'll text you both if I uncover anything groundbreaking in the case." Once he'd stepped out onto the sidewalk, he dipped his head back inside with a grin and winked. "Don't do anything I wouldn't do."

"Which would be what?" Slade shot back.

"Not much, Detective. Not much."

Lips parted from a silent gasp, I watched Jameson as he marched up the concrete steps to the glass front doors, disappearing through them without a single glance back. Of course, I couldn't help but memorize the way his perky ass flexed beneath the tailored black slacks he wore today or notice the female officer almost trip down the stairs when she did a double take as he passed.

"So, where are we going to eat?" Slade pulled the sedan away from the curb, slowing to a stop at a red light. "Want to move up here to the passenger seat so I don't feel like your chauffeur?"

Great idea.

Hand tightly gripped around the leather straps of my handbag, I unbuckled my seat belt and tossed a long leg over the center console.

"What the—"

"Light is green," I commented as I contorted my body to squeeze between the two front seats. Damnit, this was way easier in my head.

"I'm not fucking moving this shit on wheels until you're buckled up, Rain."

"You're the one who asked me to move to the front seat," I retorted, wincing when a sharp pain shot through my shoulder, which was stretched and twisted at an odd angle. "Ouch, I might need another massage. That hurt."

"Fucking hell," he griped under his breath. Two hands slid beneath my shoulders and lifted, easily helping me clear the center console that was currently acting like Mt. Everest in my climb to the passenger seat.

Car horns blared behind us, followed by cars whipping around, clearly pissed that we weren't moving at the green light, but Slade ignored it all, helping me maneuver my long legs through the narrow gap until I dropped ungracefully into the seat with a huff, hair tangled and tossed in front of my face.

"I meant for you to open the back door, take the two steps to the front door, and hop in like a sane person, Rain."

"We were driving," I grumbled.

"No, we were at a complete stop at a red light."

"Which almost immediately turned green. I saved myself from becoming roadkill."

Whispering a string of curses under his breath, Slade reached over my far shoulder and yanked the seat belt down, stretching it across my chest and clicking the latch into place.

"You don't have to be mad about it," I stated. "You wanted me in the front seat. Now I'm here."

"Rain," he sighed, rubbing at the back of his neck with his head tilted back, eyes closed.

"And I'm open on food, but not another smoothie. I need real sustenance."

He grunted some response that I couldn't understand and pressed on the gas, shooting us through the now-yellow light.

"Anything you're allergic to?"

"Nope."

"Seafood or burgers?"

"Both sit-down?" I questioned.

"Yep."

"And these are real food places? They're not blending these food options into some disgusting mixture—"

"It was one fruit smoothie with protein powder," Slade nearly yelled. "You act like I was trying to poison you."

"No, that would be me, remember?" His eyes cut my way. "Kidding."

"Seafood or burgers."

"Burgers. Or maybe seafood. No, definitely burgers. Though fish tacos—"

"Executive decision. Burgers."

I shot him a smile. "Exactly what I wanted."

Burgers, french fries, and alone time with my longtime crush.

Not sure what I did recently to be so lucky to have the past two days with Slade and Jameson in my life, but I sure as hell would make every moment count. Even if one for sure didn't see me the way I wanted him to, it didn't matter. I would still enjoy every second of their attention, lock it away in my memories for future nights when I went back to my regularly scheduled routine.

Though, after spending so much time with them, that normal routine seemed twice as lonely as it felt before.

14

———

JAMESON

The rolling wheels twitched as I shifted my weight in Rain's chair, hyperfocused on the pictures lining the wall. My frustration had mounted with every scene we investigated today. It was clear, based on the premeditated locations and lack of evidence, that this unsub hunted the victims, planned the crimes down to the last detail.

But *why* was the question I still couldn't answer.

Why these particular men?

How did they cross paths with our unsub?

A frustrated, heavy sigh rushed between my pursed lips as I swiveled the chair to study the files strewn along the desk. Resting my elbows on the top, I pressed the heel of both hands against my eyes and counted to ten, attempting to calm the swirling unanswered questions and constant intruding thoughts of her. It was a feeble, desperate attempt to keep any thoughts of Rain out and everything focused on nailing down the profile. But how could I not constantly think about her when she was entangled in this? Her name on all the reports drew my gaze every time, like a blinking neon sign.

This was my first solo assignment as a profiler, and I refused to fuck it up by being distracted.

Fingers wrapped around the slim device, I slid my cell from my pocket and pressed my boss's number, hitting the speaker icon before dropping it to the desk. The sharp ringing echoed through the quiet and desolate office three times before Rhyan's voice poured through the phone.

"Riggs."

"Hey, it's me." The chair let out a squeak as I leaned back, bouncing a little with nervous energy. "You got a few seconds?"

"For you? Always. How's the case going?"

With a huff, I let my head tip back until I gazed at the square ceiling tiles.

"Honestly, I'm not sure I'm any closer on a profile than I was on the plane coming here. It's confusing as fuck. I haven't even narrowed down the gender because of a few inconsistencies that normally point one direction or another. One second, I'm leaning toward a male unsub, then the next, something new catches my attention and I swing back to female."

Rhyan hummed, but another voice came through the speaker. "What's keeping you from identifying the unsub as female?" Special Agent Charlie Bekham cleared his throat before continuing. "I made the same mistake once, and it almost cost Rhyan her life."

I swallowed hard and swiveled the chair to face the wall lined with pictures. Leaning forward, I balanced both elbows on the top of my thighs.

"The bodies are left on display, no signs of remorse or attempting to cover them up, which we normally don't see with a female unsub. Then there's the way the unsub kills.

The amount of blood at the scene makes even some of the crime scene techs squeamish. It's a colossal mess, and—"

"How about the ME?" Rhyan questioned, cutting me off.

"Well, no, it doesn't bother her, but—"

"She is a woman, isn't she?" she continued.

"Yeah, but Rain is different—"

"Ohhhh, it's *Rain* now, is it?" I rolled my eyes at Charlie's teasing. "Not Dr. Evans? I'm guessing you were excited to see her again?"

I jerked around and grabbed the phone, glaring at the time ticking on the screen like I could force my annoyance down the line all the way to Dallas. "How do you know I knew her from before?"

Charlie scoffed. "It's me, and I'm fucking good at my job. No stone unturned and all that shit. When I searched for online connections between the victims, I might have sniffed around her background too."

"Why?" I gritted out, the edge of the phone digging into my palm beneath my death grip. The responding silence shifted my annoyance to trepidation. "Tell me what the fuck is going on, Charlie." Shoving out of the chair, I clenched the edge of the desk until all color bled from my knuckles. "Why the hell were you looking into Rain's background? Looking into her, period?"

"That was my call." At least Rhyan sounded the tiniest bit sorry for having her partner investigate Rain. "I'll explain why later, but it isn't negative, so don't worry. Let's just say I wanted to know more about this brilliant ME who caught that these cases were committed by one unsub. I'm intrigued."

My thoughts spun on hyperdrive around the implications of what Rhyan said. My Rain intrigued Rhyan. Was that a good or bad thing?

No. Fuck. Not my Rain. Not mine at all.

Except the more time I spent in Rain's orbit, the more I wanted that to be true.

The only explanation for Rhyan's request slammed into me like a punch in the gut. I straightened and ran a hand through my hair, pulling at the ends.

"You're considering her for the team."

"Hmm." I rolled my eyes at the noncommittal hum. "I guess we'll see, won't we? Now, let's focus on the reason you called. You've laid out the reasons you think a woman didn't commit these crimes, which are valid. Weak but valid based on what we've learned from other female serial killers. Now tell me why you think it's a female."

"The blitz attacks to subdue them, the fact that there aren't any hilt bruises around the stab wounds, and from what I can tell, there aren't any souvenirs taken from the bodies or scenes. The point of entry in all the home cases are narrow windows and even a doggy door."

Stepping up to the wall of pictures, I leaned a shoulder against an empty spot and stared down the row of gruesome photos, hoping the angle would help me see something new.

It didn't.

"And the alley murders," Charlie spoke up, the sound of the keyboard keys clacking beneath his warp-speed fingers filtering through. "What would lure a heterosexual man into a dark alley?"

I popped off the wall. "A woman." Stepping to the desk, I flipped open the files on the victims found in an alley. "So, what are we looking at? A past scorned lover maybe upset because the victims wouldn't call her back? Or maybe the victims rejected the unsub's advances?"

"That's an angle. Let me dig more into these guys' backgrounds. I had to focus on another case for Sam today, so there could be a few things I could uncover." I nodded like Charlie could see me. "There has to be something tying them together. A bar, a grocery store, hell, a doctor or a fucking dentist. They all came in contact with our unsub. We just have to find out how."

"Thanks, Charlie. I appreciate it, man."

"Based on what I see," Rhyan cut in, "I'd say Caucasian female, late twenties, early thirties. The anger she has toward men comes out in her daily life, so ask people if they've noticed anyone whose demeanor has changed at work or at home. They won't be able to keep this kind of anger toward a certain type of male hidden for long."

Damn, Rhyan was good. Not only was she an awesome boss who cared about every member of her team but a damn amazing profiler. Add in that her partner, Charlie, being the best computer hacker I'd ever met, and they were an unstoppable couple. They technically met on a case, so maybe they would both understand if I mixed a little plea-sure with business while I compiled a more detailed profile here in Santa Coasta.

"So, how do I stop this from happening to someone else?" I mused. "Thank fuck the unsub has a decent gap between kills, probably to learn the next victim's routine, and plan."

"Keep asking questions," Rhyan stated. "Find the answer to why these men and you'll be able to get ahead of her. Like Charlie said, we'll look into things from here, but you're at ground zero. Talk to the neighbors again. Find answers to a few of our questions and you'll be home in no time."

My stomach tightened at her comment. Did I really want to be home in no time?

That would mean leaving Rain behind.

"Yeah," I offered absentmindedly.

"Don't sound so excited," Charlie laughed. "Though I have a feeling you're not minding the long stay in Santa Coasta. Maybe because of a certain ME you worked with before?"

I groaned, though my lips curled in a smirk. "If you sing 'Jameson and Rain sitting in a tree—'"

"F-U-C-K-I-N-G."

"That's not how it goes."

"It does in the adult version. Though how that would work in a tree...."

"Can you two focus, please," Rhyan said, sounding exasperated, like our antics were annoying. But considering she was with Charlie, she put up with way more than this on a day-to-day basis. "I think we're overlooking a way that might tie all the victims to the unsub."

"Go on, please. I need something, anything," I pleaded. "What am I not seeing, boss?"

"You suggested a jaded lover or someone they rejected. And sure, there is that possibility, but from a woman's perspective, I'm thinking a different angle. One you two don't immediately think of because you're men and have never been in a situation like our unsub. What if all these men, our victims, wouldn't take no for an answer when they were with our unsub? Maybe came on too strong, called her something when she rejected them, or, even worse, assaulted her?"

Anger churned in my gut, making heat flare in my veins. I fucking hated this part of the job. Seeing all the ways men abused a woman's trust or smaller size. There were too many out there who forgot that women have a voice. The men who pushed for what they wanted, took without consent, were the worst of the worst and deserved to have their own voice taken from them. Let them see how it felt to be violated and taken advantage of.

Sadly, our justice system did not feel the same way.

Fingers massaging my gunshot wound, tracing along the muscle to help ease the insistent throb, I said, "My only question is, if there was an assault that triggered this, wouldn't the unsub have identified them in a report if she knew who it was, which would've led to them being arrested?"

"And what are the odds of the same woman having five arrogant assholes taking their interest too far? I know it happens more often than we realize, but the odds of it happening to the same woman are low," Charlie muttered, voice distant, as if he'd moved away from the phone. "I'll run a search in the Santa Coasta area for women who reported assaults and see if there's one victim with multiple cases pending. If we find nothing to go off of, then I'll expand my search."

"Charlie," I called out before he lost himself in this new search, "can you check the Santa Coasta database for our victims' names in any files? Maybe they weren't officially charged and booked in the system, which means they wouldn't pull on any reports, but if they were listed as a potential suspect or even had their name mentioned by the victim...."

"Then it wouldn't show up in their background since nothing was actually filed. That will take a little more time considering I'll have to set up a search to scan each of the written reports from the last few years."

"Ten," Rhyan added. "Go back ten years, Charlie. I think we're onto something. If my gut is right, this unsub has a list she's working from and won't stop until she's marked off every name."

"This is so fucking sick," I bit out, slamming the file folder closed, which did nothing to calm my rising anger. "If what we're assuming is true, these assholes assaulted one or multiple women and were never charged. How could the system just let these fuckers walk?"

A heavy silence poured through the phone, all of us no doubt simmering in our own rage at how unjust the system could be. The evidence needed for an arrest was great to keep the innocent from being falsely imprisoned, but it just put that much more burden on the victim and detective to gather enough evidence to prove guilt.

Sometimes we knew we had the right person but just couldn't find enough evidence to prove without a reasonable doubt that they were guilty.

"I know, Jameson," Rhyan said, the exhaustion in her voice clear even states away. "And it's worse for us because we see how often it happens on a national scale. We know it's not just Santa Coasta, it's everywhere. Listen, you're doing all you can to catch the unsub, but sometimes we need to take a step back for a fresh perspective. It's what, eight o'clock there? Go get dinner, have a beer. Pick up the case tomorrow. Charlie will create the algorithm needed to search the old Santa Coasta files, and I'll keep going over the new ones to see if there's anything else we can add to the profile we discussed earlier."

I swallowed. "I just feel guilty. What if she's... what if she's a victim herself, Rhyan? How do we—" Fuck, I couldn't finish that thought.

"You're a good man, Jameson. But we have a job to do. If she is a victim herself, then we can sympathize, and that will adjust how you approach her to ensure she gets the help she needs. But she has killed five men. We can't turn a blind eye to that." I collapsed into the chair, the exhaustion suddenly too much to stay standing. "And where are you staying, by the way? The travel coordinator said you checked out of the hotel but haven't checked into another one."

"Erm." I rubbed at the back of my neck and squeezed. "So, what happened was...."

"Go on," she encouraged, humor lifting her tone.

"The hotel was in a rough part of town, as in you might have come here to investigate my murder, so I checked out to find another place where I wouldn't end up outlined in chalk, but then Dr. Evans offered another place to stay." My features twisted in a wince. "With her."

"Oh, did she now?" Oh hell, I would never hear the end of this. I just knew it. "Well, I'm sure that is super beneficial for the case. Among other things." She paused, but I kept my lips sealed shut, not giving her any hint to how I really felt about staying next door to the woman currently consuming my thoughts. Well, half consuming—the other half was filled with murder and mayhem. "So, I have to ask, since as your boss and all, I need to know these things... did you two date when you worked together in Nashville?"

"Nope. She was married, so all we did was talk. And flirt a bit. Then there was the occasional lunch and—" I shook my head. "But she was married and nothing happened."

"But she isn't now." I blinked at the blank phone. *How the fuck does he know that?* "Don't stare at the phone, Jameson Leslie Bend." Oh, I fucking hated that bastard for even knowing my full name. Curious motherfucker. "I noticed the divorce filings when doing my bit of digging for my girl here. Not sure if you know this or not, but the divorce was messy. Looks like he took her through the ringer and still wanted more. He even wrote out the canned goods on the list of assets that he wanted."

"Sounds about right," I grumbled. "He was a fuckhead."

"You're not a fuckhead," Rhyan commented.

"Thanks?"

"I'm just saying. You're there. She's there. A spark from years before. Which is fine. I can't cast judgment on something happening between you while you're there for the job. You know how Charlie and I met."

"Best. Case. Ever," Charlie blurted.

"When I almost died?" she laughed.

"Minus that."

"Just don't let it distract you from finding the unsub, Jameson. You're there for a job, but you're allowed to still have a life while working."

But that was the problem, wasn't it?

I knew in my soul that if I pursued something with Rain, it would be a distraction. There wasn't a doubt in my mind that the moment I touched her soft fair skin, she'd instantly consume every part of me. Even more than she already did.

But I also knew I couldn't let this opportunity pass me by. If Rain wanted me, wanted our flirting to lead to more, why push aside what I'd wished for all this time because of the job?

Only one way to find out.

15

SLADE

Already done with my massive salad with three grilled chicken breasts added, I pushed the plate to the side and wiped the thick paper napkin across my lips. Across the table, Rain continued to devour her double-patty burger, little content moans escaping her along with strange happy dances in her seat with every bite. Every sound had my attention snapping to her and my mind sinking straight in the gutter.

Because hot damn, if she made those noises about food, what would she sound like if I made a meal out of her?

With a little satisfied hum, she wiped her fingers, bouncing slightly in the seat as she slurped down the chocolate milkshake she'd ordered for a drink. This had to be the single most entertaining dinner I'd ever had, and we hadn't talked about anything other than work. It was just her being one hundred percent Rain, and I was sitting here enjoying every second.

So many of my past relationships revolved around the physical side, all fucking and nothing else. This between me and Rain, the simplicity of enjoying being in each other's presence, was a breath of fresh fucking air. That didn't mean I didn't crave something physical, because how could I not with a woman like Rain?

But I wouldn't.

Which reminded me that I still needed to apologize for my slip.

"Hey, so I've been meaning to talk to you about yesterday."

Her hazel eyes flicked up to me, peering through long dark lashes that weren't goopy with mascara or as long as her hair with lash extensions. Damnit, Rain was so organically beautiful. If I looked long enough, I could see the faint scattering of freckles along the bridge of her tiny nose that faded along her cheekbones. And those eyes, when they locked on you, it was like a black fucking hole you wanted to dive into and never come up for air again.

"You mean how you gave me a migraine from the emotional whiplash?"

My heart sank. Fuck. I never meant to cause her pain. Damnit, this was just another tally mark under the reasons I couldn't want more with her.

"Damnit, Rain," I sighed and scrubbed a hand over my scruff-covered jaw. "I didn't mean—"

She held up a hand, cutting me off. "Listen, I get it. At first, I was confused, but I've thought about it, and I think I know what's going on."

"You do," I huffed. Both arms crossed over my chest, I leaned back and hitched my chin her way. "I'll bite. Tell me, what's your theory?"

Wiping her lips, she tossed the dirty napkin onto the empty plate where a burger and two orders of fries once sat. Damn, there was something sexy about a woman who wasn't afraid to eat. Though I was slightly concerned about her cholesterol levels and possible Type 2 diabetes, considering all the sugar she consumed.

"A new guy comes into town, who I know, and boom, you're actually treating me like a normal person."

My brows pulled in tight. That made me sound like an asshole. And I could correct her and say her mentioning the date she went on was the actual trigger for breaking the professional facade I wore, but then that would show my hand more than I did yesterday in her office.

"So, the way I see it is you're just competitive," she continued. "I mean, that's what made you good when you played hockey."

"Football," I grunted, but based on her responding grin, she knew that and was just messing with me.

"I don't appreciate you peeing on me, so to say—"

"Who the fuck says that?"

"People."

"I think you need to get out more, Dr. Evans."

A wide smile broke across her gorgeous face, and I released a slow breath, taking in the beautiful woman across from me. This was Rain at her most stunning. All the stress of the day gone and that brilliant grin crinkling the edges of her eyes, making them somehow sparkle.

Oh hell, I was so lost on this woman, and she thought I was just trying to mark my fucking territory. A pang vibrated through my chest at the loss of something I'd never actually had. I pressed a fist to my sternum and rubbed to ease the pressure.

Shit, am I having a heart attack?

At least Rain was a doctor.

And could administer mouth-to-mouth.

Huh. Suddenly my heart stopping and me dying for a few seconds didn't seem so bad.

"Anyway, like I said, I don't appreciate it, but it was nice. I liked us acting like friends and not just coworkers. Normally I'm intimidated by you, all nervous because you're you and I'm me." *What the fuck does that mean?* I did not like the sound of that. "But yesterday was different, and it was nice. Really nice. So don't worry, but I would love for this," she said, motioning between us, "to keep going even after Jameson is gone. It's nice having a friend, someone to talk to since everyone else treats me like the plague."

Ah fuck.

"And I get that too. I'm the strange girl because of what I do. Just sometimes I wish what I enjoyed didn't isolate me so much."

And I was officially an asshole. All those cops I'd warned away apparently took my warnings a step further and just avoided her altogether instead of keeping their eyes, hands, and compliments to themselves.

"Rain," I started, but I didn't have words after that. Because what was there to say? If I admitted to what I did, she'd want to know why, and I highly doubted that she'd believe I was protecting her.

"No, it's okay. You don't have to say anything. Just, like I said, don't go back to being a grumpy detective all the time. I think that would hurt worse than that flicker of hope that sparked yesterday that you might actually reciprocate how I feel for you being extinguished with reality."

Okay, I went to college. I wasn't a dumb man, but...

What the hell did she just say?

Those were a lot of big words used in a very complex sentence. If it didn't make me feel like an idiot, I'd ask her to write it on a napkin so I could break it down at my own much slower pace.

"Reciprocate how you feel?"

Her cheeks heated. "Well, yeah. Come on, Slade. You're *you*," Rain emphasized like that meant something. "It's impossible to not be sucked into your gravitational pull."

Reason number 161 for why I didn't deserve her.

Because fuck, she was smart, and I didn't understand most of what came out of her mouth.

"You guys good here?" I didn't look up at the server, who paused a little too close. Her sickly sweet perfume clogged my sinuses, and her bare arm brushed against my bicep as she dragged my plate closer to the edge of the table. "Wow, you took all that down. That's more than this big guy."

My hackles rose at her snarky tone directed toward Rain.

Sweet Rain, who just smiled like she didn't understand the rude undertone of the woman's comments.

"Yeah, I was hungry," she said, patting her flat stomach. "But in all honesty, I'd eat that much even if I'd had more than a smoothie for lunch." Leaning forward, she rested both elbows on the table and flicked her hazel eyes my way. That smile turned mischievous. "Do you know who this is?"

The waitress huffed. "Of course, I know who he is. My older brothers talked about him nonstop."

Rain's brows furrowed. "Your brothers? Wait, are they criminals or something? Is that—"

"What the fuck?" the waitress snapped. "Why would you say that?"

"Because you said you know who he is. The best homicide detective in Santa Coasta—"

"I was talking about him as an NFL player."

Surprise lit across Rain's face, and it made me want to thread my fingers through her dark hair and pull her face to mine for a deep kiss. Of course, this woman didn't see me as who I was but who I am.

Wasn't that all I wanted?

And here I was, pushing her away. At the very least not correcting her assumption of me posturing because Jameson was in town.

"Oh, right." Rain flicked her gaze around the restaurant, clearly uncomfortable now.

Yanking out my wallet, I slapped my credit card down on the table. "We'll take the check."

I didn't look the young woman's way, just kept my focus trained on Rain.

"Sorry," she whispered once the server walked away. "Worst wingwoman ever."

My brows flew up my forehead. "That's what you were trying to do?"

"Yes, and I clearly failed." She groaned and slumped back against the booth seat. "This is why I don't have friends."

"Stop it," I snapped. "Stop talking shit about yourself, you hear me? You're perfect. They're the idiots for not seeing how amazing you are."

Fuck. Well, that just slipped. Though every word was true.

"You don't know me, Slade. I'm awkward, anxious, and prefer the silence of my morgue to being out with the living. It's nothing new. I've always been a bit of a loner." Her fingers nervously ripped at the paper napkin, tearing it into long strips. "I think it's too far-fetched to find someone who lets me be me but will also fill that part of me that's hopelessly lonely."

I sucked in a breath and held it to keep from shouting that I could be that man.

That I could be her partner in life.

I wouldn't stifle her career. I'd let her be the amazing woman she was yet be there in the background waiting.

But I did the opposite.

"You know, Bend has a thing for you. I told you he was asking about your relationship status." The words were like poison on my tongue, slowly killing me from the inside out.

"Are you playing wingman now?" she said with a forced smile.

I shrugged. "Just saying, seems you two have a connection."

The server came back at that moment and slid the receipt and my card in front of me.

"I get off in an hour," she whispered into my ear.

Needing her out of my personal space, I raised a shoulder up toward my ear, slightly pushing her out of the way. As I signed my name on the receipt, I rolled my eyes at the phone number listed on the back of my copy.

"You ready, Rain?" I asked, pressing both hands into the bench seat, eager to get the hell out of here.

Out of habit, I scanned the restaurant and bar area, gaze snagging on a disheveled man sitting at the end of the bar, dark eyes locked on me. I met his intense stare, only breaking it when Rain walked past, heading for the door. Hand hovering over her lower back, I guided her around the full tables, noticing every time she tensed when the noise level increased from a burst of laughter or someone yelling about the game playing on the TVs.

Outside, I sucked in a deep breath of the crisp air. In my youth, I loved being surrounded by people. My favorite times were in the locker room, with the team joking and fucking around. In fact, I hated being alone. The weight of everything felt heavier if I wasn't in the middle of a crowd.

But now I was more like Rain, the complete opposite of who I was then. I loved the quiet, savored the time I could actually think by myself.

A pricking sensation, the feeling of being watched, had

every muscle tensing. It didn't seem dangerous per se, more like how it felt to be stalked by the paparazzi.

"I can get an Uber," Rain said halfway to the car.

"What?" I jerked my head around, searching the shadows for the cause of the sensation, but came up empty. "Why?"

"I heard what she said to you. Don't feel you have to hold back because I'm here." There was a sadness in her tone that told me she didn't quite believe her own words.

"I'm right where I want to be, Rain." Unlocking her door, I pulled it open and folded both forearms on top. "Tonight was fun. You're not as awkward as you think. Smart as hell, though. Some words you used I'll have to look up later."

That sadness vanished with a wide, radiant smile. The smile that made my heart ache, and I'd do anything to see it every day for the rest of my life.

Rain nodded and stuck out her hand. I gave it a hesitant look before grasping it, mine completely engulfing her smaller one.

"Friends?"

The moment I knew I would never play football again didn't hold a candle to the anguish that word out of her mouth sent through my chest.

Because I wanted so much more.

"Friends," I gritted out. "Come on, let's get you home to Jameson."

Right into the arms of a man who deserved her.

And far from the one who didn't.

16

RAIN

The ride to my place was quiet, both of us lost in our respective thoughts. Which I was thankful for, considering I didn't know what to say that wouldn't expose the utter devastation I felt at knowing I was right about Slade's actions yesterday.

Of course, he didn't want or see me the way I wanted and saw him. He was being territorial because a new man— an FBI agent, at that—came into town and immediately connected with me.

It made sense, yet it didn't. I'd really hoped Slade would refute my theory, tell me I was overthinking it all and his actions in my office yesterday were genuine. That he wanted me, wanted to cross that professional boundary. With me.

But he didn't.

Instead, he pointed out that Jameson was into me. Now, I was blind to a lot of things, but not that. Jameson made it very clear how he viewed me, never jerking me back and forth, toying with my emotions. Which was a breath of fresh air because I knew where I stood with him.

Though I also knew Jameson wouldn't take that first

step. That ball was in my court. Not because he wasn't interested, but he toed that gentleman's line carefully. It was cute. And infuriating. Last night, I'd worn my cutest sleep shorts, basically offered myself up on a platter by lying beside him on the couch. But nothing happened.

Maybe a more direct approach was needed. I just hoped once he knew I was interested in exploring our attraction while he was in Santa Coasta that he would take control. Sure, I'd had sex before, but not with someone like him.

Or Slade.

I shook my head to fling that thought right out of it.

Fantasizing about both of them would only lead to disappointment.

The sedan slowed, pulling alongside the curb in front of my townhome. With a tight-lipped smile, I gathered my things and reached for the door handle. A moment's pause, a hopeful hesitation, had me stalling. The naive part of me wanting him to say something. But Slade remained silent in the driver's seat. With a huff—though I had no right to be as annoyed as I was with him—I pushed the door open and stomped onto the sidewalk.

The door slammed behind me, making me grimace.

I may not have the right to be annoyed, but I couldn't stop.

Annoyance with both him and myself vibrated beneath my skin, whether or not it was justified.

My steps were quick as I climbed to the front stoop with the gentle hum of the car engine idling behind me. The metal key easily slid into the deadbolt before I twisted it to unlock the door. I gave in to the urge to take a quick glance over my shoulder. With the passenger window rolled up, the tint prevented me from seeing inside, but I could practically feel Slade's stare, watching and waiting for me to be safely tucked in the house behind a locked door.

A high-pitched sappy sigh escaped as I shoved the heavy wooden front door open and stepped into the foyer. After flicking the lock back in place, I fell against the wood and tapped my skull against it, trying to make sense of my swinging emotions. Sad, quickly followed by annoyed, and now wearing this goofy smile because he'd waited for me instead of driving off before I was inside.

I told him we were friends, but that didn't mean I could just erase the massive crush I had on him in a single night.

"That you, Rain?"

I popped off the door and started the slow climb up the steep stairs. My steps faltered when an amazing aroma of meat cooking wafted down the staircase. Even though I'd already eaten—a lot, per the catty waitress's comment—my mouth watered at the yummy scent. Moving quicker now, I rounded the corner and froze on the landing, mouth gaping as I took in the unfamiliar scene in my normally desolate kitchen.

Air refused to enter my lungs, the organs suddenly frozen. Every confusing thought about Slade and the night vanished, leaving only room for memorizing every bare inch of Jameson's muscular back. He was facing the stove, his defined arms shifting as he stirred whatever he was currently cooking. Those same sweats from last night that hugged his ass and generous package—it was easy to tell considering that damn material left nothing to the imagina-tion—sat low on his hips, giving a hint of the top of his butt cheeks. My fingers twitched to give the tiniest tug for them to puddle around his ankles.

I licked my lips, mouth watering for a totally different reason than seconds before. The sight of him half naked in my kitchen made me ravenous for something other than food.

In an unhurried move, Jameson glanced at me over his shoulder, a smirk growing when he found me staring, mouth agape. "Hey, welcome home." My heart did this weird flutter thing at those words on his lips. "Hope you don't mind me using your kitchen. I couldn't deal with takeout again, so I stopped by the store and picked up some things."

I dropped my bag to the floor by my feet, not caring that it was in the middle of the walkway. Toeing off one sneaker, then the other, I padded closer to the sexy, cooking man and leaned in, inspecting the questionable contents in the pan.

"Of course I don't mind. What are you making?"

The hand not holding the spatula lifted a familiar box off the counter and gave it a shake. "Hamburger Helper. Not the healthiest, but it sounded warm and, most important, easy. I'm as good a cook as you are a plant parent." I shot him a glare and crossed both arms over my chest, which only made him laugh. "Food should be ready in about fifteen minutes. I'm sure you're ready for that nightly soak and to get comfortable."

Or I could just get comfortable here by ripping all my clothes off.

Jameson ran a finger down my forearm, eliciting goose bumps in its wake. "Are you hungry? I can wait for you if—"

"No, thank you," I somehow managed around the lump in my throat. Him half naked and being super considerate had me half ready to burst into tears, the other half a second away from attacking his lips with my own. "I had dinner with Slade."

My stomach dropped upon saying his name out loud to Jameson, nervous he'd pick up on my feelings for the other man by the hitch in my voice, ending this vibrating connection between us.

"That's great. I'm glad he got you some food since you were so hungry. Well, if you saved room for dessert, I picked up a few different flavors of ice cream while I was at the store. Oh, and I bought you more beer since I drank a few last night and noticed you were low."

Tears lined my lower lids. I bit my lip to keep it from quivering from the swelling emotions. How could this man be so sweet, look like absolute sin, and be single?

"Go on," Jameson urged, brows dipped in tight as he studied me. "We can talk after you come back down."

I swallowed hard and forced my hesitant gaze to meet his worried one. "Jameson." Inhaling a deep breath for confidence, I forced the next words out. "What if I want to do more than just talk?"

He stilled, chest not even rising with a single breath. The words to retract my stupid question were on the tip of my tongue when he flicked the gas off and two powerful hands whirled me around. My lower back pressed against the rounded edge of the island, Jameson trapping me in place with both palms pressed to the marble on either side of my hips.

I couldn't meet his gaze, only stared transfixed at his heaving, bare chest.

Holy fuck, that's hot.

"What does that mean exactly, Raindrop?"

My lids fluttered shut as I inhaled his cedar-and-spice scent. A fresh wave of desire had my core trembling and warmth flashing along my cheekbones. I swallowed my whimper when two cool fingers pressed beneath my chin, slowly raising my face up to his.

"Rain?"

The need pulsing through my veins bolstered my courage to follow through with expressing what I wanted. To finally do something for myself. Arms heavy, I reached between us, searching his honey-brown eyes for any sign of hesitation, then slid my fingers along his defined chest and rippled abs, the heat radiating from his smooth skin making my breaths stutter. His responding guttural groan had my heart slamming against my chest, desperate to break free.

"It means... what if I don't want to talk?" I rasped, barely able to get the words out. "I'm tired of talking, tired of thinking and overanalyzing everything." I let all the pain and exhaustion bleed from my gaze. "So damn tired of being alone."

The corner of Jameson's lips quirked in a cocky smirk as he traced the line of my jaw. "Are you asking for a distraction, Raindrop?"

Yes. No. Hell, I didn't know. I just wanted to feel for a few hours, to not be all alone and lost in my own thoughts. Wanted to feel a genuine connection with someone like him, who I knew wouldn't play mind games or take more than I was willing to give.

"Yes," I breathed, gaze locked on his throat as it bobbed with a hard swallow before sliding down to his chest.

To his smooth chest that I was almost positive he shaved or waxed or....

Oh fuck.

When was the last time I shaved any part of my body besides my ankles when I wear those cute cropped black pants?

"But," I squeaked, "I need to shower first."

"I don't give a fuck if you've been out all day or not, Raindrop. I'll eat your sweet cunt for an appetizer right here, right now, if you'll allow me." My lips parted on a silent gasp as he ground his clearly hard cock against me. "I'll lift you up on this counter like I imagined last night and make you scream so loud your neighbors will hear you begging for more."

Liquid dripped from my core, soaking my panties. Warmth built beneath my skin the longer we stared at each other. The tip of his tongue slipped out, wetting his lower lip. A shiver raced down my spine, my shoulders trembling. A pitiful whimper caught in my throat as he ran his nose along the length of my neck. I tilted my head, giving him more access as his lips caressed my skin.

"Yeah, um, I just…. Give me ten minutes."

His dark chuckle caused the hairs on the back of my neck to stand on end. Gathering my hair in a tight grip, he held me in place, running his lips along the shell of my ear.

"Okay, Raindrop. Go have your shower, and I'll be down here waiting. Waiting to touch you the way I fantasized about those years we were apart. But promise me one thing. Are you listening, sweetheart?" I moaned instead of using words in response, making him chuckle in my ear. "If you touch yourself in the shower—" A hand slid across my hip and cupped my core, squeezing until the pressure had me whimpering in pleasure. "—think about me." I nodded, too lost in a lust haze to do anything more. "And Slade."

My lids flew open as I leaned back, putting distance between us to search his face.

"What?" I gasped.

Still holding my core, he leaned forward, brushing his lips over mine in a barely-there kiss.

"Don't worry, sweetheart. I see how you look at him, how you look at both of us. And I've always loved sharing." With that verbal bomb, he stepped back and adjusted himself with a pained grimace. "Now go shower. I'll eat. And then we can finally see how hot this fire between us can burn."

Fuck me.

Yes. Can that just be my blanket response from now until he leaves Santa Coasta?

Dizzy with the desire pumping through my veins, which Jameson caused even though he barely touched me, I nodded and turned toward the stairs, gripping the counter for support. Too dazed and lost in my dirty thoughts, I jumped, not expecting the stinging slap that landed on my ass and propelled me forward.

Mouth wide open, I whirled around, hand on my stinging butt cheek.

Without a word, Jameson winked and turned to the stove, flicking the gas back on. Whistling, he picked the spatula back up like he didn't just light my entire body on fire.

I numbly made my way up the stairs, down the hall, and into my bedroom. The door quietly clicked behind me before I slumped against it, my legs feeling more like noodles than muscle. I tipped my face to the ceiling, a slow grin creeping across my face as the reality of what I just put in motion settled over me.

Finally. Tonight, for the first time in too many years, I would let it all go.

Forget about tomorrow.

Focus on the now.

And the sexy-as-sin man half naked downstairs in my kitchen.

———

THIRTY MINUTES and about a pound of body hair removed later, I stood at the top of the stairs, toes curling around the step's edge. Tucking a few dark strands behind my ear, I gripped the railing as I leaned forward, straining to hear movement in the living room.

Besides the soft, unfamiliar voices—what I assumed was the TV—I heard nothing else. Fingers fiddling with the hem of my sleep shorts, I dared a step down, then another, slowly descending the stairs while attempting to calm my quick breaths. My nerves were so tight that I hesitated a second, wondering if I needed to bolt up the stairs to throw up.

I hadn't done this since medical school.

This being a first kiss, first touch. And this was a man I was not only attracted to physically but every sweet and dirty part of him, who was willing and eager downstairs. And I was a damn nervous wreck about it. Now that the rush of hormones from earlier faded during the shower, I was left scared shitless. I still wanted this, but how?

Did I just walk up to him and say, *"Hey, Jameson, I'm ready for you to do all the things to me?"*

I wasn't naturally sexy. I worked with dead people all day, for fuck's sake.

If I tried to tempt him with my moves or sexy looks, I'd end up looking more constipated than suggestive.

The realization that I'd one day redo these firsts hit me the hardest when I'd finally filed for divorce. At one point in my life, when I said "I do," I'd assumed I would never feel these first jitters again, but things happened and now here I was. I wasn't 'scared' per se but rather extreme stomach churning, about to pee myself nervous. Excited with a dash of terrified.

At the bottom of the stairs, I peeked around the corner, first searching the kitchen before finding Jameson lounging on the couch in the living room. Swallowing to ease my suddenly desert-dry mouth, I ventured into the living room, my heart in my throat.

"Good shower?" Jameson asked without glancing away from the flashing TV screen.

A frown pulled down the corners of my lips. "Yeah." I shifted my weight from one bare foot to the other as I eyed him suspiciously. "So, do you still want to—" I swirled a hand in the air. "—you know?"

He didn't respond. Didn't even look my way.

My nostrils flared in annoyance at the slight tic of his cheek, as if suppressing a grin. I crossed both arms, pushing my breasts together beneath my pajama top.

Oh, the bastard wants me to sweat, to make me spell it out. Well, we'll see how that works out for him.

Tiptoeing over to the couch, I sat on the opposite side, back against the high armrest with both long legs outstretched toward him.

"What was your question?" he asked, finally deeming me worthy of his attention, and twisted to face me. His gaze flicked down to my bare feet, then slowly glided up my legs until it paused at the junction. Whatever flame that dimmed while I was in the shower roared back to life as he sucked his lower lip between his teeth.

"I was wondering if you wanted to make good on your promises from earlier. Or if those were just words."

Damn. Who is this bold woman with the raspy voice and sassy words? I kind of want to be her.

Oh wait....

Jameson hummed and picked up my right foot. "I think I owe you a foot massage since Slade stopped us earlier today."

My stomach fluttered at Slade's name with Jameson's hands on me.

My lips parted, each shallow breath brushing past them

as his fingers moved, gently massaging the tightness out of the balls of my feet and toes.

"We need to discuss what this is, make sure we're on the same page." Jameson set that foot down and worked on the other. Though this time his fingers only lingered there for a minute before slowly working up to my ankle and moving to massage my calf. "When this case is done, I'll go back to Dallas." My ears perked up at that. I wanted to tell him I was from there but couldn't form words as his hands moved even higher, now working the muscles just above my knee. "If we do this, follow through on what we both want, it will only be for while I'm here and can't distract us from the case."

I licked my lips and then bit the lower one. "I get it. I understand."

"And," he drawled, "if you want to explore your attraction to Slade while I'm here—"

"I won't," I whispered, voice dropping. "We're just friends."

Jameson chuckled and shook his head, a few longer strands of hair brushing against his forehead. "Well, let me put it this way. If that dumbass gets over his insecurities and you two finally act on what's clear between you, I'm good. Don't think this means you're only mine and you have to hold back. And if you want us both"—a wicked gleam shone in his light eyes as his fingers played with the hem of my shorts—"then I'm in."

"Jameson," I whimpered as his fingers dipped beneath the cotton and continued to slide upward. Any second now, he'd notice the one article of clothing I'd skipped when getting dressed.

"Yes, Raindrop."

"I need... I want—" A forceful gasp cut off my pleading as his fingers brushed along my slick slit.

Jameson's long dark lashes fluttered closed as a guttural groan rattled in his chest. "Fucking hell, Raindrop. You're already soaking through your shorts." A shiver raced down my spine as he trailed a single finger up and down my core. "And so smooth. Is that why you needed a shower, to shave this perfect pussy just for me?"

And my legs.

And armpits.

But even my awkward ass knew his question was rhetorical. Plus, I was too lost in his touch to answer.

I jolted when the couch shifted beneath me. Forcing my lids open, I studied Jameson as he moved closer, positioning himself between my spread legs, situating one until it hung off the couch and my toes pressed to the floor.

With zero warning, two fingers slid into my tight center while his thumb flicked my swollen bundle of nerves. I released a tortured cry, my back arching off the couch, his expert touch feeling way better than my hand or my assortment of toys. Up and down my chest heaved, my stiff nipples poking through the tank top's thin material.

With a smirk, Jameson slid his free hand under my tank, calluses scraping my stomach as it moved higher. I sucked in a self-conscious breath as his palm engulfed one small breast, but it quickly exploded from my lungs when he squeezed, pinching the tip between two fingers at the same time.

"Fucking hell, you're perfect, Raindrop. Every fucking inch of you." He smirked, picking up the pace of his fingers. "Inside and out. Though I need a taste to make sure you're as delicious as I imagined."

"You've thought about me? About this?"

A startled cry ripped from my throat when he jerked his fingers from my core. Before I could complain, demand that he finish what he'd started, the room spun. Strong hands shifted me along the couch, manhandling me with more grace than I would with my long, flailing limbs. Eyes wide, I stared down at Jameson once he had me exactly where he wanted: head resting against the back of the couch, ass on the edge of the cushion with him kneeling between my spread legs, fingers hooked around the elastic band of my sleep shorts.

"Thought about you?" The soft cotton caressed down my legs. Jameson stared transfixed at my weeping core and licked his lips. Honey-brown eyes flicked up, connecting with my hazel ones, and the want and desire swirling there had me shivering in anticipation. Without breaking eye contact, Jameson dipped closer, blowing a soft breath along my sensitive flesh. "I knew it was wrong. You were married to that asshole, but there were so many nights... too many fucking nights lying in bed, fantasizing that it was your hand wrapped tight around my hard cock instead of my own."

I jolted, lids squeezing shut as he pressed his tongue to my center and licked from entrance to clit, sucking on the sensitive nub in quick bursts. My head lolled side to side along the back of the couch, stars blinking behind my lids. Without thinking, I combed my fingers through the longer section of his thick hair, fisting the ends to hold his face closer, chasing the release I desperately needed.

"Tell me something. How many nights did you dream of me, Raindrop? Of my face between your thighs, eating your delicious cunt like a damn starved man?" He thrust three fingers inside. I moaned and shifted my hips to ease the too-full feeling. "Shh, sweetheart. I want you to ride my fingers, thinking about how my dick will stuff you so full you can't move."

With one more flick of his tongue against my clit, the building orgasm ripped through my entire body. A choked scream caught in my throat as I did just as he instructed, picturing him hovering over me, fucking me into oblivion.

All at once, my tensed muscles relaxed, my thighs peeling away from where they were sealed around his head. The hand in his hair loosened, dropping to the couch beside me. Blinking past the dark spots still floating in my vision, I chanced a glance down, finding Jameson licking off my orgasm from the three fingers that were inside me.

"I have to say, Raindrop, you taste utterly divine. And with those sounds you make, plus the way you squeezed the life out of my fingers, the real Rain is a hundred times better than the one in my dirty fantasies."

Holy fuck.

Now I understood why women gushed about oral sex.

You just needed someone who knew what the fuck they were doing.

17

RAIN

Soft sheets brushed against my calves, tangling between my legs as I twisted, only to freeze when I met resistance, the fabric refusing to move with me. My lids snapped open, the darkness of the room filling my blurred vision, hazy waves distorting the outline of the dresser lining the wall. With a controlled exhale, I turned back the other way, toward the weight holding down my normally unrestricted sheets.

I squeezed both lids shut, opening them wide before repeating the motion to ensure I wasn't seeing a mirage.

Last night, after I turned into a limp noddle when he sent my mind, body, and soul into a different dimension with his fingers and tongue, he carried me upstairs and helped me into bed. Apparently, I'd passed out cold, because I didn't realize he'd plopped down next to me. In my bed. And, based on the bare leg kicked out from beneath the sheet, fell asleep naked or mostly naked.

But now that sleep wasn't coating my brain, fuzzy memories of before I fell asleep started to come into focus. I might remember, unfortunately, holding him hostage with an unrelenting hold on his waist while I begged him to sleep with me. Okay, begged was a strong word. I probably just asked nicely. Several times. That sounded more like normal me.

Fuck, he probably thought I was some... was there such a thing as a lightweight orgasmer? It had to be a thing. Because yeah, one body-shaking orgasm and I was down for the count. Then wanted to snuggle.

Oh fuck me. When we woke up, I needed to tell him I was, in fact, capable of more than one orgasm and not falling comatose. I did it all the time. By myself.

Okay, maybe that was a terrible idea. Being able to bring myself to orgasm several times using toys probably wasn't an achievement most would be proud of.

The other memories from last night flickered in my mind, sparking a simmering heat that built between my thighs. I squeezed them together, relishing the lingering ache from Jameson's thick fingers stretching me. The hand not tucked beneath my cheek slid down and dipped into my shorts. A sharp gasp rushed down my throat as I swirled the tips of my fingers against my clit while visually devouring every bare inch of the man sleeping beside me.

I swallowed as my gaze scanned along his lean chest. Careful to keep the movements slow, I gently tugged on the sheet, bringing it closer to me. Inch by inch, more of his golden skin was exposed, the streetlight peeking through the slats of the shutters helping me see as the sheet fluttered to the bed, leaving him fully bared to the chilled air.

Clad only in a pair of oh-so-tight black boxer briefs with one leg bent to the side, his arm tossed over his head, Jameson looked ready to pose for the FBI's naughty agent calendar. I licked my dry lips as I slid my face along the pillow, closing the distance between us.

He shifted, mumbling something as his arm slipped down and his palm slapped to his bare stomach. I froze, riveted on his exploring fingers as they dipped beneath the waistband of his boxer briefs and curled into what looked to be a fist. A croaked moan vibrated out of his slightly parted lips as his head pressed back into the pillow, features tightening.

Unable to stop watching the erotic show, I continued to stare as his hand jerked up and down in quick strokes. The bright streetlamps outside the bedroom window gave just enough light, exposing the swollen head of his dick peeking out the top of his boxers as the tight material shifted lower with every powerful stoke.

My quick breaths fanned across my lips, a soft gasp escaping as I moved my fingers like his tongue had against my clit. Lost in the moment, a sharp hiss caught my attention, dragging my hooded gaze up from Jameson's moving hand to his face.

His eyes were open, dark gaze locked on me, the light glinting off his straight white teeth as they bit his plump lower lip.

I stilled, knowing I was caught not only watching him but playing with myself as I did.

Muscles locked, all I could do was stare back up at him. Fire burned in my lungs, the trapped breath desperate for release. In the blanket of darkness and the utter silence of the early morning, I pulled my fingers from beneath my shorts and skated them across the smooth sheet. His hooded gaze tracked the movement, not showing a single hint of hesitation when I brushed my fingers against his hip.

"Do you know how fucking sexy it is," he rasped, voice rough with sleep, "to wake up finding you watching me while touching yourself?" Moisture slipped from my core, dampening my cotton shorts. "I haven't woken up this hard in a while, Raindrop. I must have been dreaming about you."

"You were awake?" Obviously, but that was all I could come up with. Maybe I wasn't as stealthy with pulling the sheet back as I thought. I slid the pads of my fingers along the curve of his hip, brushing the elastic edge of his boxer briefs until they met where his hand delved beneath.

"You want to help?" His voice was so gravelly it sounded like it hurt to speak.

I nodded but couldn't get my fingers to move.

Unease quickly cut through the lust fog, making me question everything.

Yes, I desperately wanted to touch him, make him feel amazing like he did for me on the couch, but it had been so long since I'd been at this pinnacle step with a man outside of my ex. Even then, those last couple of years, things were so bad we barely touched each other. What if I was out of practice, or out of date on the new hip thing to do?

Damnit. What if jerking him off wasn't enough, and he wanted me to give him head? I wanted to, but I needed some warning, time to build up to the idea of doing that, since it never was my favorite thing to do. Mostly because every time I did it was after Josh guilted me into it instead of me being desperate to please him. What if Jameson did the same thing now, pressured me, and then I hated him for it?

And we still had to work together—

Firm fingers wrapped around my chin and tipped my face upward. The earlier lust had vanished from Jameson's lax features, now replaced with concern.

"What's going on in that head of yours, Raindrop?"

"Nothing," I said, way too quickly to be true, then winced. Lip between my teeth, I avoided looking into his eyes, not wanting to find the disappointment there. But instead of huffing and getting frustrated like I'd expected, he continued to wait, giving me all the time I needed to find the words to explain how I felt. "It's just that I've seen a lot of penises, so it's not that I'm scared to touch you. It's just... been a while. Like years, and I don't exactly remember the protocol of what to do with one that still has blood flowing through it."

All the blood drained from my face the second the words left my lips.

Fuck my awkward life.

Shit, now he probably thinks I fondle them—

Jameson's roar of laughter cut off my twisted—and very concerning—thoughts. I blinked up at him, and he had his eyes squeezed shut, head tossed back, and mouth open as he laughed. After a few seconds, he calmed down, the roaring laughter dwindling to a chuckle.

"Come here," he murmured.

Before I could even shuffle an inch closer, two hands hooked beneath my arms and hauled me across him until my chest lay over his and our noses were nearly brushing as my head sank into the pillow beside his.

Honey-brown eyes searched mine.

"What I would give to take a few trips around that mind of yours," he whispered. "Listen, you mentioned that it's been a while." Heat scorched beneath my cheeks, and I tried to bury my face in the pillow to hide my embarrassment, but a tug on my hair held me in place, preventing me from hiding from him. "We can take this slow. I'm sorry if I rushed things and made you feel you had to—"

"You didn't," I blurted. "I just... I don't want to disappoint you or make a fool out of myself. I haven't been with anyone since Josh, and... what if I'm so out of practice from only touching dead people—"

A wide, brilliant smile split his face. His hair rasped along the pillowcase with the slight shake of his head.

"Raindrop," he whispered. Leaning in, he brushed his lips against mine.

I sighed at the faint touch, the promise of more. Why couldn't I be normal and just let my hormones take control and dictate my urges? Instead, I had to sit here and dissect, overanalyze, and ruin it all.

"Are you listening to me?"

I guess I didn't respond quickly enough, because a frustrated grunt escaped him just before he sealed his mouth to mine.

My lips parted on a gasp, giving him the opportunity to slip his tongue inside. With every swipe and teasing flick, he stirred the earlier ember of desire, fanning it until all my rambling thoughts faded, leaving only my pulsing need for him. I followed his retreating lips when he pulled away, not ready to break the moment.

"You, Rain Evans, are uniquely wonderful, and there will *never* be a moment where you could disappoint me." He smoothed his palm over my hair and then pressed it to my hot cheek. "My dreams are made reality just being in the same room with you. Toss in you wanting me, wanting to touch me, and you allowing me the fucking honor of worshiping your body the way it should've been all your life, and all sense of reality is blown out of the water. You can touch me or not. Being here with you is more than I ever could have hoped for. I never thought I'd have this chance to hold you like you're mine, even if it's not forever."

Tears welled, and a single drop escaped the corner of my eye, dripping from my cheek and soaking into the pillowcase.

"Can you...?" I sucked in a steadying breath. "Can you tell me?"

"Tell you what?" he asked, tilting his head to search my face.

"Tell me what to do. What you want."

His eyes widened. "I don't want to control you. When you're ready and comfortable—"

I pressed my palm against his cheek. "You're not taking my control. I'm giving it." Heart slamming against my chest, I sent him a pleading look that I hoped he could interpret. "I don't want to get lost in the nonsense I create in my head. I want to lose myself in this between us."

His gaze flicked side to side, searching my eyes. "And you'll tell me if I push too hard?" I nodded. "If I want too much." Again, I nodded, though this time I shifted along his body so I straddled his hips. He sucked in a harsh breath when I aligned his still-hard cock with my center. My lids shuttered as I moved against him, wiggling until the pressure was exactly where I needed.

"Okay, Raindrop." Jameson's hands wrapped around my hips, holding me in place. "I'll tell you a secret confession. I'm usually in the same boat as you." I tilted my head in confusion, my loose hair shifting with the movement. His Adam's apple bobbed when he swallowed. "It's why I like a partner. I enjoy losing myself to the moment, having someone else in charge. So, we'll figure this out together."

His fingers threaded into my hair. A gentle tug had me lowering until I hovered over him with both palms pressed into the mattress just above his shoulders.

"How about you use me?" His hands went back to my

hips, sealing me tighter against his hard length. His abs flexed, muscles rippling as he rolled his hips, thrusting against me. My lids fluttered closed, and a delicate moan escaped at the amazing friction.

"What about what you want?" I panted.

"I almost came the moment your hot pussy settled over me. Don't worry about me, Raindrop."

His words and my past fought as two polar opposites.

Josh always made it about him. Guilted me into doing things for him, leaving me confused and feeling used. What Jameson wanted was for me to put myself first, and he'd find satisfaction just from that. Just like he did on the couch earlier. He enjoyed that, wanted that, and not just so I'd return the favor.

"Are you even real?" I whispered, not meaning to let those words slip out. But something about the darkness around us and the vulnerability I felt in the moment gave me the courage to say what I'd wondered for a while, not just since he showed up at the crime scene.

With a wicked smirk, he shoved himself harder against me and swiveled his hips. "I'm very fucking real. Now rub that delicious pussy of yours against me until you come."

My doubts vanished. Instead, I focused on where our bodies connected, the feel of him hard beneath me. Using my palms as leverage, I moved myself up and down his rigid cock, sparkles of pleasure spreading through my body as the head nudged my clit, my movements turning frantic as I chased the encroaching bliss.

"Fuck," Jameson gritted out below me. "Even with two layers of clothes between us, you feel amazing." Using the opening where my shirt draped away from me, he slipped a single hand up my firm stomach and engulfed my breast.

The edge of his nail scraping along my pebbled nipple shot me over the edge.

Shutters racked my body as pleasure coursed through my veins. The blood thrumming in my ears muffled a manly grunt. Muscles trembling, I collapsed on top of Jameson, my chest rising and falling with his labored breaths.

For a few minutes, we lay there, not a single word spoken. The content smile on my lips pulled into a frown when he carefully maneuvered me off him and shifted toward the other side of the bed. I squeezed my eyes shut, not wanting to see him leave, only for them to pop back open at the sound of drawers opening and closing in my bathroom. The faucet turning on had me pushing up on my elbows, brows pulled in tight, studying the darkened entryway and wondering what the hell Jameson was doing in there.

Seconds later, his tall, lean frame emerged, a small hand towel dangling from his fingers.

"Which drawer do you keep your sleep shorts in?" he asked, pointing to the dresser along the wall.

"Um, the top one. But I'm fairly certain they won't fit you."

That was where he was going with this, right?

He snorted and tugged the drawer open, pulled out a pair of soft cotton shorts, and turned. "These are not for me."

The bed dipped beneath his weight as he sat on the edge beside me. Laying the towel across his bare thigh, he flipped back the sheet that I'd self-consciously pulled over me. The blast of chilled air felt amazing against my hot skin, but goose bumps sprouted along my arms and legs at the sudden change in temperature.

Jameson slowly worked the shorts I was wearing down my legs and then tossed them over his shoulder to the corner of the room. Grabbing the towel, he brushed it along my inner thighs and between my folds, cleaning the lingering wetness from my orgasm—which, embarrassingly, was quite a bit considering none of his was mixed with my own.

"I can do that." I reached down only for him to smack my hand away playfully. Each cool swipe of the cloth felt amazing, but a sliver of awkwardness kept trying to rise and ruin the sweet moment.

"Never said you couldn't, but I want to. I want to take care of you. We still have a couple of hours of sleep to get, and I figured you wouldn't want to do that in soaked shorts." He chuckled and turned a dramatic grimace down to his own lap. "I know I don't."

With one more careful swipe, he situated the clean shorts around my feet and pulled them up. Standing, he shot me a half smile and brushed a single finger over my cheek before he walked out of the bedroom, taking the towel he'd used to clean me with him.

Confused. Worried. Content. All the feelings mixed and fought for dominance.

With a groan, I flopped back on the bed and slapped a hand to my forehead.

Soft footsteps drew my attention to the bedroom door just as Jameson stepped through. Not saying a word, he dropped to the other side of the bed and rolled onto his side, facing me. I squealed in surprise when he hooked his arm around my waist and tugged, sliding me easily along the sheets until I was tucked snug against his chest.

Soft lips pressed to the back of my neck. "Sleep, Raindrop, and dream of me."

And with a sappy smile, I did just that, giving in to the weight pulling at my lids.

And falling asleep without a single worried thought on my mind.

18

JAMESON

The chair let out a screech as I leaned back, taking in the full expanse of the murder wall. Two days had passed since Rhyan helped me narrow down the profile to add our unsub being a female. Charlie had yet to come up with anything new regarding the murder victims' pasts, and as it stood, we were at a standstill with the profile.

Caucasian female, late-twenties to early-thirties, patient, methodical, quiet with underlying anger at the world that would come out at work and home, and physically strong.

That was all I had for the Santa Coasta police force to help them identify the unsub.

Being here as many days as I had, we should have a decent list of suspects compiled based on the profile, yet we had zero.

Frustrated didn't describe how I felt.

How we *all* felt.

The corner of my lip quirked in a half smirk. Well, Slade was definitely more frustrated than Rain and me, considering he was stuck working alongside us knowing something was going on there. Though we were all equally annoyed by the lack of movement in the case. None of us wanted another innocent person to fall victim to the killer, but we needed more evidence and hopefully for the unsub to make a fucking mistake.

Behind me, the office door whooshed open and slammed against the wall. The subsequent grumbled curses told me exactly who'd joined me. I swiveled around, my smile shifting to a grimace at seeing Slade for the first time today. To say he looked like shit was an understatement. The slightly pale skin and dark circles under his eyes made it clear this case was wearing on him both mentally and physically. Though I wasn't sure if it was the case or his feelings for Rain that kept him up at night.

"What's that creepy look for?" he grumbled. "You look like you shit your pants or ate something bad."

"Where have you been all day? I've missed my work bestie." I chuckled when he flipped me off, and swiveled back around. "Not that you missed anything new. This case is pissing me off."

"You and me both. Between this case and the others I spent today catching up on, I'm fucking stressed to the max with all the loose ends."

"I know a great way to ease some of that stress," I replied offhandedly, trying to keep my smile hidden.

Slade huffed. "Yeah, me too. A three-week vacation, then walking away from all this without a second look back."

Shocked at that unexpected statement, I whirled around, eyes wide. Propped against the wall, eyes closed, Slade looked seconds away from falling asleep standing up. Concern for my new grumpy and occasionally scary-as-fuck friend urged me out of the chair to take a tentative step closer to the massive man. If he fell over, it would probably register on the Richter scale somewhere and cause a whole to-do. We had enough on our plate as it was, plus Rain wasn't around if he hurt himself.

"You'd walk away from this job, the families and victims counting on you for closure?"

He peeled his lids open, though it appeared to take monumental effort. Damn, he really looked terrible. "You mean the late nights, no sleep, constant stress, only being kept alive by gallons of shit coffee? You're romanticizing it, Bend. The past few days have shown me it's time for me to move on."

I studied his tight features before the truth slapped me in the face. The past few days… meaning since Rain and I hooked up. "You stayed here, in this job, for her."

His green eyes flicked my way, annoyance simmering just below the surface, before darting elsewhere. With a grunt, he shoved off the wall, the single picture hanging near his head rattling with the force. Lowering onto the couch, he sighed and spread his arms out wide along the back. "I was over it all, ready to close the cases assigned to me and resign. Fuck knows what I planned to do after, but I knew I couldn't keep doing this. Then she showed up, literally fell into me, and I knew I couldn't leave. She was so fucking innocent, and…." He tipped his head back, sighing. "I couldn't leave her unprotected. So, I stayed just a little longer. Which turned into too fucking long."

Easing into the chair opposite him, I leaned forward, pressing my forearms onto my thighs. "You wouldn't miss it? Not the shitty parts but the ones where we get that high of catching a suspect. Solving a case. Saving a life. Finding answers, putting together clues. That overshadows the bad —for me, at least. Knowing I can make a difference."

His head popped up, and he leveled me with an intense stare, no doubt surprised by the passion in my voice.

Because I *was* passionate about our roles in keeping others safe. Sure, our job was challenging and shitty, but we helped people. From what I'd seen over the past few days, Slade was one of the good ones who cared, and he was a damn good detective. So yeah, I didn't understand why he'd easily toss it all away just because some parts weren't ideal.

"I'd miss some of it." I flicked my gaze to where his hand now massaged his right knee. "It just feels like the reason I got into this after being sidelined from football isn't there anymore."

"And that was what?"

He paused, gaze going unfocused as he stared at the ink on his hands. "I wanted to make a difference. For too long, I was entertainment. Sure, I was good, but it didn't mean anything. But for a while now, it's felt like I'm chasing my ass, always one step behind the bastards intent on hurting others. I'm an offensive-minded guy, and I've been stuck playing in a defensive role for way too fucking long."

I canted my head, considering that analogy. It didn't resonate with me because I enjoyed solving puzzles, but it clearly did with him.

"Even though a three-week vacation sounds nice," I started, picking an invisible piece of lint off my slacks, "I was going to say that one way to ease some of that stress weighing you down is to stop fighting your feelings for Rain, but you went and took it to a whole deeper level." His startled, barked chuckle had me laughing along with him. Easing back against the chair, I studied Slade. "I'm not kidding. You're draining energy fighting it."

He arched a brow and shook his head. "I'm fine on that front. Thanks, though, Mr. Matchmaker."

"Really? I see the way you look at her and then the way it

shifts to death glares when you look at me. That doesn't seem fine."

He huffed, rubbing at his jaw. "Am I jealous? Sure. Who wouldn't be? But you're better for her than I am. I'm good with it, even if it fucking sucks to see it all playing out in front of me."

I glanced at my watch and groaned. Time to end this wasted day and get some much-needed rest. My cock twitched against my boxer briefs, thinking about another night of sleeping next to Rain. Each night since we'd pushed past the professional boundaries, I fell asleep with her tucked in my arms and woke up the same way. We hadn't ventured past what she's comfortable with, which was fine with me. I'd wait as long as she needed.

I sent a quick text to Rain, letting her know I was done for the day and packing up. She'd left a while ago, saying she needed to work out, that it helped her focus. Considering we were all grasping at straws to come up with any new ideas or leads on the case, I understood her frustration and the need to break through the ever-circling questions we couldn't answer.

"Want to grab a beer?" I asked, standing with both arms high in the air as I stretched out my tight muscles. "There's no reason to stick around here. All I'm doing is making myself more frustrated, which doesn't help anyone."

A flash of uncertainty crossed his face. "Rain coming?"

Hmm, was that hope in his tone?

I forced myself not to grin. The bastard had it fucking bad for her. He just needed to man up and tell her, make a damn move. That bullshit he told her the other night about staying friends wasn't a lie, but I knew he wanted more. And more than a quick fuck. The way he looked at her wasn't only heated with desire—there was a longing there, too, for something he'd never have.

And he wouldn't if he kept being a dumbass and thinking he wasn't good enough.

The image of Rain living her lonely existence with only dead people as conversation partners put me on edge. I could be there for her via phone, but she deserved to have someone supporting her here. And Slade needed to step up to the plate and be that man. That way, maybe the knot in my gut would go away knowing she'd be taken care of when I was gone.

Which I would be.

Even if every second with her made me wish otherwise.

"Bend?"

I shook my head, running a hand through my hair. "Sorry. Fuck, I need sleep. No, she's not coming. Rain left earlier to work out. It's just us." He grunted and nodded his nonverbal acceptance to the invite. "Know a place close by?"

THE ROAR of the packed bar seemed to skip a beat, coming to a sudden stop the moment Slade walked through the bar's door behind me. Everyone's eyes widened before jerking to either stare at their drinks or diving back into the conversation that abruptly paused at his entrance. Though I still felt some lingering curiosity.

"You don't get out much, do you?" I joked over my shoulder as I moved around a server holding a tray full of drinks, heading toward an open high-top table. When two women beat me to it, claiming the table, I switched direction for two empty barstools at the end of the large square-shaped bar.

"I don't have much of a social life these days. Much to the tabloids' dismay."

I dragged my stool away from the bar, catching the bartender's attention as I sat down. I pointed to the IPA on draft, then held up a single finger. The bartender dipped his chin and reached for a pint glass in the freezer. After the full, frosted glass landed on the polished wood in front of me, I gestured to Slade, giving him the opening to order.

"Bottled water. Make it three to save you time later."

My eyes rolled to the ceiling as I took a sip of my ice-cold beer. "Lame," I muttered into the thin layer of foam.

"Fuck off. If I have a beer, you'll need a few people to drag my unconscious ass out of here. I'm running on fumes, remember?"

"So, back to the earlier conversation of you quitting. What would you do if you weren't doing this?" On instinct, I scanned the bar, looking for anything suspicious. A few stares darted away when I caught them eyeing Slade. "Fuck, how do you get used to this? Everyone staring and watching you like you're some kind of zoo animal?"

He lifted a massive shoulder in a half shrug. "Been that way for a long time, though I think most of the looks in here are from people I work with who are shocked I'm actually out."

Drumming my fingers on the bar, I studied him from the corner of my eye. "I think she'd miss you." His head snapped my way, and the plastic bottle in his hand crinkled beneath his tightening grip. "She likes you." I sipped the cold liquid, giving myself a moment before continuing, knowing my next words would either pique his curiosity or send him running. Or he could kill me. But the reward was worth the risk. "Actually, she likes the idea of both of us."

His eyes flared for half a second before his normal scowl fell into place. "Meaning what, exactly?"

"Listen, I'll tell you what I see, what I've seen the last few days. She wants more with you but thinks you see her as just a colleague, a friend. Which, what the actual fuck was that about the other night?"

"She said it first," he grumbled.

"Anyway," I snapped, "I don't like the idea of her being alone when I leave. And we all know I will. She needs someone to lean on to help her get out of that brilliant head of hers. Someone who can share the burden of fucking living and doing what we do."

"And you're what, asking me to be that guy?" He scoffed. "Not likely." Shoving the water bottles out of the way, he gestured for the bartender. "Whiskey. Neat. Top shelf."

The corner of my lips quirked once the bartender slid Slade's drink into his waiting hand. "I agree with you, though, on one thing."

"I'm afraid to ask," he muttered, spinning the highball glass on the bar, staring into the dark liquid.

"One man in her life won't be enough."

He huffed. "She told you about her parents, then." My brows rose along my forehead. "Taking that as a no." If I wasn't mistaken, he took a bit of joy in the fact that he knew something about her that I didn't. "They're poly. She didn't tell me much, but that's the gist. That's where I thought you were going with the 'one man not being enough' talk."

"That makes sense. No wonder she's okay with being attracted to both of us at the same time."

The sip of whiskey he'd just taken nearly spewed from his lips. A massive, tattooed hand slapped across his lips and swiped away a few drops as he coughed. "What the fuck did you just say?"

"Have you ever done it?"

"Done what?"

"Multiple partners." I paused, knowing I needed to tread carefully. My hope was high that the strange situation I'd found myself in could fill the void since Tallon and Remy became a couple. But getting Slade on board would take some delicate finagling.

"Does being with three women at one time count?" he said, shooting me a look. "Though, based on the context of this odd-as-fuck conversation, I'm assuming that kind of orgy isn't what you're talking about."

"And...?" I rotated a hand in the air, asking for more detail. "Did you like it?"

"What the fuck is this about?"

"Just answer the fucking question. I'm curious."

He sighed and rubbed a hand along his jaw as it worked back and forth. Then he scooted his stool away, giving him room to angle toward me.

"Who wouldn't?" Though the lack of emotion in his tone said it all. "But I wouldn't say I'd do it again. Too much fucking work."

I smiled. "All I'm saying is be open to the idea, because she is. And so am I."

"You're open to the idea of us three... together."

Lifting a shoulder, I took a long drink, letting the bartender pass by to keep our conversation from being overheard. "I've done it a few times. Always with the same guy, different women, but yeah, I enjoyed it. But I'm talking about less of the physical, more on the relationship."

"Say I consider the idea, forgetting all the reasons I shouldn't be with her. What's the upside for you in all this?"

"She gets the support she needs, and I won't hate myself when I have to leave. Listen," I sighed. Clearly, it would take more than this conversation for him to see the benefits of what I was suggesting. "All I'm saying is think about it. Between you and me, while I'm here and when I'm back in Dallas, we could offer her the type of relationship she deserves. We each bring something different to the table for her."

He shifted, angling himself back to the bar, ending the conversation.

Or so I thought.

"You asked about my orgy experience. Why? That was a few hours, and then we all went our own way. Nothing like you're talking about now. You're making it out to be more of a supportive structure for Rain."

The smooth edge of the glass pressed against my lower lip as I tipped my beer back, draining the contents. "I think you know why."

He cut his eyes my way. "Explain it to me. If you want me to really consider this." My lips parted, but he held up a hand. "And I'd have to see what she wants. Because even though you say she's interested in more, that doesn't mean she is."

For someone like Slade, the insecurity he felt around Rain was confusing. Every woman in the bar had her eyes on him, yet he still wasn't sure if Rain would want him. Did that mean he was afraid of what she'd say once she uncovered the real Slade instead of a broody detective? Or had he put her on such a high pedestal that she was more an unobtainable prize?

"I want to be around for that conversation when you have it with her." I smirked. It would no doubt lead to more than words, and I sure as hell would love to watch that. "And explain what? We're both there for her, and it works as any other relationship. At least I assume. Like I said, I've done the closed-door group activities before but not anything long term. It would take some getting used to and a lot of communication, I'm sure. But knowing now that her parents are poly, she can help guide us on that front."

"And on the other?"

"Other?"

"'Group activities,' like you worded it."

Even thinking about it got me semihard. I shifted on the barstool. "Am I expecting that? No, but if it leads to that…."

"Why?"

"Why what?" I sighed, rubbing a hand along the back of my neck. This was fucking awkward. Tallon and I just fell into the sharing routine. He was the one in control, so I just followed his orders. Even though Slade would be the dominant male in our threesome, getting him to understand that role would take some time.

"Why did you do it before? Why do you like sharing with another guy?"

After flagging down the bartender and motioning for another IPA, I braced both forearms on the edge of the bar. "Because, like Rain, I get so damn tired of being in control all the time. It's a relief to not have to think, to either simply enjoy watching or follow someone else's orders. But you have to understand that what I like isn't the reason I'm suggesting all this. It's Rain. She needs and deserves the support multiple men in her life can give her."

And if the three of us came together in the physical way, that would be a bonus.

A bonus I knew he would enjoy.

I just hoped he was open-minded enough to consider all the possibilities.

19

SLADE

The sounds of the bar faded as I stared at the bottom of my empty highball glass, lost in thought.

I didn't want to admit it, but Jameson's suggestion intrigued me. The thought of the emotional side of a relationship not falling solely on me, that there was another to help where I always seemed to fail, was fucking amazing. Maybe then I could have a long-term relationship that didn't end in a dumpster fire and expensive lawyers.

But the physical side of things....

Could I share, knowing some other man was balls deep inside my girl? Or would the jealousy stop all this before it could get started? Though knowing Jameson and Rain were fooling around now didn't diminish the longing I had for her, nor did I want to kill him. But if I were in the mix, that could change how I felt.

Then again, when I was too sucked into a case to leave at a normal time, knowing she would still be supported and taken care of could ease the pressure of feeling pulled in too many directions. Even if I left this soul-sucking job, no matter what I did next, it would consume me. I was an all-or-nothing type of man with my career, no matter the path.

"Group activities," I said after a while. I knew the long break in the conversation was him giving me the opportunity to process it all. Though I wasn't lying. I'd have to talk to Rain first. "Tell me about that."

"Like I said before, I can only tell you what I've done, but it was always one-night scenarios, not relationships. But I can't imagine it would be much different. It's not all the time, just when it happens. So, let's say if things move forward while I'm here, then you can be with her alone, or if something turns to more when all three of us are together, then that door is open." He paused, making me shift to face him. "I know it's only been a few days, but it's not like whatever this is between Rain and me is fresh. I wanted her before, and now it's possible. What I'm trying to say is I don't see this ending between us when I leave. I'll come back as much as I can to see her, even if it's for just a day."

Interesting. My respect level for the man increased with his admission. So, he wasn't just talking about this for however long he was in Santa Coasta. Jameson was considering this long term. Not sure if that added more pressure or took it off.

"I need to know the parameters."

"What do you mean?" he asked, tapping his fingers against his half-full pint glass.

"Is it all about her, or are you expecting you and me to...?"

His smirk at me not being able to finish the sentence pissed me right off. The bastard clearly loved seeing me uncomfortable.

"Honestly, that's not something I'm into."

"So you don't want to touch my dick," I said, just to see his reaction.

He froze for a second before shooting me a cautious look. "Do *you* want me to touch your dick?"

"No. Like I said, just setting parameters."

His shoulders drooped.

Huh. Not sure if I should be relieved or offended at his clear relief.

"I told you before why I like the idea of three. I enjoy giving up control when I can, when the trust is there. It's not about me being sexually attracted to the other male partner —it's about her. If she's happy being taken care of, then that's what matters, whether that's me sitting back and watching her face as she comes around your dick or eating her oh-so-sweet cunt while she sucks you off. As long as she's turned on by it and not uncomfortable, then I'm game. But no, I don't want to touch your dick. No offense."

"I don't think I could give up control," I muttered.

"Which is why if this, whatever we decide to do, happens, I think it would work. Because Rain doesn't want control either. She has a lot of false ideas in her head from that asshole ex of hers—"

"Like what?" Anger shot through me at the mention of her ex-husband. The hand resting along the bar curled into a tight fist.

"Like the fact that she doesn't understand that I find pleasure in touching her, in giving *her* pleasure. She seems to think returning the favor is a requirement, as if the only reason I devoured her tasty pussy was so she'd suck me off."

"I hope I get to meet this motherfucker one day," I gritted out through clenched teeth.

"You and me both."

His words made me pause. "You never met him?"

"Nope. He never came around the station. I'm assuming that was because he knew someone's sidearm might accidentally misfire in his direction if he did."

A snort caught in my throat. "I'll think about it. What you're saying. It's nothing I've done before, and I'm not sure I can share. If you haven't noticed, I'm a possessive asshole."

Jameson muttered something I didn't understand before raising his hand. "You ready?" At my nod, he motioned for our tab. "I'll call Rain and see—"

My phone vibrating on the bar and the name flashing on the screen cut him off. With a quick swipe, I answered Rain's call and pressed the smooth screen to my ear.

"Hey, we were—"

"Slade." My spine went ramrod straight at the quiver in her voice. Jameson noticed the change immediately and pulled out his wallet, slamming a hundred down on the bar without looking away from the phone in my hand.

"Rain, what's going on? Are you okay? Are you hurt?" My heart hammered against my chest. All the dark and demented things I'd seen people do to others flashed through my mind, making a horror film of possibilities.

"I got home and.... The police are on their way."

"Rain," I snapped as I shoved off the stool. Not caring about the people I clipped with my wide shoulders, I pushed through the crowd toward the front door. "Talk to me."

"Someone broke into my house," she whispered, the tears clear in her trembling tone. "I'm waiting outside, and...." A loud breath blew across the speaker. "I'm scared."

Ice flooded my veins. The idea of her out on the sidewalk unprotected, scared, and wanting me to be there was almost paralyzing. Outside the bar, I raced for my car, footsteps pounding behind me.

"We're on our way. Stay on the phone with me, baby. Don't hang up. We'll be there soon." The car rocked when I jerked the driver's door open. Using my shoulder, I kept the phone pressed to my ear as I started the engine and slammed the door shut. Jameson wasn't fully in his seat before I pressed on the gas.

His curses filled the car, followed by the slam of his door.

"Rain, are you there?" Heart in my throat, I flicked on my flashing lights and siren, racing through a red light.

"I'm here."

"Do you have a weapon on you?"

"No."

"We're fixing that tomorrow," I growled. A curse flew from my lips as I jerked the wheel to miss a car that pulled out in front of me. If we wanted to get to Rain in record time and in one piece, I needed to focus. "Talk to Jameson. Stay on the phone with him. Please."

He took the phone from my fingers the second I pulled it away from my ear. With her taken care of, I pressed down on the accelerator, desperation urging me to get to her in record time. The shit engine roared, the RPM needle hitting the red, the entire frame vibrating as I urged it faster. Every second we weren't there meant she was alone, vulnerable to an attack. What if whoever broke into her home came back?

What if it was someone who'd targeted her specifically?

What if it was our killer?

Sweat slicked my forehead and dripped down my temples as all the possibilities swirled through my head. All that mattered was getting to her and wrapping her in my arms. Nothing could get to her if she was with me, but I had to fucking get there for that to happen.

The normally short drive to her place felt like an eternity. When we rounded the corner to her street, the strobing red-and-white lights that filled the darkness had me sucking in a deep breath. At least she wasn't alone, but I couldn't relax until I saw with my own eyes that she was unharmed.

Not giving two shits about blocking the damn street, I slammed my foot on the brake, the tires locking up, sending the car skidding to a stop. One hand thrusting the gearshift into Park, I shoved the door open with the other, sprinting for the sidewalk the moment my feet hit the asphalt.

I cleared the curb, my quick pace faltering at the sight of her waiting on the lower step of her townhome. Highlighted by the glow of the front porch light, she had her head in her hands, shoulders curled in on herself. My normally stony heart cracked. Rain looked so small. Nothing like the strong, confident woman I was used to seeing daily.

"Rain," I called out.

Her face snapped up, red-rimmed eyes searching until they landed on me. Palm pressed to the concrete, she started to stand, but I got to her first. Wrapping my arms beneath hers, I hauled her up, securing her much smaller frame to mine. Dark silky strands wove through my fingers as I dove a hand into her hair, pressing her face into my shoulder.

"You're okay." I wasn't sure if I was trying to assure her or myself. "We're here. You're safe now, baby."

The term just rolled off my lips. That made twice tonight, and it felt right. It made her feel more like mine.

After a full minute of my too-tight embrace, I forced my hold to relax, allowing her to pull back enough to angle her face up toward mine. "Are the officers inside?"

"Yeah," she rasped.

"Rain." There was desperation in Jameson's tone that had me releasing my hold on her. Taking the opening, he pulled her into his arms and buried his face in her hair, his continued words of reassurance muffled with his lips against her neck.

The light blazing through the front windows of her three-story townhome drew my focus. The itch to know what happened and uncover the clues had me rolling my shoulders to shrug off the need for answers. But I couldn't. I needed to be out here with Rain, making sure she was safe.

But when my gaze swung back to her and Jameson, him still holding her close, I realized that for the first time I didn't have to hold back, to bear the full weight of taking care of someone alone. His brown eyes met mine in the dark. I inclined my head toward the front door in a silent question and raised my brows.

"I've got her," he responded. Hands on her shoulders, he gently twirled her around, placing Rain's back to his chest. Both arms snaked around her waist and tightened, holding her against him in a protective stance. A wave of relief slammed into me at the sight instead of making me jealous, shocking the hell out of me. "Go talk to the officers, see what the fuck is going on. Better you than me."

He was right. They all knew me. Jameson was an outsider in their eyes.

In one step, I was toe-to-toe with Rain. Her smooth skin brushed against my fingers when I wrapped them around her chin, tipping her face up to mine. Emotions warred inside me, hating leaving her but also desperate to find answers for what happened tonight. As I searched her eyes, looking for a sign that she needed me to stay, a pulse of relief hit me, finding the earlier fear gone from her beautiful face.

"Are you okay?" She nodded. "Words, Rain. I need to hear that you're okay."

"I'm good. Now that you're here." Her head thumped back against Jameson's chest. "Now that you're both here."

Again, I expected jealousy at her admission, but the way she looked up at me, with complete confidence in her eyes that I would take care of everything, that she was safe now that I was here, left no room for jealousy.

She'd called me when she was scared, knew I'd protect her and keep her safe.

Talk about a fucking ego boost.

This strong, amazing, smart-as-hell woman was leaning on me to handle the situation for her. Because she trusted me and knew I would take care of everything. And I would, especially knowing she would remain safe when I turned and walked into that house to get the answers we all wanted.

Without thinking or stopping the urge, I bent low and pressed my lips to her forehead.

"Take care of her," I ordered Jameson.

There was zero sign of the good-humored, easygoing agent I was used to seeing. The man holding my girl was someone anyone would think twice about messing with. It was the look of a man protecting the only thing that mattered to him, combined with the edge that spoke of his training and skill to take down anyone he deemed as a threat.

With that, I turned on my heels and stomped up the stairs, shoving the door open and entering the townhome. Wooden splinters crunched beneath my shoes when I crossed the threshold. Eyeing the doorframe, I took in the jagged edges and missing chunks of wood from the crowbar or something similar that was used to pop the lock.

But why didn't the alarm go off?

Inspecting the wall, I moved to the next, then the next, looking for the alarm panel.

Nothing.

My jaw worked back and forth. The alarm didn't go off because she didn't have one. I fisted my hands, resisting the urge to turn back around and ask Rain what the hell she was thinking living alone without a security system, but even in my frustrated state, I knew that would be a terrible decision. I was just so fucking pissed—not at her, at the whole situation—but my anger wasn't what she needed right now.

Marching up the stairs, I pushed the piercing pain in my knees that shot through my legs with each step to the back of my mind.

The hushed conversation between the two officers cut off, their attention jerking my way when I reached the landing.

"Detective Taylor," one stated. "What are you doing here? This isn't a homicide scene."

"Dr. Evans is a friend," I mumbled while scanning the destruction.

Pieces of glass and shattered ceramic littered the kitchen floor, and the living room looked like a few ducks had been plucked. Feathers covered the shredded couch and chair. The wires hanging from the wall suggested a TV once hung there.

"This mess, and the TV looks to be missing. Anything else?" I asked while memorizing the damage. There wasn't a pattern to the destruction, no apparent reason for destroying her furniture and kitchen. Hands on my hips, I inhaled deep through my nose and held it. This looked to be the result not of searching for anything but for the sole action of ruining her things. Rage. This was anger-fueled, which pointed to the asshole knowing Rain.

"There aren't any TVs upstairs, and someone emptied a jewelry box too. We'll need Dr. Evans to walk through—"

"No," I snapped. Inhaling and counting to three, I forced the anger and worry down deep so these two fools wouldn't see how much this affected me. "She doesn't need to see this. I'm going to look around upstairs."

Not waiting for their reply, I climbed the stairs, much slower now that the rush of adrenaline had worn off. At the top, I poked my head into one room, finding it undisturbed. The next one, not so much. Stepping inside, I instantly knew it was the one Jameson had been using since bunking with Rain. An open, empty suitcase sat in the corner, the clothes tossed around the room.

Instead of inspecting the clothes to see if they were shredded like the couch downstairs, the sharp stench of bleach had me spinning on my heels and following the smell. My eyes watered, lungs burning with each shallow inhale of the harmful fumes.

Nose to my forearm, I used my shirt sleeve to filter out the worst of it while scanning the destroyed main bedroom. Based on the powerful smell radiating from the pile of clothes, they were soaked with the corrosive chemical. Maybe even the bed too.

Tears leaking down my cheeks, I turned toward the bathroom. Smashed bottles littered the floor, the glass cracking beneath my steps as I moved toward the walk-in closet.

Light already on, I paused, taking in the mess that was like the one in the bedroom and downstairs. A tall pile of clothes sat in the middle of the floor, no doubt soaked with bleach based on the almost visible fumes in the confined space. A few tops hung haphazardly on hangers as if the fucker was in too much of a rush to toss them all into the pile, ensuring every article of clothing was ruined.

Now, I didn't know shit about shoe trends, but I knew Rain loved fancy sneakers. She talked about them all the time and was excited to show off her newest pair. All of those fancy shoes, every single one, were in a separate pile, the bleach having already discolored several pairs. A large shampoo bottle and a couple empty tubes of lotion lay nearby, probably the source of the thick substance coating the sneakers.

"What the fuck?"

I whirled around, gun in hand, at the too-close voice.

The female, who I recognized as a detective in the B&E unit, raised both hands, eyes narrowed on my gun. "Put that shit away."

I holstered it while eyeing her as she took in the destroyed closet. "You came fast."

Her lips quirked. "That's what she said." A half huff, half chuckle escaped me. "I was close, and when they said it was Dr. Evans's place, I headed this way even though it's my night off. This looks personal."

I nodded, fully agreeing. Which wasn't good. My fears of Rain being targeted seemed to be valid. Sure, the TVs were gone, but the level of destruction pointed to an ulterior motive. Making her feel unsafe or scared, maybe, and destroying the possessions that would hurt the worst, something only people who knew her would know.

"You got this?" I asked as I squeezed by her, poking my head into the bathroom, expecting to find the other detective she was always with. "Your partner here too?"

A strange look passed across her face, but it vanished in a flash. "Nah, like I said, it's our night off. She's out with some mysterious boyfriend, if I had to guess. She sneaks around with him a lot."

My brows tugged close. "Why would she hide that from you?"

The detective shrugged, though it seemed stiff. "The thrill of it all. Fuck if I know. I don't understand those mind games, which is probably why I'm still single with only my cat for company."

"Nothing wrong with cats," I mumbled. Sighing, I rubbed at my jaw, the weight of the day hitting me like a fucking four-hundred-pound lineman. "I'll make sure Dr. Evans gets somewhere safe for the night."

"Sounds good, but I want to talk to her first. See if there was anything of extreme value in the house that put her on someone's radar."

Smart.

Our footsteps pounded on the stairs as we jogged down one flight, swiveled around the second floor, and hurried down the next set of steps.

Outside, Jameson still had his arms wrapped around Rain. Her hazel eyes flicked to the woman beside me as we approached.

"Detective Gray," Rain said.

"Jennifer, remember?" the detective said, all the harsh lines from when she'd spoken to me gone when she talked to Rain. "I know it's been a tough night already, but can you list anything in the house that had a high monetary value?"

While Rain and the detective spoke, I angled my head, indicating for Jameson to step aside with me. With a light squeeze around Rain's waist, he whispered something in her ear and then moved to the edge of the sidewalk. Both of us were close enough that we could get to Rain if needed but far enough for a private conversation.

"This was personal," I muttered.

"Fuck. Did they leave a message or anything?" Jameson's gaze flicked from me to Rain, then down the sidewalk, no doubt searching for threats in the shadows.

"Not that I saw, but you've been here a few days. I want you to go inside. Look at it from your perspective. Your shit was tossed through too. They ruined most of her clothes if the lethal levels of bleach fumes are any sign. Go inside, check your shit, and grab anything of hers that's salvageable."

He winced as he massaged his left arm. "Okay. Are you thinking of taking her to a hotel, or—"

"Fuck no. You two are staying with me."

The full-body tremble, every muscle convulsing, that started the moment it dawned on me that someone broke into my home hadn't stopped. Adrenaline continued to pump through my veins, keeping me on edge as Slade drove us away from the house, leaving Detective Gray behind to finish sweeping the crime scene alone.

Damnit.

Tears welled, threatening to fall as I gazed out the back passenger window. The familiar homes surrounding my neighborhood had shifted to businesses and restaurants a while ago, yet I still hadn't uttered a single word despite the two men up front shooting worried looks my way.

Shock was still firmly in place, making me feel numb. I wanted to tell them I was fine, because physically I was. Mentally and emotionally, not so much. But even the single word felt like too much effort. So instead, I sat in the back seat, forehead pressed to the cool window, completely unresponsive.

Plus, I didn't want to tell them my suspicions of who ransacked my home.

The unshed tears burned in my throat.

My home. The place I'd once felt safe, and now that was ripped away. I could replace the furniture and clothes easily, but that sense of security the townhouse provided was gone for good.

The sensation of eyes on me had me flicking my gaze toward the front seat. Worried light-brown eyes were focused on me, scanning my face for the hundredth time since we all piled into Slade's car.

"How much longer?" Jameson asked with an exhale as he settled back into his seat.

"Fifteen minutes," Slade sighed. I met his bright green gaze in the rearview mirror. "How are you holding up back there?"

The words *fine*, or *okay*, or *all right* sat on the tip of my tongue, but I couldn't utter a single one. Instead, I raised a shoulder in a noncommittal shrug.

"You're killing me, sweetheart," Jameson groaned. "Talk to us. Anything. We know you're not okay. That's obvious. Tell us what you're feeling."

Feeling. How I was feeling.

Vulnerable. Victimized. Angry. Sad. Despondent. Guilty.

That last one sat the heaviest in my gut. I could've stopped this if only I would've told someone about the note and my fears. A part of me worried they would be mad once they found out.

I knew it was dumb not to tell anyone. I understood now that I should've treated it like the real threat it was. But I never expected this, for my ex to take things to this level of violence. Sure, he was irate about the divorce, but this, destroying my stuff and scaring me, it was beyond what I'd imagined he was capable of.

That should tell me that either I didn't really know the

depth of his anger toward me or something had shifted in his mental state since I left him behind in Nashville.

"At least the plants were already dead. No loss there. Was there anything salvageable upstairs?" The words were like sandpaper scraping my dry throat.

Mouth tacky and gross, I'd give a nonessential organ for my oh-so-yummy unicorn drink.

"The plants... I didn't mention that earlier." Slade's voice trembled with barely restrained anger. "You went into the house before you called us." A frustrated statement, not a question.

"Calm down. Don't hulk out on us." Jameson shot me a smirk to lighten the dark mood. "She told me while you were looking around inside. When she got home earlier, she used the door leading to the attached garage and didn't notice the damage to the front door. It wasn't until Rain found the destruction in the living room and kitchen that she realized someone had broken in. That was when she ran outside and called the police, then you."

It was a relief that there was zero jealousy or hurt in Jameson's tone, signaling he was upset that I'd called Slade instead of him. It was instinctual, my fingers automatically finding Slade's contact, knowing he'd handle everything. That he'd protect me and figure out a solution to the shit show that was suddenly in my life.

I cleared my throat, drawing both men's gazes toward the back seat.

Once I told them this next part, they would more than likely lose their shit. But they needed to know.

"I didn't initially see the mess and run outside. There was a noise. Upstairs. That's when I bolted," I confessed, locking my gaze out the window like the large homes on oversized lots actually held my rapt attention.

"What?" Slade practically growled. "The motherfucker who did this was still in the house?"

I winced at his scathing tone even though I knew he wasn't mad at me, more about the situation and the asshole who he viewed as a threat to my safety.

Instead of clamming up beneath his frustration, I forced myself to continue. "I ran outside and down the street, hiding behind a corner. I didn't want to be hanging out on the sidewalk alone when whoever was inside made their escape. There was no way he didn't hear me. I was quite vocal when I realized someone vandalized my house."

"That was brilliant, Rain. You realized you were in a dangerous situation and got yourself the hell out of Dodge." Jameson fully turned in the seat, resting a comforting hand on my bare knee. Thinking I would shower at home, I didn't change out of my workout clothes at the gym, so I still wore my short spandex shorts, matching sports bra, and Dri-Fit top. "Did you see them when they left? Any discernible features will help—"

"No." Squeezing my eyes shut, I shook my head. "But I might know who did it."

"A dead man?"

A snort escaped, tickling my nose at Slade's violent, yet strangely comforting, remark. "My ex-husband." Neither man said a word, the silence deafening. "I found a note on my front stoop the day Jameson arrived, when I ran home to check my hair straightener. It was tucked under my front mat."

"Do you still have it?" Jameson asked, tone soothing, but there was no missing the strain in his voice. He was undeniably pissed. Slade, too, not that I blamed them.

"No." I pressed the side of my head to the window. "It said 'I found you' or something like that. At first, I assumed it had something to do with work, but a note was too passive-aggressive for the type of people we deal with. And the verbiage 'found' made it feel like he'd been searching for me, not stalking. That would've been 'I'm watching' instead."

"Why didn't you tell us?" Slade demanded. Jameson shot him a pointed glare. Slade cleared his throat and shifted in the driver's seat. "Sorry, why didn't you tell us?" This time his tone was soothing instead of pulsing with anger.

"When I saw you two later that day, my mind automatically went to discussing the autopsy. Then Jameson started staying with me, so the fear that note generated was pushed to the background because I wasn't alone." Leaning forward, I poked a single finger into Slade's shoulder. "And don't you victim-blame me, Slade Taylor. I had no idea this would happen."

"I'm not blaming you. Fuck, do you think I would?"

I lurched forward, the seat belt snapping across my chest when the car came to an abrupt stop. My jaw dropped when he flung open his door, mine following suit half a second later. Between blinks, Slade was crouched in the street, putting us at eye level.

"Tell me you don't think I'm that kind of man. That for even half a second you believed I would blame you for what happened."

Sincerity and desperation leaked from his gravelly tone, those green eyes imploring me to believe him.

And I did. Slade was grouchy, not mean.

Heat warmed my palm when I cupped his scruff-covered cheek. "No, Slade. I don't think you'd do that. To me or any woman. I'm just... I'm feeling guilty because I didn't tell anyone, and now we're here."

"Thank fuck."

Too fast for me to react, Slade lunged forward and sealed his lips to mine. Eyes wide, I could only blink, too shocked to move.

Before the kiss registered and the fact that my unrequited crush was kissing me, Slade pulled back and cleared his throat. "Sorry about that."

Dazed, I pressed two fingertips to my lips as if I could hold the taste of him there forever. Something like "fucking finally" came from the front seat, making a hesitant smile spread across my face.

"We're almost at my place." His knees cracked as he stood, using the car frame for help. After double-checking that I was safely tucked into the car, he shut my door and folded himself back behind the wheel. "Neither of you are allergic to cats, right?"

Melting back into the seat, I replayed the brief, scorching kiss.

The anger and fear faded with the memory of his lips pressed to my own, heated anticipation simmering in its place.

Me and two sinfully attractive men forced to cohabitate for the foreseeable future. Maybe my place being trashed isn't such a terrible thing after all.

AWARE OF SLADE'S NFL background and having heard rumors of his Hall of Fame father and movie star mother, I expected his place would be nicer than mine. But in reality, it wasn't nice—it was a gorgeous modern mansion. During the grand tour, I had to remind myself to not gawk after the fourth guest room followed by the media room, gym, and game room.

Standing outside, arms wrapped tightly around myself, I inhaled deep. A hint of salt water lingered on the cool breeze that had my dark hair floating behind me as I walked along the edge of the large pool. Because of course he had a pool, complete with a cabana and a small pool house, with comfortable-looking seating along the pool deck and yet another enormous TV.

The man liked his TVs, that was for certain. I'd lost count during the tour—but to be fair, there was too much to take in to even attempt to keep count. Especially after he showed us his cat's room. That had both Jameson and me snickering, which turned into rolling laughter at Slade's eye roll.

"You have to be freezing out here in that outfit." Slade leaned against the patio doorframe, tracking my every move, either curious about what I thought of his home or worried about my mental state from the earlier incident. Another cool gust had my teeth chattering. The tiny outfit was perfect for the hot gym, but not so much out here. "Come back inside. I'm sure you're ready for a shower and to crawl into bed."

With a longing look at the steaming water that cascaded from the spa into the main pool, I weaved back through the lounge chairs toward Slade.

Movement through the glass door caught my eye. Jameson paced, still on the phone, moving from one side of Slade's kitchen to the other. With my suspicions about Josh, Jameson wanted to trace his last known whereabouts and had put in a call to a technical genius he worked with back in Dallas.

Slade's massive hands wrapped around my slim shoulders, the heat that soaked from his skin to mine immediately soothing the sharp edge to the cool night air. Using the pads of both thumbs, he brushed tiny circles against my skin, making goose bumps sprout for a whole different reason than the temperature.

"We'll figure out what's going on," Slade murmured. "You're safe here."

"I know," I breathed. Desperate to break the heaviness of the night, I tossed my head back and let out an exaggerated groan. "All my shoes. My precious, precious shoes."

Though slightly dramatic, I'd shed a tear when Slade informed me of the ruined state of my sneaker collection. Not only were they expensive, but they were broken in perfectly. I could afford to buy more, but I was not looking forward to the discomfort and time it would take to truly replace what I'd lost.

Slade chuckled. "Come on, let's get you cleaned up." Jameson looked our way as we stepped back into the house but continued talking on the phone. "Do you want to look through the clothes Jameson found in your room that were okay or wear something of mine to bed?"

I sucked in a fast breath, pulse now racing at the thought of wearing Slade's clothes. "Yours, if that's okay. I don't have the energy to sort through it all. Not tonight. I need sleep and a truckload of sugar before I'm prepared to take on that task."

Following him, I couldn't help but stare at his firm ass.

"Rain."

"Hmm," I practically panted. The entire house smelled like him. Manly and intoxicating.

"I said you can use this room."

At the clear laughter in his tone, I jerked my gaze up, finding him watching me. *Well, damn. He one hundred percent caught me checking out his ass. Whoops.*

"I'll be right back with some clothes." His soft chuckle

echoed down the hall as he continued walking deeper into the house toward the main bedroom.

Half of me wanted to go after him, see if he'd follow through on that kiss.

The kiss he'd quickly apologized for.

Shaking my head, I dismissed the idea. No need to add embarrassment and hurt to the night if he rejected my advances. I had Jameson to seek for comfort tonight. That was enough. It would be stingy to have both of them, even though the idea made it difficult to breathe normally.

Lost in thought, I startled, a little squeal escaping when firm hands slid around my waist. Before I could whirl around, a solid chest pressed to my back, fingers tightening, keeping me in place.

"I was scared shitless tonight," Jameson whispered in my ear, breath fanning along my skin, making me shiver. Soft lips swept over my neck. "Being on the phone with you, knowing you were in danger and I wasn't there. What if something had happened to you?"

I peeled his fingers away, loosening his grip enough to spin around in his arms. Two palms slid lower to cup my spandex-covered ass as he backed me across the floor until the doorframe pressed between my shoulder blades.

"I'm okay." I tried to reassure him with a weak half smile. "I was scared, too, which...." Tilting forward, I pressed my forehead to his chest, the edge of a button from his dress shirt digging into my skin. "I'm thirty-two years old. I've been on my own for a while now. This feeling, being vulnerable and unable to do anything about it, sucks. I feel weak."

His hands tightened. "You're anything but weak, Raindrop. Tonight, you needed help. That doesn't make someone weak. It makes them smart and strong."

A snort escaped me. Strong. Right. If I were strong, I

would've had a weapon on me and confronted Josh while he was in my home instead of running away.

Jameson frowned. "You're strong because you allowed yourself to lean on someone—or two someones, in this case—who you knew would catch you. Being strong doesn't mean handling it all on your own. Sometimes it means giving up control enough to allow others to help."

I blew out a long breath through pursed lips. Leaning back, I searched his honey-brown eyes. A lock of his shaggy brown hair lay haphazardly across his forehead, messed up from the stressful night and his hands constantly running through the soft strands.

"I don't want to be alone tonight," I admitted. Sure, we'd slept in the same bed the last couple of nights, but that didn't mean him sleeping with me tonight was a foregone conclusion.

Both corners of his lips twitched upward. "Then it's a good thing I didn't plan on letting you. I need some comfort cuddles tonight too."

Giving me time to pull away, he leaned forward until his lips pressed to mine. Just like Slade's, the kiss chased away all the unwanted feelings and thoughts the night had stirred up. With a content sigh, I relaxed against him, allowing his strength to keep me upright.

His tongue tangled with mine, the kiss quickly shifting from sweet to scorching. The hands cupping my ass tightened. With a tug, he sealed my lower half against his. I moaned at the feel of his long, thick cock pressing just above where my body demanded friction. The passion and need pumping through my veins had me threading my fingers through his long strands, adjusting our angle to take control of the kiss.

Jameson groaned, the sound vibrating against my lips. A

hand slipped lower to grip behind my knee, urging it higher until it hooked around his hip. The doorframe dug into my upper back, reminding me that we were making out in the hall where Slade could catch us at any moment.

The thought had more desire dripping from my core, soaking my shorts and no doubt leaving a damp spot on Jameson's slacks.

Breathing heavy, I pulled back. "Slade could catch us."

My words of caution did the opposite of cooling the moment. With a muttered curse, Jameson slammed his lips to mine, taking back control.

"Would you like that?" he whispered, moving to suck at the sensitive skin beneath my ear.

"I don't want to make him feel uncomfortable in his own home."

Jameson's dark chuckle had me shifting against him, desperate to ease the building ache between my thighs.

"Oh, he'd be uncomfortable, but not in the way you're thinking."

The idea of Slade watching Jameson and me, getting so turned on that he'd have to take matters into his own hand —literally—sent a shiver racing down my spine.

"Hmm," Jameson mused. "Seems someone else likes that idea as much as me." *Um, say what?* "But I agree. I don't want to make you fall apart in the hall. Next time, maybe."

With ease, he lifted me, my other leg automatically coming up to wrap around his waist, spreading me to align perfectly against his thick cock. My hair tumbled down my back as I tipped my face to the ceiling while grinding against him.

"Fuck, you're amazing," Jameson whispered in an almost reverent tone as he stepped into the bedroom. "And those shorts." He released his hold just long enough to smack one ass cheek. Hard. "They should be illegal. Showing off your long, beautiful legs that every fucker would kill to have wrapped around them."

"Like you do now," I said breathlessly.

"I'm a lucky bastard to be the one with you tonight, Raindrop. And I'll do everything in my power to ensure it's still me for the foreseeable future." The mattress molded beneath my back as he laid me in the center of the bed. "Well, me or Slade."

He glanced over his shoulder, a sly smile stretching across his face when he turned back.

Eager to feel his skin against mine, I gripped the hem of my tank, lifting it up and over my head.

"I don't want to stop tonight," I admitted. The need burning hot in my core wouldn't be satisfied by his fingers and tongue like it had the last few nights. "I want every inch of you, Jameson."

And if Slade joined in...

Well, that would just be icing on the cake, and at this point, I was one hundred percent okay with being greedy with these two.

21

RAIN

The stretchy fabric clung to my skin as Jameson worked the spandex shorts down my thighs, the action reminding me that I hadn't showered yet and probably smelled terrible. The moment my hand wrapped around his wrist, pausing his movements, Jameson froze, leaving the shorts dangling from one foot.

"I need to shower," I blurted. "I ran several miles tonight, and I probably smell. Everywhere."

I'd never wanted to punch myself as much as I did in that moment for adding that last word. *Why? Why? Why am I this way?* This was the exact reason my chosen career path of days filled with dead people was the perfect one for me. I didn't need to subject others to my strange awkwardness. They deserved to have easy days, not ones convoluted with placating the slightly unhinged woman.

"That doesn't bother me, but—" Jameson shrugged, sweeping the tips of two fingers along my inner thigh. "—how about some company?"

"Absolutely."

With a tiny kick, my shorts flew through the air,

smacking the wall before falling to the floor. I barely caught Jameson's mischievous grin before he put both hands on my waist and tossed me over his shoulder with ease. His shoulder dug into my gut as he hurried toward the bathroom.

With my hair hanging in front of my face, swaying with Jameson's every step, I almost missed the solid shape filling the bedroom doorway that led to the hall. But before I could push off Jameson's back and swipe my hair out of the way, the view of the doorway was cut off as we entered the bathroom.

My pulse kicked into high gear. Was that Slade, listening and watching from the hall as Jameson undressed me?

And if he liked what he saw, would he want to watch what happened next?

Water sputtering from the showerhead and slapping against the river-stone floor shifted my thoughts from Slade back to the man who slowly slid me down his muscular chest. The tips of my toes brushed the cold tile floor, though Jameson's stabilizing hold didn't loosen from around my waist until I was steady on my feet.

He took half a step back, making me immediately miss his radiating body heat and his protective hold. But as his deft fingers worked the buttons of his dress shirt, then yanked the hem from the waistband of his slacks, I forgot about everything but watching him strip. Fingers wrapped around the bottom of his undershirt, he jerked it up and over his head, tossing the white cotton to the floor beside the dark blue dress shirt.

With the tip of my tongue, I licked my lips, fingers twitching at my side with the urge to reach across the small distance to trace every dip and curve of his defined chest and abs. The clink of metal rang in my ears. My pulse raced, heart leaping into my throat as he worked the clasp of the belt free before whipping the thin leather from the loops.

Pants resting precariously on his hips, Jameson pulled a square foil packet from the pocket before releasing his hold and letting the pants puddle around his bare feet. Thumbs hooked into the elastic waistband of his boxer briefs, he inched them lower, slowly exposing his hard length.

A trickle of desire leaked from my core, sliding down my inner thigh.

Ignoring my doubts and tumbling headfirst into the irresistible urge, I lowered to my knees at his feet. Hands wrapped around both thighs, I eased them higher, shivering at the feel of corded muscle beneath my palms. I rose on my knees until his tip hovered an inch in front of my lips. I paused, nerves making me question what I absolutely wanted to do.

Long fingers dove into my hair, tangling in the disheveled mess. A sting radiated along my scalp at his not-so-gentle tug that tipped my head back. His other hand cupped my face, thumb tracing along my lower lip.

"You don't have to do this, Raindrop."

I nipped at his thumb before sucking it between my lips. "What if I want to?" His features turned strained, and a hiss radiated above the water pounding in the shower. "Just help me. Show me what you like so I'm not lost guessing and wondering if I'm doing it right."

"Sweetheart, you on your knees, saying you want to suck my dick, is almost enough for me to embarrass myself before you even get those perfect lips wrapped around me." I waited, blinking up at him. Noting my resolve, his light eyes darkened, lids drooping low. "Take your sports bra off. I want to see all of you while I fuck this perfect mouth."

All elbows, I awkwardly wrestled the tight fabric over

my head and tossed it toward the double sink, uncaring where it landed. Licking my lips, I leaned forward, the small bead of precum tempting me to try a taste. His entire body trembled at the swipe of my tongue along his slit, lapping up the small bead and rolling the flavor around in my mouth.

"Fuck, Rain." I couldn't help but preen at the tremble in his voice. I did that. Awkward, lanky me made this strong, badass man weak. "Wrap your hand around the base and squeeze." I did as he instructed, relaxing a little, knowing I wouldn't need to think or worry, only listen and do. "Tighter. Shit, yes, just like that."

I peeked up through my dark lashes, finding his intense stare locked on my lips.

"Now wrap those beautiful lips around me, sweetheart, and run that tempting tongue up and down my—fuck." He jerked, slipping deeper into my mouth. But I didn't care. He was losing control, and I loved it. "Yes. Fuck, your mouth is so damn perfect, taking my cock like you fucking love my taste."

Daring to go a little deeper, I slid my lips down his thick shaft to where my fingers were wrapped around his base.

"Look at you," Jameson said, a hint of awe in his voice. "Taking my dick like your mouth was made for me. I'm going to take control now, sweetheart. And you're going to let me, aren't you? Let me fuck this hot mouth of yours."

I barely nodded before his grip on my hair tightened, holding me in place. Unable to move anything but my eyes, I strained to look up. Lower lip secured between his teeth, face tight with tension, his abs flexed as he slid in and out of my very willing mouth.

"Fuck, fuck, Raindrop."

His hips snapped forward, the tip of his cock tapping the

back of my throat. I gagged, the action making my throat work around his sensitive head. Tears leaked from the corners of both eyes. Spit slicked my lips, but I didn't care. Not when he stared down at me like I was his entire world.

With a barked curse, he stepped backward, pulling himself free. Chest heaving, cock bobbing in front of my face, he swiped at my trail of tears. "Your throat working around my cock is the best feeling I've ever experienced. And almost had this ending before I got to feel your tight pussy wrapped around me."

Hooking both hands beneath my armpits, he hauled me up and slammed his lips to mine in a hard, passionate kiss. My eyes widened in surprise. Flickers of the past filtered through, of Josh shoving me away after I gave in to the guilt and gave him the blow job he wanted, demanding I brush my teeth, too grossed out at the thought of us kissing.

Somehow, Jameson knew my thoughts had drifted. With a frustrated groan, he swiped his tongue inside my mouth, almost like he wanted to lick the taste of himself off me.

"I'm not him," he insisted. "And I swear as long as I live, I will never, ever allow someone to make you feel less again. You hear me, Rain? You letting me slip between those pouty lips is a fucking gift that I will cherish and enjoy every fucking time you get on your knees for me."

I blinked to keep the hot tears that burned behind my eyes from falling. Jameson's gentle fingers swept down my arm until they entangled with my own. Stepping into the shower, he pulled me in after him, allowing the water to hit his back, testing the temperature. Steam billowed around us, the heat adding to the rising fire racing beneath my skin.

With the spray pelting him, Jameson crowded me, urging me back until my spine flattened against the cold white subway tile. A rough stroke and pinch on my peaked nipple had my back arching, pressing me harder into his dominant touch in a silent demand for more. A husky chuckle filled the steamy shower as his lips sealed around one nipple. Palm encasing my other small breast, he squeezed until the soft flesh molded beneath his fingers, pain and pleasure tangling together.

A hiss whistled through my teeth as he pinched the sensitive bud between two fingers and tugged, the sharp sting quickly morphing into a wave of bliss that sent a pulse straight to my swollen clit.

"Jameson," I pleaded. "I need you. Make tonight go away. Just for a little while, make me forget."

Instead of responding with words, he slid his hand down my flat stomach, fingers skimming over my mound and then slipping inside my slick core. His muttered curse had a smile pulling at my lips.

"You're so wet for me, Raindrop." Putting distance between us, he watched his fingers plunge in and out while also grinding the heel of his hand against my bundle of nerves. "Did me fucking your mouth get this pussy all nice and ready for me? My cock filling your throat makes you needy to feel me fucking your cunt harder."

My head fell back, tapping against the tile wall. "Yes. Please," I begged, past the point of caring how I sounded.

A pitiful whimper escaped me when he pulled back just enough to grab the condom wrapper off the floor of the shower where he'd tossed it earlier. Using his teeth, he ripped the packet open and tossed the trash aside before rolling the condom down his twitching cock.

An excited, lust-filled glint shone in his light eyes when he looked up through wet lashes.

"No more waiting, Raindrop. Wrap those long, beautiful legs around me." He nipped at my lower lip and then sucked the spot, soothing the sting. "And I'll give you everything you're begging for and more."

Not needing to be told twice, I slid both arms along his wet skin and wrapped them around his neck while hooking one knee around his hip, followed by the other. Chin on his shoulder, I blinked through the water droplets coating my lashes and froze. On the other side of the steam-covered glass stood the same shape as earlier, though this time closer.

Much closer.

I parted my lips, the words on the tip of my tongue to tell Jameson we had an audience, but they evaporated at the feel of him nudging my entrance and slowly pushing deeper. All thoughts and focus went to him filling me inch by inch until his hips ground against my own. The stretch of my body accommodating his thick cock was a thousand times better than his fingers. With a shallow thrust, Jameson rocked against me, his pelvis hitting my swollen nub. Wet skin molded beneath my teeth as I latched on to his shoulder to keep from screaming his name.

With a grunt, he drew back, the tip almost slipping out, before snapping his hips and slamming back inside. This time there was no muffling the raspy curse that slipped free.

The shape on the other side of the glass door shifted, drawing my glazed gaze back to Slade. My fingers trembled as I stretched a single hand toward the glass, smearing a thick line through the steam that blocked my view of him.

His vivid green eyes locked on mine immediately.

A bolt of desire zipped down my spine, making me tighten around Jameson as I held Slade's intense stare. Jameson thrust in and out, each time at a different angle, bolts of pleasure erupting from my core.

Fuck, I'd never felt anything like it.

Not with Josh, not with anyone before him.

Higher and higher, he wound me tighter with each snap of his hips and dirty words whispered in my ear. But it was when he said his next words, catching me off guard, that I tipped over that edge to bliss.

"You like him watching, don't you, dirty girl? Show Slade how fucking gorgeous you are when you come."

That shoved me into oblivion, plunging me into pure ecstasy. I sank my heels into his firm ass, desperate to feel him a little deeper as I squeezed tight around his cock. Voice cracking on a curse, Jameson's movements faltered before his full weight pressed me harder into the tile wall. When reality settled back into my awareness, his forehead was pressed beside my head, the only sounds our heavy breaths and the water splashing around us.

My tender nipples brushed against his chest with every deep inhale. I peeled both lids open, the small smile that had formed disappearing at finding the other side of the shower vacant.

Gone.

I tightened my hold on Jameson until there wasn't a sliver of space between us.

"He's gone." I tried to not let the disappointment come through in my voice.

"For now," Jameson whispered, sliding his fingers through my damp hair. "He'll be back, Raindrop. He just has to figure his own shit out first."

With him still inside me, this was the absolute worst time to ask, but I couldn't stop the words from leaving my lips.

"Why? Is it something about me—" I gasped, cutting myself off when Jameson snapped his hips and ground against my sensitive clit.

"No, sweetheart, it's his own messed-up thinking that he needs to work out. You're perfect."

"I wouldn't go *that* far."

"Then you have the incorrect definition of perfect. Because from where I stand, what I see and know about you, all of you, inside and out, that word sums you up."

I searched his face. "What does Slade have to work out?"

Jameson blew out a slow breath and planted a chaste kiss on my lips. "That's not for me to explain. But he'll come around. No one can resist your pull forever." He shot me a wicked smirk and winked.

Breaths deep and slow, muscles lax and the throbbing need from earlier sated, I relaxed back until my head lolled against the tile. Lip between my teeth, I hitched my chin toward the showerhead. "I'll wash your back if you'll wash mine."

A full smile spread across his handsome face, taking away all worried thoughts of Slade. Damn, Jameson was too attractive in a naughty-boy-next-door type of way. "How about I wash every square inch of your amazing body, eat your delicious cunt until you beg me to stop, then fuck you until your knees give out?"

I swallowed, inhaling a shaky breath.

Very naughty boy next door.

"I like your plan better."

"Good. Because I'm starving, and having you once tonight isn't enough. Now that I know what it feels like to be inside you—" He bit his lower lip and shook his head until water sprayed all around us. "—I never want to be anywhere else. Now, I'm going to put you down, and then I want you to sit on the stone bench, legs spread. Understand?" I nodded, unable to form words as a fresh wave of need pumped through my veins. "I want to look at your pretty pink pussy while I wash you clean before getting you all dirty again."

My skin easily slipped over his as he lowered me until my feet pressed to the smooth gray stone. Between the hard workout earlier and clenching around Jameson like my life depended on it, my thigh muscles trembled, threatening to give out as I wobbled toward the built-in bench and lowered myself onto the smooth stone top. Eager to please him by not having to be told twice, I spread both knees as wide as I could and leaned back against the wall, never dropping his sizzling stare.

Fisting a loofah, he squirted citrus-and-cedar-scented liquid soap on top. With a cocky grin on his oh-so-kissable lips, Jameson lowered to his knees, a hand stroking up my inner thigh. I felt like a queen with him kneeling in front of me, hair dark with water, plastered to the sides of his face with rivers cascading along his tan skin. I sucked in a shallow breath, a shiver racing down my spine.

"Now, while I get you clean," he said, rubbing the soapy loofah up my calf, "you put those fingers to work and keep yourself soaked and ready for me."

Lids squeezed shut, I blew out a breath, zero hesitation as my fingers trailed down my sternum toward my pulsing center.

Tonight was for forgetting, getting lost in pleasure.

No random thoughts, no worries about my ruined home.

Tomorrow I'd deal with reality.

22

SLADE

I barely made it to my bedroom after that live porn show before my pants were undone and my fist was wrapped around my throbbing cock. Twice I'd jerked off in the shower to the memory of her face pinched with pleasure and the sounds of her sweet moans in my ears. I hadn't recovered, hard and able for another round after coming so hard I saw stars.

Yet here I was the next morning in the shower again, my soapy hand wrapped around my rock-hard dick, squeezing and jerking, desperate to find relief for the erection that woke me up leaking from my dirty-as-fuck dreams of Rain. Forearm pressed to the tile wall, I used it to support my weight as my thigh muscles quivered.

"Fuck, Rain," I muttered under my breath. I pictured her on all fours, ass in the air, as I slammed into her over and over, my hips bruising that firm ass that teased me last night in those damn short shorts.

Without my consent, Jameson's face popped into my brief fantasy. This time he was watching like I had last night, not touching himself or Rain because I'd ordered him not to.

That sent me over the edge. My hand pumped harder, shooting ropes of cum onto the shower wall. Breaths coming in shallow pants, I pressed my forehead to the cool tile and dropped my spent cock. Lips parted, I inhaled deeply, nostrils flaring as the evidence of my fantasy swirled down the drain.

The churning disgust that usually overwhelmed me after jacking off to the image of Rain never happened. Last night, she'd caught me watching as Jameson fucked her against the shower wall. There was no disgust or horror in her soft hazel eyes, only heat and desire. She liked me watching, and based on the timing of when her face pinched in pleasure, she got off on the idea of it—or hell, maybe even the idea of me joining.

Maybe Jameson's words last night at the bar weren't the ramblings of a crazy asshole after all.

Somewhat sated, I rushed through my normal routine and then stepped out of the shower, grabbing a warm towel off the heated bar. As I rubbed it over my hair, a sharp inhale snapped my focus toward the sound, barely catching a flash of dark brown hair. Rivulets trailed down my legs and upper body, but I ignored the water dripping all over the bathroom tile as I marched toward the door, wrapping the towel around my waist as I walked.

"Rain," I called. The woman who I'd just jerked off to stopped her hurried retreat, hand tightly gripping the doorframe. "Did you need something?"

"Clothes," she rasped, voice slightly breathless. "Last night you said I could borrow some."

"Damnit, I forgot." *Because I was too busy watching you,*

then jacking off to the memory. "I'll find you some. Give me a second."

My wet bare feet slapped against the hardwood floors as I paused in front of the dresser. In the mirror hanging on the wall, I eyed her frozen frame where she'd yet to turn around. I hadn't heard her call out my name when she entered the bedroom. How long had she been standing there before I caught her? Did she see me beating off in the shower, watching me like I did her last night?

I rolled my eyes at the twitch of my cock beneath the towel. *For fuck's sake.* If this kept up, my dick would be raw from how much I'd need to jerk off to keep it from punching through my pants every five minutes.

"You can, um, finish." My hand tightened around the athletic shorts I was pulling out of the drawer for her. "The shower, I mean. Or drying off." Her hair dipped farther down her back as she tipped her face to the ceiling. "Not that I was watching. Or saw anything."

My lips curled in a silent smile. "Are you sure about that? Because I know I saw plenty last night."

She fell to the doorframe, the wall literally saving her from crashing to the floor. "Right. Well, I just saw your tattoos. All of them."

I chuckled at her obvious embarrassment. If she saw all my tattoos, the ones that covered my entire chest, arms, and thighs, then there was no way she missed my recently spent cock slapping between them. That was where most women's eyes went when they saw me naked. It always intrigued me if hunger or fear would emerge once they took in my size.

What could I say? I was fucking huge everywhere, and my dick was no exception.

"Here you go." When she still refused to turn around, I

couldn't help but chuckle. "Do you still want the clothes, Rain?"

"What? Oh, yes. Of course. I just put these back on before grabbing a shower and...." She muttered something under her breath. The tips of her hair whipped across my bare skin when she whirled around. Her hazel eyes didn't meet mine; instead, they slid down my mostly naked body. "Oh, you have a towel on now. Good. That's good."

Though her tone said otherwise.

"Take the clothes, Rain." There was only so much of her staring at where my towel now tented that I could take. "I'll get dressed and make breakfast. We can figure out a game plan for restoring your place and replacing the essentials before we head to work."

Her narrow shoulders rounded as her head bobbed up and down. "Yeah, that makes sense. I honestly don't even know where to start."

"I do," I assured her with confidence. "Replace the things you need right away, file a claim with your insurance, and start putting back together what last night took away."

Rain huffed. "Like my sense of safety?"

Knuckle beneath her chin, I tipped her face up to mine. "That will come with time, baby. Not that you need to go back there anytime soon. You can stay here, safe, with me for as long as you need." I swelled with pride at the immediate relief my words had on her tense posture. "But we'll start with replacing those shoes you love so much. Go shower, and I'll meet you in the kitchen with my iPad to get started."

Her eyes flicked between mine, indecision clear, before she propelled forward, wrapping her arms around my waist. "Thank you." With one more tight squeeze, she hurried down the hall.

I watched until she disappeared into the room she and Jameson had shared last night.

And I had to wonder.

Would we be sharing mine tonight?

***

Dressed in a pair of joggers and a T-shirt, I lumbered toward the kitchen. My steps faltered at finding Jameson already up, sitting on the breakfast nook bench, feet up and laptop open on the wooden table. His attention flicked from the screen, and he hitched his chin in greeting.

Not a morning person, it seemed.

I began gathering all the shit needed for my morning smoothie and turned on the coffee. When the roar of the high-powered blender reverberated through the entire kitchen, I chuckled, the sound swallowed by the noise, at the feel of Jameson's hateful glare burning into my bare back.

"Is that really necessary at this hour?" he groused the second the sound cut off.

"Yep." Without turning, I tilted my head toward the coffee machine. "Coffee is ready."

"Thank fuck," he mumbled.

While he made his coffee, I poured my breakfast into a fresh glass, storing the extra in the fridge for Rain, and pulled out a stool from beneath the counter.

"What are you working on?" I asked.

Knowing the taste wasn't the best, I gulped down half the contents in two swallows and set the glass on the island. It was healthy and fast, which was why I drank it first thing in the morning. The pain meds I'd taken before walking in here would make my stomach churn if I didn't get something to eat fast. The nausea and cramping started within the past few months, which was probably a sign that the pills were ruining my stomach lining and liver, but I had to walk, and that was the price to pay. At least until I gave in to Rain's advice about the cortisone shots.

My shoulders shook with an involuntary shiver.

Jameson shot me an annoyed look before settling back on the bench and taking a sip of the steaming liquid in his mug. "Our technical profiler sent over what he found on her shit of an ex."

The stool's legs scraped across the tile, the damn thing almost tipping over as I abruptly stood before he was even done talking. Shoving at his shoulder, I forced him farther into the booth so I could sit beside him.

"Fucking hell, we both don't fit in this shit." Not like he had a choice in moving or not. "Why do you have to be so damn big?"

"Better to beat your ass with, asshole. Drink your damn coffee and show me what he found."

A soft meow came from the living room, stopping my next words. Leaning to the side to see around a large potted plant, I searched the couch and found Sneaks on his back, paws in the air, twisted in an S-shape with his big eyes blinking at me. "Sorry, buddy, not this morning. This is more important than your belly pets."

"Belly pets," Jameson mocked. "Seriously. Did that cat take your balls, or did you hand them over with a smile on your face for him to play with?"

"Fuck you."

"I thought we established that's not my thing." I chuffed a laugh into my smoothie, sending some of it splattering against my face. Jameson's responding grin was sharp. "Serves you right for making such a loud breakfast."

"You can have all the undisturbed silence you want back at that rat-infested hotel."

That shut him up. "Noted. Thank you for these fine accommodations. The bed was great, but the shower space was even better." He shot me a wink. "Perfect for two."

"We're sitting way too close to discuss this shit."

"What? That you saw my ass as I fucked—"

"Oh, you're both up."

Rain shuffled into the kitchen, hands working to secure a lump of damp hair on the top of her head in a messy bun. I stifled a groan and heard Jameson clear his throat, doing the same. My shorts hung low on her lean hips even with them rolled several times. I didn't think about it then, but now I was fucking hating myself for giving her a black tee instead of a white one since it was obvious by her pointed tips that she wasn't wearing a bra.

Hands on her hips, she scanned the kitchen with a frown. "Thought you were making breakfast?"

I held up my glass and gave it a shake. "There's some in the fridge for you too."

Her tiny nose crinkled. "Um, thanks, but I need a little more than that." She held her phone close to her face, thumbs moving across the screen. "What's your address?"

After rattling it off, I shifted my focus back to the computer screen while keeping one eye on Rain as she skipped—literally *skipped*—to the coffee machine.

"He has five credit cards maxed out," Jameson muttered under his breath so only I would hear. "He drained his accounts last month, and there hasn't been activity since. Charlie is running him through a facial recognition software at airports, bus terminals, train stations, that sort of thing, but that will take time."

"So, we have no idea where he is." Twisting on the

bench, I pointed to the counter. "Rain, the iPad is there if you want to look for your shoes."

A few seconds later, her very full mug thumped to the table across from Jameson and me before she slid into the opposite bench seat. Eyes full of mischief flicked from me to Jameson and back again.

"Don't you two look cozy," she chuckled. "What is that you're working on?"

"Do you have insurance information handy?" I asked instead of responding to her question. I didn't want to hide the information about her ex, but maybe the fact that we had no idea where he was would go over better after her first cup of coffee. Or never. Fuck, I wanted to keep all this stress far away, maybe encase her in bubble wrap.

Which was dumb. Rain was a strong, independent woman who didn't need me to shield her from the world. But that didn't mean I would stop trying, or that the urge to protect her would vanish.

"Yeah," she said with a sigh. "I guess I should call them before we—"

"Text me the information and I'll handle it," I offered. When she glanced up from the iPad with a shocked look, I shrugged. "You take care of replacing everything you need immediately. Clothes, shoes, bathing suit...." I gave her a smirk that had most women pulling up their skirts for me.

Instead, Rain just looked confused. "Why would I need a bathing suit immediately?"

"You saw my pool, and you have a day off coming up."

"You know my schedule?" she asked, brows raised.

The chuckle that rumbled in my chest held zero humor. "I think you'd be surprised what all I know about you."

Crimson flared across her cheeks before she dipped her

face back to the screen. The bench back shook with Jameson's quiet laugh.

"So, Slade mentioned something yesterday that I found interesting," Jameson said, tone bland, like he was talking about the weather. "Your parents are in a poly relationship?"

The sip of coffee Rain just took sputtered back into her mug. Grabbing a napkin out of the holder at the end, I handed it over for her to wipe up the droplets dotting her chin.

"Um, yeah. Why?"

Wood groaned as Jameson shifted, angling himself so he could lean back on the wall. "Just interesting. I've... played in the poly world but never heard of anyone who made it work in a long-term relationship. How does it work exactly?"

Sneaky. Sneaky motherfucker.

Forearms to the edge of the table, I leaned closer, very interested to hear her response.

"Um, okay, was not expecting this conversation today. But I'll be honest, it's better than thinking about the growing to-do list to get my house back in order." Her lips curled down in a frown. "Who do I even call to clean up and get rid of the ruined furniture?"

Reaching over, I tapped her wrist, urging her to look my way. "I'll take care of it. Just like the insurance."

"Right, thank you. That's—" She blew out a breath, lips vibrating. "—a huge relief. I can do it, but it's nice knowing I don't have to tackle all this on my own. Same as last night—and thank you for letting me stay here. Really. Not having to figure out a hotel and immediately think of where to get clothes for the next day was...." Her lower lids filled with tears before she jerked her gaze away. "Thank you. I don't know how I can repay you."

"I know of one way," Jameson said around the fakest cough ever. Only to be cut off when my foot connected with the side of his leg. Hard. "Fucking hell. Remember, we're not all part giant."

And just like that, the worry and weight that lingered just seconds ago disappeared from Rain's tight features as her smile grew at our antics.

"Right, well, my parents. Not sure what Slade told you, but my mom is an anthropologist and supports the idea that monogamy doesn't work for long-term relationships. Especially for women like her and me."

"Meaning what?" Jameson prodded.

"Independent, successful, driven. She's studied different cultures and observed that those who incorporated a group-relationship style were happier and more fulfilled. It helps that my dad was fully behind the idea too. Though not for the reasons you'd think. He didn't want the poly relationship so he could see other women. It's only ever been my mom for him. He likes it because he's driven, too, and can't give Mom everything she needs and deserves. Not money wise, but more to do with time and emotional capacity. Growing up, it was always my mom, dad, and Uncle Sam in our house. Obviously, Uncle Sam isn't related at all, but it's what they tell people to avoid the stigma of my mom having two men living with her."

"So, it's those three? Always?" I asked, mind blown at the idea of a long-term poly relationship. Though not in a bad way. Maybe with another's help, I could actually make a marriage work.

"Yep. Now, don't ask me about their sex life." Her shoulders shook with an exaggerated shudder. "I'd plug my ears and run away anytime Mom started raving about it. But yeah, it works for them because they make it work. My mom loves them both equally, and they each bring something different to the relationship." Raising her mug with both hands, she took a long sip, gaze skipping between us over the rim. "Why are you asking me about this?"

Jameson cleared his throat and tapped the top of his laptop. "Per my guy, no one has seen or heard from your ex-husband in over a month. Does he have family he would've gone to who could help him fly under the radar?"

Rain just blinked, mug frozen midair where she'd been slowly lowering it to the table. Fingers wrapped around the bottom, I tugged it out of her hold before she dropped it from the shock of the conversation's detour while kicking Jameson again under the table.

His soft pain-filled grunt made my cold heart happy.

"Oh, um, no family. He was young when his parents passed and didn't keep in contact with any aunts and uncles. Honestly, I don't know of anyone who would take him in. He burned bridges fast. And what do you mean, no one has seen him or heard from him? Doesn't he have a job, coworkers who have seen him?"

I shared a quick look with Jameson. "You don't know if he did or didn't have a job?"

"Nope." She tugged the mug back her way with a fake scowl. "Get your own. I signed the divorce papers and moved on without a single look back. He stopped calling and texting about a year ago. Finally free of him and about to move on with my life without him holding me back, I cut all ties. That makes me sound terrible," she muttered into the mug before taking a sip.

"Not at all," Jameson stated with enough force that it snapped her attention to him. "You got away from that manipulative leech and were smart enough to not keep any ties for him to drag you back into his self-absorbed world."

The alert of movement on the front porch had me swiveling the iPad and tapping on the doorbell app. A scowl pulled at my face, finding an unknown kid at my door. "What the hell is—"

"That will be breakfast," she cheered. "A proper breakfast, not that smoothie crap. I'll be right back." Before I could scoot out of the bench, she was already jogging away.

With her handling the delivery, I tapped the internet icon to see what she was scrolling through. The site for her favorite sneaker brand filled the screen with four pairs of sparkly shoes in the shopping cart. Knowing I had limited time, I hurried to add a few more shoes in her size to the cart before tapping the Apple Pay button, completing the purchase.

With a satisfied smirk, I swiped my almost-empty smoothie glass off the table and leaned back, quite proud of myself.

"Oh hell. What did you do?" she hedged, eyeing me when she came back. The brown bags crinkled as she set them on the table. "You look way too pleased with yourself."

My mind went straight to the gutter at her innocent words.

"Nothing." I cleared my throat. The last few sips of thick liquid filled my mouth as I tipped the glass back, draining the contents. "All right, I'm going to get ready for work. We'll leave in an hour." Standing, I hooked an arm around Rain's waist and yanked her to my side. "Send me the insurance information, and I'll handle it today. Understand?"

Eyes wide, she nodded.

"Words, Rain."

"Yes, sir."

With a grunt, I marched out of the kitchen, needing to take yet another shower.

This time, I'd be envisioning those same words on her lips as she obeyed my every order.

And loving every second.

23

JAMESON

I was a horrible man. Her crazy ex destroyed her house, we had a serial killer to catch, and all I could think about was finding spare time to have her again. Scrubbing a palm over my face, I stared at the laptop screen, silently begging my notes to answer the plethora of hanging questions.

Spoiler alert: it didn't work.

Something helpful might be there, but my brain was being pulled in too many directions to notice. Between the break-in, knowing Rain's ex was somewhere out there toeing that line between stalker and violent threat, and the sexual tension that simmered between me, Rain, and Slade, I couldn't focus for shit.

Which was problematic considering focusing solely on the case was the reason I came to Santa Coasta. My frustration with the case in general didn't help either. It'd been a week, and I still didn't have a strong profile to give to the detectives to help narrow down a suspect pool. And that messed with my head big-time.

Sure, this case was multifaceted with zero evidence and still no firm connection between the victims, but I should've had something solid by now. Doubt crept in every time I looked at the case files and couldn't find anything new. Maybe Rhyan was wrong to hire me and I wasn't cut out for the profiler job. When I'd worked those cases with Cooper, I had someone to lean on, but alone, it was clear I was fucking it all up.

Elbows pressed onto the desk, I held my face in both hands.

"I'm a fucking joke." The words were muffled by my palms. "I need help."

A desperate groan rumbled in my throat as I pressed Charlie's number and hit the speaker icon.

Balancing two cups of coffee in one hand, Slade walked in as the ringing filled the office.

"I'll call you right back. I think I have something for you." The call cut off as quickly as it'd been picked up.

"That your tech friend?" Slade set one to-go coffee cup in front of me while taking a sip of his own. I eyed the cup, unsure of the quality of coffee inside the plain white cardboard. "It's from a decent place around the corner. Not great but not terrible. Come on, you know I wouldn't poison you with the shit they serve upstairs."

Blowing out a slow breath, I snagged the full cup and leaned back in the chair. "Everywhere I turn, I hit a fucking roadblock. This case is...." I took a sip, wincing as the steaming liquid burned my tongue.

"Challenging," Slade offered.

"Making me debate all my life choices."

His bark of laughter made the corners of my lips tug upward. Hand wrapped around the back of the sitting area chair, he dragged the piece of furniture closer to the desk and carefully lowered onto the cushioned seat. I hid a smile behind my cup at the hilarious vision of his massive frame perched on the edge of the small teal armchair.

"After all this time together, I didn't realize you were so damn dramatic." I shrugged, the swirling doubts still clawing at my confidence, and he whistled. "Oh shit, you weren't joking."

"No, I'm not. This is my first case flying solo, and I'm fucking failing everyone."

Slade kept his intense, all-seeing stare locked on me as he took a long drink from his coffee. "And you're thinking that because we don't have a solid list of suspects after you've only been here—alone, like you pointed out—a week?"

"Among other things, yeah," I muttered, lips hovering over the plastic lid.

"Listen." A creak came from the chair's joints as Slade shifted his weight forward. "I'll be real honest with you right now." My heart sank into my stomach. *Fuck, I knew he would agree with me. How could he not?* "You're being fucking dumb." My head popped up. "You have a basic profile, which is a shit ton more than I had before you got here. Caucasian female, late-twenties to-early-thirties, lives in or around Santa Coasta. Smart, educated on how to not leave evidence at a crime scene, so either a crime show addict or has worked with police or forensics before. Just because we haven't found her yet doesn't mean you're failing. It just means we work that much harder to be as smart as she thinks she is."

"I hate those damn forensics shows. Educating criminals on what not to leave behind."

Slade smirked. "Thank fuck that them learning what to not do or leave behind and actually following through are two very different things."

I lifted my cup in the air and tipped my head. "True that."

The chime of my cell pulled our attention to the device. Tapping the green circle, I then hit the speaker icon. "Hey, Charlie. Please tell me you have something that can break this damn case wide open. I need something, anything."

"That's a big ask, but I might have just that." I flicked a hopeful expression to Slade before focusing back on the phone. "I did a deeper dive like you asked, and something came up for the second victim. At seventeen, he was accused of sexual assault by a woman with prior arrests for solicitation. His name was mentioned in her statement, but it doesn't look like it moved past her accusation."

The cup crumpled beneath Slade's tightening fist. "Because some old-school assholes don't believe those women have the right to say no." The obvious anger caused his voice to shake. "Tell me the idiot who took the statement still works here so I can go have a few words about 'her body, her choice.'"

"I don't know who said that, but I like you already."

"Sorry, you're on speakerphone," I explained. "That was Detective Taylor. It's just us two in the office. You're good to talk freely."

"Sorry to tell you, Detective, but that officer retired a while ago and passed away from health-related issues last year." My shoulders deflated. "But they listed her name on the statement. Carly Rogers, and she still lives in Santa Coasta. From going through her bank account and work history, she moved on from that life and now works full-time at a small diner named Bec's."

My brows flew up my forehead. "Isn't that where you took me that first day I was here?" Slade nodded. "I know the place, so just send me her home address and—"

My phone lit up with an incoming text.

"Already done. But that's not all I have." My jaw snapped shut at that. "There was a second assailant she accused, but I couldn't find a name. Her statement just said there was another present during the assault." My stomach dropped. "And I'm not done. Your first murder victim was named as a person of interest in a date rape case but never charged. There wasn't any evidence. The victim came in days after the assault, and it looks like they swept it under the rug before anything official was filed."

"Are there recordings from either the accused being interviewed or the original report from the victim?" Slade asked. "Depending on those, we could get lucky. Video recordings are now required for statements and interviews."

"I don't see anything, but the recordings library is massive. I'll search through those next. But that woman's name is Pam Chase. I'm sending you her work and home address." He paused, but I knew he wasn't done. "Bend, when you interview these two, stay alert and be careful."

"What about me?" Slade chuffed.

"I don't know you. You're on your own. Bend's boss is my partner. A lot more rides on his safety than yours." Humor laced Charlie's tone, making me smirk. "Just kidding. I guess you matter too."

"Thanks," Slade groused. "You're thinking either of these two could be our unsub?"

"Maybe," I offered instead of waiting for Charlie to respond. "Though if that's the case, it still leaves us with a major question left unanswered."

Slade's brow furrowed, working through my words. I

knew the moment he figured out what I meant. "How would she know the other murder victims if she only went after the man who attacked her?"

I dipped my chin in a firm nod. We had more questions, but at least now there was a warm lead to investigate. Better than I'd started the day with.

"Thanks, Charlie. These are solid leads to look into. I'll let you know what we have after meeting with those women." After hitting the red dot to end the call, I stood and stretched both arms over my head, grumbling at the ache from my bullet wound. "Are you coming with me or sticking around here to work other cases?"

Slade slowly stood. "Coming."

At the door, I paused and sent a concerned expression over my shoulder. "This time, let me ask the questions. Their past trauma mixed with your size and demeanor—"

"I take offense to that. I'm all fucking sunshine and roses."

A snort escaped as I pushed open the door. "Right. You keep thinking that in your alternate reality, but here in the real world, you're unapproachable and could scare these women. Let me take the lead, and if we sense they're uncomfortable, we back off immediately."

"Should we call Rain, then? The women might feel more comfortable with her there with us. I don't want to cause them any additional pain just to work this angle of the case."

I started to agree but stopped. "If one of these two women is our unsub, I don't want Rain anywhere near them. Is there someone else we could reach out to?" The female detective from last night immediately popped into my head. "Call that detective who came by Rain's place—Detective Gray, I think. See if she's free. I can easily prep her if the women aren't comfortable with me conducting the interview and she needs to ask the questions."

Outside, the warm afternoon sun made a rare appearance, breaking through the gloom and amping up the heat index. Thankfully, I'd dressed down today in just a pair of navy slacks and a white button-up, no tie or vest. It felt amazing, not nearly as constricting as my full suit, but I hated looking less professional, especially when conducting interviews. Though somehow Slade pulled off this look daily, always forgoing a tie and most of the time a jacket as well.

Standing beside the turd mobile, waiting for Slade to finish the call with Detective Gray, I leaned against the hot metal and pulled out my phone. A smile tugged at the corners of my lips as I scrolled through the few texts Rain sent to the group thread while out shopping to replace her ruined clothes and pick up some basic necessities.

"She's busy today, but her partner volunteered to help. She'll meet us there." I turned, phone still in hand, as I listened to Slade while responding to Rain. "Shoot me the address and I'll get it to her. I think you're right, having a female present is a solid idea."

"You sound surprised," I huffed as I climbed into the passenger seat while forwarding the text from Charlie to Slade. "I have all the great ideas." A slow, mischievous grin spread across my face. "You seemed to agree when you watched last night."

"Fucking hell," Slade muttered. After forwarding my text to the detective's partner, he steered the turd mobile out onto the street. "Let's not talk about that right now."

I held up both hands in surrender.

Barely two minutes had passed in silence when he

tossed up his hand in frustration. "Fuck, fine. Yes, I liked it, okay?" He blew out a breath and rubbed a hand along his jaw. "And I'm not going to lie. How she described her parents' relationship this morning... it's intriguing."

"Why is that?" I was almost certain I knew the answer, but he needed to realize it, too, if the three of us had a chance of working.

"I've already failed at three marriages. And I know for a fact that I was the reason none of them worked out. I'm terrible at communicating and being there emotionally, which both apparently make up a big chunk of healthy relationships." He shifted his bulk in the seat, changing hands on the steering wheel like he was uncomfortable with admitting all this out loud. "It could be nice to not carry the full weight of the relationship on my shoulders." He cut me a pointed scowl. "I still don't want to touch your dick."

My laugh rumbled through the car. "And I still don't want you touching it. Just stating that again, for the record, so there's no gray area in that regard."

"Let's just see how it goes. I don't want to push her into anything."

I arched a single brow at his oblivious ass. "Yeah, pretty sure she'll push *you* once she knows for sure you're open to the three of us."

"I still don't deserve someone like her. She'll figure that out pretty quick."

And there it was. The dip in his tone spoke to how the idea of having Rain and then losing her was his deepest fear.

"What if she realizes that this, the three of us, is what she needs? Or if she sees all these hang-ups you think you have and doesn't give two shits? Rain knows your age, knows you've been married, and hell, she knows you can't move without complaining—"

"Are you going somewhere with this?"

"I wasn't finished, asshole. She sees all of that and still lights up when you enter the room. She called you last night when she was afraid and needed someone. Rain called *you*. Not me. You're the one she knows will run through a brick wall to keep her safe. Sure, I might understand her a little more emotionally, but she sees you as her protector. Everything you're concerned about, she already knows, and she still sees you as the man who can make everything right again."

He said nothing for the rest of the drive, which was fine. He needed to realize soon that it wasn't just him infatuated with Rain. She felt the same. It was on her face any time he was in the room, and then the way she fell apart last night with him watching confirmed it all. My cock shifted at the memory of her tightening around me, her cries ringing in my ear.

"Looks like the partner beat us here," Slade mumbled, pointing at a dark blue sedan parked along the curb. A woman with short brown hair leaned against the car, turning our way as Slade pulled in behind her.

Out on the sidewalk, I adjusted my sidearm to a more comfortable position on my hip and moved in unison with Slade toward the waiting detective.

"Detective Savage?" She dipped her chin at Slade and shoved off her car, hands firmly in the pockets of her blazer. "I've seen you around, but we haven't formally met." He motioned to himself, then me. "Detective Taylor and Special Agent Bend with the FBI."

Her dark eyes cut over and drilled into me. I stilled, sensing any sudden moves would be a terrible decision.

Instead of small talk, she went straight into the reason for the meetup.

"Jen gave me the rundown on why you wanted a female present. It's best if I approach her first, address why we're here, and make sure she's comfortable with you two entering her space." I arched a brow, truly impressed with the idea, which she must have caught. "I worked the sex crimes division in LA before moving here."

"It's a smart approach. Let's do it the way you suggested. Detective Taylor and I don't want to make this uncomfortable for them. But I want to warn you to be alert. One of these women might be our unsub."

She rolled her shoulders and shot me a scathing glare. "I will not let you walk in there and accuse them of—"

I tossed up both hands, palms out. "I'm telling you this for your safety. If things feel off, then you get out of there. These women have been through enough already. I swear we'll treat them with the utmost respect."

"Good, because I doubt they got that the first time around," she spat, still clearly furious. "Follow me and wait down the hall. Once I get her permission for you to enter, I'll wave you two inside."

No one spoke as we were buzzed through the metal security gate and made our way through the complex. All the doors faced a small courtyard of sorts filled with colorful flowers and neatly trimmed bushes. The complex appeared well-kept and safe. Behind my dark lenses, I searched the roofline for cameras. If she was our unsub, then video of her coming and going during the times of the murders would be huge. Or it could give her an alibi without us even having to ask if it wasn't her.

Detective Savage held up a hand in a silent command for us to wait and then ascended the flight of metal stairs toward the second level. Her quiet knock resonated in the silent courtyard, followed by a murmured voice.

"I don't think she likes us," Slade said offhandedly.

"After seeing everything she has, and no doubt the injustice that comes with these types of crimes, I'm not sure I'd like anyone of our gender either." Adjusting my stance, I eased a little more into the shade and slipped my sunglasses off. "One thing I learned from my sisters is we, males in general, have no idea how exhausting it is to constantly be on alert like women have to be these days. We walk into a bar and look for an empty stool or our friends. They walk in, assess the crowd, and immediately pick out the threats and saviors."

"Threats I get—men who look sleazy or something like that—but saviors?"

"Big men who look like they would kick ass for an unknown woman in trouble. Women have a gut instinct for that sort of thing. At least my sisters say they do. Women have to do twice the work to ensure they're safe compared to us. Driving alone, living alone, running alone —like I said, exhausting and sometimes demoralizing. Which, if you want to hear my theory, is one reason women are so drawn to you. They see you, a big-ass man and protector, and immediately know they're safe when you're around."

"And here I thought it was my money and fame," he said with a smirk.

"I'm sure that helps."

"And my huge cock."

I shook my head and turned at the movement on the second level, finding Detective Savage waving for us to come up.

"You know," I said as I trailed behind Slade up the stairs,

"you have a strange fascination with your cock and people wanting to touch it."

He chuckled. "Isn't that a guy thing?"

"Touché."

All humor vanished the moment we walked into the small apartment. Sitting on a tiny cream love seat, perched on the edge, the woman we came to see glared at us with a defiant look in her hard gaze.

"Ms. Rogers, I'm Special Agent Bend." I flashed her my credentials, then pointed to Slade, who showed his badge. "And this is Detective Taylor. We wanted to ask you a few questions about an accusation you made several years—"

"So now the police give a shit?" she hissed. "Years have gone by with those two assholes free to do the same thing to others as they did to me." She stood, wobbling a little. I fought the urge to reach out and steady her. As if feeling my internal debate, she swung a glare my way. "And now that they're dead, you come asking questions, believing me."

"Ma'am—" Slade started, but she slashed a hand through the air, cutting him off.

"No, I didn't do it. I work too many hours to squeeze in the time to murder those bastards. But I sure as hell am glad someone got them. I'll sleep a little better at night knowing —" Her voice cracked. After clearing her throat, she shot a tentative peek at Detective Savage. "I changed my mind. I won't answer any of your questions, sorry. You three need to leave."

With no resistance or complaint, Slade and I hurried back out the way we came. At the bottom of the stairs, we stopped to wait for Detective Savage, who no doubt stayed behind to do damage control.

"Did you catch that?" Slade mumbled under his breath in case anyone was listening.

I nodded. "Yep."

At least the visit wasn't a complete waste.

We now knew one of the other murder victims was the additional attacker she'd mentioned in her original statement.

Why else would she say she was glad someone killed *them*?

24

RAIN

"And that's the last of it." The shopping bag handles slipped from my fingers, tumbling onto the already crowded bed. "I'm ready for a bath and sleep. In-person shopping is exhausting. Ordering everything online is way easier."

"Exhausting but instant. Now you don't have to wait for things to be delivered," Slade said at my back.

I smiled over my shoulder, smothering a laugh at him peering around the tall stack of shoeboxes and searching for space to set them down.

"Did you get something for your court appearance tomorrow?" he asked.

I jerked a thumb toward the closet where a new pantsuit waited inside the black clothing bag. Testifying in court or being called upon as an expert witness was not my favorite aspect of the ME job, but it happened frequently, and having a sharp outfit or two on rotation was a must.

My fingers fumbled through the tissue paper in a Nordstrom bag, searching for my new soft pajamas, when my stomach growled loudly. Looking up through my lashes, I found Slade's standard scowl directed my way.

"What?"

"Rain. Did you eat lunch?"

I scoffed. "What kind of question is that?"

His lips pressed into a thin line. "A valid one by the way you're deflecting and the sounds coming from your stomach."

"A gentleman doesn't comment on the sounds coming from a woman." I cringed. "Stomach. A woman's stomach. Or any bodily functions, really. We're not nearly as secure in ourselves as—"

A thick arm wrapped around my waist and hauled me against his chest, making me squeal. My hair slipped over one shoulder as I leaned to the side, searching Slade's face.

"Let's get one thing straight." Closing the gap, he paused when our noses brushed. "I'm no fucking gentleman, baby. But you'll find that out for yourself soon enough."

I swallowed hard, throat dry as my breaths quickened. "When?" Because from the way my body heated with his possessive hold and the darkened look in his eyes, I was ready now.

What was I thinking? I'd been ready since the day I met him.

"Soon." The earlier scowl transformed into a cocky smirk. "But right now, I need to feed you and Jameson dinner. It's past eight, and we're all hungry."

I licked my dry lips, about to tell him I didn't want to wait until later, but he closed the distance, brushing his lips over my own before sealing them together.

The world slowed to a stop. Nothing around us mattered except for the dominant feel of the kiss and his possessive hold around my waist. A gentle vibration came from him, the moan barely audible but enough to urge me closer.

Turning, I wrapped both arms around his chest, fingertips barely touching along his spine as I sealed my body to his. Liquid heat pulsed through my veins as his firm length pressed into my stomach. I shifted, rubbing against him, making us both gasp as pleasure skyrocketed through every cell.

After another moment of him kissing the soul out of me, Slade pulled back, grumbling a curse.

"If we start this." He pressed his forehead to mine, his quick breaths fanning across my face. Good to know I wasn't the only one struggling to regain some composure. "I won't stop."

"Fine by me," I rasped, swaying into him. "Food is overrated anyway. The body can go days without it."

His light chuckle caught me off guard, but it was the wide smile and the emotion I couldn't read behind his green eyes that made my heart skip a beat.

"Later. All good things come to those who wait." Sliding his hand along my arm, he entangled our fingers and raised my hand, planting a kiss on the palm. So simple, yet it was as if he'd licked my core with the way my entire body sang with tingling pleasure. Holy hell, he was good, and I was way out of my league here. "Did you buy a bathing suit like I told you to?"

"Two, actually."

"Good girl," he praised.

Those two words sent my stomach flipping. Pressing my thighs together, I attempted to ease the steady throb the entire five-minute encounter had created, but it only made it worse.

"Go ahead and put one on, then meet us out by the

pool," he ordered. "I'll cook everything I got from the store on the grill outside. And don't worry, the water is heated. Jameson is already in."

Well, there went that argument.

"Will you swim?" I asked, slipping my hand free from his to dig through the mountain of bags for the one that held the swimsuits.

"Maybe." Still feeling his presence hovering in the doorway, I chanced a look over my shoulder. His gaze was locked firmly on my ass. "Or maybe I'll just watch."

He disappeared around the doorframe, leaving me frozen, jaw slack. Would he just watch me, or me and Jameson? Because he'd said "meet us" by the pool.

I so wanted to find out.

Clothes tumbled through the air as I tossed bags over my shoulder, hurrying to find the one I needed. A wash of relief was chased by a tsunami of excited anticipation when I pulled the tiny bloodred bikini free from the tissue paper.

I'd bought it with them in mind, knowing the color would look amazing against my skin, and the scraps of material were perfect to accentuate my long, toned legs and firm body. I might not have curves like I wanted, but I still looked good and knew how to highlight my tall, lean frame.

After cutting the tags and securing the barely-there bathing suit, I pulled the long sheer black cover-up from the bag and slipped my arms through the billowing sleeves. Despite knowing the two men waiting were in fact attracted to me and both had already seen me naked, nerves made my steps cautious as I tiptoed down the hall.

The sound of splashing water had me easing around the living room furniture toward the open glass door. Pausing, I leaned against the metal doorframe, taking in the panty-dropping scene. In a movie-worthy move, Jameson pushed himself out of the water, his arms flexing and showing off every defined muscle as he emerged from the pool. I wiped at the corners of my lips to make sure the massive amount of saliva collecting in my mouth hadn't escaped.

Water ran in hundreds of rivers along his bare skin, the already tight boxer briefs now suctioned to him. His firm ass cheeks bunched with every step he took along the pool deck. My hand shot out, holding on to the door to keep me upright when he stopped beside a bare-chested Slade standing in front of a large steel grill. Even though I had a glimpse earlier that morning, seeing his tattoo-covered skin still sent my mind and hormones reeling. The designs blended perfectly, like they were all done at the same time instead of the years I assumed it took to accumulate.

When both turned their full focus on me, a shock raced through me like I'd gripped a live wire with two hands. The burst of energy made me tremble, and my heart skipped a beat before racing like I'd just run a full marathon.

"You coming out, Raindrop?" Jameson asked, moving away from Slade toward where I stood frozen. "The water feels amazing."

With a shaky breath, I stepped away from the doorframe, the wind catching my cover-up and exposing my mostly naked body to both men.

Jameson stumbled a step but recovered quickly. "Holy fuck. And I thought you naked was the hottest image I'd ever see." Dipping one finger inside the sheer material, he pushed it aside, exposing my shoulder to the cool night air. "This is a very close second."

Words failed me, my heart hammering too hard against my chest to take a full breath, so I simply smiled and shrugged. The feel of their eyes, knowing they traced every part of me and committed it to memory, was empowering instead of the opposite like other men made me feel. These two knew me. Knew my quirks, saw me for more than my body. They respected me and wanted me.

And that intoxicating combination almost had me crying.

How long had I longed for a complete, well-rounded relationship? To have brain-stimulating conversations, easy banter, and attraction? This, what was building between the three of us, had it all. And it felt natural. Sure, my parents' relationship helped open my mind to the idea of being attracted to more than one person, but even if they hadn't, this would still feel normal.

"Hey, you okay?"

The concern in Jameson's voice had me pushing up to my tiptoes and pressing a chaste kiss to his lips. Peering over his shoulder, I caught Slade watching.

"Yeah, I'm great, actually." Pinching his waistband between two fingers, I snapped it against his skin. "No swimsuit shopping for you?"

He draped his arm across my shoulders and directed us toward Slade. "I didn't have time to buy any, and his swim trunks aren't actual trunks." Leaning closer, he pressed his lips to my loose wavy hair. "They're practically Speedos. And I'd rather go skinny-dipping than wear one of those."

"They're not Speedos," Slade grumbled, but the twitch of his lips was proof he wasn't upset at all. "They're what you're wearing right now, just a little shorter. A shit ton more comfortable than loose board shorts."

"And they show off your biggest asset," Jameson chuckled.

My eyes widened at the innuendo.

"We all know it's not my bubbly personality that attracts women." Jameson laughed at that, his body shaking against mine. "Grilled salmon with a honey balsamic glaze, roasted brussels sprouts, and seasoned red potato squares. Does that sound good to you both?" Slade asked.

My stomach rumbled in response, and I pressed a hand to it in hopes it would help keep it quiet. "Good? Sounds delicious. You plan to make it all?"

"I like to cook," Slade said with a nonchalant shrug. He pointed the tongs toward the side of the house. "I have a garden where I grow fresh herbs and a few vegetables. It's fun to experiment, but tonight I'm going with something basic."

"Basic," I stated. "Basic is me ordering fish tacos from DoorDash. This is gourmet."

His answering grin was almost shy and sweet. "Well, hopefully you like it. We'll eat in about forty-five minutes. I'll put the salmon on last."

"Come swim with me," Jameson whispered, his lips hovering along the sheer material covering my shoulder.

Without waiting for an answer, he interlaced our fingers and tugged me toward the sparkling water. The underwater lights slowly changed from purple to pink to blue, giving the entire scene a surreal feel.

The light fabric swept down my arms as Jameson helped me out of the cover-up. I chanced a look over my shoulder. Slade watched, those green eyes sweeping up and down my body the same way I felt Jameson's taking in every bare inch from the other side.

The intensity of the moment, one I'd never felt in my life, suddenly became too much.

Shooting them both a wicked grin, I leaped from the edge and dove gracefully into the deep end of the pool. Warm water caressed my skin as I glided from one end of the pool to the other without coming up for air. At the shallow end, I crested the surface.

Before I could blink, an arm wrapped around my waist.

For one second, one breath, I relished that arm.

Until it tightened and a wicked laugh sounded above the water lapping against the tile. Between heartbeats, I broke the surface and went sailing through the air. A half giggle, half shriek filled the air, something that sounded like it came from a little kid, just before I crashed back into the pool. Bubbles drifted up all around me as I slowly sank toward the bottom, enjoying the calm and weightlessness for a few precious seconds. When my ass hit the smooth bottom, I kicked off, rocketing back toward the surface.

My wet hair slapped side to side as I searched the pool for the soon-to-be dead man. Not that I could do anything about it, but it was fun feeling playful. I hadn't had this lightness in my heart in way too long. I felt younger, happier, despite nothing changing but the way these two men made me feel.

"You," I yelled, though I couldn't hide my laugh when Jameson pointed innocently at the very dry Slade. "You're going down."

"Bring it on, Raindrop. Do your worst."

After several failed attempts at trying to dunk Jameson, I called a truce and swam to the edge. Hands on the sandstone tile that surrounded the pool, I pushed myself out of the water, twisting so my wet ass slapped to the stone with my legs still hanging in the warm water. Out of nowhere, a large fluffy towel was wrapped across my shoulders. When I turned my face up, smiling in thanks at Slade, he stroked a finger down my cheek and went back to the grill.

I watched him, so very thankful for the one-eighty change in the man I used to think only saw me as a coworker. I wanted to ask what happened but didn't want to jinx it in case he suddenly changed his mind and went back to that wide professional bubble.

Hands wrapped around my ankles and slowly slid up to my calves, turning my attention to the man nestled between my knees. The water lapped against his chest as he stared up with those honey-brown eyes, his hands kneading my sore muscles as they inched higher and higher.

"Thank you," he whispered.

"For what?" I laughed. "For sucking at water games?"

"Based on last night, your sucking is nothing to be ashamed of," he commented with a slow grin. Though as soon as it formed, it faded just as fast. "Today was tough. The interviews...." With a sigh, he moved forward until he could press light kisses along the inside of one knee before switching to the other. "Tomorrow. We can talk about it tomorrow. Right now, I just want to get lost in tonight. Forget the reason I'm here, why we're both staying here, and live in the moment like our jobs don't darken our souls a little more every day."

His wet strands slid through my fingers as I raked them along his scalp. Lids closed, he pressed a cheek against my inner thigh. Scraping my nails down the back of his neck, I watched as his skin pebbled beneath my touch.

"I love you." I stilled, unsure if I'd heard him right. "I know it's fast, and you don't have to say it in return, Raindrop, but I do. Fuck that—I *have*. I might have loved you when you were still married."

Tears filled my lower lids. I completely understood what he meant because I felt the same. It was more than a crush, more than friends, even back then.

"Just know that we'll figure this out." He pointed to me,

then himself. "Because I'm not letting you slip out of my life again without a fight."

Holding him steady, I leaned forward and pressed my lips to his in an emotion-filled kiss, letting all my pent-up feelings for him flow from my heart into his.

"I'm not just saying this because you did. I wouldn't do that to you. But the truth is, I feel the exact same way about you, Jameson. It started back in Nashville and never stopped for me. Maybe that makes me a terrible person, but—"

"It doesn't."

I shrugged a single shoulder and pressed a soft kiss to his lips. "I love you. More than I should considering the time frame, but like we've both said, this is more than the now."

Jameson inhaled deeply. "Fuck, that sounds amazing coming from your lips. I can't wait to hear it again, and again, because there is no getting rid of me now, Rain."

"Good." I gave him an adoring grin. "I needed tonight," I said, leaning back on my elbows and tipping my face up to the dark night sky. "I haven't felt this free and amazing in ages."

With a smile on my lips, I dipped my chin, only for my breath to catch at the hungry expression on Jameson's face. Keeping his hooded gaze locked on me, he turned just enough to nip at my inner thigh. A gasp parted my lips. The hand on the opposite knee crept higher until his fingertips dipped beneath the red material of my bikini bottoms.

His brows lifted a fraction, a silent question if I wanted this.

I licked my lips and shifted along the smooth tile, spreading my legs in invitation to continue. This was what I needed. A night with no stress, no work. Free-falling into the sexual pull that clicked higher with every look and touch from either of them.

The thin ties at my hips unraveled beneath his deft fingers. My abs contracted with every quick breath, making the water drops fall over my side and drip to the pool deck. Inch by inch, he drew the scrap of material lower, exposing my core to the soft cool breeze.

Movement in my periphery had me resting my chin on my shoulder. Dinner forgotten, Slade had moved closer, now perched on the nearby lounge chair, tree-trunk legs spread wide with his elbows pressed on top of both thick thighs.

His stare took in every exposed inch of my trimmed mound as Jameson's finger slowly stroked along the slick middle. Knuckles white, he restrained his hands clasped between his knees, as if holding himself back from smacking Jameson's hands away to replace them with his own.

Heart thundering, I sucked in a shaky breath at the amazing sensation of Jameson's tongue following the same path of his probing fingers.

"Pull your top down, Raindrop," he whispered, lips teasing against my slick core. "Show Slade how fucking perfect your tits are for sucking. I bet he won't be able to resist wrapping his lips around you."

Wet hair cascaded down my spine as my back arched, my head tipped back at the swell of desire his words sent rushing through my veins. Elbows on the pool deck, I dipped a finger beneath the red triangle-shaped material and pulled both sides down. A desperate moan escaped me at the night air brushing against my hard nipples.

"Fuck."

I barely turned toward Slade's voice, lips parted. His heated gaze flicked up from my naked chest to my face. A fresh rush of desire soaked my center at the heat and possessiveness in those glittering green eyes.

"Are you going to eat her cunt or just play with it all night?" he snapped at Jameson without breaking eye contact. A shiver zipped down my spine at the dominance in Slade's dark tone.

Without a word, Jameson pulled my lips apart with both thumbs, leaving every part of me visible to his hungry stare, and sealed his mouth over my swollen clit, sucking in quick succession before dipping lower. A frustrated grumble carried on the breeze a second before my ass slid along the smooth tile until my backside hung dangerously over the rounded edge of the pool. With an ass cheek in each hand, Jameson squeezed before spreading me wide again, holding me less than an inch from his face.

"Look at how perfect this pretty pink pussy is," he said, tone soft and hungry. His breath fanned along my hot, slick center, making me tremble on the deck.

"I want you to fuck her with your tongue." I squeezed my lids shut at Slade's command. "And you, baby, pinch those tips, imagining me biting hard enough to leave a mark."

Jameson thrust his tongue deep into my core before flattening it to lick upward and latch on to my clit. Over and over, he repeated the teasing cycle.

There wasn't enough air. My mind spun as he pushed me higher and higher. The coolness of the night was gone, the lust-fueled heat thrumming in my veins causing sweat to slick my overheated skin.

"Now, Rain." Another shiver whispered through me at his tone. The first brush of my fingertips along the curve of my breast caused goose bumps to sprout across my skin. "Look at me." My sealed lids snapped open, immediately finding him. "Do you hear that, baby? That's not the pool.

That's Jameson eating your soaked pussy and fucking loving every drop you're giving him." I tried to shift in Jameson's hold, but it tightened, keeping me exactly where he wanted me. "Now, baby. This is what I want you to do. Are you listening?" Lips parted, dry from my fast pants, I nodded. "Every time Jameson pushes his tongue into your perfect cunt, you pluck at those perfect tits."

A pitiful whimper sounded over the whirl of the pool's jets as I did exactly as he instructed. Every pinch and tug wound me tighter, my hips thrusting, grinding myself against Jameson's face as my orgasm built.

"Are you close, baby?"

I nodded, unable to utter a coherent word.

I didn't break Slade's stare when he stood and moved to the lounge chair directly beside my head. The thick outline of his hard cock beneath his shorts had my trembling fingers reaching, desperate to wrap around him. But he gently grasped my wrist, stopping me. Keeping my hand hostage, he moved it lower, a wicked gleam in his hooded gaze.

"Jameson. Move back."

I hissed in complaint when Jameson pulled away, leaving me hot and desperate for his mouth. Licking his lips, Jameson smiled at my exaggerated scowl. "Don't worry, Raindrop. We won't leave you this wet and needy for long."

Before I understood what Slade had planned, he tangled our fingers together, slid two of mine and one of his into my drenched core, and thrust deep, curling the tips to brush along my sensitive walls. My entire body trembled at the stretch and overstuffed feeling.

"Please," I begged, my other arm shaking, barely holding my weight.

Teasingly slow, Slade pulled our fingers free, the

evidence of my arousal glistening on our skin. He hitched his chin at Jameson, who moved back into place and pushed his tongue inside.

"Open up, baby." I parted my lips, giving Slade access to slide our slick fingers against my tongue. "Now suck like I'm in your mouth, stretching your jaw so wide it fucking hurts." His free hand gently wrapped around my throat and squeezed. "Suck like you're desperate to lick up every fucking drop I give you."

The combination of the taste of myself, having my mouth full, and his dirty words shot me over the edge into oblivion. With a pleasure-filled cry, I clamped my thighs around Jameson's head, hips bucking to keep the blissed-out feeling from ending.

All while I exploded and slowly came back together, I licked and sucked our fingers, imagining Slade's cock filling my mouth, tapping my throat. Muscles trembling, my arm gave out, but a massive hand cupped my head, easing me to the smooth tile.

I blinked up at the dark sky, a lazy smile pulling at my lips.

Who knew life could be like this? Though I knew it wasn't common, this was special beyond words.

I wanted to keep them, keep us just like this.

Forever.

25

RAIN

"That was amazing." I swiped the thick cloth napkin across my lips before tossing it onto my empty plate. "I can't believe you cooked everything on the grill."

The corner of Slade's lips twitched upward. "I knew I wouldn't want to miss out on all the fun by being stuck in the kitchen. I'm glad you liked it."

I twisted in my seat to check on Jameson, finding him exactly where I last saw him—still asleep in one of the lounge chairs, covered up with a towel, his barely touched beer beside him, the glass slick with condensation. My mostly dry hair moved across my back as I shook my head and turned back around to see Slade watching me.

"What?" I asked, reaching for my beer. "You're looking at me funny."

"Are you sure you're okay with this?" he asked. Grabbing his highball glass, he rolled it between his palms. "Me and him."

Nodding, I took a long drink, giving myself time to think over my response. One that would make sense to anyone other than myself.

"Jameson is...." I sighed and pressed the icy bottle to my hot cheeks. "He's emotionally supportive. He gets me and somehow understands even when I haven't worked it out yet myself. He makes me laugh, and even before this happened between me and him, he wanted to be around me. Back in Nashville, he was really one of my only friends. I looked forward to seeing him every day—maybe more than I should have, considering I was still married, but I did."

"You tried to find a sliver of happiness in a shitty situation. You clinging to Jameson during that time is understandable. And from what you've both said, he helped you see through the bullshit your ex made you believe as truth."

I stared at the beer bottle, swiping the cold drops of condensation as they worked their way down the brown glass. "Yeah. He made me believe in myself again." I peeked up through my lashes. "And then there's you. I feel safe with you, like nothing can hurt me if you're around. You make the weight of doing all this, doing everything on my own, not feel so fucking heavy. Even when you were still grumpy Detective Taylor." Slade snorted and took a sip of his whiskey. "I knew I could count on you. I don't have that in my life, outside of my parents. And you being you made me feel cared for and not so invisible, I guess."

"You've never been invisible to me," Slade rasped. "Not one day has gone by since I met you that I didn't want to see you, to see you smile or laugh or hear you rattle off some random-ass thought."

"Well, you know you'd always get that last one with me," I laughed.

"Rain." The beer bottle hovered just over my lips. My stomach dipped at the heaviness of his tone. "I don't think I can do this with you." I stopped breathing, and my heart dropped to my stomach. "Not if it's something you only want for just a fun fuck or while Jameson is here."

"I don't understand," I whispered. The bottom of the glass thumped to the wooden table. "You do or don't want me?"

His green eyes locked with mine. "I want you so fucking much that I know if I have you once, I'll never let you go."

"Oh." Dumbest response ever to the hottest, most possessive and perfect statement. "Why do you think I would want you to let me go? Look at you, Slade. You're famous, rich, hotter than the seventh circle of hell, and can have any woman you want. I should be the one worried about that."

So why wasn't I? Why hadn't I worked up at least five worst-case scenarios for how all this was a terrible decision and I'd end up mortified or dead at the end? Even now, sitting with Slade, my thoughts didn't wander.

It was them. It had to be them keeping me from spinning out of control and anchored in the present.

"I don't want any woman. I want you." *Swoon.* "But only if you can see this being more. I'm past all the one-night stands and quick fucks, Rain. I want more with you. I'm not saying I'll turn you down if that's all you want from me, but don't expect me to let go easily when you toss me aside."

"Slade." I reached over and gripped his wrist. "Why would I do that?"

This was crazy. This amazing man was worried that *I'd* be the one who wouldn't want *him*. Did he ever look in the mirror or see the heads turn anytime he walked by? Because I sure as hell did.

"I'm over ten years older than you," he said through gritted teeth.

"I'm aware, considering I might have done a little

stalking when we first met. Nothing too deep, just dating back to when you were born." He offered me a half smile. "I'm okay with the age difference."

"I can barely walk in the mornings. My body is used the fuck up and—"

"Still looks fucking climbable."

"What?" he chuckled.

"Just saying. For someone like me, who's all legs and arms, your size is an enormous turn-on. I can run and jump on you like a flying squirrel, and you won't fall down."

"That's oddly specific. Thought about that a lot?"

"You have no idea," I muttered into the beer bottle. "It seems you're only focusing on the things that could turn me off from us. How about I tell you what makes me *want* a relationship with you?" He nodded in agreement, though it was slow and unsure. "You understand all aspects of my job. You don't make me feel creepy about what I do or zone out when I ramble about my dead bodies." His lips curved at the corners, and I snorted. "Or think it's strange when I claim the dead bodies as my own. You realize the long hours I have to put in, recognize I'm independent but still do things for me without me having to ask. You just do it because you're always putting my needs first. And I'm not saying all this because of the past few days. You've shown bits and pieces of the amazing man you are over the past year. I see you—the real you. I just hope I can offer you, and Jameson, something in all this."

"You being you is all we need," Slade whispered. Glass edge to his lips, he tipped it back, draining the remaining liquid before setting it down on the table.

"I'm pretty sure I'm getting the better end of this deal," I admitted, tucking a lock of hair behind my ear. "I meant to ask you earlier. How close are we to the ocean? Every now and then I feel like I can hear waves."

"Very close. There's a spot I know that's hardly ever crowded that the three of us can check out."

A wide smile split my face. As if hearing me talk, a powerful gust of salt-laced cool air whipped around the backyard, causing a chill to slip down my spine. I pulled the cover-up tighter around my body to fight the cold.

"Come on." Pushing off the chair's armrests, he stood, rounded the table, and held out a hand to help me up.

I eagerly slipped my palm against his, shivering at the way his massive hand engulfed mine. "What about Jameson? Should we wake him up and bring him inside too?"

"We could, but we're not going inside," Slade tossed over his shoulder, leading me past the outdoor furniture. He inclined his head toward the spa that pushed a waterfall over into the main pool. "Care to join me? The heat helps my muscles and moving the next day a little easier."

"I would've said yes without the additional therapeutic benefit," I said with a huffed chuckle. "But add that into the mix and of course I'll join you."

With gentle hands, he helped me out of the cover-up, draping it over the back of a nearby chair. Keeping a steady hold, Slade assisted me over the knee-high stone ledge. The steaming water caused a prickling sensation everywhere it caressed as I slowly eased myself into the spa. With a sigh, I leaned back, resting my head on the edge.

I tracked Slade as he grabbed two dry towels off the rack and dropped them onto a chair. With zero flare or teasing, he hooked both thumbs into the waistband of his loose shorts and tugged them down. The black cloth pooled at his feet. I nearly swallowed my tongue as I took in the oh-so-short black swim trunks that fit snugly around every thick inch of his legs and... well, everywhere.

He was perfection in a rock-solid body. The tattoos that covered his chest down to the middle of his abs, with his size, gave him a menacing vibe until I looked into his bright green eyes and knew deep down in my gut that he'd rather kill himself than hurt me.

"You okay there, Rain?" he chuckled as he lumbered into the spa. The water rose around me, lapping at my shoulders. "You look like you're not breathing."

"Pretty sure I forgot how to the second you pulled down your shorts," I admitted honestly. Licking my lips, I leaned forward to swim over to his side. Bold from the earlier group activity and our conversation, I placed a hand on either shoulder and sank down onto his lap, my knees on either side of his hips. "Hi."

"Hi." He gave me that rare, shy smile. Reaching up, he cupped my face between his hands. "I wanted this with you but never allowed myself to believe it would happen. You deserve so much better than what I can offer, Rain, but I'm so fucking thankful that you're here with me."

Holding me in place, Slade pitched forward, closing the distance and sealing his lips over mine. I immediately molded against him, loving the way he dominated the kiss, took control so I didn't have to. It differed from Jameson, who controlled because I asked him. With Slade, it was in his nature, which was clear in the way he took what he wanted while making it amazing for me.

Pulling back, chest rising and falling with my quick breaths, I licked my lips, savoring the lingering taste of him. Mimicking his hold, I rubbed both thumbs along his cheekbones. "You're not the only one who's imagined this. After working with you all day, I'd go home and think about you.

Imagine your hands on me, holding me, on too many nights to count."

His wide hands dipped beneath the water and grasped my waist, squeezing in a tight, possessive hold. "Like this."

Between the heated water and the lava flowing beneath my skin, sweat slicked my exposed shoulders and drops dripped along my temples.

"Lower."

He chuckled. "Is that so?" I gasped as he slid me closer, dragging my slick core against his impressive cock. "Who said you're in charge, baby?" My heart stopped, but the steady pulse between my thighs shifted into a painful need. "Tell me. Are you a good girl who does what she's told or a naughty one who enjoys being punished?"

Leaning forward, I pressed my cheek to his neck, rubbing my core along his rigid length as I stroked myself higher toward orgasm. "Depends on the mood, I guess." My lips moved over his skin, kissing and sucking up his neck. "I'll be whatever you need me to be," I purred in his ear.

"Naughty it is tonight, then."

I trembled at the thrill that raced through me. "Why am I naughty?" I fake pouted.

He caught my lower lip between his teeth and tugged. "Because you think I need you to be anything other than you, than what you want. So next time"—his smile turned sharp—"you'll know the answer is always whatever you want to be, baby."

My breath stuttered in my chest. How was he real? Considerate, good-looking, and all mine. There had to be a catch, something horrible about him that would make him not so damn perfect.

"And naughty girls get punished, don't they, Rain?" I stared wide-eyed at Slade, unsure what he wanted me to say.

"Are you on birth control?" I swallowed hard to keep from choking on my spit and nodded. "Are you okay if we play with me bare?"

And there went every brain cell, all turned to mush. Somehow, I mouthed, "Yes."

"I can't fuck you tonight." He laughed at my pitiful whimper at that remark. "As you saw this morning, I'm not a small man. Anywhere. We'll need to get this"—he grabbed my mound and squeezed—"all stretched and ready for me so I don't hurt you."

"I'll be okay." Nothing a few stitches wouldn't fix. I mean, having Slade inside me would be worth the ER visit.

He shook his head. "I'm not chancing it. But that doesn't mean we can't play. But I'm serious, Rain. If you push me, everything stops. Understand?"

"Yeah, yes. I understand."

"Good girl." With a hard shove, he moved me off his lap but held on to my bottoms, slipping them down my legs with the movement. "Now turn around and face the pool, hands on the stone ledge and legs spread."

I did as he asked, the flow of the water over my bare center oddly arousing as I moved to the other side of the spa. My nails scratched along the stone ledge, my nerves ramping higher the longer I waited for him to touch me.

"Fuck, you have an amazing ass." A sharp slap followed immediately by a burning sensation across my butt cheek had my lips popping open on a gasp. "Look at how gorgeous your fair skin turns." He grabbed the whole cheek in one hand and squeezed. "Nice and red." Another hard spank landed on my other cheek, making me cry out. "Shh, baby. You're the one who was naughty, not me. And remember what you said. No pushing me."

"Yes, just... fuck." My head dropped forward. "Do something."

"Oh I will, baby. Just be patient." The strings of my top whispered against my skin before vanishing completely when it fell into the water. Palm splayed along my back, he ran it up and down my spine. I arched beneath his touch, pressing my ass higher into the cool night air—which earned me two more stinging spanks. "Fuck, I love seeing my handprint on your ass."

The pain shot sparks straight to my clit, making it pulse with every slap of his hand against my skin. I loved it too.

My lips parted to beg for more when his thick cock moved between my spread thighs, drying up my words and stealing my breath. My core squeezed, aching to be filled, spasming with need.

"Now, you're going to be a good girl and not move. I'm going to give us a preview of what we both want but without hurting you. If you move, baby, I walk away and leave you desperate and begging for me."

His hand dove into my hair, fisting at the base. With a sharp tug, I followed his pull, face tipping higher and back arched.

"Let's see how much we can both take," he growled.

With a tap of his foot against one ankle, he spread my legs even wider and stepped closer until his skin brushed against my sore backside. Fingers beneath the water, he parted my folds and angled himself so his dick nestled between them.

My heart beat too fast, breaths shallow as I waited for him to move, not daring to even adjust my stance, too afraid he'd stop like he threatened. At the first slide of him between my thighs, his wide head tapping against my clit, my lids fluttered closed as I soaked up every sensation rocketing through my veins.

"Fuck, I can feel how wet you are even with the water. So slick for me, baby. Does the idea of me prepping your pussy to take my huge cock turn you on?" I tried to nod, but his hold on my hair kept me from moving. "Or maybe it's just thinking about me stretching you so fucking wide, touching every inch inside your tight cunt, that's making you soak my dick right now."

"All of it," I somehow managed to get out.

I stilled, not even breathing when he pulled back, but instead of moving forward like he had, working himself against me in quick pulsing strokes, he nudged at my entrance. "Tell me to stop if you're not comfortable."

"Please," I breathed. Like I would stop him, not when every inch of me was homed in on where just his thick tip stretched my entrance wide. The slight burn faded, leaving me desperate for more of that amazing feeling deeper inside me.

"Fuck, I knew you'd feel perfect. So damn tight, strangling just the tip of my cock." Slade's hand moved around my hip and dipped between my legs. Using the tip of a single finger, he circled my clit, pressing just hard enough to be teasing. "That's it, baby. Imagine me so deep inside you that there isn't an inch of you I won't touch."

I trembled, my core squeezing, trying to pull him in deeper, but Slade didn't move.

In and out in tiny thrusts he moved, each time a fraction deeper.

"I can't wait to see you stuffed full of my cock." His lips trailed up and down my spine before settling over my ear. "With Jameson making you choke on his."

With a pinch and twist of my swollen clit, he shot me

over the edge into complete ecstasy. My core pulsed and squeezed around the inch of him inside me, desperately trying to take him deeper as my orgasm raced through me.

"I'm going to come inside you," Slade grunted, nipping at my neck. "Tell me now if that's not okay."

I nodded, not caring about the burn on my scalp, which somehow made the aftershocks of my orgasm burst to life again.

"Come with me." Dropping my hair, he sealed his hand around my throat and squeezed while drawing me back until my spine hit his hard chest. The new angle pushed him even deeper. "Now, baby."

My body instantly responded to his words, trembling all over again with a fresh rush of bliss. Teeth sunk into my shoulder, Slade cursed as he swelled even thicker and came inside me. Body trembling with restraint, he kept me perfectly still as he held himself back to only shallow thrusts.

The fingers around my throat loosened, falling lower until his palm engulfed one of my breasts, squeezing in a gentle massage.

"Fuck, Rain." I nodded, unable to form words just yet. "I can't wait to have all of you." With a soft kiss to my neck, he pulled out and stepped away. Immediately the cool night air engulfed the part of me out of the water, making me shiver. "Come on, let's get you to bed."

The water moved around me as I waded to the edge where Slade had already gotten out and had a towel secured around his hips. My lips tugged down in a frown, making him chuckle.

"You'll get to see all of me soon enough. This isn't a just-for-tonight thing between us. We have plenty of time for you to explore me."

I took his offered hand and stepped out of the spa, legs a little wobbly. He pulled a large, soft towel around my shoulders until I was wrapped like a human burrito. A squeal of delight raced up my throat when Slade scooped me into his arms.

"You're in my bed tonight."

As we walked toward the house, I noticed Jameson wasn't where I last saw him, his lawn chair empty and beer gone. My cheeks heated knowing he had left while Slade and I were in the spa, which was dumb considering we'd all messed around earlier in the pool. The cold AC air made me shiver in Slade's arms when we stepped into the house, the glass door clicking shut behind us.

"I was thinking you two would turn into prunes out there." I followed Jameson's voice, finding him in the kitchen working on his laptop. His gaze landed on me and softened. "I put your pajamas in his room, Raindrop." Pushing away from the island, he stood and moved our way. Sliding a few rogue hairs away from my forehead, he pressed a gentle, love-filled kiss to my lips. "Good night, sweetheart. I love you."

One more kiss and he turned, going back to whatever he was working on before we walked in.

With a lovesick sigh, I relaxed even further against Slade.

A good night indeed.

I'd be sleeping beside Slade. The only thing that could make it better was if Jameson snuggled in with us. That might never happen—or maybe it would as the guys' relationship grew. All I knew was right now, I'd take all I could get. Soak up every moment with these two amazing men.

And be grateful for every single second we were together.

"I'll be around if you have questions. Thank you, and let's go find her," I stated with a firm nod.

As the group filed out of the room, I studied the officers' and detectives' behavior. While delivering the profile, I'd spotted one in particular toward the back of the crowd who appeared uncomfortable, fidgety almost, unlike the others, who were either attentive or blatantly annoyed at having their time wasted by my bullshit.

A scoff or eye roll was normal. There were many old-school thinkers out there who didn't believe in profiling and how it can help identify an unsub quicker and with fewer casualties. Certain aspects of the profile added another layer of complication. Some men were unsympathetic toward the unsub because of the reason she killed. The comments after I'd suggested she or someone very close to her was a victim of sexual assault were sexist and disgusting. After one jackass asked why the unsub couldn't just get over it and move on, Slade came to stand beside me, crossing both arms over his wide chest.

The comments immediately stopped.

But while I delivered the details, Detective Gray wasn't angry at the profile, more troubled. I didn't know what her odd behavior was about, but I sure as hell would look into it later. Standing beside her, Detective Savage diligently listened and took notes while I spoke, occasionally slicing death glares at the officers who made the inappropriate comments about the unsub.

"That went better than expected," I said offhandedly to Slade as we walked out of the bullpen, heading for Rain's office.

"I can't believe those fuckers said that shit," he grumbled while rubbing a hand over his face. "I need some fucking coffee after that."

"You are looking a little tired there, Detective. Something keep you up late last night?" I shot him a smirk as we turned a corner. "Or should I say someone?"

"Actually had the best sleep in a long time with her beside me. I'm fairly certain I molded around her like she was my personal body pillow." My barked laugh echoed down the hall. "Thanks for letting me have some one-on-one time with her last night."

Palm wrapped around the doorknob, I pulled the door to Rain's office open and went straight for the fancy coffee machine. I held up an empty mug in Slade's direction, a silent question if he also wanted some. At his grunt in confirmation, I turned to the machine and grabbed a prefilled pod.

"If this is going to work, we can't be selfish with her." The machine whirred to life. I focused on the streaming dark liquid as it splashed into the white mug, mind spinning back to earlier. "A few of the questions earlier were valid. We haven't narrowed down how the unsub identifies her targets. Then once she does, there's the question of *how* she gets their personal information to find and stalk them."

Finger hooked through the handle, I pulled the mug out from under the spout and handed it to Slade. Mine was almost done brewing when he finally answered.

"The two past assault accusations that we tied to the current case happened years ago, so we can rule out her waiting for one to happen and then reacting. We have five bodies in under a year. She's getting her intel somewhere now."

"Agreed. So, her assault happened within the past two years to trigger the start of this mission she's on." Hot mug in hand, I settled in the armchair and blew across the black surface. "We should look into reports filed in the last five to ten years."

"And where nothing happened after she came forward."

I nodded and texted one-handed, asking Charlie to look into that angle. "So maybe one victim was her assailant, but we haven't found the accusation or case file yet. It still doesn't explain how she finds out about the other attacks to target the other men. Who would have knowledge about local sexual assault cases, past and current?"

"Stating the obvious, police officers or detectives." That sent my mind snapping back to the anxious detective from earlier. "But I would've heard if any were a victim of a crime, more so if they were sexually assaulted," Slade continued.

I deflated. He was right. That would be talked about and moved to the top of the caseload, labeled top priority. No one would let it go unsolved. And I was almost positive the unsub's assault happened recently, within the past year or so. She wouldn't be able to hold back her rage at the injustice done to her for long. Which meant Slade would know about it if it happened in Santa Coasta.

"So, who else would know about an assault without an actual case filed, which would have shown up on our searches?" I asked, and we both paused, racking our brains.

"Therapists," Slade muttered eventually. "Nurses or doctors who treated the victims. Counselors at victim centers, support groups—either the leaders or other members who heard others' stories."

I blew out a breath. "Fuck, that's a lot of people to talk to."

"Social media," he mused. "That's how she could get their personal information. People are idiots these days with what they put out there for anyone to see. A name is all that's needed, and then boom, she has everything necessary to find them."

My cell phone vibrated along my thigh with an incoming call. Setting the nearly empty mug down on the coffee table, I swiped my thumb across the screen to answer and immediately hit the speaker button.

"Charlie. You're on speakerphone." I set the phone next to my coffee mug, and Slade shifted on the small couch to lean forward, gaze locked on the screen. "You already have something for me on that search I asked you to run?"

"It's why I'm calling. It'll take a bit to get those records pulled. Remember that snuff film site the fuckers who took Remy and Tinley ran?"

"What the hell?" Slade hissed.

I waved him off. "Yeah, of course I remember." How could I forget the two psychopaths who targeted Tallon's sister and our former one-night stand? "I thought all that was wrapped up. What's going on?"

"I found a back door and now have the various IP addresses of their full past subscriber and viewer list. Anyone who ever logged in to the site, I have a way to backtrace them." The excitement in his tone stirred the same within me. This was huge. Anyone who was into watching live torture and murder needed to be behind bars before they tried to mimic the same themselves. "I'm working with the agency and Interpol as I dig up personal information on these bastards. We're talking hundreds of people, Jameson."

"Wow." I slumped back in the chair and swiped a palm across my mouth. "That's beyond...." I couldn't come up with the right word. "That's fucking amazing, Charlie."

"I'll still work on stuff for the team, but this has me more bogged down than normal, so there won't be a quick turn-around like you're used to."

"Not a problem. Great work, Charlie. Really fucking fantastic."

I tapped the screen, ending the call. Slade stared at me, brows raised.

I sighed. "It's a long, gruesome story. I'll tell you about it after we catch our unsub. So, where should we start today? We need to find out where she's identifying her next victims."

I waited for Slade to respond, wondering if he was listening as he scrolled through his phone until he spoke up. "Let's start with the crisis center angle. That would give our unsub plenty of assaults to select her victim pool from. I found two centers close. We can talk to the directors and counselors, give them the profile and see if anyone has worked there or visited frequently that hits the mark."

"Smart."

He huffed as he stood. "Don't sound so surprised, asshole."

"Just saying, brawn *and* brains. Who knew?"

He flipped me the bird. "Oh, fuck off. You're just jealous, skinny boy." There was a grin on his face as he spoke, one that had made an appearance more frequently over the past couple of days.

As we walked to his car, I couldn't keep my smile from growing despite the afternoon ahead of us. When I left Nashville, leaving behind everything I knew and my friends, I'd assumed what Tallon and I had was a once-in-a-lifetime friendship, one I wouldn't find again.

Now it seemed that maybe Slade could not only be that friend I'd wanted, but maybe he needed one just as much as I did.

ELBOW PRESSED to the white marble countertop in Rain's kitchen, I tipped the beer bottle against my lips, savoring the cool liquid as it slid down my throat with each sip. It had been a long fucking day, even worse than the previous. Meeting and talking with directors and counselors at the two centers left me hollow and angry. Too many victims were treated like what happened to them was their fault by the people who were meant to help them. I knew victim blaming happened but didn't realize it was so prevalent.

But it was, and far worse than I'd ever imagined. Hearing accounts of how the victims were treated by officers or even hospital staff made my stomach roll. How anyone could blame the victim, pushing their own beliefs or opinions on the case, was infuriating. We were supposed to help, provide justice, not make things worse by either not believing them or having a biased opinion.

Desperate to ease the helpless feeling, I downed the last of my beer and stood to toss the bottle in the recycling bin. Hands on my hips, I took in the kitchen and dining room. The desolate emptiness had the helpless feeling weighing even heavier on my chest. Though it was better than how it was before. Working his rich asshole magic, Slade had the destroyed furniture cleared out and the place cleaned in record time. If I hadn't seen it two nights ago, I wouldn't believe it was the scene of a rage-filled crime.

"I sent over the pictures from Dr. Evans for reference. She also pulled past charges to show the price she'd paid for the furniture and clothes that were destroyed. And add repairing the door to the cost of things needing to be replaced. Your office should have enough to get a basic quote started."

The poor insurance agent looked seconds from pissing his pants beneath Slade's scowl.

With a huffed laugh, I opened the fridge, pulling out two beer bottles. After popping the tops off both, I made my way over and handed one to Slade.

After an awkward goodbye from the insurance guy as he sprinted down the stairs, Slade and I were alone in Rain's townhome. Lifting the beer, Slade took a quick pull, cringed, and held the bottle out to examine the label.

I snorted. "Don't be an alcohol snob. It's decent beer. Drink it and be fucking merry." I clinked the bottoms of the bottles together in a forced cheers. "We all done here?"

He shot an odd look out of the corner of his eye as he tipped the bottle back. "Not yet. I'm waiting for a friend."

"A friend," I drawled. "What kind of friend?"

He sighed and dipped his head forward. "A security friend. There should've been a system installed in the first place." I smiled around the bottle pressed to my lips. "So, I'm having someone come out and put in the same one as mine."

"Good thinking." Shoulder to the wall, I scanned the empty townhome. "But what the hell will we do until then?"

I pulled out my phone to check the time. "Wait a second. You're telling me a security company agreed to come here to install a brand-new, state-of-the-art security system at 10:30 at night?"

"We have the time. Rain won't be home for a while. Floaters always take forever. He didn't mind coming by tonight."

"Did you give him a chance to say no?"

His lips curled at the corners. "He had a choice, though I'm not sure he knew that. And as far as what we can do while we wait, fuck if I know—" The almost-smile faded as he reached into his pocket. Pulling out his cell, he swiped the screen and pressed it to his ear. "Taylor. Yeah. Where? This just happened? Okay, we're on our way."

Standing tall, he rolled his shoulders and hitched his chin toward the beer in my hand. "Finish that. Duty calls. There's a homicide across town near some bar. I'll call my security guy and reschedule for another day," he grumbled.

With zero hesitation, I strode to the kitchen and dumped the remainder of my beer into the sink.

Time to make myself useful.

On the way to the crime scene, we barely spoke, both of us tired from the long day and lost in thought. He explained that dispatch didn't have any details about the murder, which meant this might or might not be the work of our unsub. Though the short time frame between this murder and the last made me believe it would be unrelated.

Or she was spiraling, and this could be the first of many new victims.

The flash of blue-and-white lights filling the windshield had me sitting straighter and situating both shirt cuffs back over my wrists. In true Slade fashion, not caring where he parked, he pulled up alongside a cruiser in the middle of the street and cut the engine.

A small crowd gathered up ahead, their curious murmurs filling the night as I stepped out of the car. At the crime scene tape, I flashed my credentials at the officer keeping everyone back. With a nod, he raised the bright yellow plastic and gestured for me to go through. With each step closer to the scene, I scanned the area, taking in every detail, only to have my gaze jerk back to a familiar face that appeared between two uniformed officers' shoulders.

"What the hell?" I nodded in agreement at Slade's statement, somewhat dumbstruck because what we both saw made little sense. "You go find out what the fuck that's about, and I'll check out the scene," he said. "Per dispatch, Rain will be here as soon as she can."

With a clipped nod, I marched over to the small group that huddled around the woman at the mouth of the alley. Detective Savage's wide, wild eyes met mine as I approached. Once I had a clear view, I scanned the dark crimson dots covering the front of her wrinkled blue blouse and the same color that coated her wringing hands.

"We're getting her statement now," one officer said without looking my way when I paused beside him. His words were blunt and cold, obviously dismissing me. Not that I gave a fuck. "To recap, Detective Savage here was headed to the bar next door to meet some friends when she heard a sound down the alley that made her stop. Describe what you heard, Beth."

"The noise," she whispered, face pale and lips trembling. "It was like a watermelon being broken open. Someone muttered under their breath, and then the sound came again and again." She swallowed. "I didn't have my gun or radio since I'd planned to have a few drinks tonight." Tears built in her lower lids. "My boyfriend just broke up with me. My friends and I were meeting up to help me drown my sorrows."

"What happened next?" I jerked my eyes to the officer, who'd stopped writing her statement.

"I heard a female voice, like a cry or a plea. I couldn't *not* go, you know? Not when someone was clearly in trouble, so I took off down the alley. It was dark, but I didn't see anything until I reached the parking lot around the back. That's when I found him, the guy. On his back... there was blood. So much blood. It was everywhere. I checked his pulse but didn't find one, so I started CPR just in case."

"Did you call 911 or anyone else to let them know what was going on?" I asked.

Her short hair, sweaty and stuck to her face, barely moved with the slight shake of her head. "I yelled for help, hoping someone would hear me, and finally someone came running down the alley. I kept doing CPR until it was obvious he wasn't... that he was...." She looked away and curled her shoulders inward.

The officer reached out and placed a comforting hand on her shoulder. But she jerked back, eyes wide, putting distance between them.

"Sorry, Beth. I'm sure you're jumpy after witnessing all this," he said. She studied him like a cornered, wounded animal. "We'll need your clothes—"

"What about the girl?" she asked, scanning the officers before settling on me. "I heard a woman's voice. I know I did."

"Detective Taylor is over there now," I said, breaking her stare to look toward the parking lot. "If someone is in trouble, he'll take care of it. You two"—I inclined my head toward two of the officers standing off to the side—"pull the security footage from the bar and surrounding buildings. Detective Taylor and I will talk to the bartender inside once we're done out here."

"Come on," an officer said to Detective Savage, gesturing toward the ambulance. "You can change in there so we can bag…"

Their words faded as I stepped away, heading down the short alley toward the crime scene. A yellow halo of light from a flickering streetlight illuminated Slade's massive frame standing over a lump on the asphalt. Hands on his hips with a deep scowl on his face, he looked pissed.

Great. Whatever he saw didn't seem good.

27

SLADE

Something didn't add up.

I narrowed my eyes at the body like that would help make the pieces fit together, but no surprise it didn't. The way his head was smashed in from several blows to the back spoke to a crime of passion, full of rage. Yet there was no trauma to his face or anywhere else on his body that I could see.

Checking my phone for an update on Rain's arrival, I scowled at the empty screen. After shooting off another text asking for her ETA, I slipped it back in my pocket just as I felt Jameson pause beside me.

"Damn," he muttered. "That's a lot of anger to do that to a head." I nodded in agreement. "Wonder who he pissed off."

"Do you see what I'm seeing?" I asked, pointing toward the victim's pants, where the belt and top button were undone. "Why in the hell would he wear his pants like that?"

Jameson squatted beside the body for a better look. "No clue. Detective Savage said she heard a noise, came to see what was going on, and found him like this. The shirt's messed up from where she attempted CPR until she realized he was gone."

"Hmm." The heels of my shoes ground along the pavement as I swiveled to look her way, but the area was empty. "Where did she go?"

"Change out of her clothes so the officers could bag them for evidence."

"Good."

"I also asked for them to pull security footage from the bar and surrounding area."

"Thanks," I said absentmindedly. "Where is Rain? Have you heard from her? She should be here by now."

Jameson stood and pulled out his phone. "Nothing from her. Maybe she got hung up on that floater longer than she expected?"

"Then why isn't she responding?" I moved around the body for a different angle. "Think she'd let us put a GPS tracker on her?" Jameson let out a surprised scoff. "What? Her ex is still out there and has me on edge. I don't like her being alone when we don't know where the fuck he is."

"I agree, but she's a grown woman and can handle herself. But please, by all means, ask her if we can chip her. I want to see how that goes down."

I shot him the bird at the restrained laughter in his voice. "Not a chip, just an app for her phone. A way for me to track her movements when she's not around one of us."

"Yeah, that sounds so much better," he chuckled. "Savage said she heard a woman call out. That's why she came to intervene. Maybe she was mistaken, because I don't see anyone else."

I nodded while processing the new information. "Do

you think this is the work of our unsub and she's suddenly ditched her signature?"

"The only way she'd do that is if she's spiraling, and we're fucked if she is. That means the murders will be closer together, and she might even ditch the surveillance piece and start targeting any man she sees as a threat. Although it would benefit us."

"How?" I mused, not seeing any upside to a woman this angry losing all sense of control and structure.

"That means she'll make a mistake. Leave evidence behind or maybe even get caught in the act, like tonight, maybe. We'll know more once we pull this guy's background. If he has any kind of sexual deviance on his record, then he might be victim number six."

"Please don't tell me you've touched my body."

I spun around at Rain's voice, sucking in a breath as she emerged from the shadowed alley. Dressed in a knee-length pencil skirt, high heels, and a loose Kelly green blouse that brought out the green in her hazel eyes, she looked fucking gorgeous.

"Which body are we talking about?" Jameson jokingly mused.

"Ha ha," she scoffed. Pausing beside me, she shot me a questioning look. "What?"

"Nothing. You just look...." I stopped and cleared my throat. Telling her I wanted to jerk up that skirt and fuck her from behind as her palms scraped the brick building was completely inappropriate considering we were at a crime scene.

"*Fuckable* is the word he's looking for," Jameson said, voice low so only we three could hear. "And I agree. I don't think I've ever seen you in a skirt."

"But you've seen me in far less," she said with a smirk.

"Yeah, but this"—he waved a hand up and down her delectable body—"is very sexy. Put a pair of thick-rimmed glasses on and you could fulfill my naughty librarian fantasy."

Her head tipped back with a laugh. "I'll see what I can do when we get home."

Home.

That one word coming from her lips had hope filling my chest. It was too soon to feel this way, but I'd fantasized about it for so damn long that maybe it wasn't. Whatever this was between us had been building for longer than a week, and I'd just finally gotten the chance to act on it.

"I'll go out on a limb and say COD is head trauma," Rain mused as she popped on a pair of latex gloves. "But I'll know for sure after the autopsy. Beth said—"

"Beth?" I cut in.

"Detective Savage. I saw her when I arrived and stopped to talk for a few minutes. She's shaken up by what she saw."

"Can't blame her," Jameson said, gesturing to the man at his feet. "I've seen a lot of crime scenes, and this one makes my stomach turn. Seeing someone's head cracked open like a broken egg with the brain matter—"

I held up a hand. "Please stop so one day in the future I can eat eggs again. Can you check for any other wounds, Rain?"

She nodded and opened his shirt. Nothing looked bruised or damaged except for the marks where Detective Savage attempted CPR.

"Any chance he has a wallet on him?" I asked.

"Are you asking me to search another man's pants?"

"Only a dead man's, in the current state or soon to be," I gritted out, the idea of her touching anyone besides me or Jameson making jealousy spike.

"You're so sweet when you get all murder-y." Reaching into his front pocket, Rain withdrew a thin credit card holder and flipped it over, showing me the license on the opposite side. "As you requested."

After snapping on a pair of gloves, I took it from her and angled it into the light to read the name.

"Parker Jacobs." I studied the picture, then looked at the victim's face. "That's him all right." Grabbing an evidence bag from the nearby crime scene tech, I dropped the card holder inside and sealed the tape. "Let's show this to the bartender and see if she remembers any—"

"Did y'all hear that?" Rain stood quickly, teetering on her high heels. I wrapped a steadying hand around her elbow to keep her from falling onto the body.

"Hear what?" I asked, hand automatically sliding toward my Glock.

Rain's lips dipped into a frown. "I don't know. It sounded like someone talking or muttering, maybe."

"Did you clear the scene?" I snapped at the officer hovering close by.

His eyes went wide as he nodded. "We did an initial sweep, but did we search inside every car? No. We needed to get the scene taped off quick. A drunk couple almost tripped over the body."

"I'm on it," Jameson said, his voice carrying over the now deathly quiet parking lot. "You stay with Rain."

Without waiting for a response, he pulled his gun free and started toward the row of parked cars.

"It could've been nothing," Rain whispered. "I might be mistaken—"

"Or not. They didn't completely clear the scene if they didn't check the cars. Plus, there's another point of entry where—"

"Someone get the fucking medics over here. Now!" Jameson's bellow rang through the night.

Stunned, I didn't react when Rain jerked out of my hold and started toward Jameson, where he stood waving both arms in the air a few cars down. Before she could get close, I wrapped an arm around her waist.

"Let me go," she hissed. "I can help."

The insistent urge to keep her from danger told me to keep her close and not let go, but as much as I wanted to protect her, I also needed to let Rain be Rain at the same time. My jaw worked back and forth as I debated what to do.

"Fine. Together, though."

With a huff, she nodded in agreement.

The second we rounded the bumper of a car, giving us a clear view of what Jameson found, Rain dropped to her knees beside the woman lying face up on the pavement. Fingers pressed to the woman's slender throat, Rain's shoulders sagged, signaling she'd found a pulse and the woman was alive. Next, Rain shifted to examine the woman's eyes, lifting one eyelid and then the other while shining her cell's flashlight into them. The unknown woman moaned, head lolling side to side in protest.

"I can smell the alcohol on her from here," Rain muttered to herself. "But this seems like more than the effects of too much to drink. Her breathing... it's shallow. Too shallow." She turned her face up to mine. "We need to get her to the hospital now in case she took something or was unknowingly drugged."

I glanced toward the opening of the alley, where the ambulance lights still flashed. "Can I move her?"

"I don't... I don't know. There aren't any signs of neck or spine trauma, but—"

Good enough for me.

One arm beneath her neck, the other under her knees, I cradled the woman to my chest. Knees and lower back screaming in pain, I lifted the limp body into the air. Careful to not jostle her too much, I slowly jogged toward the opening of the alley where the medics had finally appeared.

"Pull out the gurney," I demanded.

One look at the woman in my arms spurred them into action, one hopping into the ambulance to pull out the rolling bed.

Once it was out and secure, I gently laid her on the thin padding. "She needs oxygen now. The ME thinks either alcohol poisoning or drugs. We need to get her to the hospital immediately and run a full toxicology panel—"

"Slade." I twisted around to face Jameson, who had a small baggie with trace amounts of white powder inside pinched between two fingers. "Rain searched the dead fucker's pockets and found this. Look familiar to you?"

"Is that fucking ketamine? Damnit." Before the EMTs could shut the back doors, I hauled myself inside the ambulance. "Stay with Rain. Run point on the investigation for me until I get back. I'm going with her." I nodded to the EMT holding the doors, and he slammed them shut, sealing me inside.

Anger and worry mixed, sending my blood pressure skyrocketing. I watched as the EMT cleaned the inside of the unconscious woman's arm, readying it for the IV. My stomach rolled as the needle pressed against her skin.

Nope.

Hard pass.

Passing out and adding more work for the EMTs was not my goal for riding along.

I shifted along the hard seat, turning my focus to take in the woman's disheveled clothing. The buttons of her top were undamaged, nothing ripped, though the hem had risen slightly, exposing some of her stomach. Her jeans were a different situation. The button was gone, as if torn off, the zipper broken and undone. In fact, they didn't look all the way pulled up, the waist sitting below her hip bones.

I swallowed, throat and mouth dry.

The dead fucker's pants undone, hers ripped and not all the way on at all, pointed to an interrupted assault.

And my gut told me only one person would have that violent a reaction.

The mounting evidence pointed to the one thing we didn't want.

Our unsub was spiraling.

IT WAS WELL past three in the morning when I finally stepped through the front door. Every time I moved, pain flared, slowing my steps. My keys crashed to the side table where I rested my badge and gun. Not bothering with the lights, I moved through the dark hallway toward the kitchen.

I paused for half a step, seeing Jameson sitting on one of the counter stools, laptop open in front of him. A highball glass filled with ice and brown liquid sat near his hand, one of my expensive bottles of bourbon beside it.

"Helped yourself, I see," I grumbled, not really caring but not sure what else to say. My brain was just as exhausted as my body. Though seeing a beautiful woman asleep on the couch eased some of the tension from my too-stiff muscles. "Find anything after I left?" I whispered, not wanting to wake Rain when she looked so damn peaceful and perfect.

"There were zero cameras in the bar or around it." My

hand hovered over the cabinet handle, pausing at the anger vibrating in his tone. "The bartender remembered them, but the asshole paid in cash, so she couldn't really remember how many he had versus her. They were drinking the same thing: cranberry vodkas. Bartender said the woman seemed fine when they left, nothing that caused her pause, and she was too busy to say for certain if he did or didn't put something in her drink. Most of the patrons who were there earlier in the night were long gone, so I couldn't question them."

"Tiffany," I said, finally snapping out of my daze and pulling down a highball glass. "The woman you found, her name is Tiffany Gardner. They gave her something in her IV when we arrived at the hospital after I told them we suspected she was drugged with ketamine. It didn't take long for her to wake up and be conscious enough to tell me the basics. She went there with him willingly, though she thought his name was Brad. They met online two weeks ago, and tonight was their first time meeting in person."

My hand trembled, making the empty glass shake on top of the granite. Jameson shot me a worried look before grabbing the bourbon and pouring me two fingers. Instead of sipping it like the delicious liquor deserved, I tipped the glass back, downing the contents in one gulp, savoring the burn down my throat. The heavy bottom clinked against the counter, and I tapped a finger against the side.

"Is she going to be okay?" Jameson asked, caution in his tone as he poured more bourbon into my empty glass.

"Physically, yeah. Emotionally?" I shrugged. Pulling a stool out from beneath the counter, I sat on the edge, grateful to be off my feet for a few seconds. "Find anything else at the scene?"

"No, but we bagged and tagged the shit out of the area." He twisted on his seat. "Why?"

"Why what?" I asked into the glass.

"Why did you go with her? She was in good hands."

I rolled the smooth glass between my palms. "After talking with the victims and those at the crisis center, I wanted... I wanted her to know I was there for her. That I was one of the good guys in her corner, no matter what she needs."

"You're a good man, Detective Taylor."

"Don't tell anyone," I grumbled, barely managing a smile. Shifting, I looked at the couch, almost to make sure she was still there and not an illusion my tired brain conjured. "She been asleep for long?"

"She tried waiting up for you. Hell, she wanted to go to the morgue and do the autopsy tonight."

I huffed. "Sounds like Rain."

"But I convinced her to come with me. The guy will still be dead tomorrow."

"Tomorrow," I sighed, "is my day off and hers too."

"Then we get back on the case the next day. I think we all deserve some time off. Don't you?"

We sure as fuck did.

After polishing off the drink, I stood, shoving the throbbing pain that radiated from every exhausted cell to the back of my mind. "I'm going to bed."

"You better wake her up and let her know you're home or she'll be pissed. She was worried about you."

Releasing a slow breath, I made my way to the living room. Standing beside the couch, I stroked a knuckle up and down her cheek. "Rain," I whispered, not wanting to startle her awake. "I'm back, baby. Headed to bed."

Her long dark lashes fluttered, lids slowly opening. "Hey. Sorry, I must have fallen asleep."

"It's okay, just wanted to let you know I'm home. Go back to sleep, baby."

"No," she pouted, making my lips twitch in an almost smile. "I'm coming to bed with you."

The blanket floated to the floor when she tossed it aside and swiveled to stand. Grabbing her outstretched hands, I helped her off the couch. Still half asleep, she shuffled ahead of me, Jameson's laugh following us down the hall.

In my room, I pulled back the covers, waiting until she crawled in before folding them back. "I'm going to take a shower," I whispered.

She muttered something and rolled over, snuggling deeper into the pillow.

For several seconds, I stood there, memorizing her serene face.

She was here. With me, in my bed. Something I'd imagined too many times to count. And the reality was way better. When I pictured Rain waiting for me in my bed, I didn't imagine this constricting feeling in my chest at the sight of her.

Walking away from her was difficult, but the pull of the shower lured me into the bathroom, stripping as I went. Under the scalding spray, the pelting water eased some of the tightness in my shoulders and back.

Lost in thought, my mind went to the drastic difference between Rain's reaction to me coming home so late and tired compared to previous women in my life.

Rain didn't complain or scream that I always put work first. There were no demands for me to change and conform to what they needed. She accepted me. All of me—the good, the bad, and the terrible.

With my face to the water, eyes closed, the recognition of what the heavy, swelling feeling in my chest was hit me like a punch to the gut.

Love. This suffocating, amazing, all-consuming feeling was love.

I had fallen hopelessly in love with Rain.

28

RAIN

The sound of the shower cutting off roused me from the light sleep I'd slipped into after he tucked me into his bed. Rolling to my side, I folded both hands beneath my cheek and stared into the dark, listening as the shower door whooshed open, followed by Slade's footsteps. A minute later, the sliver of light pouring beneath the closed bathroom door winked out, and then the door opened.

The mattress shifted as Slade slid beneath the sheets, his body heat immediately adding to the warmth under the bedding. A smile curled my lips when his thick arm wrapped around my waist and his hard body sealed against my back, molding around me as if he wanted us touching in as many places as possible.

With a slow exhale, I wiggled against him to erase any lingering distance.

"You should be asleep," he whispered in my ear. Moving my long, loose hair away from my neck, he softly kissed my skin. Him pressed against me combined with that simple kiss ignited a spark in my center.

Breaths shallow and quick, I shifted again, this time

grinding my backside against his thickening length. My lower belly twisted and fluttered, the scorching heat burning through my veins. There was no way I could close my eyes and fall back asleep now. I wanted him, needed him to ease the throb between my thighs his proximity caused.

As if he'd read my mind, Slade dipped a hand beneath my sleep shirt, palm pressed against my bare stomach while his fingers shifted back and forth. Each teasing swipe that came dangerously close to brushing against the underside of my breast made my breath hitch.

"Don't feel like sleeping?" he murmured, the soft seduction in his tone making me shiver. "I'm taking that as a no."

The laughter in his voice caressed my skin. My back arched, pushing my ass even harder against his now fully rigid cock.

"Slade," I breathed. "Please."

I wasn't even sure what I was begging for at this point. I just needed him to touch me more, to touch me everywhere with his fingers and lips, and to hopefully finally feel him inside me. He'd teased me last night, letting me feel his massive size in my hands. I was slightly terrified to see if he would fit but more nervous and excited to try.

Jameson wasn't a small guy, and feeling him stretch me, brushing every nerve ending deep in my center, was amazing.

And I just knew Slade's thick girth would feel just as magical.

Painstakingly slow, he inched his hand higher. His groan when he reached my breasts vibrated from his bare chest along my back. One massive hand palmed my breast, fingers pinching and twisting at the hard tip.

"I need to suck on these pretty tits, baby. Take your top off."

Gripping the hem, I tugged it up, wiggling a little to get it over my head. It fell from my fingertips, disappearing over the side of the bed. On my back, I waited for Slade to follow through with his words.

Except, instead of his lips on me, the bedside light flicked on. I blinked, chasing away little black dots dancing in my vision at the sudden change. My hair slid along the pillow as I twisted to frown at Slade, but the hungry look in his eyes as he took in my naked chest had me swallowing the protest.

"Do you know how many nights I lay awake with my cock strangled in my fist, imagining you in my bed, begging me to do whatever I wanted?"

A fresh rush of desire had moisture leaking from between my thighs. I internally cringed, knowing I was no doubt soaking my thin cotton shorts. But I couldn't find it in me to be embarrassed, not when two hot-as-Hades men found every part of me amazing. I was confident in all aspects of my body because of him and Jameson in a way I'd never been before, even before Josh.

"Take those shorts off so I can see all of you."

Thumbs hooked into the waistband, I yanked them down my thighs and kicked them off. A rush of cold air hit my lower half when he pulled back the covers, tossing them over the end of the bed.

I almost swallowed my tongue at the sight of him kneeling beside me on the bed naked, hand slowly working up and down his massive cock. A pitiful whimper escaped me, unable to look away from his white-knuckled grip.

"You like that?" I nodded, and he gave his dick a hard tug, a droplet of precum slipping out. He looked at the drop, then at me. With a wicked gleam in his green eyes, he swiped it off with his thumb and stretched it out toward me.

"Suck it off, baby. Give me a preview of what that amazing mouth of yours can do."

I greedily sucked his thumb between my lips, only for them to part on a gasp when thick fingers stroked along my slick center. A moan had me humming around him, and I sucked harder, loving the way his eyes flared when I pulled it deeper into my mouth.

"Hmm, seems like someone is in a good girl mood tonight." I nodded, making his hand move with me. "Good girls get rewarded." *Thank fuck.* "What do you want, baby?"

Unable to speak, I wrapped a hand around his steel-hard cock and squeezed. His hiss filled the quiet room, spurring me on. Tightening my grip, I pumped my hand up and down, forcing more precum to slip free. Pushing up to my elbows, I leaned to the side, eyes on him, making sure he understood what I wanted.

Him in my mouth—and not just his thumb.

With a cocky smirk, he pulled the digit free, swiping my saliva along my lips. "You want to taste me directly from the source, baby?" He wrapped his hand around mine, constricting my grip even tighter. "Then come and have a lick. Pull me into that mouth of yours I've envisioned too many times wrapped around my cock, choking on me until all you can taste and feel is me."

I tightened around the fingers that plunged into my core. Closing the distance between my lips and his cock, I used the tip of my tongue to lick up the tiny drops straight from his slit.

"Oh damn, baby." His hips tilted forward, pushing him past my parted lips. Jaw stretched wide, tongue flat, I took him deeper, loving the feel of this powerful man shuddering because of me. "That's it. Now let's get you ready for me."

With that warning, he added another finger into my

core, palm grinding against my clit. I tried to pull back, the feeling too full and too much, but his hand on the back of my head kept me in place. "You want to watch?"

I stilled. Eyes tipped up, I saw Slade's attention was focused behind me. I squeezed his fingers, realizing we had company.

"By the way her cunt nearly broke my fingers, I'd say she's interested."

"I'll never turn down the chance to see our girl fall apart, whether it's for you or me."

Jameson's voice amped up my need, knowing he was behind me somewhere, watching, enjoying seeing Slade with his fingers between my thighs and my lips wrapped around his cock.

"Keep working that hot mouth around me, baby," Slade growled. "One more finger. If you can take all three, you can have me."

My eyes went wide before slamming shut as the stretch pushed the boundaries of pain. I whimpered around his cock, making him twitch on my tongue.

"Holy fuck." The sound of furniture moving somewhere in the room had my ears straining to figure out what was happening around me. "That's so damn hot, Raindrop. Seeing your pink pussy stuffed full of his tatted fingers, it's fucking erotic as hell."

Slade moved in and out in shallow pumps, driving me higher. At the flick of his thumb against my clit, I shattered, crying out around his cock. A snap of his hips had him tapping the back of my throat, making me gag and tears drip from the corners of my eyes.

Without warning, he pulled away. With the back of my hand, I wiped at my messy mouth, blinking through the tears.

"Damn, you're perfect. But as much as I like the feel of your throat working around my cock, I think I promised your tits some attention." Hand to my shoulder, he gently pushed, forcing me to lie back on the bed. "Can you see?"

Chin to my chest, I gasped when I saw Jameson sitting in an armchair at the end of the bed. Sleep pants pulled low, hand wrapped around his cock, he smiled. "Knees up and spread them, Raindrop, so I can see every delicious inch of you."

Complying, I let my head fall back onto the pillow, shivering at the brush of cool air along my hot, slick core. The first brush of Slade's lips and then tongue against my pebbled tip had me arching off the bed, my body instinctively urging him to take more. Fingers still moving in and out, Slade wrapped his lips around me and sucked my nipple into his mouth, teeth scraping along the sensitive flesh.

"Play with your clit, Raindrop." Looking down my body, over the hand between my legs, I sucked in a breath at Jameson's darkened gaze locked on my core, his own hand moving up and down his cock. "Come around those thick-ass fingers stuffing your pussy, knowing his monster cock will feel that much better."

One hand wrapped around Slade's cock, I moved the other between my legs and circled my sensitive nub. My hips bucked off the bed, moving and jerking with the steady rhythm of Slade's fingers thrusting inside me.

With a hard bite to the curve of my breast and a sneaky finger moving around to press against my back hole, I detonated. Slade slammed his mouth to mine, swallowing my scream as I broke into a thousand pieces, everything too much yet not enough at the same time.

Blood pounding in my ears, I slowly came back to earth,

breathing like I'd just run several miles instead of experiencing a soul-shattering orgasm. Vision a little blurry, I blinked up at Slade's smirking face, his cocky, self-assured features slowly coming into focus.

"You think you're ready for all of me?"

Two seconds ago, yes. Now, I really needed a nap and a gallon of water to replace all the fluids I felt slicking between my thighs. But a gentle brush of a finger against my overly sensitive nub sent fresh energy flooding through my veins.

At my nod, Slade removed his thick fingers. A distinct wet sound made me cringe. But instead of being grossed out or saying a word about it, Slade stuck those three fingers in front of his mouth. Green eyes locked on me, he ran his tongue along each digit, licking them clean.

"Damn, you taste better than in my dirty fantasies, baby." One-handed, he pulled his shorts down to his knees and kicked them off the bed. He glanced over his shoulder. "You, sit by her head and suck on her tits. Keep her soaked for me while I work my way into her tight cunt."

I stared wide-eyed as he shifted to kneel between my open thighs, unable to look away from his long, thick shaft. A flicker of doubt weaved its way through my mind, making me wonder if I could take someone his size.

"It'll fit, baby. I promise. And then I'll make you feel so fucking good when you explode around my cock, strangling me like you did my fingers."

All doubts vanished when the bed dipped by my head just as Slade lifted my hips, sliding my ass onto his thighs. Jameson smiled down at me. It turned a bit wicked a second before a sharp pinch radiated from a pebbled tip where his fingers twisted and tugged.

"I don't think I can," I whimpered, though as renewed heat flowed through me, I knew that was a lie.

"Shh," Jameson shushed. "Let us take care of you, sweetheart." Grabbing my hand, he wrapped it around him, tightening my hold to what he wanted before pulling away. He ran the tip of his finger over a sore spot on my breast. "Looks like Slade marked you here. Guess you need mine on the other."

With a wink, he lowered his face to my chest and ran the tip of his tongue along Slade's bite mark. All the air rushed from my lungs, but Slade nudging at my entrance had me sucking it back in with a gasp.

Inch by inch, Slade worked his way inside me with gentle thrusts, the burn of me stretching to accommodate his large size only lasting a moment before turning to blissful pressure. I pumped my hand up and down Jameson's cock while he sucked and nipped at my tender peaks.

Slade's groan vibrated through the room when he bottomed out inside me, his hips digging into my thighs. With the angle, lifted off the bed like this, all I could do was take everything he gave, completely at his mercy as he slid out before jerking me back onto his dick.

My lids sealed shut, I lost myself to all the overwhelming sensations.

It didn't take long for my core to quiver with my impending orgasm. Slade must have felt how close I was because he picked up the pace, this time snapping his hips when he moved me toward him, hitting deeper and forcing a moan from my parted lips.

"That's it, baby." Voice strained, fingers digging into my hips, he sounded seconds from coming too. "We come together. Now."

His barked command rattled through the room, and I

couldn't stop my body from listening even if I wanted to. I squeezed around him, the feel of him rubbing against my walls sending bursts of tingling pleasure from my core to the rest of me as I trembled along the bed. Slade's hold tightened further, his rhythm stuttering as he came inside me.

I barely registered hot liquid landing on my chest or Jameson's hand controlling my movements along his shaft as I drifted into an almost comalike state, too sated and weak to even open my eyes or move when the two men moved on the bed.

When Slade pulled out, I winced at the sudden empty feeling left behind.

"He'll be right back, sweetheart," Jameson whispered as he stroked a hand along my sweaty hairline. "He's just getting a rag to get you all cleaned up."

Somehow, I managed a nod and smile. A warm cloth brushed along my chest and another at my abused center, each stroke careful and gentle.

"Sit up, baby."

Grumbling under my breath, which made them laugh, I let them maneuver me to a sitting position. Soft cotton slid over my head, and my arms threaded through massive armholes. I inhaled deeply, sighing at the distinct scent of Slade.

"Good night, Raindrop," Jameson whispered against my cheek. "Love you so fucking much."

My lips moved to respond with the same sentiment, but no words came out.

Without my consent, a dark tidal wave consumed me. Fully sated, happy, and most of all, loved, I fell asleep with a smile on my lips.

29

―――――

RAIN

Careful to not jostle the sleeping giant beside me, I inched out from under the soft, warm sheets and tiptoed out of the room without making a sound. Far enough away from the room to not wake Slade, I released my held breath and dropped my shoulders from around my ears. He wouldn't care if I did accidentally wake him up, but the man worked his ass off and needed the extra sleep. Especially since it was technically our day off.

Not that my early-morning-loving brain cared.

If I could sleep in like normal people, I would, but my internal alarm clock went off at five every morning no matter the day. My body didn't care that it was my day off, too, and I could stay in bed until lunch if I wanted. But I was fine with it today, considering there was a very important body waiting for me at the morgue.

If what Jameson suspected was true, the man murdered last night was victim number six for our serial killer. Getting to the office and literally picking up any and all clues from the man's clothes and body could offer the break in the case we needed.

Pausing in front of the room I shared with Jameson, I pressed an ear to the thin opening. Soft snores poured through, signaling he was sound asleep like his friend in the other room. I nudged the door open with a single finger and poked my head inside. Legs tangled in the disheveled sheet, Jameson lay sprawled on the bed like a starfish, arms and legs going in different directions.

A very naked and apparently dreaming happy dreams starfish.

I had the urge to crawl in beside him, snuggle him close, and put that very awake part of him to use. Squeezing my eyes shut, I forced my feet to not carry me toward the bed. Not this morning, even if now the sated and sleepy parts of me were wide awake, too, and ready to play.

I couldn't play today. One of Jameson's early requirements when we started all this was to not get distracted from the case. And I wouldn't, even with the tempting scene in front of me.

The body at the morgue could hold keys to the case we desperately needed, and I wouldn't be the reason progress slowed.

After finding a pair of leggings, a sports bra, and a T-shirt in the shopping bags I had yet to unpack, I slipped into the bathroom to shower and change. Since it was technically my day off, comfortable was okay; my normal business casual attire wasn't required.

Before opening the bathroom door, I flicked off the lights, then tiptoed toward the hallway door.

"Hey," Jameson grumbled, voice deep with sleep, stopping my sneaky retreat. "What are you doing?"

"Go back to sleep," I whispered, changing direction and perching on the edge of the bed beside him. He was disheveled and oh so cute in the mornings. I pushed some wild hair away from his forehead with a soft smile. "I'm going up to the morgue for a little while. I'll be back before you and Slade even know I'm gone."

Eyes still closed, he rolled his head along the pillow. "I don't want you going alone. Not safe. I'll come with you."

My lips curled, broadening my smile. He was too adorable for words. "No, stay here and get some sleep. You need it."

"So do you," he pouted.

Oh my goodness, grumpy morning Jameson was tearing down all my defenses. One more pouty lip and I would dive into bed with him, completely ignoring my responsibilities and the case.

"Go back to sleep. When I come back, I'll bring breakfast —as in actual food, not the nasty grass concoction Slade drinks."

"You sure?" I swallowed a laugh at the hope lifting his tone. Jameson and I agreed when it came to food and eating. "I can be ready in—"

"I won't be gone long. Promise. I won't start the autopsy, just process his clothes for trace evidence. That way, if I find anything, it'll be on its way for analysis at the lab in San Diego today." As natural as breathing, I leaned forward and pressed a chaste kiss to his soft lips. "I'll be back soon."

He grumbled more protests, but by the time I closed the door behind me, I was fairly certain he was back asleep.

Grabbing my handbag and keys, I deactivated the alarm by the front door and headed out, already plotting my route to work. I needed important things on the way: first, my yummy unicorn drink and maybe a donut.

Or two.

It was my day off, after all.

SUGARY, icy goodness in hand and two donuts fueling me, I hummed, lips wrapped around the wide straw as I practically skipped down the hall toward the morgue. Most of the lights were still off; no one was here at the insanely early hour but me, which was perfect. I worked best alone, in the quiet, with no one to disturb me except for my own random thoughts.

My steps slowed to a stop.

When was the last time I lost myself in a thought tornado that didn't just distract me but intruded in my day-to-day life?

A couple of days, a week maybe, which was crazy considering it had happened several times a day before the guys forced their way into my daily routine. Maybe being alone, left to my own thoughts as much as I was before Jameson and Slade, took a harder toll on my mental health than I'd realized. And now that I had companions, two men who stuck to me like glue and helped keep me distracted from those intrusive thoughts, I didn't have the opportunity to get swept up in the tornado.

The anxiety was still there. I was a doctor and knew sex —even amazing, soul-changing sex—and companionship wouldn't cure anxiety. But it sure as hell seemed to ease some of the more debilitating symptoms.

Or maybe science had it all wrong and several orgasms a day kept the doctor away, not apples.

I snorted and shook my head. Pretty sure I would lose my license if I submitted a formal study request to see if my theory was correct. Though I wouldn't mind being a test subject with Jameson and Slade as my partners.

Ah, what a way to sacrifice yourself for science.

Something tapped at my shoulder, jerking me out of my

thoughts. With a startled gasp, I whirled around, the tip of my ponytail snapping me in the face with the quick movement. Blinking back at me, standing so close we could smell each other's breath, stood the slightly odd crime scene tech.

"Dr. Evans," he said, dry lips pulling into a Joker-like grin. "I'm so glad you're here."

Swallowing hard, I held the drink protectively to my chest and took a giant step back, putting much-needed space between us. "Oh, yeah, I came in to, you know, work."

He just blinked, slate-gray eyes trained on me for several uncomfortable seconds without saying another word.

"I'm just going to...," I stated slowly and hooked a thumb over my shoulder toward the swinging doors that led to the morgue. "Have a good morning."

I stilled, my blood turned to ice when his hand latched on to my wrist, preventing me from making my hasty escape. Focusing on the patches of irritated skin along his hand and wrist, I inhaled deep, willing my heart to stop pounding. I couldn't think with the sudden rush of adrenaline that had kicked in my fight-or-flight instinct.

"I wanted to thank you for not telling anyone."

Oh fuck. What in the hell is he talking about? If I said "You're welcome," would he just move on? But my curious brain wouldn't let me find out.

"Tell anyone... what exactly?" I whispered.

His thin lips pulled tighter into a wide grin. "Come on, Dr. Evans, you know. You noticed at the crime scene the other day. The one at that house, with all the blood."

But I didn't know. Damnit, I needed to alert someone, but my phone was buried somewhere in the deep dark depths of my carry-all handbag.

My gaze shifted to my office, just a few feet from where

we stood. If I could get inside, I could lock the door and call for help.

Could I break the tech's weak hold, sure, but he'd done nothing to harm me. And until that happened, I didn't want to hurt him because I'd overreacted to his need to talk to me.

"And what exactly do you think I noticed?" *Shit, what is his name? Ugh, I really need to up my people skills.*

He held up his free hand and twisted it one way, then the other, giving me a clear view of the angry red and irritated patches of skin that matched the one still holding my wrist. "I knew I would get in trouble if anyone found out. The last thing I want is to be on my manager's radar for needing special supplies."

Special supplies?

What the...?

With a practiced move, I easily broke his weak hold on my wrist to grip his. Holding his hand a few inches from my face, I studied the irritated skin. His words and condition finally clicked, making total sense.

"The latex," I breathed. "You're allergic to the latex gloves." He nodded. "And you think you'll get in trouble for telling your manager you need a different type?"

His slim shoulders rose in a shrug. "I need this job, and I love what I do, so I don't want to jeopardize that."

All my fear and tightness drained, leaving me slightly light-headed. "You won't get in trouble for needing different gloves, I promise. I'll order new ones myself from my expense account just to ease your concerns. Are you allergic to any other material?" His stringy dark hair shifted with the slight shake of his head. "Okay, until the new ones arrive, put a barrier between your skin and the gloves. Thick lotion or Vaseline. I'll make the order a rush and be sure the new ones are here tomorrow. Sound good?"

Totally was not expecting the man to close the space between us and wrap his arms around me. Thankfully, my quick reflexes saved my drink, a few condensation droplets slipping down my hand when I held it high in the air. Standing as stiff as one of my dead bodies, I stared wide-eyed at the white wall over his shoulder and waited for the unsolicited hug to be over.

To this guy's credit, it wasn't just him. Touching the living really wasn't my favorite pastime.

Except for Slade and Jameson.

And Sneaks. The reclusive cat had grown on me.

"Thank you." Finally moving back, he nodded toward the lab where we processed the evidence before shipping it all to the main lab in San Diego. "I'll go to work now."

I watched him walk off, afraid if I took my eyes off him, he'd hug-attack me again.

When he was safely inside the lab, I hurried into the morgue, not stopping until I had several metal tables between me and the doors. Hand lightly clasped around my throat, I inhaled deeply and counted to five before slowly releasing it, hoping that would calm my racing heart.

I wasn't in danger. I was safe. But even though the threat I'd suspected was not actually real, dread and worry still churned my stomach.

Something felt off, not counting the strange encounter, but I couldn't put my finger on the reason.

Shaking my head to dislodge the unwarranted feeling, I set my handbag and drink on the desk along the side wall and tapped the space bar on the computer, eager to check my emails. Hopefully, the lab had identified the type of shoe the unsub wore from the print we'd pulled at victim number five's home. Or even better, narrowed down the cat breed from the strands I'd pulled from victim number two's clothing.

The unease faded to excitement at finding the emails I'd waited impatiently for in my inbox. Clicking on the first one from the lab, I read the findings. The shoe print wasn't enough to go by, unfortunately, considering it was only a partial heel impression. Disappointing, but that was okay since we'd profiled that she ditched all her clothes after the crime.

The next email had me sitting up straighter. They'd found a match for the cat breed.

"Maine coon," I muttered under my breath. *Huh, never heard of it.*

I opened a browser and typed the breed into the search bar. Instantly, pictures of enormous cats appeared on the screen along with articles about the breed's temperament, care instructions, and diet. Scrolling through the images, I laughed out loud at a few of the funnier ones and, after losing at least twenty minutes to hilarious cat memes, minimized the screen.

Shifting back into work mode, I jotted down a quick note to update Jameson and Slade on these findings and attach the email to the case files. Accurate documentation throughout the case was essential; the last thing I wanted was to be the reason a suspect went free because of a clerical error.

Standing, I shrugged off the light jacket I'd slipped on in the car and draped it over the back of my chair, trading it for my white lab coat. It might not be an autopsy day, but I still needed to dress the part while pulling evidence. After checking the drawer number for last night's victim, I yanked open the cooler door and slid the metal rolling table along the smooth tracks.

Just like I'd requested, the body was still in the black bag, barely touched, even his shoes still on, ready for me to go over his clothes and body with a fine-tooth comb.

"All right, all right, all right. Let's get this party started, shall we? Shit, I forgot your name already. I'm a terrible person." Moving back to the computer, I double-tapped the keyboard. "Parker. Okay, so we'll start by going over every square inch of your clothing with my light and magnifying lens. Cool? Cool. Well, I guess you *are* cool since, you know, you've been in the cooler all night."

Even I rolled my eyes at that one. The lame jokes needed to stop if I didn't want to grow old all alone and eventually get eaten by my plethora of cats.

Oh, maybe a few Maine coons. They were cute.

More than an hour passed with me totally engrossed in pulling what looked to be foreign hairs and other particles off the victim's clothes, placing everything into tiny evidence baggies to send to the lab. Nothing jumped out as abnormal until I rolled him over. On his back, between his shoulder blades, was a single hair that gave me pause. Pinched between my tweezers, I held it beneath the magnifying glass and rotated it, allowing the bright light to reflect off the long blonde hair.

Odd.

The woman we'd found in the parking lot was a redhead, and Detective Savage was a short-haired brunette. I'd found hairs from each of them on the front of the victim—or at least what appeared to be theirs to the naked eye. DNA would confirm my suspicions. This one was not only a different color but the texture didn't even look like a normal hair. I rolled it between two gloved fingers, squinting at the blonde strand, when it hit me.

Fake. The hair was synthetic.

I flicked my gaze to the back of the victim's head. I couldn't confirm anything until I did an official autopsy, but what if this hair was attached to his back because he was attacked first from behind by the unsub? With the damage done to the back of his skull from the unsub slamming it to the pavement, there was no way to confirm my theory. Tapping my fingers on the metal table, I worked through the various possibilities.

Our unsub might have been watching, conducting her normal surveillance, when she realized Parker had drugged the woman in the parking lot. No way could our unsub let him hurt that woman and do nothing. Which was why this crime scene was so different from the others. It was a blitz attack, unplanned and sloppy.

Something tickled in the back of my mind from the night before. After placing the hair in a tiny evidence baggie, I headed out of the morgue toward the tiny crime lab. It wasn't much more than a place to process the evidence collected at the scenes before shipping it off to San Diego for analysis.

The moment I burst through the door, the tech from earlier jerked his head up, clearly startled by my abrupt entrance.

"Last night, you guys bagged everything in the alley, right?" He nodded, eyes wide. "Great, perfect." Hands on my hips, I took in the massive number of brown bags. "Any chance you remember bagging and tagging a blonde wig? I feel like I remember someone making a joke or funny comment about it. But I have zero clue where it would be, or maybe it's wishful think—"

"I actually just got done processing it." He held up the brown bag in front of him. "Long blonde synthetic hair. I swabbed the band that goes around the head for trace DNA.

And there was some red splatter that I assumed was blood, so I swabbed that too."

I wasn't a hugger, but I so wanted to hug him at that moment. Though the urge passed quickly when he leaned over and wiped his nose on the sleeve of his lab coat.

Gross.

"Please let the lab know we need a rush on those results. As fast as they can. I think our killer wore it while she attacked the victim."

Leaving as quickly as I came, focus fully on the tiny baggie in my hand, I smiled as I made my way back to the morgue on memory alone. This could be the key piece of evidence we needed to find the unsub, or at least possibly the incriminating evidence needed once we had her in custody.

Too focused on the major find, I didn't notice the person hunched in the morgue's corner when I pushed open the doors and stepped inside. It wasn't until a putrid stench, one that wasn't filling the room when I left, engulfed my nose, making me gag, that I jerked my head up and scanned the room.

My heart slammed to a halt before jolting back into a frantic rhythm.

"Josh?"

At least I *thought* it was my ex. If it was, he hadn't showered in weeks, if not months. A ratty beard covered his face, deep lines etched around his eyes and along his forehead. One thing Josh always had going for him was his good boy-next-door looks, though that ship had sailed from how he appeared now. And that rancid stench that first caught my attention wafted from his direction in nauseating waves.

His hand was frozen in my purse. No doubt I'd caught him stealing my wallet.

"What are you doing here, Josh?" I asked with more force this time. Now that the initial shock had worn off, anger quickly filled its place. "You need to drop my shit and get out of here. Now."

He blinked and slowly stood to full height, losing the rounded spine and sagging shoulders.

"You."

I rolled my eyes. "Well, yeah, me. This is my place of work, and you need to—"

"You ruined everything," he hissed and took a menacing step closer.

A sliver of fear wormed through my rising anger. This wasn't the man I'd married, not that he was ever that great. I had no clue what he was capable of now. Sidestepping a steel table, I put it between us as a barrier.

"We had it good, everything we wanted. Then you went and fucked it all up. You're a selfish bitch for not caring what happened to me or anyone else. Didn't care or even try to work things out between us, just fucking left to start this new life."

My hands tightened into fists at my sides. His accusations, calling me selfish for wanting something for myself, or calling me a bitch for not agreeing with him, weren't anything new. In fact, calling me self-centered was his go-to, breaking me down so I would give in to whatever he wanted.

"No, you had it good because I supported us. I went to work every day, worked my ass off, and you just sat at the apartment drinking or fucking around on me."

"I supported you," he roared and tossed both hands out. The movement parted his heavy coat. With the way it swayed, it seemed one side weighed more than the other. "I gave you everything, even put my career on hold so you could have yours. And this is the thanks I got. A wife who left me when things got tough, just tossed me aside when I gave you everything I could. It might not have been all that you wanted, but I did what I fucking could for someone like you."

Wait. Is he right? Did I give up after he'd supported me, gave up his own life for—

I shook my head. No. After college, he'd worked a string of short-term jobs and was fired from every single one for outbursts at customers, not showing up, or even one time making the female staff uncomfortable. He didn't put his career on hold for me. He'd never had one to begin with.

"And now look at me," he sneered, daring another step closer. "Look at what you did to me. Left me all alone and heartbroken, and I couldn't recover. You were my everything, and you just tossed me aside when it suited you."

"No, it wasn't that way, and you—"

"And now you're with them." His eyes narrowed as they swept up and down my body. I wanted to cover myself, hide from his leering observation even though I was fully clothed. "A fucking whore. Just like your mom."

Unshed tears clogged my throat, burning as I swallowed them down.

"You were wrong. Just admit that and we can forget this whole thing. I'll take you back because that's what good husbands do—not that you deserve it."

"'This whole thing' being our divorce that was finalized? Or maybe the fact that you destroyed my home," I screeched, pressing up to my toes as my anger reached its boiling point.

"You didn't deserve all that nice new stuff when I'm living like this." He tossed his arms out wide, propelling another wave of body odor through the room.

I waved a hand in front of my face, which was like

jerking a red flag in front of a bull considering the situation. And the next thought that escaped didn't help.

"Not going to lie. You smell like my floater yesterday that was pulled from the ocean—"

"Stop," he yelled. "Stop it with the dead body shit. No one gives a flying fuck, Rain. No one. Everyone thinks you're creepy and disgusting, and you know your looks aren't helping you any. They all put up with your crazy-ass sayings, tolerate you being around, because it's their job."

Suddenly the door swung open and the tech from earlier—who now, faced with crazy Josh, didn't seem nearly as creepy—walked in brandishing....

What the actual fuck is going on in my morgue?

"Are those nunchucks?" I asked with a startled laugh.

He nodded, not breaking his steely stare at Josh.

"Where the hell did you—" I cut myself off and sliced a hand through the air. "Never mind. We'll have a talk about bringing weapons to work later. You need to go get someone with...." I didn't want to say "an actual weapon" and hurt his feelings. He did just insert himself into a potentially dangerous situation for me. "Training," I finally managed.

Boom. Nailed it. All feelings left intact.

"No," Josh hissed, drawing my full attention back his way—to the gun gripped in his hand.

Well, shit.

This just went from bad to "a week-old liquefied body in a tub" bad.

"I'm not leaving without you, Rain. You're coming home with me, and we're going to make this work."

"Um," I muttered, jerking my gaze around the room, looking for any type of weapon. If I'd prepped the area for an autopsy, there would be lots of sharp and deadly tools to chuck his way. "I'm pretty certain there are two men who will absolutely disagree with you on that plan."

Josh's lips curled into a snarl. "I'd like to see them try."

Well, if I knew my guys, he wouldn't have to wait long.

Because the longer I was away from them with no communication, the sooner they would be here.

Now we just had to wait. And hope Josh didn't get trigger-happy.

30

JAMESON

The rising sun's glare through the glass door, burning my retinas, was offensive and fucking rude. Grumbling under my breath, I shifted on the living room couch to face the kitchen to save myself from being blinded. Sneaks hissed at me for interrupting his bath and darted off toward his room. I rolled my eyes at the animal and shot another annoyed look out toward the pool deck.

In its defense, the beautiful sunny day wasn't to blame for my bad mood. It stemmed from the worry of not hearing from Rain. She'd promised she wouldn't be gone long, but now almost three hours had passed since she left, and the knot in my gut wound tighter with every minute that ticked by.

"Who pissed in your cereal?" Slade rumbled as he shuffled into the kitchen. It took him all of five seconds to realize I was alone in the living room. "Where's Rain?"

I took a slow sip of my coffee. "She left just after five this morning."

"For where?" He leaned both forearms on the island.

Sleepy Slade was gone, intense and terrifying Slade now wide awake and glaring at me.

"The morgue." I stared into my dark coffee. "But that was a while ago, and I haven't heard from her. I know she's somewhere safe, but...." I took a sip, trying to give myself a second before making him worry too. What if I was wrong and had no reason to be nervous? "I don't know. Something feels off. I can't explain it."

"Did you text her?" The urgency in his voice had my concern kicking up another notch.

"Yes, once, but—"

My phone vibrated along the coffee table, and I released a relieved breath. But that relief changed to confusion at Charlie's number filling the screen.

I swiped to answer the call and put it on speaker. "Charlie—"

"Where is Dr. Evans?"

Coffee sloshed over my hand, dripping onto the rug, when I lurched to stand at his panicked tone. "What?"

"Just tell me where she is, Jameson. Now."

Fuck, I couldn't breathe. If something had happened to Rain while I sat here drinking my fucking coffee, I wouldn't forgive myself. "She went to the morgue earlier this morning."

"Fuck," he cursed under his breath. "And where are you or Detective Taylor? Are you with her?"

"We're both at his house. What the fuck is going on, Charlie?"

A heavy breath blew across the mouthpiece. "I set up an alert to let me know if her ex's face appeared in video. Well, I got a hit this morning, about thirty minutes ago, and I just now looked to see where he'd popped up."

Dread sat heavy in my gut, churning the earlier sips of coffee. "Where, Charlie?"

"At the fucking Santa Coasta police station. He walked right in, bypassed the person working the desk, and I lost him when he turned down the hall that I suspect leads to the morgue. I can hack into their system, but—"

"It'll take time." I looked up. Slade was nowhere to be seen, but I overheard his raised voice echoing down the hall, ordering people around. "We're leaving in less than thirty seconds. Thanks, Charlie. We'll handle it from here."

"Report back," he demanded. "I want to know that she's okay."

With a nod he couldn't see, I ended the call and hurried to the room with my clothes. Pulling on a T-shirt, I swiped my credentials and sidearm off the table. Then I hurried back into the living room, almost getting run over by Slade as he stormed past me while yelling at whoever was on the other end of the line.

"Just fucking get someone down there to monitor the situation. Call me before making a move. We treat this like a volatile domestic hostage situation. We have no idea what he'll do if he feels trapped."

At the front door, he launched a pair of shoes at my head before grabbing a pair for himself. Racing after him, I skidded to a stop, changing direction from the turd mobile to his matte black G-Wagon. I climbed in, barely having time to shut the door before he took off, tires screeching.

A couple minutes into the silent drive, a sharp shrill poured through the speakers, cutting the rising tension.

"What do we know?" Slade answered after pressing a button on his steering wheel to accept the call. If I weren't almost about to puke from worry, I'd admire the interior and all the fancy buttons of the cool-as-hell SUV.

"One man holding a gun, Dr. Evans, and a man we think is a crime scene tech are in the morgue. The man and Dr. Evans are arguing, but the tech is down. I repeat, the tech is down."

"What the fuck did he do? Shoot some innocent guy trying to intervene?" I hissed. The officers outside the doors needed to know exactly who they were dealing with, understand that barging in without us could result in the standoff ending in a way that would rip me in two. "This man is delusional and armed. He's a pissed-off narcissist who's lost control of the one person he needs and will do anything—and I repeat, *anything*—to gain that control back."

"And he thinks that's Dr. Evans?" the man on the phone asked.

"Precisely. His life probably fell apart after she filed for divorce and left, so he blames her for everything that's wrong now." This wasn't good at all. "Do not go inside that room unless you feel like Dr. Evans's life is in immediate danger. If they're arguing, then Rain is doing her job—stalling. Once we get there, I'll go in alone, so I'll need a vest—"

"What the fuck are you talking about?" Slade said, flicking his angry glare my way. "You're not going in there alone."

"Trust me," I snapped and hit the End Call button. "I know what I'm doing. If we want to get her out of this unharmed, then you'll send me in alone. He'll feel cornered and ganged up on if we both go in there. I'll talk to him, and hopefully Rain remembers what I coached her on last night."

"What's that?" His hands tightened around the wheel.

"Before you came back and she fell asleep, we talked about what to do if she found herself alone with him. That she knows him better than any of us, which we could use to our advantage. She'll either need to give in to what he wants, which I'm assuming is her"—Slade's curse vibrated through the SUV—"or figure out a distraction that will break his focus and give us an opportunity to move in."

"You thought this might happen," he mused. "Why didn't you tell me?"

"I hoped it wouldn't, but I've profiled this guy, and I figured it was a strong possibility. I just wasn't sure when or where. She knew the risks of going out alone, but she's Rain. No one can keep her sheltered or caged when she has her mind set on something. I wanted to cover her in bubble wrap and keep her locked in your house until we caught this fucker, but that's not Rain."

"Now what?" Slade said after a minute. The station was now within sight.

"Now—" I blew out a steadying breath. "—I put my training to work and get our girl out of this unharmed."

The moment we stepped into the station, a flurry of movement and shouts greeted us. By the time we made it downstairs, I was wearing a borrowed vest, since mine was back at the house, and a Santa Coasta PD jacket over it. Not only did the light jacket cover the vest, but it also hid the gun tucked into the back of my sweats.

"If you sense shit is going south, you give the word and we're there."

I nodded at Slade as I secured an earpiece that would allow them to hear everything I did. "You know I won't put her safety at risk. This is our best chance to get everyone out of there unharmed. I've got this."

"I know you do," he said confidently. "It's that crazy-ass fucker in there I don't trust."

I huffed a laugh, unable to force a real one with the

tension thrumming through my veins. Taking a step toward the doors, I sucked down a deep breath to calm my nerves. Slade's massive hand slapped between my shoulder blades, jerking me forward a single step. I turned to glare at him over my shoulder, but the worry and concern in his green eyes chased away any irritation.

"Josh Evans," I called, projecting my voice. "I'm coming in, unarmed."

"Who the hell are you?" he asked from the other side of the doors. "What do you want?"

"I just want to talk," I said, trying to keep my tone even. "To understand your demands so we can all walk out of this and no one gets hurt."

A pause. A too-long fucking pause that had my heart jumping into my throat.

"Only you," he yelled.

My shoulders dropped several inches. The tightness in my muscles had my still-healing bullet wound throbbing, but I pushed the discomfort to the back of my mind.

Cold from the steel door soaked into my sweaty palm as I sealed it to the metal and pushed it open just enough for me to wedge through but keep the horde of officers behind me out of view. The last thing we needed him to know was he wasn't getting out of here without handcuffs.

Unless it was in a body bag. But I really didn't want it to come to that. Every life I took in the line of duty added another dark mark on my soul.

The stench of body odor and alcohol smacked me in the face the second my foot crossed the threshold. Breathing through my mouth, I kept my gaze locked on Rain's ex and the gun he had trained on her.

It took every ounce of effort to not rush him and slam the bastard to the floor.

Not yet.

Hands in the air, I forced myself to not look at Rain. "I'm only here to talk. What is it you want, Josh?"

The man looked nothing like the picture I had of him. This man in front of me had nothing left to lose, and that was clear by his current irrational approach to turn his life around. Holding the ME at gunpoint in the morgue only a few yards from hundreds of armed officers proved he was past the point of thinking clearly or negotiating.

I had to hope Rain knew that, too, and had a distraction that would help me get a shot in before he killed us both. Because there was only so long we could keep him from recognizing the inevitable—that he'd backed himself into a corner.

"You," he hissed, eyes narrowed on me. And just like I knew he would when he recognized me as one of the men in Rain's life, the gun's barrel swung my way. Despite the fact that a gun was pointed at my chest, relief soothed some of my nerves since it wasn't aimed at Rain anymore. "You're why she left me."

He had no idea how true that statement was.

"Tell me what you want, Josh," I said calmly.

"I want my wife back!" he yelled, voice shaking with the rage running through him.

"Wife or life?" I stated slowly.

"Fucking both. She doesn't deserve to leave me, take everything I worked for away." I nodded along without rolling my eyes, which I considered a major win for the day. "I made her. I supported her, and then she turned around and became a whore, just like her mother."

I forced my face into a blank mask. Showing any kind of reaction to his lies could get Rain and me both killed.

"And she—" He swung the gun back to Rain, who

squeaked. *Ah, fuck.* "She"—the gun shook in his hand—"ruined everything."

"I understand," I placated. "What do you want her to understand, Josh?"

Damn, I needed that gun pointed back at me. I had a vest on. Rain was vulnerable to any shot.

"That she can't leave me. No one leaves me. I deserve better than—"

"Oh my," Rain exclaimed, cutting him off with her shocked tone and snagging his confused attention. "Is that an Australian jumping spider?" she shrieked, pointing just over Josh's shoulder.

With a high-pitched squeal, Josh whirled around, searching the walls and floor for the made-up spider.

If I had the time, I would have high-fived Rain for giving me the distraction I needed. But I had to act fast before Josh realized there was, in fact, no spider.

Withdrawing the gun from the back of the sweats, I aimed it at his chest just as Josh whirled back around, face red and nostrils flaring. Guess he figured it out faster than I'd expected. His wild eyes focused on the stun gun in my hand, he jerked his very real gun in my direction. Without hesitation, I pulled the trigger, sending the leads and lines straight for his chest.

Unfortunately, at exactly the same time, he pulled the trigger too.

31

SLADE

The second I heard the ear-rattling bang, I burst through the morgue doors, gun at the ready. Swinging the barrel left and right, I surveyed the room before shoving it into my holster and storming toward the fucker jerking along the ground as the electric current continued to pulse through his entire body.

I could pull the leads free, but I wouldn't. I could also easily angle my holster toward the fucker's head and my gun could accidentally go off, but I wouldn't. Because that would mean prison, and I was way too bougie for that shit.

A dark spot formed on his pants, adding to the stench wafting off him.

"Disgusting prick," I grumbled.

Using the tip of my shoe, I not so gently rolled him over and pulled both hands behind his back, securing a set of cuffs around his wrists. His incoherent mumbles told me he was still conscious, but clearly the stun gun did its job and kept him incapacitated until I could restrain him.

With the immediate threat taken care of, I swiveled around on the balls of my feet, gaze searching the last place

I saw Rain. Her voice drifted from the other side of the room, toward the doors. Jameson sat on the floor, hand pressed to his chest, with Rain ripping at his shirt.

"Check on him, please," Rain said when I stopped by her side, tipping her head toward the tech now sitting up, rubbing his head. "Damnit," she snapped at Jameson, "I need to see where you're hit."

"The vest stopped it," Jameson said, voice strained.

Shaking my head, I squatted near the tech, who seemed to sway where he sat. "What happened to...?" The object beside him caught my eye. "Are those nunchucks?" Taking in the red welt on his forehead, I stifled a laugh. "Did you hit yourself in the head with those things?"

His cheeks flushed bright red, which stood out against his pale skin. He must have hit himself, then smacked his head on the floor, knocking him unconscious.

"We'll get you some medical attention now that we've neutralized the threat. You gonna make it until the medics can get down here?"

He nodded and curled in on himself.

Well, shit.

"Listen, it looks like you tried to protect Dr. Evans, am I right?" Again, he nodded, still not speaking. "Well then, no need to be embarrassed. You tried to do something instead of running away from the danger. No matter the outcome, you did good, kid."

When I turned back around, both Rain and Jameson were gawking at me.

"What?"

"Oh nothing," Jameson wheezed. "Nothing at all, you big teddy bear, you."

"Oh, fucking hell," I groaned as I stood. Pointing at the tech, I shot him the scowl that made most grown men run screaming. "Don't you tell a single soul I was nice to you. Got it?"

"Yes... yes... sir."

Knowing my grumpy asshole reputation would stay intact, I stepped over to Rain and Jameson.

"Good job." I held out my fist, which he tapped with his own. She'd gotten his T-shirt and vest off while I handled the kid. "Way to go on not dying."

"You should needlepoint that shit," he grumbled, wincing as Rain poked and prodded around the large red area on his chest. "You scared the shit out of us, Rain."

"Yeah, well, first, I didn't do it on purpose. And two... okay, I don't have a second point. Is he going to be okay?" Her gaze flicked to her ex as two officers dragged him out of the morgue. "I'm honestly not sure how I'll feel either way you answer that question."

"He'll be put away for a long time. Are you okay?" I squatted down to be at their eye level so they could stop straining their necks. I brushed a knuckle down her cheek. "I was so fucking terrified something would happen to you."

Her responding smile was weak. "Thanks to Jameson, I'm okay. Shaken up, but I knew you two would come."

"So... spiders?" Jameson huffed before squeezing his lids shut and groaning. "He's afraid of spiders?"

"Deathly. Like can't even see them in a movie or show without having to leave the room."

"Smart and beautiful," I muttered with so much fucking pride filling my chest.

"We need to get you to the hospital," Rain demanded.

"Nope. Nothing a little rest and TLC won't cure." He shot her a wink. "Know anywhere I can get both? I mean, it is our day off."

"Oh," she exclaimed and leaped up. "You'll never

guess—"

"Dr. Evans, you're okay."

We all turned to find Detectives Savage and Gray moving around, the officers still lingering in the morgue. Fuck, she still had to give a statement, which would take a while.

I eyed the dead man on the table, knowing the rising temperature in the room wasn't good for it.

"Want me to put your body away?" I asked Rain.

Her hand came to her heart, and I swear tears gathered on her lower lids. "You called it my body." At first, I thought I'd said something wrong until she leaped off the floor and lunged toward me. Arms wrapped around my neck, she pressed her lips to my ear. "Thank you."

"For what?" I murmured into her hair while wishing all these people were gone so I could kiss the fuck out of her.

She pulled back, and sure enough, a single tear dripped down her cheek. "For accepting my quirks. Especially the dead body stuff."

"It's a part of who you are, Rain. If I can't accept all of you, then I don't deserve any of you."

She nodded and wiped at her eyes. "Thank you. And yes, if you could put him back in his locker, I'd appreciate it. I wasn't planning to do the autopsy today anyway, but definitely not now."

"Who was that guy?" Detective Savage asked.

I kept one ear on the conversation while I wheeled the dead fucker toward the cooler.

"My ex. Long story short, he's a narcissist who thought his downfall was my fault because I had the courage to leave his verbally and emotionally abusive ass."

I chuckled under my breath. That about summed it up perfectly.

"Want me to kill him?"

I whirled around at the bitter tone in Detective Gray's voice.

"What? No. Then I'd have to do the autopsy, and I never want to see that man naked again."

The entire room burst out laughing. Exactly what we needed to cut through the tension from the too-close call for both her and Jameson.

"What were you about to tell us?" Jameson asked after I put the body away and came back to the small group. He held out his hand, and I wrapped mine around it to help him stand. "You seemed excited about something, Rain."

I watched as she dipped her hand into the front pocket of her lap coat and pulled out a tiny evidence baggie.

"Do you know what this is?"

I leaned in close and squinted, only barely able to make out a single blonde hair. "Is that our killer's?"

"Nope. It's synthetic, but you'll never guess what someone bagged and tagged in one of the nearby dumpsters last night." Her growing excitement had her bouncing on the balls of her feet. "Time's up. A wig. A blonde one that, with the naked eye, looks very similar to this hair that was found on the victim."

"Holy fuck," Jameson exclaimed beside me.

"Exactly." She beamed.

"But you can't pull DNA from a strand of fake hair," Detective Savage said, reminding us all that she and her partner were still in the room.

"No, but I can from the band around the inside of the wig. Sweat is a great source of DNA."

"Holy shit," I muttered. "You're telling me you think we have our killer's DNA?"

She nodded so forcefully that her ponytail popped up

and down. "I've already had the wig swabbed and asked for the results to be rushed. We could know something within the next two weeks."

"That's only if they're in the system," Detective Gray stated. "Right?"

Is that worry in her tone?

"Right, but even if she isn't in the system, we'll have it to compare to a suspect's. It's a win-win either way."

"That's a fantastic find," Jameson said, draping an arm over her shoulders. "Almost makes up for being shot by your ex."

The doors swung open, and the chief walked in, a mix of concerned and pissed in his no-nonsense expression.

"I'll talk to him," I sighed. "You"—I pointed at Detective Savage—"take her statement." Swinging my finger to the other detective, I tilted my head toward the piss on the floor. "And you call someone to clean that shit up."

Without another word, I turned on my heels and marched toward the chief, ready to do whatever it took to get Rain out of here sooner than later. I had grand plans of not letting her out of my sight—or hands—for the foreseeable future.

POPCORN, two beers, and a glass of bourbon in hand, my bare feet slapped on the hardwood floors as I made my way back toward the media room where I'd left Jameson and Rain. We'd been home for a few hours and decided we all needed a distraction after the insane start to the day. Rain was okay, but Jameson and I both knew it would take more than half a day to recover, and we would be there by her side for every step.

At Sneaks's room, I poked my head in, finding him dozing in his hammock. His gray gaze met mine, and I gave him a nod, which I swore he returned before turning over and putting his back to me.

Asshole.

But I loved him.

Thank fuck Rain wasn't allergic to cats or I would've had to buy Sneaks his own house next door.

"There's no way. It's impossible." I paused outside the media room, listening in on the conversation going on inside. "Everyone has that one place." My ears perked at Rain's words. *What in the hell are they talking about?* "And I'm going to find yours."

Well, this just got interesting.

When I pushed the door open, their heads snapped my way, both sporting wide smiles. Rain straddled Jameson's hips as he lounged on the massive sofa. He shot me a wink before turning his attention back to Rain.

"Do your worst, Raindrop, but I'm telling you I'm not ticklish." He gripped her hips, thumbs sliding under her loose top. "But I know you are."

Her hazel eyes went wide. "Don't you dare, Jameson Bend. What have I ever done to you?"

In a practiced move, Jameson switched their positions, Rain's back now pressing into the soft cushions.

Grabbing both of her hands in one of his own, Jameson held them high above her head, stretching Rain out beneath him. The position tightened her shirt around her braless breasts, the hard tips poking the soft cotton. My feet guided me deeper into the room, my gaze locked on the two staring at each other, fanning the growing heat building between them.

Popcorn, my drink, and one beer discarded on a side

table, I moved to stand beside them. Rain's hair rasped over the cushion, and those sparkling hazel eyes met mine.

"Save me," she breathed, though the way she wiggled beneath Jameson, making him groan, told me they both were okay right where they were.

"I don't think so, baby." Bottle dangling between two fingers, I swept the hard, cold bottom along her neck, down her chest, and brushed it against her taut nipples. With a gasp, she tugged at Jameson's hold, trying to get away. "Pull it down."

Jameson acted immediately, knowing exactly what I wanted. Finger hooked in the top of her loose tank, he pulled the neck down, exposing both breasts. With a wicked smirk, I repeated my previous action, the slick glass now sliding directly against her sensitive peaks.

Rain groaned, back shifting along the couch. "Slade, why are you so mean?"

"Oh, baby, you haven't seen anything yet."

Jameson and Rain both stilled and looked up at me.

I shrugged, then pressed the smooth glass to her sternum before dragging it toward her belly button. "Tell me, baby, how adventurous have you been with this amazing body of yours?"

Her throat worked with every hard swallow.

"Do you use toys when you play with yourself?"

She nodded.

Jameson shifted lower, taking her shorts with him when it was clear where I wanted to press the bottle next.

"Have you ever played with things not meant to be toys in this tight cunt?" She shook her head. "Hmm, we can work up to that." Jameson cursed, and I grinned. "What about that ass of yours that I love so much, baby? Anyone ever taken you there?"

"No," she whimpered. "Fuck, Slade."

With a chuckle, I slid the bottle along the inside of her thighs before dragging it through her slick core. "Don't worry, we'll work up to that too." Stepping back, I licked the side of the bottle, shining with her arousal, not taking my gaze off her. "Jameson, on the floor. We're going to make our girl forget everything but us. Hell, I want you to tongue-fuck her so good she forgets her damn name."

I swallowed a laugh at how quickly he slid off the couch. Lying on the rug, he yanked his sweats down, kicking them off to the side.

Hands wrapped around Rain's waist, I hauled her off the couch, holding tight until she was steady on her feet. I swept my gaze up and down her delectable body, upper teeth sinking into my lower lip to quiet my rumbling groan.

"Leave your top just like that." It looked so fucking dirty with her top pulled down and tits spilling out. I wrapped a hand around my cock and squeezed. "Take your shorts off and sit on Jameson's face."

"What?"

Whirling her around, I landed two sharp spanks on her perfect ass before ripping her sleep shorts the rest of the way down her legs until they pooled at her feet. Her the puppet and me the master, I plucked her off her feet and moved her so she stood over Jameson's face. His hands moved up her thighs, fingers dipping into her slick core. Rain's lids fluttered shut and she swayed forward, but my grip on her shoulders kept her upright.

With Jameson playing with her below, I leaned in and sucked a nipple between my lips, pulling and nipping at the peak. Her fingers gripped either side of my head, holding me to her chest like I had any intention of letting go.

Easing her down, I helped her settle over Jameson's face,

positioning her core right over his mouth. I pulled back, popping her nipple from my lips. Hair mussed, cheeks flushed, Rain looked completely lost in the moment. Perfect. Exactly where we wanted her after the traumatic day.

"Now, you're going to let Jameson lick every inch of your sweet pussy while I have some fun with this perfect mouth of yours."

Hands on her hips, Jameson lowered her until he could lick every inch of her cunt. Rain tossed her head back, long dark hair swaying against her back as she latched onto my shoulders to keep herself steady. Her hands in mine, I shifted her hold to my hips when I stood and pulled the band of my shorts down until it nestled just below my rock-hard cock.

"Are you ready for me, baby?" Eyes hooded, she nodded. "Good, because I've been dreaming of your mouth on me again. This time I won't be gentle." Threading my fingers into her hair, I held her in place and flexed my hips forward.

The first brush of her lips, followed by her tongue swirling around my swollen head, had me gritting my teeth to keep from plunging down her throat. The heat from her mouth strung me even higher as I pumped in and out, inching deeper with each thrust.

But it was her scream of pleasure as she came on Jameson's tongue, the vibrations against my shaft, that had me losing control and pushing forward until I tapped the back of her throat.

Chest heaving, I stared down at the woman I loved and brushed a sweaty strand of hair off her forehead.

"You're so fucking perfect, baby. Now relax your throat for me, because I'm going deeper than your smart mouth has ever been fucked before."

32

RAIN

Eyes wide, tears leaking from the corners, I nodded, his thick cock shifting deeper in my mouth with the movement. Tingles of bliss still sparkled through every cell after the orgasm Jameson's tongue ripped from me. He didn't give me a second to recover before he latched onto my clit and sucked, building another orgasm right on the heels of the first one.

Jaw as wide as it could go, I flattened my tongue and relaxed my throat, preparing for Slade to follow through on his promise. Using the grip on my hair, he tipped my head back and slowly inched forward. I gagged, throat working around him, but he pushed farther still.

"That's it, baby. Oh fuck, your throat is magic. Breathe through your nose, swallow—" His guttural groan and full-body tremor when I obeyed had me moving my hips faster, grinding my core against Jameson's face. And by the sounds coming from between my thighs, Jameson definitely approved.

Three fingers plunged into my channel, replacing Jameson's talented tongue, shooting me over the edge again. With a curse, Slade jerked out of my mouth, his cock popping from my lips, and hauled me upright.

"Jameson, on the couch." Slade slammed his lips to mine, tongue swiping inside my mouth, dominating the kiss like only he could. The world spun. My entire body felt light and free. I didn't protest when he guided me backward, the edge of the couch tapping the backs of my knees. "Sit on his cock, baby." My core pulsed, squeezing around nothing, making me whimper. "Shh, we know what you need, Rain."

Different hands wrapped around my hips and guided me backward. The tip of Jameson's cock brushed between my thighs before slipping past my entrance. My lips parted on a gasp at the stretch, the angle making him hit every inch of my sensitive walls. Fully seated, ass on Jameson's stomach, I pitched forward, hands slapping to his knees.

Unable to stop, I rocked against him, causing a burst of pleasure to race through me.

"That's it, baby. Ride his cock while you swallow mine."

I barely comprehended his words before Slade's massive cock pushed past my lips and slid down my throat. I coughed and gagged, but that only spurred him deeper, which had me moving faster on Jameson's cock.

"Oh fucking hell," Jameson cursed. He moved me up and down his shaft, impaling me with every thrust of his hips off the couch. "I won't fucking last long with her cunt strangling the life out of my cock."

"That's it, baby. Make your pussy suck every drop out of him."

I shuddered around Jameson, and my moan vibrated along Slade's shaft.

The second Jameson sneaked a hand around to flick my clit, I shattered. Crying around Slade's cock, I pushed at his massive thighs, but he only snapped his hips forward, lodging himself deep in my throat as he came at the same time. I swallowed his cum while squeezing and jerking around Jameson, who was so deep inside me I felt every twitch of him as he came.

Slade pulled back, spent cock slipping past my lips. Falling onto the couch beside Jameson, he pressed a tatted forearm against his eyes. Soft lips trailed up my sweaty spine. Our combined heavy breathing was the only sound filling the room.

With Jameson softening inside me, I leaned back until I rested against his chest.

"That was fucking amazing, Raindrop," Jameson whispered in my ear. Gathering my hair, he moved it to the side so he could rest a chin on my shoulder. "And don't think for one second that we're even close to being done with you."

"I'll need a fucking minute after that," Slade said beside us. "I'm an old fuck, remember?"

Jameson's responding chuff had a smile spreading across my face. "Don't worry, old man. I'll take care of our girl while you recover."

"What about me?" I laughed. "Do I get to recover?"

"Would you want to, Raindrop?" His breath whispered past my ear. "Or would you rather keep playing and see how many orgasms I can wring out of your perfect pussy before the old man can rebound and fill you full with his monster dick?"

Decisions, decisions.

Not really.

Who would say no to being worshiped by him?

By them?

"Play." I sucked in a breath, feeling him twitch inside me. "Make today about us, all three of us, not him. He doesn't get any headspace. Never again."

"As you wish, Raindrop. It's my pleasure to make you so blissed out that all you can think about is us. And I'll do it every day you allow me."

I never wanted this to end, but soon reality would come crashing back in and I would need to face the trauma I knew lurked in the dark recesses of my mind.

Tomorrow. Tonight was about us.

And only us.

"I KNOW, MOM," I huffed into the phone as I paced the length of the pool deck. The late-morning sun heated my skin just enough to chase away the chill in the air. "But I'm okay. I'm sorry you guys were so worried."

"It wasn't your fault," Mom said with a sigh. "I don't like you being so far away. We didn't even know you were in danger until it was all over. Now here we are three days later, and I'm still anxious every time I see your name pop up on my phone, worried something else terrible has happened to you."

Dropping onto a lounge chair, I leaned all the way back and closed both lids. "So, I'm calling for a purpose this morning—"

"To schedule a FaceTime call so we can meet the two men you're seeing?" There was no mistaking the smirk in her voice. "I knew you'd come around. Do you think you'll stop at two or—"

"Mom," I laughed. "Stop it right there. I'm not building an harem."

"Works for some societies."

"But not for me."

It wasn't too long ago that I didn't remember what to do

with a penis attached to a living body, and now I had two to wrangle. Definitely not interested in making things more complex than they already were.

Not that I minded. Having those two, knowing they were mine and I was theirs, was the best feeling ever. I was supported, loved, needed, and wanted. Everything I'd ever wanted and never knew I needed all meshed into two amazing—and well endowed—men. Our unique relationship was growing deeper, faster than expected, but that was okay. Even if we hadn't talked through the details of how it would work once Jameson left.

And possibly me too.

Which brought me back to the reason for calling Mom. Blowing out a slow breath, I gave myself an internal pep talk for telling her about the conversation I'd had with SSA Riggs yesterday. Because if I knew Mom, she'd blow it all way out of proportion and have me on the next flight home to start house hunting.

"So back to the reason I called.... I sort of have a job offer."

"I didn't know you were looking."

"I wasn't. This job just fell into my lap, so to speak. Jameson's boss was impressed with my findings, how I connected the murders here, and she offered me a job. With her profiling team. In Dallas." I cringed at the sharp inhale from the other end of the line. I really didn't want Mom to get her hopes up, but I also needed her advice. "I'd review reports of cases where an ME is involved, checking for discrepancies and finding connections that might have been missed. Or actually flying to the small towns where the team is needed and only a coroner is available."

Mom hummed, but in the background, I heard her pounding footsteps as she ran up the stairs. "And this would be with the FBI, you say?" I rolled my eyes at her loud tone. Obviously, she was trying to not so subtly let Dad know we were discussing something big. "In Dallas?"

Damn, could she have said that any slower?

"She's coming home?" I heard Dad ask.

"Mom," I whined. "Don't get his hopes up. Or yours or Uncle Sam's either. I haven't decided what I'm going to do." The heavy pause made guilt fill my chest. "Yes, it's an excellent opportunity, but I'm not sure I'm ready this early in my career to leave the day-to-day aspects of this job. I love what I do, and I don't know if I'm ready to step away from all that."

"Rain," Mom said in that soft voice she always used when she was about to impart something she viewed as wisdom, "do you really love the day-to-day aspects, or is it the problem-solving that comes with it? Don't think about this offer as stepping away but gaining more responsibility, doing what you love on a grander scale. And no one says you have to stay in this job for the rest of your life. It could be a steppingstone to get you into a chief medical examiner role somewhere."

Damnit, I hated when she was right.

"I just wanted to let y'all know about the opportunity. I'm still thinking it over and told SSA Riggs I would have a decision for her soon. Now, enough about me. How are things at home?"

"We're all good, honey. I don't have another trip planned for a while. Your uncle is away for a few weeks." It always made me snort when she called him my uncle. It started back when I was younger so their lifestyle didn't affect how others treated me at school, and it kind of stuck. "And your dad—"

"Is fucking tired," he called out, making me snort. "Here,

give me that phone." There was a rustling noise and them bickering about Mom hogging me, and then Dad's deep sigh came through the line. "Hey there, Rainy Day. Is there a trial date set for that motherfuck—"

"Language," Mom chastised somewhere in the background.

"That ass of an ex of yours?" he corrected.

"Not yet. He's going before the judge soon, though. I've heard he plans to plead not guilty despite half of the police force witnessing what happened that day."

"I never liked that guy," he muttered.

"I know, Dad. So, you're tired? What's going on?"

"Just tired of herding cats." I barked a laugh. "I can't keep up with all the new ways people have invented to cheat the system or hurt each other." He paused. "I'm debating retiring sooner rather than later. Let someone younger step in with new ideas and more damn energy than my seventy-five-year-old ass."

"You're not seventy-five." I could almost hear his mustache brush against the phone with his growing smile. He'd called himself seventy-five for years now. Saying that was how he felt the number just didn't match up.

"Still. Time for me to travel, explore while I still can. You seriously thinking about taking this job in Dallas?"

"Maybe," I muttered. At the whoosh of the glass patio door opening, I turned to face Jameson and Slade as they stepped outside. "Hey, listen, I need to run. Talk to you and Mom later. Love you."

After his quick goodbye, I ended the call and set the phone beside me.

"You guys headed to the station?" I asked.

"Yep." Jameson bent down and pressed his lips to my forehead. "You'll be right behind us, right?"

I nodded, holding a hand to my forehead, shielding my eyes from the sun as I shifted my gaze to Slade. "Right behind you. I don't have anybody waiting for me." I paused. "Get it? Any. Body. Anybody."

"I'm laughing on the inside," Slade said with an indulgent grin. Holding my chin between two fingers, he tipped my face all the way up and pressed a searing kiss to my lips. When he pulled back, his green eyes searched my face. "You sure you don't want to ride with us?"

Careful to not let my anxious, twisting emotions show, I shook my head, dislodging his hold. "I'm taking the chief's advice and taking things a little slower. Who knew a lazy morning could be so enjoyable?"

"Everyone, Raindrop. Everyone." Running his hand down my hair, Jameson tugged at the ends. "We'll either be in your office or at Slade's desk. Come find us when you get there, okay?"

It made me want to hug them both, knowing they didn't want to leave me alone but still did. I would push them away if they didn't. I was fairly certain they knew that too. Well, Jameson did and then communicated—a.k.a. strong-armed into understanding—my need for independence to Slade.

"You know I will."

"Did you tell your parents?" Slade asked, shoving both tattooed hands into the pockets of his slacks. "About the job offer?"

I nodded. "Of course, they're excited about the idea of me being close, but I told them I'm still thinking about it. I'm not sure if I'm ready to leave all this. I love my job and the people I work with."

Jameson shot Slade a strange expression, but Slade completely ignored him. With a huff, Jameson waved goodbye and headed inside, grumbling about stubborn assholes.

"What was that all about?" I asked.

"Nothing, baby. Enjoy your lazy morning. Turn it into a lazy day if you need to. And don't think you're fooling me. I know you're not telling us how you're really feeling after the incident in the morgue, but know I'm here to listen when you are. Bye, baby. Love you."

With that L-word bomb, he turned on his heels and strode inside, leaving me gaping after him.

Love. You.

Me?

I flopped back onto the lounge chair with a huge grin on my lips.

"The sexy man I fantasized about for almost two years just said he loves me. At least I think he did." I popped back up, smile now more of a grimace. "What if he said 'more you,' meaning he wants more of me later?" Lip between my teeth, I worked it back and forth. "Or 'door you,' for like 'adore you'?"

A pitiful whimper escaped, and I slapped my face down into my awaiting palms.

Love was a big step. Not that I didn't feel that way about him and Jameson. My heart was so full of love for those two men that sometimes I wondered if it would burst, spilling red glitter and cartoon hearts all into my chest cavity. It was honestly too much when I thought too hard about them and our future. I couldn't breathe. And when I watched them joke around and work so well together, it was as if this between the three of us was years in the making, not weeks.

How could I go to Dallas and leave Slade?

How could I *not* go to Dallas and work side by side with Jameson?

Either way, I left someone behind. Someone I loved. And I knew deep in my gut it would feel like I was missing an appendage if I didn't have both men in my life.

I'd tried to live in the moment the past few days, to not think about the future too much, but now it was here.

We were so close to identifying the unsub. Hopefully, the DNA would come back in the next day or two, giving us a name. But then this perfect dreamlike existence—minus being held at gunpoint and my place being destroyed—would end.

I wasn't ready for that.

Not one bit.

Add in my mixed emotions about going back to the morgue and I was an emotional mess. The place where I was held at gunpoint, where I'd watched the man I love get shot. I didn't know he had a vest on under the jacket, and I really thought I'd lost a piece of my heart—and hearing, because it took forever for the ringing to stop.

So yes, my lazy mornings and calling it quits earlier than usual were at the chief's orders, but it was really me avoiding the one place I used to consider my sanctuary. Now it just reminded me of my fear.

My thigh vibrated with an incoming call, pulling me out of the thought tornado I was on the verge of being sucked into. With a wide smile, figuring it was Jameson or Slade already checking in on me, I flipped my phone over, both brows flying up over my forehead at the name on the screen.

Huh. Wonder what she could want.

With a shrug, I swiped the screen and held the smooth surface to my ear. "Detective. What can I do for you?"

"Hey, um, I was wondering if you were free. I need... I need some help."

"Help?" I asked, tilting my head to the side, not understanding the waver in her voice.

"Yeah, someone to talk to. Now, if that's okay. I just—"

I scooted off the chair and stood. "Of course, it's okay. I'm glad you called, and I completely understand the need to talk things through after what happened. You were there when my ex tried to kill me." When she didn't respond, I blew out a breath. *Okay, too soon for that joke. Noted.* "Where should I meet you?"

"I'm at a friend's place. Can you meet me here, say, thirty minutes?"

"Sure, of course I'll come to you. Just text me the address and I'll swing by on my way to the station."

"Great, wow, okay. Thank you so much, Dr. Evans. I didn't know who else to call, and I really could use some help right about now."

"Not a problem. I'll see you soon."

After disconnecting the call, I tapped the side of the device against my palm. I needed to let Slade and Jameson know I would be later than expected, but I also didn't want to break the detective's trust. She'd called me, wanted to talk to me for a reason, and she sounded scared. The last thing I wanted was for her to be embarrassed because her moment of weakness, needing someone to talk to, was broadcasted to another detective.

Opening our group text, I shot them both a quick message and hurried into the house.

Looked like my relaxing morning was officially over.

33

―――――

JAMESON

"You know she's holding something back, right?" I said while reading the report from victim number six's crime scene for the hundredth time.

"She was held at gunpoint by the man she used to love in a space she's always felt safe." Slade rolled his eyes and tossed the file folder to his desk. "I can't focus on anything while we're waiting for those results. I have a stack of ten other cases I need to be working on, but this one is consuming me."

"Same, but it's my only job while I'm here, so I have zero guilt about being single-minded." I waited a beat before shifting the conversation in a different direction. One we absolutely needed to discuss. "I think the move would be good for her. Especially after what happened a few days ago."

I studied his face to read his reaction. Knowing Slade, he would want what was best for Rain, and going to Dallas and taking a job with the FBI was the best thing for her if she wanted the position. But the dumbass wouldn't come out and tell her how he felt about the news and what that meant for them. I knew he thought he was doing right by her by not putting his thoughts and feelings into the mix to sway her decision, but him not fucking communicating was doing just that, even if he didn't realize it.

"You need to tell her how you feel about her and the job offer," I urged.

"I did. This morning."

I leaned forward, resting my chin on my hand, elbow pressed to the top of his desk. "Oh really? And when was that?"

"Before I walked out."

"And what exactly did you say?"

His green eyes slid my way and narrowed. "I said 'love you.'"

My elbow slipped off the edge of the desk, head plummeting several inches before I caught myself. "You said 'love you,' casual as fuck, and what, just walked away to come to the office?"

"Yep."

Clearly, I would be the communicator in our little trio.

"Okay, Romeo. Listen up, and I mean this in the best way possible. I mean it, all the love, but you're a fucking idiot."

"Why am I an idiot?" He tossed both hands in the air in exasperation. "I communicated how I felt like you've harped on me about and—"

I held up a hand, cutting him off, when Charlie's name flashed on my cell phone.

"Would you randomly drop the L-word to your girl and then walk away?" I asked Charlie, smug as fuck, knowing he would be in my corner on this.

"Pretty sure I was bleeding out after saving Rhyan's life when I told her. Though truth be told, my memory is foggy considering I was minutes away from dying."

Well, fuck. "Oh."

"Are you ready for me to drop a fucking bomb on you? The reason I called?"

"Give us a second," I said and inclined my head toward the hallway. "We need to get to Rain's office where we have some privacy, and I'll put you on speakerphone."

"How's Rain doing? Do you think she'll take Rhyan's offer?"

"Not sure," I said as Slade and I walked side by side toward the morgue. "And she's okay. Working through the trauma of it all, but she'll get through it. That woman is one of the strongest I've ever met. Outside of my mom." I sucked in a breath. "And sisters. Do not ever tell them I put them last or they'll slit my throat."

Inside Rain's office, Slade sat on the couch and me in the chair. I slid the phone from my hand, dropping it on the coffee table between us.

"Okay, talk," I said after hitting the speaker icon.

"You know how you asked me to run search history as a Hail Mary for anyone with a Santa Coasta emergency services login who looked up the address and personal contact info on the murder victims? Well, the search I had running in the background just caught that motherfucking Hail Mary pass."

"Who?" Slade and I asked at the same time. We exchanged an excited glance.

"Detective Jennifer Gray."

Ominous silence filled the office.

"Anything else match up?" I asked, mind whirling with the reasons for her to have searched the personal information for our victims outside of her being our unsub. "Do you know the timing of when she searched them?"

"Anything else as in connections related to the profile,

no. Besides her gender and now this that's the only thing I can find that points to her. And as far as the searches go, they were done weeks before the victims turned up dead."

"The timeline makes sense if she was stalking them," Slade muttered.

"And she was acting shifty that day when I presented the profile to the department." This all pointed to Detective Gray being our unsub, yet it didn't feel right. Especially since it didn't explain why the killings started. "Okay, we'll go talk to her. Thanks, Charlie. Let me know if you find anything else."

After hanging up, I stared at my clasped hands for several seconds, lost in thought.

"Do you feel off about this too?" Slade asked.

I nodded and blew out a heavy breath. "We have to talk to her, though. Figure out why she would have searched our victims before they were victims. You ready to do this?"

"Yeah." After he stood, he stretched his arms overhead. "Damn. That collagen Rain has me add to my morning shakes is the fucking bomb."

"No one says 'the bomb' anymore, just FYI." I beat him out the door with a smirk on my face.

"So what, now you're giving me advice on how I communicate my feelings *and* slang usage?"

"Just trying to tell you what all the cool kids are saying these days."

"Which is?"

I thought about that for a second. "No fucking clue."

Our combined laughter rolled through the hall as we made our way back to the area where all the detectives, no matter the division, had their desks or offices. When we rounded the corner that took us to the bullpen where Detective Gray's desk sat, I skidded to a stop and slammed my forearm against Slade's chest, holding him back from continuing.

"Who is that talking to Detective Gray?" I asked, eyeing the man in a suit standing by her desk. I sure as hell hadn't seen his face around the station; I would have noticed and remembered a man like him. He looked lethal, as if he were taking in every aspect of the room, calculating and assessing without really looking. I'd seen it before with former Special Forces, which this guy certainly was. Buzzed dark hair, medium build, and that stillness all pointed to a man who could kill me with the plastic stapler near his fingers.

"No clue. Never seen him around before, but I think I see a badge. Let's go find out who's talking to our suspect."

Almost like he heard us, the man's attention snapped our way as we approached, studying each of us with a steely gaze. It made me equally tense and impressed.

"Everything good over here, Gray?" I asked, noticing the greenish tint and fear in her eyes.

Her long hair shifted with her quick headshake. Before I could ask another question, she bolted out of the chair, sending it flying backward, and raced out of the room with a hand slapped over her mouth.

"What was that about?" I asked the man who had yet to say a word.

He held out his hand, the movement making his jacket part, revealing the gold badge Slade had gotten a glimpse of earlier. "Detective Hudson Mott, LAPD."

I shook it as I introduced myself, followed by Slade.

"What was that all about?" I asked again, tilting my head in the direction Detective Gray went. "And you're a little too far south for LA, aren't you?"

In a smooth movement, he dipped both hands in his pockets. "Honestly, I'm not sure why she ran off. I came down here to check in on my old partner and was told to talk to Detective Gray when I arrived. I haven't heard from her in a while, and she isn't responding to my check-in calls or texts, so I figured I'd make the quick drive down and talk to her in person."

"Check in? Why would you need to check in on your old partner?" Slade asked.

"She wasn't herself when she left, and I...." Detective Mott's gray gaze slid around the office, noting the detectives within listening range. "Is there somewhere we can talk in private? It's not something I want to air to her colleagues. I assume she left to be somewhere no one knew what happened."

Turning on his heels, Slade searched the room and then stalked off to one of the empty offices. Mott and I followed, and once the door closed, Mott continued. "After three years together, my partner left abruptly, put in a transfer to Santa Coasta PD without even telling me and moved here with that damn massive house cat of hers."

"What made her leave?" A memory nagged in the back of my mind, but I shrugged it off, needing my full attention on Detective Mott.

"The long story? Over a year ago, we were investigating a string of sexual assaults in the area. All the women were at home, in bed for the night, when attacked. We worked the cases hard, out there every day to drum up fresh leads, and...." His jaw worked back and forth like he hated saying his next words. "I guess we got too close, so he targeted Beth. The bastard broke into her house and did the same to her as he had all of his other victims, but this time he inflicted physical torture." Lifting his hands, Mott cracked his knuckles, stare focused just over my shoulder. "He carved the word *mine* into her stomach and left her for dead. After she came back to work, the stares and whispers were too much, and the fact that I still hadn't caught the bastard while she was healing—"

"Wait. Did you say Beth?" Slade asked, eyes wide.

"Yeah, Beth Savage. She was my partner. Do you two know her? Don't let her know I told you about—"

I held up a hand, stopping him. "Holy fuck. It's her."

"What the hell are you talking about?" he demanded, straightening to his full height, which was just a few inches shorter than Slade. But that didn't diminish any of the terror his predatory stillness inflicted. "I asked that detective about Beth when—"

The door swung open, and Slade and I turned toward it. Detective Gray stood in the doorway, just as pale as she was before. A light sheen of sweat lined her upper lip.

"I didn't know," she whispered. "Please believe me, I had no idea. I thought... I thought she was doing drugs or something, not—" She rushed to the corner of the room and vomited into the trash can.

"Someone tell me what the fuck is going on," Mott stated in a tone that demanded no hesitation or risk a very painful death as he stared at the vomiting detective. "Where the fuck is Beth?"

"Like I stated earlier, I'm Special Agent Bend, and I'm with a Dallas-based profiling team." His steel-gray eyes bored into me, clearly telling me to get to the fucking point. "I was brought in to help identify an unsub who had murdered four men by that point, who we recently learned were all sexual predators on various levels."

Mott continued to stare at me. Right, he didn't know our profile and how we'd all just connected the dots of our unsub being his old partner.

"Our profile for this unsub is late twenties to mid-thirties, Caucasian female, with recent trauma which pushed her to commit these vigilante-type murders on men who were accused or at least identified in an assault but never arrested. We still aren't clear how she's picking these men, but we found out a few minutes ago that Detective Gray's login was used to find the victims' personal information before they were victims."

Mott's nostrils flared with each restrained breath. "She wouldn't do this."

"The woman, your friend you knew her as before, didn't commit these crimes. I agree with you. But she's not that person anymore. The trauma changed her. Twisted up the way she views right and wrong. She's taking the law into her own hands to find justice—"

"We never caught him. *I*," he gritted out, "never caught him."

"Why Santa Coasta?" Slade asked.

"After she put in the transfer, I asked the same question, along with a few more than that, but she said there was an excellent support group down here. A group of women met up once a week at a local center, all of them women who'd either reported an assault and nothing came of the statement, or the assailant was never caught...." He locked his stare on me. "Fuck."

"Fuck," I reiterated. "That answers the question about how she's identifying her victims."

"You don't get it," Mott said through his clenched jaw. "She's one of the good ones. Fights for advocacy for the victims. She makes every voice heard, no matter who they are. Beth is a damn good detective, a hell of a partner—" He cut himself off and cleared his throat.

Fuck, this was hard to watch. I couldn't even imagine the internal turmoil going through the man.

"Where is she?" Slade demanded. "Savage. Where is she right now?"

"I don't know," Gray responded, still bent over the trash can. "She should be here, but she didn't show up for our shift. I've called her all morning. I even drove by her house. Her car wasn't there, and no one answered when I knocked."

My cell was in my hand between blinks, calling the one man who could find a needle in a stack of needles.

"Charlie," I barked the moment he picked up. "Ping Detective Beth Savage's cell. We need her exact location right now. We're almost certain she's our unsub."

"Plot fucking twist," Charlie whispered over the sound of his fingers flying along the keyboard. "Okay, her cell is on, which is good for us. It's pinging about twenty minutes away. Give me two seconds and I'll have an exact location for you and real-time satellite images so you know what you're walking.... Okay, address sent. Satellite image pulling up now. It looks like a row of older homes. What does Savage drive?"

"Her car?" I asked Detective Gray.

"Jeep Wrangler. Black."

I rattled off her response to Charlie.

"Yep, that's out front and.... Hold on, there's another car parked behind it. I can see the plates. Running the number now...."

I held my breath, waiting to hear who the car belonged to. Future victim, accomplice, unsuspecting neighbor.

"Oh shit. Oh fucking shit. This can't be right. Quick, what kind of car does Rain drive?"

I snapped my gaze to Slade's, who didn't hear the urgency in Charlie's rushed words. I swallowed hard to keep my stomach contents down.

"A white Tesla." Slade took a menacing step closer,

knowing I was talking about Rain's type of vehicle but not the context. "Please fucking tell me it's not—"

"Get to that fucking address now," Charlie ordered. "I'll try her cell phone until she picks up."

Not needing to be told twice, I bolted out of the room knowing Slade would be hot on my heels. Her text earlier mentioned she had a quick errand, not that she planned to meet with a fucking serial killer. Alone. She wouldn't do that, not to us, to me and Slade or herself.

Which meant only one thing.

She had no idea what she was walking into.

34

RAIN

Cute house. That was my first thought about the bright blue cottage-style home as I pulled along the curb. The flower beds needed some love. Not from someone like me who killed everything she touched. Maybe that was why I liked my career path so much.

They were already dead.

Snickering at myself for my lame-ass joke, I climbed out of my car and stepped into the street. Tossing my handbag over my shoulder, I blew out a breath and shook both hands to dispel my irrational anxiety, making me feel nervous and a sense of dread sit in the pit of my stomach.

I wasn't the best at normal social interactions, but this woman called me to talk. Obviously, Beth didn't feel comfortable talking to her partner about whatever bothered her. I couldn't back out just because my anxiety told me to tuck and roll away from the situation.

The soles of my new sparkly tennis shoes slapped on the cement walkway as I approached the house. The sun hit the gold glitter, shooting pretty rays along the green grass. Smiling, I jumped up the two front steps and raised my knuckles to knock but the door swung open before my skin could touch the black painted wood.

"Beth," I called, that dread sensation growing at the oddness of the door opening on its own.

Pushing aside the bombarding worst-case-scenario thoughts of me walking into a trap or a butler ghost opening the door for me, I wedged through the small gap and quietly closed the haunted door behind me.

You never know. The ghost might get super poltergeist-y with loud noises.

"Rain."

Wide smile on my face, I turned toward Beth's voice only for my lips to slowly fall. Several blinks later, I still didn't understand what I saw playing out in front of me.

"Um. So." Yep. Apparently, when confronted with a woman I somewhat knew holding another obviously terri-fied woman with a gun pressed to the stranger's temple, I was reduced to two-letter words. And like the antisocial person I was, I stated the obvious because what else was there to say? "Is this what you wanted to talk about?"

Even the hostage rolled her eyes.

What? I was used to dealing with dead people, not life-and-death situations.

They came to me already dead, for fuck's sake. I was not equipped for this.

"I messed up," Beth whispered, wild, bloodshot eyes pleading with me from across the small living room. "I didn't know.... She wasn't supposed to be here."

"Whose house is this?" I asked, taking in all the exits and possible weapons.

The woman sobbed. "My boyfriend's—"

"How could you be with a man who rapes women?" Beth

shouted in the hostage's ear, making her whimper and attempt to pull away from the arm keeping her in place.

It all clicked then.

How could I be so fucking dumb?

Beth is our unsub.

Our serial killer is Beth.

And I am in so, so, so much shit.

The strap of my purse slid down to the crook of my elbow, reminding me I had a lifeline in its deep depths. If I could get to my phone, then I could call for help to get me out of yet another shitty situation.

This was really becoming a trend, and I did not like it one bit.

"Listen," I said slowly, mimicking the tone Jameson used the other day on Josh. I shivered just remembering the helpless feeling of standing there with a gun pointed at me. And that was exactly how Beth's hostage felt, and who knew for how long. "Let me just call someone—"

"No," Beth screeched, jerking the woman in her arm, which made her scream.

Which made *me* scream.

If the cops weren't on their way, they had to be now.

Surely the neighbors knew a group of women screaming wasn't the norm. Or maybe it was and—

The insistent vibration in my purse stopped my tornado thoughts. I wasn't sure how, but I knew that constant buzzing meant *they* knew.

My guys knew I was in trouble.

Now I once again had to keep my shit together long enough to be saved.

Maybe Beth and her hostage like dead people jokes.

35

SLADE

We parked three houses down from the one Savage and Rain were holed up inside. Eyes on the location, I secured my vest while Jameson and Mott did the same. The LA fucker tagged along, jumping in my car without a word before I took off from the station. Which didn't bother me, considering he looked like he could not only hold his own no matter the situation but possibly the whole county too.

The fucker radiated deadly.

Exactly what we needed since Jameson and I were floundering, too emotionally invested in this to think clearly. Our girl was inside that house, and we were helpless. Again.

I fucking hated this. I should've pieced it all together sooner, known that the damn killer was one of us from the start. I felt like a damn fool letting Savage get away with literal murder right under my nose for months.

"Hey." Jameson slammed his fist against my shoulder hard, jerking me out of my head. "There was no way we could've known. None of us. Now that we have all the information and see how the profile fits Savage, of course all the clues make sense and point to her. But we didn't, and now we move fucking forward and get everyone out of this alive."

His features pulled into a grimace while he tightened the Velcro strap around his chest, reminding me that he'd walked into the line of fire last time. It was my turn to face the unknown and save our girl.

"I'm going in this time," I demanded, mind already made up. Hopefully, this ball of guilt would go the fuck away if I was in there with her. I'd put myself between her and the danger, no matter the risk to myself. "You went in first last time and—"

"Don't go all Donkey Kong on me, big guy, but you're actually not." I shot him my signature glare. "Oh no, that doesn't work on me anymore. You've shown me your softer side, so I know you're just a big ole cinnamon roll inside that giant, tough exterior."

"Am I interrupting something?" Mott asked, looking between us, thumbs hooked into his vest. "Because that's my partner and friend in there, and I don't want you trigger-happy fuckers anywhere around her." He leveled me with a cocky smirk. "I'm going in."

I stretched my neck one way and then the other, preparing to fight the asshole for the right to go in first. Though this might be the first time in my life that I doubted I'd be the winner. "It's our girl in there, so—"

"Our?" He pointed to me and Jameson in question. "Nice. Congrats. But that doesn't change a single fucking thing. You're both too emotionally invested in this for all the wrong reasons for my liking. You'll shoot first and ask questions later."

I opened my mouth to argue, but Jameson spoke up first.

"He's right." He shot me a sympathetic look and shrugged. "All kidding aside, Mott is our best option. We have no idea what's going on in there. If Savage is spiraling like we believe based on the last crime scene, seeing her old partner, someone she trusts and considers on her side, could help pull her back from the edge."

Jameson turned to Mott. "I can tell you're used to going into hostile situations, but this is different. If you do exactly as I tell you, we can get both of them out of this unharmed. But if you go off the script—"

"I won't. Tell me."

"You need to remind her of who she was when you two worked together, of who she is without the trauma twisting her up inside. Bring up happy memories, anything that will remind her she's not this person. Assess the situation as best you can and play to win. You understand what I'm saying?"

"Yeah." He turned to look at the house over his shoulder. "But know if it comes down to it, I'll take the shot. If she's intent to hurt anyone else, I'll do it."

Some of my anger faded at the desolation in his tone. This was fucking hard for him, knowing he might have to take down someone he'd counted on to cover his back for years. I couldn't imagine.

"If you do this right, you won't have to."

He shot Jameson an annoyed look that made me smirk. "No fucking pressure, right? Get this right or my old partner dies." Jameson cringed. "It's fine. Fuck. Okay, comms on?"

"Check" from Jameson.

"Check." Me that time.

"And check," Mott muttered. "Backup in route?"

"Five minutes out," I responded.

"But we won't send them in unless you give us the signal that they—we—are needed. What's the word you want to use for 'all hell has broken loose'?" Jameson asked.

His lips quirked. "What's y'all's safe word? I feel like that might be best with us three."

Despite all the odds, I barked a laugh. "It's not like that, fucker."

"Whatever, I'm cool either way. You do you, buddy. Fine, my go word for 'get your fucking asses in here because shit just hit the fan' will be *pineapple*." With that, he started down the sidewalk, jogging at first before outright sprinting toward the unknown danger waiting for him in that house.

Huh. With Mott in the mix, maybe this whole situation wasn't fucked after all.

Now all Jameson and I could do was listen and wait. Checking my clip, I slammed it into place and leaned my ass against my car.

Waiting to see if my entire world was about to crumble around me.

36

RAIN

"Do you want to talk about it?" I asked like a dumbass. "Please, Beth. This isn't you." I gestured to the woman in her arms.

As I said the words, a strong waft of copper—a very familiar smell considering my line of work—came from somewhere in the house.

"Oh no." Beth wouldn't look me in the eye when my gaze followed my nose down a hall that led to the bedrooms. "Beth, what did you do?"

Without thinking of the consequences, only my training, I started down the hall, following the overwhelming smell of blood. At the end, the door was open to the main bedroom, where my fears were confirmed. Splayed out on the bed was a mess of what used to be a young man. The overkill with this one went above and beyond any of the others.

And there was something else different.

Steps hesitant, I inched closer to get a better view of the word written on his stomach in blood.

No, not written.

Carved.

I pressed my fingers to my gaping mouth, unable to look away from the gory scene.

"He deserved it." I whirled around, finding Beth, the woman still restrained in her arm, standing in the doorway. "They all did. Do you know how many lives he and the others have ruined?"

The stranger's face grew pale, her eyes glassy as she stared at the ceiling. Anywhere other than the massacre on the bed. The ceiling was the best place to look, considering it was the only clean spot in a room sprayed in blood.

"I don't. Do you want to tell me?" I said calmly.

"No one listened. Nothing happened. No one was held accountable," she whispered, staring at the floor. Hell, even she couldn't look at the body. "But they are now. They won't hurt anyone else."

"Not on your watch?"

She nodded. "No one else will lose that sense of safety in their own home, or their trust in basic decency."

"Sounds like you know a lot about that," I said softly, empathy filling my tone. It all made sense. I didn't know the details, but I didn't need to. This woman was a victim herself, that much was clear. And the fact that she wouldn't look at her handiwork told me she didn't enjoy the kill.

The result, sure, but not the act like a sociopath would.

I considered that a check in the positive column.

"That she does."

I stood up taller at the unfamiliar male voice that echoed down the hall.

Beth jerked the woman around so hard the hostage stumbled, moving just enough for me to see who'd spoken. Hands held up in surrender, a man I'd never seen before walked down the hall, his eyes trained on Beth.

I didn't know who he was, but the way he moved and tracked Beth's every breath told me he was capable of getting us all out of here alive.

"Hudson?" she whispered, eyes glassy with unshed tears.

"Hey ya, B."

Her hold loosened for half a heartbeat before she tightened it around the woman's neck.

"What are you doing here?" She shifted to keep us both in her line of sight as this Hudson walked confidently into the bedroom. Points for the man who didn't even flinch at the bloody mess on the bed as he came to stand beside me.

No, not beside. Just in front of.

Damnit, this guy—whoever he was—just put himself in the line of fire if Beth decided one victim wasn't enough today.

"I came down to check on you, B. You weren't returning my calls."

Her hand twitched. "I've been busy."

"Beth, sweetheart, this isn't you. What are you doing?"

Her back straightened, and she rolled her shoulders. "This is me now."

"No, it's not, B. It's not and you know it. I know you, remember? I'm your partner, your friend who you tell everything to. And after years of working together, I know this"—he hitched his thumb behind his shoulder—"isn't you."

"They deserved it," she whispered. "They hurt people, Hud. Like that guy hurt me."

"Oh, sweetheart." The hurt and pain in his tone cut through my heart. "They might have, but you know this isn't how it's done. You give the victims a voice. You listen—really listen—to them and help them. I'm sorry I couldn't do the same for you."

I forced myself to not reach out and grip his shoulder. The agony in his voice was almost too much.

"But what about her?" he asked. "Did she hurt those women?"

"No. I didn't... I didn't know she would be here. She just showed up when I was about to leave, and... I didn't think about...." Her voice trailed off as her gaze went unfocused.

"Look at her, B. She's terrified. You know how that feels, don't you? Remember how it felt to be so helpless, under someone else's control who wanted to hurt you?"

Oh, this guy was good. Appealing to her as a victim herself rather than the vigilante who killed those responsible.

She looked at the woman, really looked at her. I saw it the moment Hudson's words rang true.

"I didn't mean to," she whispered. "What happens now? I won't... I refuse to go to jail. You know how they'll treat me. There's only one way out of this, Hud. You know it and I know it."

Her pleading eyes fixed on his.

"Put the gun down and we can talk about it, B."

Slowly, the gun lowered and the arm restraining the hostage loosened. The moment she was no longer held up, the woman slumped to the floor. Eyes still open, she was a human puddle at Beth's feet, probably a few seconds away from passing out cold. Wanting to help her, I took a step closer, but Hudson's forearm snapped out, holding me back.

"We'll get you help. You're a victim, Beth. We'll get you the help you need and deserve, and I'll be with you every step of the way. Hand me the gun, sweetheart, and let's get out of this unharmed, all of us. Don't make me do what you know I'll have to do if you decide this is the end."

The light caught on a single tear as it trailed down his

cheek. Flicking my gaze back to Beth, I held a breath, waiting for her decision.

Understanding and resolve flickered behind her eyes when she blinked away the unshed tears. Looking my way, she blew out a slow breath.

"I'm so sorry."

Slowly, ever so slowly, she raised the gun.

Hudson called out to her, but I didn't listen. Knowing what was coming, I sealed my palms to my ears and squeezed my eyes shut, whispering a simple apology to my guys that I'd done this to us.

That our happily ever after had turned out to only be happy until now.

Through the earpiece, I strained to hear Mott's words as he talked Savage off the ledge, telling her to hand him the gun. It said a lot about his trust in the woman that he didn't ask her to drop it and kick it away.

We would know shortly if that call was a smart one or not.

"All clear in here. Gun is secure, everyone unharmed except an unknown male very dead in the main bedroom."

For half a heartbeat, I fell into the well of relief his words offered, washing away all my worry and fear.

Slade, not so much. Like a starter gun went off, the bastard sprinted toward the house.

And let me tell you, he still moved fast as fuck for an old guy.

With a curse, I chased after him, wincing every time my feet slammed to the concrete, the jolt reverberating up to my still-sore chest. Being shot fucking sucked, no matter where the bullet landed.

Loud, soul-shattering sobs greeted me the second I

stepped over the threshold. Creeping down the hall, I followed the sound toward the distinct smell of blood.

My heart remained lodged in my throat until I saw Rain with my own eyes, unharmed and wrapped in Slade's massive arms.

Instead of heading to my girl, I squatted next to Mott and Detective Savage, who was curled up on his lap, her sobs somewhat quieted as he stroked a hand along her short hair.

Careful to keep the barrel pointed anywhere but at us, Mott handed me a gun. Immediately he wrapped that hand around Savage, squeezing her even tighter against his chest. His lips moved, but the soft whispered words were lost in her hair. Which was fine. They weren't meant for me.

Standing, I tucked the gun into the back of my pants for safekeeping and shifted my attention to the unknown woman lying on the floor. I cocked my head to the side, utterly confused about how she fit into the situation.

"She's okay." Rain's voice cracked. When I looked up, unshed tears lined her lower lids. "I checked her pulse. It's strong. She probably just got overwhelmed and passed out. Which is totally understandable. And just a heads-up, I just might join her." I shared a concerned look with Slade, who tightened his hold around her just in case she fainted. "I'm going to have so many thought tornadoes about this one."

Her voice had changed, the tone monotonous and the cadence off. And what the fuck was a thought tornado?

"Rain?" I stood abruptly, hand outstretched toward her even though I knew she was safe with Slade.

"Baby?" His tone was tinged with desperation.

"I'm just going to—"

Before she could finish, Rain's eyes rolled into the back of her head, and she slumped into Slade's protective arms.

Well, fuck.

SLADE

I would never let her out of my sight again.

Ever.

It didn't matter what Rain wanted or didn't, I would stick to her side, carrying two sidearms and maybe a handful of knives.

Okay, I did actually care what she wanted, but fuck, she'd nearly killed me when she passed out in my arms last week.

I wrapped my hand around the refrigerator's handle. Jameson mentioned, several times, that I needed to send the EMTs and hospital staff who'd attended to Rain a fruit basket for acting like an overprotective silverback gorilla.

His words, not mine.

Grabbing a bottle of water off the shelf, I headed back outside where Jameson and Rain waited, enjoying the beautiful early afternoon without Rain's family hovering over their still-recovering daughter. Her mom, dad, and uncle arrived three days ago after learning about yet another danger their daughter had faced and were staying in the guest/pool house. That location was at Rain's request despite having enough guest rooms in the main house. Apparently, the three of them were loud when cooped up together, and she didn't want to hear any of that.

And when she put it that way, I readily agreed.

Plus, it gave Jameson and me privacy to show Rain how much we loved her and were so fucking thankful that she was okay by worshiping her body as often as possible. And I had no plans to stop anytime soon.

The second Mott disappeared into that house, I knew without a doubt that if she took the job in Dallas, I would go too. There wasn't anything holding me in Santa Coasta. I didn't love my job, the house would sell easily, and my parents... well, those two were never in the country, so it didn't matter where I lived.

Stepping out into the warm air, I inhaled deeply and smiled at Jameson and Rain playing in the pool like two children. Thankfully, the other three were checking out the beach, meaning our trio had a few hours to ourselves.

"Here you go," I said, offering Rain the bottle of water when she swam up to the ledge. "Keep hydrating. The doctor said—"

"I'm a doctor, too, you know." She took the bottle, eyeing it with disdain. "And I say I've had enough water for four people." Setting the water down on the stone, she blinked her dark lashes up at me. "Can I have my unicorn drink delivered now?"

"Come on, Slade. Like you can deny this woman anything." Jameson swam up behind her and curled around her back. "A bit of sugar won't hurt anything, right, Doctor?"

"You two are impossible." Though the growing smile on my lips said I wasn't as annoyed as I made it sound. "Fine. After you drink that bottle of water. Deal?"

She pushed her lower lip out in a full pout. "Fine. You're bossy," she said with a twinkle in her hazel eyes.

"You love me bossy." I flicked my gaze over her shoulder at Jameson's chuffed laugh. "So do you, jackass."

"No complaints here," he said, kissing down her shoulder, licking up the lingering water droplets. Rain's head dropped back, her lips parted on a soft moan.

With a long look toward the glass doors, I calculated the time her parents left and how long they planned to stay at the beach. Smirking, I hooked both thumbs into my shorts and jerked them down, leaving me in my swim shorts.

"Fuck, I'll never get tired of seeing you," Rain whispered, eyes locked on the outline of my semihard cock.

"Same, baby. Now take off that scrap of lace and bend over so Jameson can fuck that perfect cunt while you remind me why your mouth is like fucking heaven."

How was this my life?

After ruining everything I ever touched, I finally had it all.

Who knew I just needed a plus-one in the equation to make it fucking perfect?

Forever.

EPILOGUE

RAIN

Seven months later

At the sound of the garage door, I clicked off the TV, silencing the Dallas news reporter's next words. There were still a few boxes we needed to unpack, but the house was mostly done. After I accepted the job with the FBI, it took a month for my replacement to arrive, and then we made the long drive to Texas. Thankfully, Slade had flown out a couple times and found a house he deemed acceptable.

Tossing the remote to the coffee table, I rolled my eyes, remembering him constantly complaining about the lack of ocean nearby.

It was cute in a spoiled little kid type of way.

Jameson walked in, go bag in one hand, laptop bag in the other. Seeing me on the couch, sitting straight up in anticipation of his arrival, he dropped both to the floor and strode toward me. Leaping off the couch, I wrapped my arms around him and pressed my face to his neck.

"Someone is happy to see me," he chuckled as his arms

banded around my back and tugged me even closer. Nose in my hair, he inhaled, his tight muscles automatically softening. "Fuck, it's good to be home."

"I missed you. Two weeks is a long time."

He sighed, his breath blowing my hair. "I know. I'm sorry, Raindrop." He pulled back to look at me. Honey-brown eyes scanned my face, brows narrowing. "What's wrong?"

"Nothing."

Lie. Such a bald-faced lie. After the last few days, I should've been used to it, but I wasn't.

I hated lying to both of them, but it was necessary. Things had to stay even and everyone on equal footing if this would work between us.

Grabbing Jameson's hand, I pulled him toward the massive kitchen that any chef would be envious of, following the scents of cooking meat, garlic, and fresh bread.

His back to us, Slade glanced over his broad shoulder as we entered and hitched his chin in greeting to Jameson. "You catch that sick fucker?"

I dropped Jameson's hand and moved toward the island, strategically putting myself between the two.

"Yep." At the fridge, he yanked open the door and pulled out two beers. "Sneaky-ass fucker, but we got him before he could hurt any more kids. The sick asshole preyed on the parents' trust. No one even suspected him because he inserted himself into the investigation early on and kept the cops running in circles." Popping off the top to both, he took a sip from one and set the other in front of me.

Where it stayed. I didn't even attempt to wrap my hand around it.

"Until you showed up," Slade tossed over his shoulder,

attention back on the beef Bolognese sauce on the stove. "Hope you're hungry."

I sure as hell was, though the delicious smells were making my stomach roll with nausea.

Bottle raised, hovering right in front of his mouth, Jameson eyed me, his suspicion shifting to concern.

"Rain?"

With a quick headshake, which made the room spin, I slapped a hand over my mouth and bolted to the powder room right off the kitchen. My knees hit the tile floor a second before the delicious lunch Slade made me earlier came back up, not tasting nearly as amazing as it had a few hours ago.

I felt them in the doorway, didn't need to turn around to verify both stood there waiting for an answer. An answer they'd probably already pieced together themselves. The fact that I'd kept the news and morning sickness—now apparently all-day sickness—from Slade the past three days was a testament to how distracted he was with talking about becoming the next chief of police with my dad.

"Have some important news to share with the class, Raindrop?"

Head still in the toilet as another wave of nausea had me dry heaving, I raised a hand in the air, middle finger straight up. Their combined chuckles made hot, emotional tears prick behind my eyes.

"Surprise," I rasped, finally feeling well enough to scoot back and lean against the wall. Because I sure was when those two pink lines showed up on the pregnancy stick. We really should have used condoms when I was on antibiotics a while back. Not that I was upset or devastated by the unexpected, yet completely welcomed news. When I took them both in, their wide radiant smiles and the tears glimmering in their lower lids had a sob welling in my chest. "I'm pregnant."

"Oh, Raindrop." Reaching down, Jameson scooped me off the floor and pulled me in for a tight hug. I shook against him with every heavy sob, tears now leaking down both cheeks. "I'm at a loss for words for how stupid happy I am. I never—" His voice caught. Pulling back, I watched in awe as his own tears slipped down his jaw. "I never thought it was in the cards for me to have a family. And when I found you, and then Slade, I thought it couldn't get any more perfect."

Slade's arms encircled my waist and gently tugged me out of Jameson's hold. With my spine to his chest, Slade rested his chin on my shoulder and splayed both massive hands across my still-flat stomach.

"A baby," he murmured. I nodded, gnawing on my lip, unsure what that odd tone meant. "I'm going to be a dad."

"Are you happy?" I whispered.

"Happy? I'm in fucking awe, baby. How long have you known?"

I winced. "Three days."

His dark chuckle rumbled in my ear. "Naughty girl, not telling me the moment you knew."

"I wanted us to be together. All of us."

Jameson leaned a shoulder against the doorframe. "Hmm, I agree with Slade on this one. Quite naughty indeed. And you know what happens to naughty girls, Raindrop."

Yes. Yes, I did.

And knowing what was to come and feeling a hundred times better now that my stomach was empty, I shot Jameson a wink and broke out of Slade's hold to bolt out of the room. A wide smile stretched across my face, the earlier emotional tears gone. I took the stairs two at a time, knowing I needed the head start if I wanted a chance to brush my teeth before they pounced. A shiver of anticipation raced through me at hearing their pounding steps right behind me.

I had no idea how my life could get more perfect than this.

Though nine months from now, I knew it would be even better.

ALSO BY KENNEDY L. MITCHELL

In Clear Sight: A Small Town, WITSEC Interconnected Standalone Series

Safe Haven - FREE Prequel

Guarded by the Marshal

Cherished by the Agent

Saved by the Officers

Hidden by the Doctor

Protection Series: A Dark Romantic Thriller Interconnected Standalone Series

Mine to Protect *

Mine to Save *

Mine to Guard *

Mine to Keep *

Mine to Hold *

Mine to Love *

Mine to Share

Mine to Shelter

*Now available in audio!

SEALs and CIA Series: A Navy SEAL Interconnected Standalone Series

Covert Affair

Covert Vengeance

More Than a Threat Series: A Connected Bodyguard Romantic
Suspense Series

More Than a Threat

More Than a Risk

More Than a Hope

More Than a Threat Series Boxset: Complete Series

Power Play Series: A Protector Romantic Suspense Connected
Series

Power Games

Power Twist

Power Switch

Power Surge

Power Term

Standalones:

- Finding Fate - Dark, Captive Romantic Suspense

Memories of Us - Contemporary, Small Town Romance

ACKNOWLEDGMENTS

It's always bittersweet when a book is officially done. Having been written, revised, edited, proof read, beta read, formatted... A lot goes into making the words inside the book you just read make sense. I'm a story teller not a grammar person AT ALL. But the bittersweet part comes from saying goodbye to the characters I worked so hard creating and building but knowing their stories will be read by you and so many others makes it all okay.

So thank you for reading this book and any of my others. I hope my words and characters were able to pull you out of reality for just a little while, transporting you between the pages and into these character's lives. That's what I love the most about reading, is getting a break from life for a chapter or two so I hope this book brought that to you.

I can't say thank you enough to my alpha readers. Chris, Em, Kristin and Darlene, thank you so much for reading the barely readable chapters I send you and helping me shape the story to what it is today. I am so very very grateful for your support and all the time you put in reading all to help me and my characters.

The book wouldn't be readable without my amazing editor Kristin and proofreader Sarah. Thank you both for turning my story into something beautiful. Your attention to detail and focus to identifying every inconsistency in these 112K words is astounding. And I'm sorry that I did not get this section edited or proofread. #Mybad

And last but not least thank you to my amazing ARC readers. Your role is so so so tough and I'm so very appreciative of you. I don't know how you do it, reading under a time constraint while still reading other books and managing your busy lives. So thank you, really. For giving me a piece of your downtime to help this book be successful. I hope you liked it, but even if you didn't I appreciate the time you took to read my words.

Then of course there is you the reader. The one who gave this unknown author a shot. THANK YOU! Because of you I continue writing these dark thrilling stories. Every email, review, and comment on posts I read and cherish. If you loved the book I'd FLOVE for you to leave a review and hopefully pick up another KLM read.

Until the next book, happy reading book lovers.
KLM

ABOUT THE AUTHOR

Kennedy L. Mitchell lives outside Dallas with her husband, son and two very large goldendoodles. She began writing in 2016 and has no plans of stopping.

She would love to hear from you via any of the platforms below or her website www.kennedylmitchell.com You can also stay up to date on future releases through her newsletter or by joining her Facebook readers group - Kennedy's Book Boyfriend Support Group.

Thank you for reading.

9 781962 509060